HEARTS AND EVER AFTERS

REGENCY ROMANCE COLLECTION

JOYCE ALEC

Hearts and Ever Afters
Regency Romance Collection

Text Copyright © 2018 by Joyce Alec

First printing, 2018

Publisher
Love Light Faith, LLC
400 NW 7th Avenue, Unit 825
Fort Lauderdale, FL 33311

AN EARL'S AGREEMENT

By Joyce Alec

1

London 1836

Miss Lucy Donoghue sighed happily to herself and settled back a little more against the cushions of the window seat in the library. Looking out of the window at the beautiful gardens below for a brief moment, she let her mind drift to thoughts about life and love, picturing herself as the heroine in the book she held in her hands.

Her parents would be horrified if they knew she was reading such a book, considering these novels to be both unorthodox and entirely unhelpful to a young woman of quality.

Lucy could not agree.

The books opened up a world far beyond the trappings of society, where one could find someone of worth who sought love over expectation. They told her that matrimony could happen between two individuals who held a deep and long-lasting love for each other.

It was certainly not what she saw in her own parents' marriage. There might be affection of sorts, but nothing akin to love existed between them. Her father, the Earl of With-ington, held a great deal of power within society. For whatever reason, he had a shrewd mind and could accomplish wonders within his business dealings, which garnered him a great deal of respect from the gentlemen within his acquaintance. His wife—Lucy's mother—had the ability to look down her nose at almost anyone, even those above her own title, to the point that a great many ladies sought her favor. Lucy had heard it said on more than one occasion that to have Lady Withington's favor meant that you were accepted within society.

Lucy, for herself, had very little interest in the subject. She attended balls and other events with her parents with good grace, but much preferred to spend her time in quiet pursuits, such as reading or discussing what she had read with anyone willing to engage with her. She had heard her mother exclaim that she had never wished for a bluestocking for a daughter, yet Lucy had not found herself caring one whit.

She was the second child, with the first, her brother Jonathan, already married and settled. Of course, he was the apple of her parents' eyes, especially because he had done as he was expected and married well. Their father had sent him to the country with his wife, giving them one of his many holdings as a wedding present. In due course, Jonathan would inherit the earl's title and take on all of his responsibilities.

Lucy had never been close to him. He had always been willing to do what he was asked, whereas she wished for more. She still remembered the day their mother had pressed a certain young lady's suit onto Jonathan. On that day, she had known in her heart that her brother would marry within the year—and so it had come to pass. Jonathan had married Lady Victoria Bentson within a few months, and now, after a year, had already produced the heir to the earl's title.

Jonathan was everything she was not: proper, compliant, and entirely respectable. She was not particularly good at the pianoforte, she shunned needlework, and she attempted to further her own knowledge through reading and discussion.

No one wants a bluestocking for a wife, she thought to herself, recalling her mother's words and ignoring the sharp twist in her heart at the memory.

Sighing to herself, Lucy picked up her book from her lap and snuggled back against the cushions, propping the novel up on her knees. Here, hidden away in the window seat, she was able to enjoy her love of prose without anyone interrupting her. Her parents had, on many occasions, sought her out, though they had never been able to find her hidden amongst the curtains in the library. Thankfully the housekeeper had something of a soft spot for Lucy, and so never once told her parents where she might be, even if she was fully aware of it.

"This cannot go on much longer, Charles!"

Her mother's shrill voice reached Lucy's ears, making her jump with surprise. Slowly closing the book, she wondered whether to pull open the curtains and announce her presence, but then her parents would know one of her favorite hiding places and all would be undone.

Instead, Lucy remained entirely still, thinking that she might stop up her ears with her fingers. She did not want to eavesdrop, did not want to hear her parents' private business, which was not hers to know.

"Whatever shall we do with her, Charles? Did you see her at the ball last evening?"

Lucy swallowed, nerves beginning to flurry through her stomach. They were discussing her. Her cheeks warmed at the thought of the last ball she had attended with her parents. Her mother had caught her deep in discussion with two other gentlemen, talking about the merits of the Scottish Poor Law in relation to the English law. What had made it worse was that both gentlemen, while titled, had been of a lower standing than her father, and Lucy knew she was expected to marry either within a similar rank or, preferably, higher.

"She is becoming wild!" her mother screeched as Lucy heard her father slam the door with his usual lack of consideration. "Discussing the Poor Law, discussing poverty, and the workhouse! That is not the kind of subject a young lady needs to talk about. She should be fluttering her fan and seeking to ensure her dance card is full."

"Did she not dance at all?" her father asked, his voice grave. "I can scarcely believe that. Lucy is one of the most beautiful and most eligible young women at such events."

"She did dance some," her mother replied slowly. "But her beauty and eligibility mean nothing, Charles, not when she is so lacking in other ways."

Lucy's grip tightened on her book, her fingers growing white as she forced her anger back under control. She had no need to simper and smile, since none of the young men her parents favored was of any interest to her. In fact, she considered them all quite dull! They looked at her as though she were simply some kind of adornment, one they could wear on their arm, but care very little about.

No, she did not want that kind of man for a husband. Instead, she sought someone who actually had some semblance of character, someone who appreciated her desire for knowledge and wish to better herself. She needed a husband with whom she could talk, a husband who enjoyed spending time in her company instead of simply expecting her to turn up to societal events with him.

Love? She smiled softly, her parents' voices fading into the background. Perhaps love, and if not love, then certainly affection, for she was sure that affection could, and would, grow to love.

Lucy was determined not to ever allow herself to marry

someone who had utterly no regard for her, nor she for him. That kind of marriage would only turn out to be similar to the bond her parents had, a bond that was brittle and liable to snap at any moment. Her lip curled with distaste.

She was more than aware that her father had a few mistresses throughout their marriage, for he often shouted it at her mother when he drank too much whiskey. No, her parent's marriage was a decidedly unhappy one, and certainly not one Lucy sought for herself.

"I do have a friend that would be a fine match for Lucy," her father said slowly, his voice suddenly capturing her attention again. "I know he is keen to wed once more, but no one has caught his eye as yet."

Her mother snorted. "And you really think Lucy might be the one to do so?"

"As it happens, the gentleman is interested in some kind of partnership with me."

Lucy gripped her book tighter and tighter as the seconds ticked on. Surely he was not about to suggest that she be pushed into another man's arms as some kind of business agreement.

"Then you think Lucy might wed him, and secure your partnership?" her mother asked quietly. "Who is this man? That does not make sense, Charles."

"Of course it does," her father blustered, sounding both irritated and angry that his wife had questioned him. "Have you not just finished telling me that Lucy is struggling to find a suitor? Lord Hutton is quite desperate to be in partnership with me, I believe, and will do exactly as I ask, I am sure of it. He will take Lucy off our hands, make her more than respectable, and my holdings will be more than secure with his additional funding. What issues can you foresee, my dear?"

There was silence as Lucy held back her shriek of refusal

and despair. She clenched her fists and pressed one to her mouth; tears began to roll unchecked down her cheeks.

"And if she does not agree?" her mother asked, a worried ring to her voice. "What then?"

Her father chuckled. "She will have no choice but to agree. Our stubborn, rebellious daughter is about to realize that she will do as she is told, or she will be out in the cold. She will lose all respectability and, without funds, what exactly is she to do?"

Clapping her hands together, her mother let out a squeal of glee. "Wonderful! It is about time that girl learns her place."

"I shall speak to Hutton as soon as possible," her father finished, his footsteps carrying him across the floor. "Shall we, my dear?"

Lucy kept silent until the sounds of their footsteps died away, leaving her entirely alone once more. Putting her head in her hands, she allowed the pain and hurt she felt bubble to the surface as fresh tears began to fall. Her parents had, unwittingly, alerted her to their intentions, but she had never expected them to be so cruel. Was she really so much of a burden that they would push her onto Lord Hutton, a man almost the same age as her father?

No.

Lucy dried her eyes and lifted her chin, staring out of the window. She would not allow this to happen. She could not. Now that she knew exactly what her parents intended, she would have time to try and find a way out.

Unfortunately, her mind was so cluttered and her emotions so fraught that she could do nothing more than stare out into the gardens, the book slowly falling from her fingers and landing with a bump on the floor.

2

L ucy hugged the wall, keeping as much to the shadows as possible. She had not wanted to attend the ball, given what she had heard only this very afternoon, but she could not allow her parents to guess that she was privy to their conversation.

Pretending that all was well had been difficult, but not entirely unmanageable, although she had hated the sudden gleam in her mother's eye as she discussed the upcoming ball and the various gentlemen that Lucy might meet.

She had managed to escape her parents' attention almost immediately and had rushed to where she would be least likely spotted. It was not her usual behavior, of course, but she had to discover whether or not Lord Hutton was there—and if her parents were intending to speak to him that very night.

Her stomach rolled with distaste as the man himself came into her line of view, mopping his red, sweating face with a large, yellow handkerchief. His balding head gleamed in the candlelight, his rotund figure adorned in swathes of bright yellow and green fabric. It was an almost comically grotesque sight. Lord Hutton, of course, was known to be wealthy, and it

was only because of his status that he was given so much
leeway by society. However, Lucy found him utterly
detestable. Shivering, she imagined his pudgy hand taking
hers, his large fingers sealing her to him. Shaking her head,
she diverted her gaze. She could not allow this to happen.
She would not allow her parents to even introduce him
to her.

Unfortunately for Lucy, that was exactly what unfolded in
front of her. To her horror, she saw her father shaking Lord
Hutton's hand, his eyes searching the crowd. Lucy knew exactly
who he was searching for, her stomach rolling with alarm and
anxiety.

Her feet moved before she even thought about where she
was going. Practically clinging to the wall, Lucy walked slowly,
ducking behind tall gentlemen so that she remained hidden
from view.

A blast of cool air hit her, making her heart beat a little
faster. Cool air meant a door.

Moving as carefully as she could, she caught sight of the
open French doors. The orchestra began to play and couples
took to the floor, leaving her a little more exposed. Her breath
hitched as she scrabbled for the door leading to the gardens,
keeping herself low as she hurried outside.

The darkness welcomed her like an old friend, wrapping
itself around her and hiding her from the prying eyes of Lord
Hutton. Lucy drew in a long breath and scurried further into the
gardens, wishing she had brought her shawl. The path was lit by
only a few stray lanterns, bathing her steps in shadow. Lucy did
not know what to do or where to go, realizing that she was only
delaying the inevitable.

Her slippers grew cold and damp as she left the path and
crossed the grass in search of a quiet place where she could be
alone. If she remained on the path, she might very well come

across courting couples, which would bring her only embarrassment.

Stumbling further into the gloom, she managed to find a small, enclosed arbor, encircled by a thick hedge and revealing a small bench within. A single lantern lit the way, and, to Lucy's surprise, she found it slightly warmer inside, hidden from view.

The arbor was exactly the place she needed, somewhat sheltered from the cool night air and giving her the privacy to gather her scrambling thoughts. Sitting down heavily on the bench, Lucy put her face in her hands and tried desperately not to cry. She struggled to see any way out of her predicament while Lord Hutton's leering face swam into her mind.

She had no doubt that her father would do exactly as he said, for he had always been a hard-hearted man. That was why he had been so prosperous in his business dealings: a man with a tender and compassionate heart would not be willing to make some of the callous decisions he had.

If Lucy refused to marry Lord Hutton, she would find herself without a home and without funds—and then what was she to do? Find employment somehow, even without references, without the proper attire? She would be cleaning the homes of her counterparts, easy pickings for any gentlemen who had his eye on her. Could she run to the country? Stay with her brother?

Lucy sighed to herself, knowing that Jonathan would not come to her aid so easily. He was too straight-laced and would most likely return her to her parents' home, instructing her to do as she was told. No, he would not be any kind of help.

For the first time, Lucy wished she had some kind of close friend to whom she could turn. Of course, she had acquaintances, but none of the other young ladies had ever seemed remotely interested in what she considered her passions. They were too interested in discussing their latest achievements, whether it was on the pianoforte or just how many gentlemen callers they had. Lucy had never formed a particular bond with them, nor with anyone else.

This left her entirely alone, she realized. Her heart sank and moisture began to cling to her lashes. Her shoulders began to shake as she finally understood how desperate her situation truly was. So lost was she in her sorrow that she did not hear footsteps, followed by a sudden gasp of shock.

"I do beg your pardon, miss."

The voice caught her attention at once, and, hastily wiping her eyes, Lucy glanced up at the tall figure in the doorway of the arbor.

"Oh, no, it is quite all right," she murmured, hating that her privacy had been intruded upon. She said nothing else, hoping that the intruder would leave her in peace. In the gloom, she could not make out his face, and as her heart began to pick up its pace, she hoped desperately that he was not about to attempt anything discourteous.

Her face warmed with embarrassment. Perhaps he had been planning a liaison in this very place and she had put his plans awry. She would not leave, however, for that would mean returning to the ball where she was sure Lord Hutton would be waiting for her. No, that simply would not do.

"I do apologize for the intrusion," the man said, not making any sign of leaving. "But I have noticed that you seem to be in some distress. Can I assist you in any way?"

"Not unless you can prevent my father's dictates from being enforced, no," Lucy replied before she could stop herself. "Please, do not let me bother you."

"It is of no trouble," he responded, gesturing to another bench to her left. "May I?"

She hesitated, still unable to see his face in the darkness. Her nerves jangled as a loud warning sounded in her mind that she absolutely should not be ensconced with a gentleman in a garden arbor, no matter how kind he appeared.

"You are reticent, of course," he said, as if reading her thoughts. "How rude of me not to introduce myself. I am Lord Caldwell.

Lucy's eyebrows lifted with surprise. "Why are you not enjoying the ball? Won't your parents be searching for you?"

Lord Caldwell sat down carefully, and the bench groaned loudly. "I needed some fresh air. My mother is currently enjoying the ball, but my father, the Marquess of Blackinstore, has gone to Paris on business of some sort. first son of."

Lucy nodded into the darkness, thinking hard. Any man with such a title could be one of two characters: either they went out of their way to throw their wealth and title around, treating others entirely abysmally, or they took their responsibilities seriously and spent their years working hard so that they might one day be ready to take on their father's title.

As of yet, Lucy did not know which character Lord Caldwell might be, although his voice was warm and friendly, which gave her some hope that he might be the latter. "I am Lady Lucy Donoghue," she said heavily. "Daughter of the Earl of Withington."

He inclined his head. "How very nice to meet you, Lady Lucy Donoghue." A momentary pause left them in silence. "Might I ask what has upset you so?"

She let out a harsh laugh. "You may well ask, Lord Caldwell, but given that there is nothing you can do, then I see very little point in discussing it."

"It might help lift your spirits somewhat," he responded.

Letting out another sigh, Lucy stifled a sob and, instead, cleared her throat. "You are a gentleman, and titled at that, so I do not think you will be able to understand the quandary in which I find myself."

"Ah."

"You may marry whomever you choose," she continued bitterly. "As for me, my path is set." Brushing moisture from her lashes, Lucy tried not to give into the fresh tears that threatened to overwhelm her once more.

"Your parents have chosen your fiancé, then?"

"Sadly, yes. Although, I have not been introduced to the man yet, nor been told of their intentions. I was lucky enough to over-hear them."

"And you are hiding from them," Lord Caldwell finished thoughtfully. "A wise choice, Lady Lucy."

Hearing the slight humor in his tone, Lucy bristled. "I did not expect you to understand, Lord Caldwell," she snapped, emphasizing his title so that he would not forget her earlier point. "Why don't you return to the ball if my situation causes you such humor?"

Anger coursed through her veins, making her tremble with frustration. Why had she spoken to him? Was it simply because she had no one else to talk to, or because he had appeared to be kind? Irritated with herself, Lucy closed her eyes tightly, aware that she should not have revealed a single piece of her situation to a stranger.

"Is your betrothed so terrible?" the gentleman softly asked. "Surely the daughter of an earl will be wed to a fine, upstanding gentleman. I have heard of your father and know of his reputation within society. I doubt he would throw you away on some undeserving—"

"I am to be wed to Lord Hutton," Lucy cut him off through clenched teeth. "Something about helping my father with a partnership of sorts." She waited for Lord Caldwell's jovial response, but received none. The seconds ticked by slowly, the atmosphere suddenly growing tense.

Without warning, the gentleman got to his feet, pacing

across the arbor. "You cannot mean the elder Lord Hutton?" he asked, his voice growing louder with each word. "But his son is recently married, is he not?"

"I was not aware he had a son," Lucy said quietly. "So yes, I do mean the elder."

Lord Caldwell paused in his steps, turning to face her, although she could still not make out his features. "But that is quite ridiculous!"

"I am glad you think so," Lucy told him. "I am also glad that you no longer laugh at me."

"That is because I can understand your distress!" he exclaimed, walking over to her. "Why your parents are insisting on such a thing, I cannot understand."

Lucy let out a harsh laugh, knowing exactly why her parents had chosen this course of action. "I am not the daughter they wish for, Lord Caldwell. I much prefer books and the expanding of my mind to practicing the pianoforte or learning the latest gossips that visit my home. In short, they have given up on me, and so have decided that I should be taken off their hands in the easiest way possible." Pressing her hand to her brow, Lucy winced as pain sliced through her heart once more. "It seems I am nothing but a commodity, useful for bartering and trading and securing my father's part-nership."

Lord Caldwell said nothing, simply stared down at her for a long moment. She managed to glance up at him, her vision blurry with unshed tears, managing to make out his features somewhat. Blinking hard, she took in his dark hair, the way his lips were drawn into an angry line. She could not tell what color his eyes were, only that they were focused entirely on her. He appeared to be tall with broad shoulders, every inch the gentleman.

"You appear upset, Lord Caldwell," she said eventually. "I

assure you, there is no need to be so on my behalf. You have enough troubles of your own, I am quite sure."

"That is true," he said quietly, coming to sit beside her.

Astonished, she made to move away, only for him to grasp her hand in his gloved one.

"I mean you no harm, Lady Lucy," he continued. "Please, do not run from me. I might, in fact, have something of a solution for you."

Lucy found herself unable to take her hand from his, the warmth of his body soaking into her chilled limbs. Instead of running, she turned her head to look into his eyes, taking in his serious expression.

"You are not funning me, I hope, Lord Caldwell," she warned. "I have no idea what possesses you to offer to help me, but in truth, I have no other options available to me."

"No, I am not funning you in the least," he replied. "I have had dealings with Lord Hutton in the past and will do anything in my power to keep you from him."

Lucy let out a long breath, knowing she had to at least listen to him. "Well then, Lord Caldwell. What is it you suggest?"

3

L ord Caldwell cleared his throat. "My mother is also pressing me to wed soon," he said slowly. "As of yet, she has not picked any lady in particular, but I fear it will not be long."

"Someday the title of marquess will be yours," Lucy said with a roll of her eyes she was sure he could not see. "Of course she wants you to wed! You will need to produce an heir." Heavy irony lined her voice, as she once more grew inwardly weary with society and its heavy dictates.

"You are correct," he replied without a trace of humor. "But I find myself not quite ready to enter such a state. Perhaps, with both of our situations, there might be one easy solution."

"Such as?" Lucy asked, struggling to see where he might be coming from. "I cannot see any—"

"We become betrothed."

His words shocked her, dragging her breath from her body. She stared at him, breaking into laughter. "You cannot be serious."

"Of course I am," he said, sounding a little affronted.

"And what should we do when the time comes for us to

wed?" she questioned, thinking this was possibly the most ridiculous suggestion she had ever heard. "I will not lose my reputation over a broken engagement."

He did not answer for a moment. "If you are forced to marry Lord Hutton, then you will have no reputation to worry about."

Lucy closed her eyes as his blunt words hit her square in the chest.

"You may break the engagement, Lady Lucy, and I shall take full responsibility."

"And what exactly will you say?" Lucy found herself asking, faintly. She could not understand why she was already so willing to consider this, but she had to admit that he was quite right. She would have no reputation to speak of if she was married to Lord Hutton.

"I will say some such thing about a mistress, fueling rumors and the like. I am sure you will have the ton on your side, full of sympathy for you, whereas, hopefully, the rumors will push any willing lady from my side for another good few months. Besides, I hold the honorary title of earl, and one day I will inherit my father's title and fortune. Your parents should be pleased with the decision. All in all, I think it will work out well."

Lucy shook her head. "But nothing will stop Lord Hutton from wedding me once our engagement is at an end. The problem remains."

Lord Caldwell chuckled. "I can see that you are right, but it will, at least, give you some time to consider what else you can to do extricate yourself from his grip." He leaned forward, and Lucy felt her breath catch in her chest. "If you do not agree, and it is entirely up to you whether you do so or not, you must steel yourself for what will happen the moment you step back into the ballroom."

Lucy did not need to ask what he meant, knowing that her parents would have Lord Hutton introduced to her almost immediately. He would then take her to the dance floor, dance at least two dances—if not three, which would then ensure that all of the society knew there was an attachment between them. She would not be able to refuse without making a scene, bringing shame to both herself and her parents.

"I... I cannot see any other way," she said softly. Her mind was scrambling to think clearly, but she simply could not even begin to think of any other solution. "Though this is quite ridiculous, Lord Caldwell," she said, a little more strongly. "I have not even seen your face, and now we are to be apparently engaged?"

"Well," he answered, getting to his feet. "There is one easy solution to that particular predicament. Shall we walk in the gardens?"

Lucy swallowed and rose, suddenly very aware of the man's height. He waited for her, taking the crook of her elbow in his gloved hand to lead her back into the gardens.

"So," he said as they came to a lantern. "What do you think of me now, Lady Lucy? I am not, perhaps, the most attractive gentleman of your acquaintance, but I hope I will do."

She lifted her face and looked up at him, and fire burst through her veins immediately.

Lord Caldwell was a very handsome gentleman. She had not expected to see such a kind face looking back at her, a gentle smile curving his lips whilst mirth twinkled in his eyes. His dark hair was neatly styled and there was not a trace of stubble on his firm jaw. For a moment, Lucy was robbed of speech, becoming aware that her lips were parted in a most unladylike manner

"You will do, of course, Lord Caldwell," she replied, closing her mouth with a snap.

"And you are more than acceptable," he said, bowing. "Quite stunning, if I may say so. I must confess myself surprised that you have been passed over."

She took his proffered arm and began to walk back towards the house. "You forget that a bluestocking is singularly unattractive," she murmured, warmth settling in her core. "Are you sure you are aware of what it is you are letting yourself in for, my lord?"

His chest rumbled. "I look forward to our many conversations," he responded quietly. "Now, shall we find your parents and let them know of our happy news?"

Lucy swallowed and nodded, her mouth going dry at the thought of introducing the man to her parents. They were either going to be remarkably pleased or incredibly put out, their plan to engage her to Lord Hutton dead in the water. Her parents would not refuse him, of course, given that his title was greater than that of Lord Hutton, but she was already anticipating the displeasure in her father's eyes. This would ruin his plan for a partnership, after all.

"How shall we do it?" she asked, breathlessly. "After all, we have not exactly been seen in one another's company."

Stopping in his tracks, Lord Caldwell turned and smiled at her, making her heart jolt at once. "Do your parents often see you in company at balls?"

She shook her head. "In truth, they very often leave me alone." She managed a strangled laugh. "I believe they have given up on me."

Lord Caldwell's smile widened. "Then we shall simply say that we have had a few conversations over the last few weeks and have, this night, decided that we will suit very well together."

Lucy managed a smile. "And your mother will accept that?"

"My mother will accept any woman I present to her," he said, with a trace of irony. "She is desperate, you see. So long as you are from a good family and with a decent dowry, I can promise you that she will be delighted. Shall we go in?"

Nerves swirled through Lucy's stomach, pushing themselves through her veins. Unable to form words, she clung to Lord Caldwell's arm as they walked towards the French doors, hardly able to believe that she was about to do this. Her life would change for a time at least, no longer able to have the solitude she had always loved. There would be visits and courting and conversations, for they would have to give the impression of being a happily betrothed couple, of course.

"A waltz has begun," he murmured as they stepped into the ballroom. "Shall we, my dear?"

Lucy looked up at him, aware of how he had addressed her and finding it both exciting and terrifying in equal measure.

"It might help calm your nerves," he continued softly. "Come now, Lady Lucy. Courage!"

Lucy lifted her chin and allowed him to sweep her onto the floor. Within moments, they were amidst the rest of the dancing couples, and she was held tightly in his arms. Thankfully for her, Lord Caldwell appeared to be a wonderful dancer, not putting a foot wrong as he glided across the dance floor.

"Relax," he whispered, giving her a bright smile. "We are meant to look wonderfully happy! Remember, we have only just become engaged."

She managed to slightly loosen her grip on his shoulder, holding his hand a little more gently.

"There you go," he chuckled, his chest rumbling as his eyes sparkled with mirth. "Now you look much happier, my dear."

Lucy drew in one long breath after another, aware that she would have to face her parents soon after this dance ended. They would be surprised to see her on the floor, of course, in a gentleman's arms, and even more astonished to discover she was engaged!

The music ended all too soon, and Lucy found herself being escorted from the floor on Lord Caldwell's arm.

"Your parents or mine?" he asked with a quick grin.

"Mine, I think," Lucy said, dampening down her anxiety. "I believe they are upon us."

"As is Lord Hutton," Lord Caldwell growled, evidently spotting the large gentleman following her parents.

Pasting a wide smile on her face, Lucy stepped forward and greeted her parents in an excited tone.

"Lucy," her father began, attempting to draw Lord Hutton forward. "I—"

"Father," Lucy interrupted, her hand now on Lord Caldwell's arm. "Let me introduce you to Lord Caldwell, the first son of the Marquess of Blackinstore." She looked up at him with what she hoped was an adoring expression. "Lord Caldwell, this is my father, the Lord Withington, and my mother, Lady Withington."

"How wonderful to meet you both at last," Lord Caldwell murmured, bowing heavily.

She saw the astonishment in her mother's eyes, though she immediately covered it with a deep curtsy. "How wonderful to meet you, my lord," she murmured, her eyes drifting towards Lucy. "I saw both of you on the dance floor. How delightful that my daughter has managed to acquaint herself with such a fine dancer."

"Not just acquaint, Lady Withington," Lord Caldwell said carefully. "I know this is very hasty, and I must apologize for not seeking you out first, Lord Withington, but I simply could not wait a day longer to ask for your daughter's hand."

"Her hand?" Lord Withington repeated, staring at him. "You mean—"

"We are engaged!" Lucy interrupted, flashing a bright smile at them both.

There was a stunned silence as both of her parents gazed at her as though she had quite lost her senses. Lord Caldwell pressed her hand gently with his, as if asking her to bide her time before speaking again.

"Lord Withington," came a disgruntled murmur. "I thought you said—"

Lucy's father coughed loudly, stepping directly in front of the angry face of Lord Hutton. "How wonderful," he said loudly. "My hearty congratulations to you both."

"Thank you," Lucy heard Lord Caldwell reply as she held her mother's gaze. "I do hope you can forgive me for not seeking an audience with you first."

"But of course," her father said, shaking Lord Caldwell's hand. "I understand. The first foray into love and all that."

"Quite," came Lord Caldwell's reply.

Lucy drew in a long breath and stepped forward to press her mother's hand, leaving the safety of Lord Caldwell's side. "You see, Mama," she said softly, "I have found someone to marry me after all."

Her mother's befuddled expression slowly cleared. "And one day you will be a marchioness," she breathed, excitement filling her expression. "I can hardly believe, it Lucy. I had not even imagined you had formed any kind of attachment of late, given that we hardly see you on the dance floor."

"It is short, I grant you," Lucy said, thrilled that her mother appeared to be taking this so well. "But I care for him deeply, and I believe he feels the same. It is my heart's desire to wed him, Mama. I am so glad you approve."

"It is more than I ever hoped for," her mother responded gleefully. "Just wait until I tell Lady Cuthbert the news!"

4

L ucy hummed to herself as she wandered along the hallway, her mind filled with thoughts of the prior evening. She had managed to get very little sleep last night, as she had so much to think about.

Lord Caldwell would be calling today, and already there was talk of an engagement ball. Thankfully for her, his mother had been delighted, just as he had said she would be. She had grasped Lucy's hand as though she would never let her go, apparently exclaiming that she had never believed her son, Edward, would actually find himself a bride. Lucy introduced her mother to the lady and had left the two of them in deep discussion, apparently both as thrilled as the other.

The same could not be said of her father. He was pleased, of course, for having a potential marquess as a son-in-law was nothing to be disappointed about, but his plans for a partnership with Lord Hutton had been broken to pieces.

Lucy had not even been introduced to Lord Hutton, what with all the excitement of the evening, but she had caught the displeasure on his round face as he glared at her. A shudder ran through her as she remembered how he grasped her father by the arm and spoke to him in rapid, hushed tones, gesticulating wildly at one point. His face had been bright red, beads of sweat trickling down his face, and his crooked teeth more than evident as he grimaced and growled.

Lucy had to admit that she was more than delighted with the outcome, meaning that she would not have to even entertain the idea of being engaged to Lord Hutton any longer. Lord Caldwell, however, was entirely another matter. Lucy could not deny that she found him handsome and believed him to be of a warm disposition and kind character.

Would another gentleman of her acquaintance do what he had? He had taken pity on her and helped her in the most admirable way. She found herself enjoying being on his arm, relishing the warm congratulations that had come from all parties. No longer the wallflower, she was the talk of the town, although there had been a great deal of amazement that she had managed to capture the heart and the hand of the earl.

She rolled her eyes, knowing that it was almost unbelievable. No earl would truly want someone like her for a bride. It was just as well, then, that their engagement was nothing more than a façade.

"This is utterly ridiculous!"

Her mother's voice echoed from her father's study, evidently having a heated exchange with her father.

"She is engaged to an earl, who will one day become a marquess!" Lady Withington exclaimed. "Lord Hutton has nothing on that. Besides, Lord Caldwell seems to make her happy."

"Lord Hutton still wants her for his wife," her father said heavily. "He wants this partnership as much as I do."

"Then work out a partnership without Lucy being part of the bargain," her mother answered firmly. "You cannot wish her to end her engagement with Lord Caldwell, surely!"

There was a brief pause. "No, of course I do not," came the eventual reply. "Lord Hutton is angry, however, because I promised him our daughter's hand."

Lucy caught her breath, leaning against the wall for support. Her mother's shrieks began soon after, echoing down towards her. Apparently, she was furious that her husband wanted their daughter to still consider Lord Hutton. Lucy's engagement to Lord Caldwell was much more advantageous.

"I will sort the matter out, I assure you," her father pleaded, apparently quailing under his wife's fury. "Lord Hutton will have nothing to complain of soon, I promise."

"He had better not ruin this engagement!" her mother screeched, slamming something down heavily. "I will not have our daughter's new position ruined simply because of some old man's fancy."

Lucy's stomach rolled at her mother's words, but, on hearing footsteps, she rushed along the corridor and into the silence of the library.

Sagging against the door, she let out her breath, unease rippling through her. Her father had promised her to Lord Hutton, which meant that Lord Hutton had every right to be angry, for her father did not give his word without fully intending to fulfill it. Would he demand some kind of recompense? And, if so, in what form?

More than ever, Lucy was grateful for Lord Caldwell. Had he not stepped in when she had needed him the most, she might be awakening this morning to find herself betrothed to the repugnant Lord Hutton, who clearly wanted her to be his wife in all senses of the word.

Lucy knew very little of the intimacies between husband and wife, but the thought of him extracted another shudder from her. Lord Hutton was a leech, and she would not allow him to even touch her, not once. Should he ask for a dance, she would refuse him. Now that she knew his intentions, as well as what her father had promised, Lucy swore to herself she would not go near the man.

A short rap on the door startled her, and she opened it to find the surprised face of the maid looking at her.

"I beg your pardon, miss, but your mother wishes to see you."

"And you were sent in search of me, were you?" Lucy replied with a wry smile. "Where is she?"

"The drawing room, miss," the maid answered, bobbing a curtsy before Lucy dismissed her.

Wondering what it was her mother could want, Lucy made her way to the drawing room, only to find her mother waiting for her with a tea tray on the table. Apparently, they were to have a discussion.

"Yes, Mama?"

"Sit, my dear," her mother beamed, her face wreathed in smiles. "We have so much to discuss and I had hoped we might start this very day!"

"What could you mean, Mama?" Lucy asked, blankly.

Her mother let out a loud trill of laughter. "Oh, my dear! You are engaged now, so of course we have a great deal to discuss. There is your trousseau, and of course, your wedding gown as well. I think we should also go to the modiste and purchase a few more." She ran a critical eye over Lucy's dress. "We must fit you in the best gowns now. After all, you are the talk of the town."

Lucy swallowed the sudden ache in her throat and attempted to smile. She had not truly considered what might happen when she told her mother about her supposed engagement. In truth, she had never before seen her mother as delighted and as happy as she was now. What would happen when it all came to an end? Would her mother be heartbroken?

"I do not think I need new gowns, Mama," she replied quickly. "Lord Caldwell has proposed to me already, so it is not as though I need to catch his eye."

"Nonsense," her mother declared, pouring the tea. "You are to be seen all over town, my dear. In fact, I have arranged for the carriage in around one hour."

"The carriage?"

"Yes, yes," her mother answered, almost impatiently. "To the modiste, of course!"

Lucy hated the thought of being swathed in fabric, of being pinched and prodded. "Mama, Lord Caldwell is coming to call this afternoon."

Her mother waved a hand. "We shall be back before he arrives, of course. You need not worry, Lucy." Her face softened as she handed Lucy a cup of tea. "You have done very well, my dear. I never imagined you would capture such a man. To think that you will be a marchioness one day..." She trailed off, regarding her daughter with something like wonder in her eyes. "I hope you know just how proud I am of you, Lucy."

The ache in Lucy's throat reappeared almost at once, and she managed a wobbly smile. Her mother had not often spoken to her so, and she still remembered what Lady Withington had said about her only the day before, but still, the words hit her heart with a great deal of force.

"Thank you, Mama," she murmured, furiously blinking so that no tears would slip down her cheeks. "I do hope you like Lord Caldwell."

"Of course I do!" her mother exclaimed. "He is handsome and titled. What is there not to like?"

Those words haunted Lucy all through her fittings, allowing her mother to dictate the color and cut of the gowns whilst she stared at herself in the mirror. Was that all there was to Lord Caldwell—his title and handsome features? She did not want to admit it, but she knew almost as little about him as her mother did. It did not seem quite right to know so little about one's betrothed, even though it would not last all the way to matrimony. He was of a kind heart, having taken her out of her miserable predicament and promising that he would bear the burden of the broken engagement when the time came.

Did Lucy want to know more about him? Would that not put her into dangerous territory? She stared at herself in the mirror, noting the slight blush in her cheeks. Her mother was right; Lord Caldwell was a wonderfully handsome man. She could not pretend that she was not attracted to him, for even the memory of his smile sent a shiver through her.

She would have to spend a lot more time in his company over the next few weeks, until their betrothal came to an end. She would have plenty of time to get to know him, but Lucy reminded herself that she would have to ensure her heart was not in the least engaged by that time. It would not be a good thing to fall completely head over heels for Lord Caldwell, only for their acquaintance to come to an end. She certainly did not want to add a truly broken heart into their already complicated relationship.

"Ah, yes!" her mother exclaimed, her voice intruding on Lucy's thoughts. "This is lovely. I believe you can keep this on for the time being, Lucy. Lord Caldwell will simply adore it, I am sure."

Lucy lifted her eyes to the mirror and found herself clad in a beautiful day dress. Its warm red tones highlighted her brown eyes, whilst also illuminating her golden hair. It was one of the loveliest dresses she had ever owned.

"What do you think, Lucy?" her mother asked, grasping her hand in an unexpected gesture of affection. "Will your betrothed like it?"

"I am sure he will, Mama," Lucy whispered, unable to take

her eyes from her reflection. "In fact, I am not sure he will recognize me!"

"Wonderful," her mother sighed happily. "Then we will purchase it, and then we must return home at once. It would not to do keep Lord Caldwell waiting."

Lucy stepped down onto the floor, brushing her hands over her skirts in an attempt to calm her jangling nerves. She had not expected to feel this way, not after only just meeting the man the day before!

Control your heart, Lucy, she warned herself, following her mother out to the front of the shop. *There is no use in falling in love with the man, especially when it is all a sham. Remember that it is all a pretense.*

Stepping out into the cold, Lucy lifted her chin and tried to smile, pretending she did not feel the sinking of her heart.

5

L ucy drew in a long breath and tried to smile as the door opened and Lord Caldwell was announced. Deep within her heart, she wondered whether he had changed his mind over their engagement, having had the night to think on it. Not that much could be done about it now without causing a severe scandal.

"Lord Caldwell," she murmured, curtsying gracefully before lifting her head to look at him. "How are you this afternoon?"

His smile was warm, alleviating her nerves almost at once. "I am all the better for seeing you, my dear," he said, taking her hand before bowing to her mother, who was gushing with sentiment. Lucy gave him something of a wry smile before sitting down, allowing her mother to witter on for a few moments before delicately clearing her throat.

"Shall I ring for tea, Mama?"

"Oh, yes, yes, do," her mother replied, her face more animated than Lucy had seen in a long time. "You shall stay for tea, shall you not, Lord Caldwell?"

"It would be my pleasure," Lord Caldwell answered, his eyes

twinkling as he glanced towards Lucy, apparently entirely at ease with her mother's overly enthusiastic manner.

Lucy smiled back and allowed her mother to continue her discussion with Lord Caldwell, noting that something warm was settling in her stomach. Was it because she was glad to see her mother so happy? Or was it because Lord Caldwell appeared to be such a kind gentleman to be so willing to entertain her mother's enthusiasm?

"And, my dear Lady Lucy, how are you today?" Lord Caldwell asked the moment her mother paused for breath. "I am sure after last night's commotion, you must be exhausted!"

Heat rippled up into her cheeks as she remembered how he had found her in the garden arbor, and her ridiculous exclamation about how handsome he was. "I am quite well; I thank you," she mumbled, dropping her eyes for a moment. "I am glad your mama thinks me acceptable."

"More than acceptable, I assure you," he replied, his smile widening. "In fact, she has requested that we throw an engagement ball, but I insisted that I ask you first before she begins making any plans."

Lucy opened her mouth to answer, only for her mother to interrupt with a gasp and a clap of her hands.

"A ball! How wonderful! Yes, of course we should have an engagement ball. It is very kind of your mother to think of such a thing. Lucy would be delighted with such an event, is that not true, Lucy?" Her mother turned to her for a moment but gave her no time to answer before turning back to Lord Caldwell. "You must allow me to help in some way."

Lord Caldwell reached for one of her hands and patted it gently. "My dear lady, my mama has requested that you call upon her at your earliest convenience. I believe she hopes you might organize the ball together, as it will give you the opportunity to get to know one another a little more. In addition, with my father currently out of the country on diplomatic business, I believe she could do with some company."

Watching her mother with amusement, Lucy saw the way her eyes widened and her mouth formed a perfect circle as she was robbed of speech for a moment.

"What say you, Mama?" Lucy asked drily. "Shall you write to her this very moment?"

She had not expected her mother to take to her suggestion immediately, but to her surprise, Lady Withington stood up in a flurry of skirts and practically rushed from the room, saying something about how it was an excellent notion and she would press her note into Lord Caldwell's hand before he left.

Clearly, her mother had not realized that she had left Lucy and Lord Caldwell completely alone. Even as a betrothed couple, this was not entirely seemly.

"Well," Lucy murmured, suddenly unsure as to where to look. "I think you have my mother in the palm of your hand, Lord Caldwell."

"She appears to be quite delightful," he replied, leaning forward in his chair. "But I am not sorry that she has left the room, for it gives us some time to speak freely."

Lucy's stomach swirled with sudden nerves. "I do hope you are not regretting our scheme, my lord."

His surprise was evident. "No, not in the least!" he exclaimed, his dark eyes searching hers. "Are you?"

"Not at all," she responded, aware of just how quickly her heart was beating. "My mother has never been so delighted, as you can see!"

His eyes lit with humor. "Neither mine," he said, his lips quirking into a smile. "It appears you have done what so many other ladies could not, according to Mama. She is utterly besotted with you, even more than I am!"

Lucy managed a smile, her breath catching as she took in the warmth in his eyes, the easy smile on his lips. Had he meant such a sentiment, truthfully? Or was he simply playing the part?

"I must confess I was a little surprised to hear that Mama wished to throw an engagement ball for us both, but given the circumstances, I was unable to do anything but agree." Lord Caldwell's hand reached for hers, his fingers brushing her skin. "I do hope you are not upset."

Jolted by his touch, Lucy felt tension ripple through her body, making her more than aware of just how close he was to her, despite being in an entirely separate seat.

"You believe I might be upset over a ball, my lord?" she asked, hating that she was a little breathless. "It is quite the contrary, I assure you." She gave him a tight smile, relieved when his fingers left her hand and he sat back in his chair.

"I am glad to hear it," he replied quietly.

Lucy, deciding to be honest, lifted her chin. "In truth, my lord, I have had very little attentions from my parents who, as you were aware, practically wrote me off. Since yesterday evening, that has changed entirely! My mother is insisting on a trousseau and even a few new gowns for our betrothal period." She shook her head as a slightly sad smile crossed her lips. "I cannot remember the last time mother was so willing to spend both time and money on me."

Her words trailed off, her eyes leaving his only to land across the room, focusing on nothing in particular. Her mother's attentions would die away again the moment Lucy's engagement came to an end, and Lucy knew she would feel the loss keenly. For the first time in many years, she felt as though there was nothing of ill-feeling or frustration between herself and her mother. It was a feeling Lucy realized she truly appreciated.

"You must make the most of this then, my dear," Lord Caldwell said gently, his words intruding on her thoughts. "Your mother may give her sympathies towards you for some time after our engagement comes to an end. Now that she knows you have the ability to catch the eye of a man who is, one day, to become a marquess, she will not push you towards Lord Hutton again."

Lucy frowned, remembering the strange conversation she had heard taking place between her parents only earlier that afternoon.

"I do not believe Lord Hutton is entirely thrilled with our betrothal," she said wryly. "I heard my father talking earlier."

Lord Caldwell snorted. "I care very little for what Lord Hutton thinks," he muttered darkly. "And whilst I will admit that the man is not used to being refused what he wants, I am delighted that I have saved you from his clutches."

At that very moment, the tea tray arrived, preventing further discourse on the matter. As Lucy prepared to pour the tea, her thoughts would not leave the discussion she had heard previously. She knew very little of Lord Hutton, but if what Lord Caldwell said was true, then they would have to take care around the man. Not that she intended on seeing him again, but if he was going into partnership with her father—even without her hand as part of the deal—then there was a chance she might be introduced to him at some point in time.

Lord Caldwell cleared his throat and accepted a cup from her gratefully. "Perhaps we ought to get to know one another a little more," he suggested, smiling at her. "After all, when someone asks me about my betrothed, I think it would be best if I knew the answer to their questions. Otherwise, I do not give the impression that I am a man in love!"

Laughing softly, Lucy felt her cheeks warm as he grinned at her, the butterflies not entirely gone from her belly. If only he were not quite so handsome, then she might not feel such unsettling things. "I think that would be a welcome idea, my lord," she said before delicately taking a sip of her steaming tea. "Although

I must warn you that you may find some of my answers uncon-
ventional."

To her surprise, he let out a loud laugh, his eyes crinkling at
the corners as he chuckled.

"Lady Lucy," he said, "that is precisely why I think you are so
well suited to me, even if this is all a sham. I have never had any
interest in the run of the mill, finely dressed, and slightly
vacuous young ladies of the ton. Instead, I have sought to find
someone who is, by all intents and purposes, a little less 'run of
the mill.' In short, my dear, I find your unconventionality a truly
desirable trait."

"Oh," Lucy murmured, wondering why she struggled to find
words to form any kind of reply. "Then I am relieved, Lord
Caldwell."

"Shall I begin?" he asked, settling back in his chair. "Why
don't we start with your favorite novel of late?"

6

"Should you like to go for a drive this afternoon, Lady Lucy?"

Lucy looked up at Edward and graced him with a smile. "Yes, I believe so."

The drive would be their first outing as a newly betrothed couple, and Lucy could already feel the swirl of nerves settling in her stomach. This was the third time Lord Caldwell had called upon her at her parents' home, but as yet, they had not taken any kind of outing outside of the four walls.

"Wonderful," he replied, smiling at her. "The phaeton is just outside."

Within a few minutes, Lucy found herself in the phaeton, fully aware that she would be spotted by a great many people within society. Thankfully, the phaeton meant that she did not have to bring her maid with her, something she was greatly relieved over, for it meant that she and Lord Caldwell could have a free conversation, which was something she was growing to appreciate.

"How are you, Lord Caldwell?" She glanced up at him, catching the swift smile that crossed his face.

"I have been thinking, Lady Lucy. Now that we are betrothed, I think you may call me Edward, if you wish it."

That was quite proper, but still, Lucy felt a blush rise to her cheeks. "Then you may address me simply as Lucy," she murmured, wondering why she felt such a rush of pleasure when he spoke her name.

"Lucy," he said, smiling at her. "That is such a lovely name. And may I compliment you on your attire. I believe I was over-come by your beauty when I first laid eyes on you this afternoon!"

She laughed. "We need not pretend that much! No one else can hear what you are saying."

To her surprise, he did not laugh, but rather held her gaze for a moment. "I mean every word, my dear Lucy," he said quietly. "You are a beautiful creature and I am glad to have you on my arm."

Lucy swallowed and spoke not another word, as she did not know what to say. This was meant to be a pretense, after all, although surely it did not matter if he complimented her on her appearance. It was not wrong if he found her desirable. In the same way, she thought him handsome.

"I have embarrassed you now," he said, breaking the sudden awkwardness. "I do apologize. It must seem quite strange to you to accept such compliments from a man you barely know, even if I am meant to be your betrothed."

"In truth, Edward, I very rarely receive any kind of compli-ment," she replied with honesty, "so I am, perhaps, less used to accepting them with grace. I thank you for your kind words. Mama has insisted on practically an entirely new wardrobe, and only this morning I found myself at the modiste for a final fitting!"

He chuckled then, his tones rich and warm. "It is amazing what an engagement can do to one's parents, is it not? My own mother has smiled at me a great many times since I first announced our news. Indeed, I cannot remember the last time she was so enamored with me!"

Lucy joined in his laughter, appreciating his wit. "But you must tell me, Edward," she said, growing a little more serious. "Why have you never married?" At his surprised look, she colored but continued on bravely. If they were to pretend to be betrothed, she believed she ought to know. "You are handsome and titled, so surely there must have been some young lady who caught your eye at some point."

Edward looked at her again, just as the phaeton turned into Hyde Park. "I suppose that is true. Many young ladies have caught my eye." He shook his head and gazed across the park. "But in truth, Lucy, I do not wish to marry someone who cares only for balls and fripperies." His eyes flicked to hers. "I believe I have spoken to you of such a thing before. If I am to marry, I want a wife with whom I can have a pleasant and engaging conversation, as well as someone who will be an excellent hostess and can fulfill the duties required when the time comes for me to take my title." He threw her a quick smile. "Perhaps I am too severe with my requirements, but as yet, no one has met my standards."

Lucy felt her heart sink into her slippers, but she forced a smile onto her face. "Mayhap you will meet someone very soon, Edward. Maybe even before our betrothal comes to an end! I have heard it said that a newly engaged man often draws more ladies than ever before."

He scrunched up his features with distaste. "I should not care for any woman who did that kind of thing," he replied firmly. "A betrothal signals the start of a serious attachment, not one that can simply be given up for someone—or something —new."

She raised her eyebrows, surprised to hear such an opinion.

"I believe many men take on a mistress," she murmured quietly. "It is almost expected, is it not?"

Frowning, Edward shook his head. "Not for me, Lucy," he said. "When I marry, I will make my vows with the utmost seriousness, committing myself to one woman for the remainder of my life. I know such a stance is almost laughable, but I intend to stick with it."

"You astonish me greatly," Lucy murmured, both surprised and delighted to hear the words from his lips. "I had not expected a gentleman with such a title to have your attitude. Even my own father..."

She trailed off, shaking her head to herself as she was reminded of the lack of love shown between her parents, and how her mother had told her on more than one occasion that any husband should be expected to have a mistress.

A gentle hand touched her own, startling her from her thoughts. "What hopes do you have for matrimony, Lucy? You will not accept a man who intends to take a mistress, I think."

Laughing, Lucy smiled up at Edward. "No, indeed not!" Her smile became a little dreamy, her gaze wandering across the park as she glanced at all the other carriages. "You may call me ridiculous, Edward, but I hope for love. I have seen the kind of marriage my parents have, one where there is no affection between them whatsoever. I do not want the same for me. I desire love, but I suppose I will have to settle for affection."

"Do not ever settle, Lucy!" Edward exclaimed, grasping her hand suddenly. "You cannot, I beg of you. Stick to what it is you desire and know that it is within your grasp."

Her entire body buzzed with awareness as he looked into her eyes, the fervency in his expression making her breath catch in her throat. He did not look away, did not drop her hand, and small explosions began to go off in her head. Without warning, he leaned closer, and she could feel his breath mingling with hers.

Was he about to kiss her? She had never been kissed before, closing her eyes with a welcome expectation.

"Ah, Caldwell!"

A voice had Edward jump back into his seat, his back ramrod straight as he turned to speak to another gentleman sitting astride his horse.

"Brownly," Lucy heard him say, finding herself a little dazed. "May I present my betrothed, Lady Lucy Donoghue. Lady Lucy, my dear friend Lord Brownly."

"Betrothed!" Lord Brownly exclaimed, doffing his hat and smiling at her. "How wonderful. May I offer you both my sincere congratulations."

Gathering herself, Lucy managed to smile up at him. "I thank you, my lord. It is a most happy state."

"I am sure it is," Lord Brownly said, his eyes twinkling at her. "I dare say your mother must have been in alt with the news, Caldwell?"

The gentlemen both laughed aloud, making Lucy smile with a genuine happiness. It was nice to see Lord Caldwell so relaxed, so at ease with someone who seemed to be a genuine friend. She allowed the conversation to wash over her as the two gentlemen talked, realizing anew just how little she knew of her betrothed. She knew nothing of his friends, of his hobbies, or even whether he preferred port over brandy.

She supposed that this was the case with many engaged couples, but it did not sit right with her. Even if this was a pretense, which was soon to come to an end, she found that she wanted to know more about him. *Just as a friend*, she assured herself, denying the spark of heat she had felt between them just a few moments earlier.

"What do you think, my dear?"

Edward's question made her start, and, flushing, she dropped her eyes. "I must beg your pardon, my lord. I did not hear your question."

"Too busy daydreaming of your wedding day, no doubt," Lord Brownly interrupted, smiling at her. "That is just as it should be, of course. I was simply asking if you would care to join me for dinner next week? It is just a few friends, of course, nothing overly grand. I am sure we shall have some musical accompaniments and the like after dinner. Perhaps you might grace us with a song, Lady Lucy?"

Her flush deepened. "I confess that I am not particularly skilled when it comes to such a thing, Lord Brownly, although I would be happy to be an avid listener."

"Then you will come?" he asked, placing his hat back on his head. "I would very much like to get to know the lady my friend has so obviously fallen head over heels for!" He gave her a wide smile, clearly unaware of just how unsettled his words had made her.

"I would be delighted to attend," she managed to reply, twining her fingers together so as not to betray her emotions. "I thank you for the invitation."

Nodding to Lord Caldwell, he said, "A week from today, then."

Lucy watched him ride away, just as Lord Caldwell picked up the ribbons and began to continue their way around the park. They rode in silence for some minutes, as though neither of them knew what to say.

"I hope I did not embarrass you just then," Lucy murmured, feeling more than a little self-conscious. "I know ladies are meant to be masters of the pianoforte and spend their time practicing the arts, but I confess that I have never shown much interest in such things."

Turning to face her, Lord Caldwell gave her a wide smile,

which sent yet more butterflies to her stomach. "I should not be embarrassed by you in any regard, I think, Lucy. You are quite wonderful."

Heat crept up her spine and into her cheeks. "You do not mind?"

He shook his head. "No, of course not. Although I must confess myself a little embarrassed that I did not know you preferred to listen over performing." With another shake of his head, he glanced at her. "I have enjoyed our conversations over the last few days," he continued, his hand reaching for hers for just a brief moment. "We are meant to be engaged, and I believe one should know things about their betrothed. I believe I know more about you now than I did only a few days ago, yet I feel as though there is so much more for me to discover!"

Lucy smiled, delighted that he had put into words the exact sentiment she had been feeling. "I agree, Edward. Although I will admit that I find myself quite at ease with you already. It is as though we have been friends for a very long time, even though I have only known you for a brief period."

"I feel exactly the same way," he murmured, studying her for a moment longer. "Perhaps we should take one of the quieter paths within the park, instead of following society's routes. We might then have a little more privacy to talk."

"That would be wonderful," she said softly.

He did not reply but simply took the phaeton further into the park, turning to the left and then to the right until they were almost entirely alone. Lucy sighed happily to herself, feeling entirely safe with Edward and knowing that they were about to have a most enjoyable conversation together. It seemed that he was an extraordinary man.

7

"There," Lucy's maid smiled, looking down at Lucy's hairstyle. "I think you are ready, miss."

Lucy smiled and got to her feet, walking over towards the full-length mirror in the corner of the room. What she saw utterly astonished her.

"Good gracious!" she breathed, taking her reflection in. "I look quite..."

"Beautiful, miss!" the maid interrupted, clapping her hands together and beaming at her.

"You have done a wonderful job," Lucy murmured, running her hand down over her new gown. "Thank you."

The maid bobbed a curtsy, although Lucy could see the blush in her cheeks at Lucy's praise. "Is there anything else, miss? Remember you have your necklace laid out for you on the dresser."

Lucy shook her head. "No, that will be all. I will be down presently."

The maid nodded and walked from the room, leaving Lucy entirely to her own thoughts.

Staring at her reflection once more, Lucy felt her cheeks heat as she thought of what Edward's response might be. Even she was astounded at what she saw, having never before allowed her maid to put so much time and effort into dressing her.

Her hair was done up in an elegant style, adorned with a few pearls that caught the light when she moved. The gown was a new creation, done in the latest fashion of course, but it was a wonderful shade of gold with a sheen of red gossamer over the top. It brought out her coloring, highlighting her chocolate-colored eyes and blonde curls. In truth, Lucy barely recognized herself.

Lifting the shimmering necklace from the dresser, Lucy fastened it around her neck and tried not to allow her nerves to grow any more than they already had. The drive with Edward last week—as well as the three outings that had taken place thereafter—had all gone wonderfully well, and she had found herself enjoying his company more and more. They were never short of conversation, talking about many subjects of interest to both, from science to her favorite novel.

Lucy smiled to herself as she remembered the surprise evident in his face when she had launched into her thoughts on the most recent laws brought before Parliament. Not that he had laughed at her, or shown any kind of derision. In fact, his face had almost glowed with appreciation. They had talked and laughed, and she found herself sad and disappointed when the time had come to return her home.

Tonight was the dinner with Lord Brownly, and Edward would be calling for her in a few moments. Lucy could no longer deny that her initial attraction to him was slowly growing into something more. It was as though he was the gentleman she had been waiting for but had never had the opportunity to meet. It did not surprise her, given how large society was, though now that she had found him, she knew that she simply did not wish to give him up.

The engagement was meant to be broken in a few weeks, but Lucy was beginning to wonder whether she might ask him to consider making it of a longer duration. Perhaps, in time, he might come to feel for her what she was beginning to feel for him, and he would want to make their arrangement something permanent himself.

"Do you wish to marry him, Lucy?" she asked her reflection, feeling the answering warmth in her heart as she thought of it.

In truth, she did not want their engagement to come to an end. She wanted to marry him. In her heart, Lucy knew that there would never be another gentleman like Edward, one who managed to capture her heart in the way he did. He did not look down on her for her interest in things that most other ladies shunned, but encouraged her in them. Their discussions were lively, and the warmth in his eyes when he smiled at her always made her glow inwardly.

There had been times when he had touched her hand, and even one occasion when his ungloved hand had taken hers for a good few minutes. She had hardly been able to breathe—such were the sensations sparking in her chest. Was it possible that he might feel more for her than he had initially intended?

Her stomach swirled with butterflies. Schooling her features into a serene expression, Lucy opened the door and went downstairs. She was not waiting but a minute when Lord Caldwell was announced. She rose as he stepped in, only for him to stop short and stare at her, his mouth hanging open.

Lucy swallowed the sudden lump in her throat as his eyes traveled over her, hoping desperately that he was pleased with what he saw.

"My goodness, Lucy," he said, haltingly. "You are exquisite."

Heat rose into her face at once. "I thank you, Edward. You cut quite a dashing figure yourself."

A strange expression came over his face as he stepped closer, taking her hand and pressing his lips to her palm. Lucy's breathing quickened as his lips brushed her skin, moving a fraction closer when he raised his head.

They were standing very close together, she realized, far too close than what was regarded propriety.

We are meant to be engaged, she reminded herself, looking up into his face. *And we are alone, at least for a few minutes.*

"Lucy, I—" she heard him say, his voice husky and filled with emotion. She opened her mouth to ask him what it was he wanted to tell her, only for his lips to brush hers.

Startled, Lucy stepped back and raised one hand to her mouth, touching her lips with her fingers.

"I apologize," Lord Caldwell muttered, looking around in an entirely self-conscious manner. "I know this is meant to be a sham, Lucy, but my heart does not believe it."

Lucy drew in a breath, the tension leaving her shoulders, and she drew close to him again. She had never been kissed before, but it seemed entirely right to be doing such a thing with Edward. He was looking down at her uncertainly, possibly wondering whether she might slap him for his actions, which only made her smile.

"Perhaps we should be going, Edward," she said quietly. "We do not want to keep Lord Brownly waiting."

"You are not angry?" he asked, relief evident on his face.

She shook her head and, reaching up on her tiptoes, pressed her mouth to his. Stars exploded inside her as his arms slid around her waist, holding her tighter against him than ever before. He broke the kiss after a few moments, releasing his hold a little. Lucy laughed softly when he let out a long breath of relief, as though he hardly believed what had happened.

"I think we have much to talk about," he murmured, lifting her chin with one gentle finger. "Unfortunately, now is not the time for that."

She gave him a slightly wry smile. "No, it is not. Perhaps tomorrow?"

He nodded. "Tomorrow sounds wonderful. Shall we go, my dear?"

Lucy took his proffered arm while warmth settled in the pit of her belly. This was working out perfectly.

LUCY LAUGHED as Lord Brownly finished the punchline to his joke, appreciating the way Edward's eyes lit with humor. She could still not believe that he had kissed her, heat flooding her core as she remembered her own intense response. There was a developing affection for him that she could not deny, and even now, as he smiled at her, Lucy felt her cheeks heat.

"May I offer a toast?" Lord Brownly asked, getting to his feet. "My warmest congratulations to my dear friend, Lord Caldwell, and his most beautiful betrothed, Lady Lucy Donoghue." He raised his glass and gave Edward a grin, followed by a slight bow to Lucy. "I wish you a lifetime of happiness."

A flush hit Lucy's cheeks as the entire table raised their glasses to herself and Edward. Glancing at him, she saw him watching her with a deep warmth in his eyes that ricocheted through her and had her heart almost exploding with happiness.

You are not truly engaged yet, Lucy, she reminded herself. *He kissed you, yes, but you have not discussed what this might change, if it changes anything. Accept their congratulations but keep your mind clear.*

Drawing in one long breath, Lucy settled her mind and waited patiently until the cheers had come to a close before returning Edward's smile. He was studying her with a dawning speculation, as though he had only just realized what future they might have together, were he to take the next step with her. So much promise presented itself in that one look, so much hope, that Lucy could barely prevent herself from rising from the table and dragging him from the room so that they might talk.

A sudden commotion outside the dining room door brought those thoughts to a swift end as loud voices broke into the genial atmosphere.

"What the devil?" Lord Brownly muttered, rising to his feet. "Whatever is going on?" Turning to his guests, he gave a swift bow before marching to the door. "Do excuse me, please," he murmured, walking from the room.

"I'd best go with him," Lord Caldwell said, pressing one hand onto Lucy's shoulder as he passed. "Please, carry on, everyone."

Lucy could do nothing but sit silently. The murmurs around the table began to grow in number as the voices of Lord Brownly and then Lord Caldwell added to the commotion.

"She is his betrothed," she heard Lord Brownly state, his voice loud enough to hear. "You have no right to come here and demand such a thing. Remove yourself from my house before I have someone do it for you."

Lucy's stomach tightened, wondering if this was to do with her. If so, then who was it who had come to Lord Brownly's home in some strange attempt to accost him?

Within a few minutes, all had grown quiet, and the door opened to admit Lord Brownly and Lord Caldwell back into the room. Lucy kept her eyes pinned on Lord Caldwell, but he only smiled and then gave a tiny shake of his head, warning her that he could not speak of what had gone on at this precise moment. Lucy knew then that whatever had occurred had had to do with her, and her stomach dropped to her toes.

"A very strange occurrence," Lord Brownly said, resuming

his seat. "But it has all been dealt with. I do beg your pardon for the intrusion, but we can continue on now. Port, gentlemen?"

Lucy rose from the table with the other ladies and they all excused themselves to the drawing room, leaving the gentlemen to their port. She heard the other ladies begin to discuss immediately what might have happened and who it had been outside the door, but she kept her thoughts to herself. A few ladies glanced in her direction, as though they suspected she was involved, but nothing direct was said.

It was with some relief that she saw the gentlemen arrive in the drawing room, having chosen not to linger over their port.

"And now to the musical performances!" Lord Brownly cried, clapping his hands. "Which of the dear ladies wishes to stand up first?"

Lucy slowly moved into the shadows in the darker corners of the room, knowing that she would not stand up even if she was asked. She was relieved that Lord Brownly knew not to expect her to do so, glad to see a young Miss Edwards seat herself at the pianoforte and begin to play. The other guests took to their seats almost at once, although Lucy caught Lord Caldwell looking through them, searching for her.

Lifting her hand, she saw him catch her eye and carefully move towards her.

"You are hiding, I see," he murmured, his mouth so close to her ear that it caused her to shiver. "Are you well?"

"What on earth went on out there?" Lucy asked, not answering his question. "Was it to do with me?"

She refused to look away from him, her eyes searching his face as he pressed his lips together, struggling to find an answer.

"I have no wish to alarm you," he said quietly. "The matter is dealt with, I assure you."

Lucy shook her head, refusing to accept his response. "Please, Edward. Do not hide things from me."

Sighing, Edward caught her hand in his, squeezing it gently. "It is only for your good, but I see that you will not be dissuaded. Come, shall we take a walk in the gardens? Tis late, I know, but we might slip away without being noticed—and I have heard that engaged couples are shown a little more leniency by society!"

"And you will tell me?" Lucy asked, tension coursing through her body.

"I will," Edward promised, lifting her hand on to his arm. "Come, my dear. Let us make our escape."

8

The gardens were cold, making Lucy shiver, and Edward immediately removed his jacket and pressed it to her shoulders.

"We cannot have you catching a cold now," he said with a lilt to his voice.

"But you will be cold now," she protested, although she could not help but pull his warm coat a little more closely over her body.

"I will be all right," he reassured her, his eyes catching the moonlight as he smiled. Then he stopped and took her hand. "We have much to talk of, do we not?"

Lucy found herself letting out a breathless laugh. "I believe so, Edward." She lifted her face. "But of what do you wish to speak?" Quirking one eyebrow, she made sure he was aware that she would not forget her questions about what had happened outside the dining room.

He sighed heavily, shook his head, and grinned. "You are quite incorrigible, my dearest Lucy," he murmured, sliding his arm around her waist before beginning to walk with her once more. "But I believe I like that about you."

"I did hear a little snippet of what was said," Lucy admitted quietly. "Something about someone who was engaged... and I was worried that I was the one being discussed."

There was a lingering silence, which made Lucy's heart beat faster. Was she right?

"You do not miss much," Edward said after a few moments. "Yes, it was about you, I'm afraid. About the both of us."

"Oh?"

His clasp around her waist tightened "Lord Hutton was here."

Lucy stopped dead on her feet, despite the way Lord Caldwell urged her to walk on. "Lord Hutton?" she repeated, her breath wavering slightly. "What do you mean, he was here? Did Lord Brownly invite him?"

Edward shook his head at once. "No, not at all. He does not hold the man in high regard, much as I do." Lucy saw the way his face grew puzzled. "In truth, I am not sure how he came to know we were here."

Trying to control her anxiety, Lucy drew in two long breaths before speaking. "And I presume he wished to speak to me?"

"I'm afraid it was more than that," he answered. "He told first Brownly, and then myself, that he had some claim over you. That you were betrothed to him first. Apparently, he was going to attempt to procure a Special License."

Lucy's eyes widened as she stared up at Edward, hardly able to comprehend what he was saying. "He was going to attempt to marry me?"

Edward shrugged. "I have very little idea what his intentions were, in truth. He seemed quite crazed, and I grew concerned over his behavior. You must be careful, Lucy."

"I am glad now that you have told me the truth," Lucy murmured, leaning forward so that her head rested on his chest. "It means that I am at least aware of what Lord Hutton intends."

To her surprise, a quiet growl came from Edward's chest. "I do not like it, Lucy. That man is determined to have you, for whatever reason." He pressed a gentle kiss to her hair and Lucy smiled despite the anxiety she felt. "I believe we must call our faux engagement off, my dear."

"What?" Stepping back, she looked at him in confusion, wondering what precisely he meant. "You wish to call our engagement off?"

Chuckling, Lord Caldwell took her hand. "No need to look so fiery, my love. You have misunderstood me. I wish to call off our faux engagement." His expression softened. "You will marry me, won't you?"

Confusion parted to make way for delight as a soft smile spread over Lucy's face. "So, this is just to protect me from Lord Hutton, is it?" she teased, refusing to answer his question. "Or is it because you kissed me earlier today and now feel obliged to wed me?"

"You are toying with me now," he growled, sliding his arms around her and lowering his head. "I might have to kiss you again if you continue."

Lucy could feel her heart beginning to pound in her chest, her hands reaching up of their own accord to twine around his neck. "Tell me the truth, Edward."

He sighed and pressed his forehead to hers. "In truth, Lucy, I have found you a most wonderful companion... and a beautiful one at that. I must confess that I have some affection for you."

It is not love, Lucy thought to herself, a strange pang of sadness echoing through her chest. *But perhaps love can come from it.*

"And I will admit to feeling the same," she replied. "In time, I believe I will love you, Edward."

"I remember that you said you will not marry without love," Edward continued, his voice barely louder than a whisper. "I do not wish you to forgo what you have long hoped for. Therefore, let us have a prolonged engagement, Lucy, so that what I feel might develop into the deep love and affection you have been waiting for."

"Do you truly believe you can come to feel those things for me?" Lucy asked hesitantly. "I will marry you without them."

He laughed quietly. "But I would not have it. I believe that I already feel the beginnings of love rooting in my heart."

She sighed then, letting out her breath and thinking through all he had said. "Very well," she murmured, her fingers now toying with his hair. "I accept your terms, Edward." Her tone grew mischievous once more, in the hope that he might do as he had said and kiss her again.

"Minx," he murmured jestingly before lowering his head and kissing her firmly.

⁓

LUCY COULD HARDLY SLEEP a wink the following night, her heart and mind too full of all that Edward had told her. When she finally arose, it was late morning, so she sought out her mother. Lucy found herself suddenly filled with a desire to throw herself, headlong, into the wedding plans.

"Oh, Lucy!" her mother exclaimed the very moment she stepped into the drawing room. "I have been waiting for you to appear!"

"How was your visit, Mama?" Lucy asked, smiling as she sat down opposite her mother. "I do hope that Lord Caldwell's mother, Lady Blackinstore, was kind to you."

"She was very kind, indeed!" her mother cried, her eyes lit with excitement. "She is wonderful. I can hardly believe you are going to be her daughter-in-law—and one day, the Marchioness of Blackinstore." She shook her head, evidently still struggling to take it all in. "The ball has been arranged. It is to happen in four days hence."

Lucy's mouth dropped open. "Four days, Mama? Is it to happen so soon? What of the guests?"

Lady Withington let out a long, trilled laugh. "Lucy, you are going to have to get used to your new status. Those who receive an invitation, even if they are already requested elsewhere, will simply give their apologies to the others and ensure they attend our ball."

"I see," Lucy murmured, not sure whether she particularly liked that idea. "I do not want anything over the top, Mama. You know how much I have disliked balls in the past."

"Nonsense," her mother said shortly. "You will appreciate every moment of it, Lucy. It will be all about you and Edward."

Thinking that she liked that idea even less, Lucy braved a smile and sat back with an inward sigh. She supposed that her mother was right, in some regard. She would be a marchioness one day, and society would expect her to, at least, be visible. Attention would follow her wherever she went.

Marrying Edward means your life will change entirely, she reminded herself, her stomach rolling with an instant anxiety. *Are you prepared for that, Lucy?*

It was not something she had considered before, knowing that their engagement was to be nothing more than a pretense of short standing, but now that it was real, now that an actual wedding would be planned, her future appeared entirely changed.

You will be a marchioness, said the little voice in her head. *The title will be heavy with responsibilities. You will not be able to hide in the shadows or keep to the corners of the room any longer. Everyone will want a piece of you.*

Swallowing, Lucy gnawed on the side of her lip, letting her mother's monologue wash over her as she thought. She had been so caught up with Edward's kisses and the deep affection she had for him that she had not once considered what it would mean to actually marry the man.

Looking over at her mother, Lucy remembered what she had promised herself before she had ever met Edward: she would not marry without love.

Edward had promised her that.

Her life would change, that was without doubt, but would it be worth it to have Edward by her side, knowing that he loved her more than anything else in the world? They had so much in common, and Lucy knew she would never again find a man like him; someone who found her love of knowledge and desire to further herself as an estimable quality. No other man of a high status would think such a thing, for even her own parents had referred to her as a 'bluestocking' in such a condescending tone that it had ripped into her very soul.

Could she manage all the changes that came with marrying Edward, in the hopes that the love she hoped they would share would overcome all the obstacles in their path?

Her thoughts were broken by her father walking, unexpectedly, into the room.

"Lucy!" he exclaimed, looking somewhat surprised to see her. "I thought you would be abed still."

"And I thought you would be in your study, Papa," Lucy replied, not getting up to greet him.

After what had occurred the prior night with Lord Hutton, she felt her father was responsible for promising her to him without even asking her permission. In addition, she wondered how Lord Hutton had known she would be dining with Lord Brownly.

"It is just as well you are here, for I have something to ask you," she said, trying to conceal her anger.

"Oh?" he asked, distracted for a moment by the tray of pastries in the center of the table.

"Lord Hutton was at the dinner last night."

Lucy watched through slightly narrowed eyes as her father froze for a moment, the pastry halfway to his mouth.

"When I say he was at the dinner," she continued, "what I meant to say was that he attempted to join us, although I cannot quite work out how he knew I would be there with Lord Caldwell."

Her father shrugged, although he would not meet her gaze. "Mayhap Lord Brownly told him."

"I doubt it," Lucy declared. "Lord Brownly does not care for him. You will be quite surprised when I tell you what Lord Hutton wanted, I am sure."

Her mother cleared her throat and shifted in her chair, glancing uneasily between Lucy and her father. "What did he want, Lucy?"

"Me."

Lucy pursed her lips and stared at her father, refusing to remove her unrelenting gaze from him.

"What can you mean?" her mother gasped, her hand at her heart. "You are engaged to Lord Caldwell!"

Lifting one eyebrow, Lucy glanced at Lady Withington. "He told Lord Brownly—and then Lord Caldwell—that apparently I had first been betrothed to him, and he was currently attempting to procure a Special License so that we might marry immediately."

"Oh, no," her father whispered, his face going sheet white as he dropped into a chair. "No, Lucy, he did not."

"Yes, he did," she firmly responded. Lucy was glad to see her father's reaction, hoping that he might tell her all since she was not meant to know any of it. "Father, I don't understand what is going on. What did you say to Lord Hutton?"

Lord Withington sighed and shook his head. "You will hate me, I am sure, but I had promised Lord Hutton your hand. You were to meet him the very night you became engaged to Lord Caldwell. If I had known that you were interested in another, then I would never have done such a thing."

"Did you tell him where I was?" Lucy questioned.

"No," he assured her. "I did not. Unfortunately, it appears that Hutton is not a man who gives up easily. He wants what he wants, and is used to having every one of his wishes fulfilled. That includes your hand in marriage."

Lucy swallowed, and she steadied herself to speak her following words. "Am I that disappointing a daughter, Father, that you would push one of your potential business partners on me, even though he is even older than you? Do you truly care for me so little that I was simply to be used to further your partnerships?"

The Earl of Withington could not answer, his mouth opening and closing like a fish.

"I do hope you have sorted this mess out, Father," Lucy finished, rising from her seat as gracefully as she could. "I want you to make it quite clear to Lord Hutton that I owe him nothing. I will never be his, and he is not to come near me again."

Her father gave a swift, jerky nod, and on seeing it, Lucy swept from the room.

9

The next few days were quiet, although Edward came to call her every day. The preparations for the ball were well underway, and Lucy found herself rolling between excitement and terror. Her mother had sent her to the modiste on at least four separate occasions, ensuring she would be the best dressed young lady the ton had ever seen. Lucy had to admit that the gown was the most beautiful thing she had laid her eyes on, not that she would let her mother know that. She supposed she would have to get used to wearing the latest styles and fashions soon enough, realizing that she did not find the idea altogether distasteful.

"Lord Caldwell."

The butler opened the door and announced her betrothed, making a flush of excitement rush through Lucy's frame.

"Oh, goodness!" she exclaimed the moment he stepped through the door. "What on earth has happened to you?"

Edward was sporting a spectacular black eye, and Lucy was sure she saw a lump on his jaw. Rushing over to him, she grasped his chin and gently turned his face to her.

"Nothing serious," he promised, wincing slightly as her

fingers carefully probed the bump. "Just taken a bit by surprise, if I'm honest."

Lucy guided him to a chair, ringing the bell for tea before sitting down next to him, ignoring the need for a maid. "Who did this to you?"

He gave her a tight smile. "I want to keep this from you, but I know you will get it from me anyway. I am afraid that Lord Hutton is the man responsible."

"Lord Hutton?" Lucy gasped, wondering how the elder gentleman had managed to strike Edward and leave him in such a state. "How? Why?"

A slow flush crept up Edward's face. "As I said, it was something of a surprise. I was walking home from White's last evening, and a fellow struck me as I rounded the corner. In fact, the first blow almost blinded me, which was why he got another in there."

Lucy began to shake with anger, her fingers digging into her skirts. "I told my father to deal with the man! I wish to goodness he had never made such a promise to Lord Hutton!"

Edward shook his head. "He is a man with a poor reputation, for he is known to get his way no matter what." His jaw worked for a moment, as though he wanted to say more but was forcing himself to keep his mouth shut.

"What is it?" Lucy asked softly. "Please, Edward."

He turned to her, his eyes worried. "I know it sounds ridiculous, but I am sure he attempted to push me in the way of an oncoming hackney. Thankfully, he is not as strong as me. I managed to stop him, but still…"

Lucy went completely still, her eyes widening as she took in what Edward had said.

"I know you do not know Lord Hutton well," Edward continued, as though trying to justify the claim he had just made. "But there is a reason he is disliked within society. He has a shrewd mind, but with it comes a cruel streak that pushes him to do whatever he can to get what he wants."

"Has he killed anyone before?" Lucy whispered, her cold fingers finding his.

He shook his head. "Not that I know of." Sighing, he dropped his shoulders "Perhaps I am being quite ridiculous and mistaking the entire situation."

"Then why else would he strike you?"

Shrugging, Edward looked down at her, his battered face making her wince inwardly.

"Who knows? Mayhap because I would not give him what he wanted, which was to back out of our engagement so that he might marry you himself. He was simply relieving himself of some of his frustrations."

"Or perhaps we have underestimated his threat," Lucy murmured, lifting her hand to press lightly along his bruised face. "I cannot understand why he is so determined to marry me!"

"Because he always gets what he wants, or what has been promised him," Edward said heavily. "You do not know him as I do, Lucy. He will not simply let this slide. He sees it as a slight, I believe, so he is doing whatever he can to correct that."

Lucy felt heat rush to her cheeks. "My father seemed disturbed when I told him about what had occurred at Lord Brownly's dinner."

"It may be that he did not fully know the man's measure," Edward mumbled. "Do not hold him in such low esteem, Lucy."

Wanting to protest, Lucy opened her mouth, only for a knock to come at the door, followed by the maid with the tea tray... and her mother. It seemed their conversation would have to wait until another time.

"Promise me you will be careful, Edward," she murmured just as her mother sat down.

He found her hand and squeezed it gently. "Of course," he replied, looking deeply into her eyes. "Nothing will come of this, I am sure. Do not worry so."

Lucy tried not to let anxiety swirl around her heart, but found she could not quite manage to do so. Instead, she simply let her mother talk whilst she thought on all that had occurred, wondering if there was any way Lord Hutton was going to be able to ruin her wedding plans.

"And the engagement ball is going to be a wonderful occasion," her mother chirped, her gaze focusing on Lucy, who tried her best to smile. "It is but two days hence and I confess that I am more than a little excited!"

"Of course you are," Lucy agreed, not feeling even the least bit excited. "I am sure it will be wonderful, Mama."

"Thank you for everything you have done," Edward interrupted, patting her hand. "Now, if you will excuse me, I was hoping to take Lucy out for a short walk."

His eyes warmed as he studied her, making her smile. Evidently, he was aware of just how much she was affected by what he had just revealed to her. She loved that he could tell that about her, and that he was looking to care for her needs.

"A walk would be just the thing, I think," she murmured, getting to her feet and smiling at him. "Shall we go?"

Two days later, Lucy was still not at ease with all that had happened. Lord Hutton had not made any further appearances or attempted to hurt Edward further, but the gnawing sense of unease that coiled within her made her increasingly anxious.

Even as she gazed at her reflection, now clad in the most beautiful gown she had ever owned, with pearls sparkling in her hair, Lucy could not muster up much enthusiasm. The ball would be wonderful, she was sure, but she would not be able to enjoy it until she was sure Lord Hutton would not show up unexpectedly.

Edward had assured her that the footmen would be doubly on their guard and that Lord Hutton would not be permitted to set foot on his grounds. However, Lucy's nerves still stretched taut. Murmuring her thanks to the maid, Lucy picked up her reticule and made her way down to the drawing room, where she found her father pacing the floor. He stopped the moment she entered, his eyes widening slightly as he took her in.

"My goodness," he exhaled, putting down his glass of brandy and coming towards her. "I barely recognized my own daughter! You are looking lovely tonight."

"Thank you, Papa," Lucy replied, leaning forward to kiss his cheek. "You are quite resplendent yourself."

"And now it seems we are left waiting for your mother," he said, walking back over towards the brandy. "Although that comes as no surprise."

Lucy snorted inelegantly. Her mother was known for taking her time when it came to her appearance, and the engagement ball of her only daughter was going to be an occasion where she could really shine.

"Lord Caldwell is a good man, Lucy," her father continued, not quite managing to look at her. "I am glad for you. I... I also wanted to apologize for pushing Lord Hutton towards you. It was meant for your good."

Shaking her head, Lucy refused to accept those words. "No, Father. It was meant to be for *your* good. Do not attempt to soothe your guilt by pretending you meant for me to have a happy life by Lord Hutton's side. Surely you can admit that." Her voice grew stronger as she let the tension she had felt for some time flood through her words.

Her father sighed, his shoulders slumping. "There is no

hiding the truth from you, Lucy, is there?" He shook his head, sighing heavily. "I should never have said anything to Lord Hutton. At the time, I thought he would be a good business partner and, in many senses, he still would be. That is one of my biggest failings, Lucy. In all my years of business, I have never truly considered a man's character before joining with him in partnership. When it came to Lord Hutton, I took the same approach. Had you not announced your engagement to Lord Caldwell, I believe I would now be insisting that you marry him —and what utter folly that would have been!"

Taken aback by her father's honesty, by the guilt that ravaged his features, Lucy sat down carefully, making sure not to crumple her dress.

"What do you mean, Father?"

Pulling his kerchief from his pocket, Lord Withington mopped his brow before continuing.

"I have discovered that Lord Hutton is not a good man, Lucy. When I told him of your engagement, he was furious." Swallowing, he glanced at her before returning his gaze to a point above her head. "It now appears that he is not used to being denied what he has been promised."

"Father!" Lucy exclaimed, her eyes widening in horror. "He has not hurt you, I hope?"

He let out a strangled laugh. "No, not yet. His threats have become more and more violent, but in letter only. I do not believe that he will carry through with what he says. However, I must confess to being somewhat more vigilant these last few days."

Her heart sank into her slippers. "Father, Lord Hutton assaulted Edward, and Edward believes that he was attempting to push him in front of an approaching carriage!"

Her father did not seem in the least bit surprised, only more apologetic. It did not make Lucy feel any more at ease. "I am sorry, Lucy. He is a man possessed, it seems. Hopefully, when you are married, he will give up the chase and find something— or someone—new on whom to focus his attentions."

Lucy suppressed a shudder. "God help whoever that is," she murmured, squeezing her hands together tightly at the thought. "Father, promise me you will be careful. I cannot help the feeling that Lord Hutton has malicious intentions he intends to carry out. I just do not know when or where."

"Of course I will be," he assured her, coming towards her and bending to take her hands. Lucy was shocked to see the tears glistening in his eyes, realizing that her father was, possibly for the first time in his life, truly repentant. "Can you forgive me for my hand in all this, Lucy? I know that I have been in the wrong."

Her throat constricted, and, for a moment, Lucy could not get the words out. "Yes, Papa. I forgive you."

His lined face crumpled, and getting to his feet, he walked away from her and back towards the fireplace.

10

"L ucy!" Edward exclaimed, catching her hand the moment she stepped out of the carriage. "You are utterly breathtaking."

Lucy's heart skipped a beat and she took him in, seeing the way his gaze warmed with heat as he studied her.

"Truly exquisite," he breathed, leaning a little closer.

Her stomach tightened as his head lowered and he caught her lips with his for a brief moment, his hands settling around her waist. She forgot all about Lord Hutton, about her father's confession and subsequent apology. There was only Edward.

"I wish we could remain like this," he whispered in her ear, one hand reaching up to catch her chin. "But I believe Mama is waiting for us. I must apologize that my father is still out of the country on diplomatic business, although he has written to me to let me know he is equally thrilled about my impending marriage."

"I am glad to hear it," Lucy said softly. "Although you are right when you state that your mama—and my parents also— will be waiting for us." She laughed quietly as he let out a soft groan of frustration. "I do not think the ball can begin without us."

Edward sighed heavily but did not release her. "Then let me say to you now, Lucy, that my heart is filled with love for you." His voice softened as he gently rested his forehead against hers, and Lucy felt her breath catch in her throat. "I have fallen so deeply in love with you that I cannot bear to think of being apart from you. Our marriage cannot come soon enough."

Not caring about whether her parents saw her or about keeping Edward's mother waiting, Lucy flung her arms around Edward's neck and kissed him deeply. She felt tears flood her eyes as their lips met, knowing that the same love was in her own heart. It had been growing slowly, rooting itself in her heart the first time they had met, and it was now fully blossoming.

Reluctantly, she broke their kiss, holding his dear face in her hands. "Edward," she whispered, her racing emotions pushing at her already shaky composure. "I love you, too."

He smiled gently. "I am very glad to hear it," he murmured softly. "It seems we shall both go into this marriage with what we have always hoped for."

Lucy gave him a shaky smile, trying desperately not to let the tears drop from her eyes. Edward tenderly brushed his thumb over her lashes, the gentleness in his face tugging at her heart.

"Shall we go in, my love?" he asked. "The guests will be arriving soon, and it would not do for them to find us out here instead of in the receiving line."

"I do not think I should mind that, even if there was something of a scandal," Lucy murmured, wishing she did not have to let him go. The moment seemed too precious, too important, to let go of it so quickly.

Edward chuckled and stepped back, putting her hand on his arm but leaving his own hand there to linger. Lucy found herself walking towards the house beside him, caught up in a whirlwind of sensations. She was abuzz with feeling, thinking that she was walking on some kind of gentle clouds instead of solid ground. Edward was everything she had always wished for.

After greeting Edward's mother and accepting her effusing congratulations once again, Lucy took her place beside her betrothed and prepared to meet their guests. Soon, she found herself curtsying over and over again, her hand taken by the gentlemen and her cheek bussed by the ladies. It felt as though her smile was becoming a permanent fixture on her face, the line of guests almost never ending.

"Perhaps a few moments to rest?" Edward murmured as the line slowly came to a close. "We are to dance soon, but I can tell you are tired already!"

The thought of dancing with Edward made her heart skip a beat, though Lucy had to admit that she would very much like to sit for a short while.

"A glass of something, perhaps?" Edward continued, his hand on the small of her back. "There is a small alcove just along this way, where you can watch the proceedings below stairs whilst keeping yourself hidden."

"Thank you, Edward," Lucy replied, truly grateful for his consideration. "I would like to sit for a few minutes, if it is not too much trouble."

He grinned at her. "The ball will wait for us both, my love. You may rest for a full hour if you wish it!"

Lucy laughed, letting him lead her towards the small alcove just along the hallway. She soon found herself looking down on the ballroom, seeing the great many guests that filled almost every space. Suddenly she felt the need to hide from them for a few minutes, knowing that she would be the center of attention any moment now.

How much her circumstances had changed. She had gone

from being a wallflower to having almost every eye on her. It was unbelievable.

"I will only be a moment," Edward said softly, bending down so that he might look into her eyes. "Are you sure you are well? You look a little pale, although still utterly resplendent."

Lucy could not help but frame his face in her hands, the love she felt for him almost overwhelming her to the point of tears.

"I am just so very happy," she murmured, seeing the answering light in his eyes. "And a little overwhelmed, I will confess."

He smiled at her before brushing her lips with his. "You mean more to me than you could ever know."

Watching him walk away, Lucy heaved one long sigh, happiness filling her heart and soul. She was so deeply in love with this man, and knowing that he loved her in return was more than she had ever dreamed about. His title or status did not matter, for that was not a measure of a man. Edward's kind and selfless character were what continued to draw her to him. He lacked the arrogance that came with so many titled men, always gracious and more than generous. Closing her eyes briefly, Lucy sent up a quick prayer of thanks that she had met Edward that day in the gardens. How different her life might have been otherwise!

Opening her eyes, Lucy sat quietly and watched the guests mingle, hearing the orchestra preparing to strike up the next dance. Rows formed and the dancers began. Lucy smiled to herself as she watched them, wondering when it would be time for herself and Edward to take to the floor. Surely it would not be too long now.

A sudden dart of worry hit her as she realized just how long she had been sitting there alone. This was now the second dance she had watched to completion, with the third soon to begin. Where was Edward?

Lucy got to her feet and leaned over the balcony rail just a little, her eyes searching for Edward.

Perhaps he has simply been caught up in conversation, she told herself. *Or mayhap his mother wishes to speak to him. You are becoming anxious over nothing.*

Lord Hutton's face floated before her eyes as the fear and worry she had felt earlier that evening flooded her once more. Surely Edward's prolonged absence had nothing to do with Lord Hutton? Edward had reassured her that the man would not be allowed to set foot on his property, had he not?

Her breath coming in shallow gasps now, Lucy searched in vain for Edward, her eyes landing on the wide-open French doors. She froze, her eyes lingering on the darkness. It was a little too early in the evening for the doors to have been opened, which gave her pause. Her hands grasped the rail tightly as she waited, suddenly certain that the doors had something to do with Edward.

A figure dressed almost entirely in black slowly made its way through the crowd towards the French doors. His gait was slow, possibly due to his opulence. The only flash of white was his shirt, but other than that, he was almost entirely hidden in the shadows of the room. Lucy gave a strangled cry as the figure turned to glance around him before disappearing through the French doors, clearly believing that no one had seen him.

It was Lord Hutton.

Hurrying down the stairs, Lucy struggled to catch her breath, fear pouring through her veins and making her heart pound frantically in her chest. Edward was gone, she knew it for certain. He would not have left her alone for so long.

"Lucy!" her mother exclaimed just as Lucy found herself at the steps that led to the ballroom. "We have been looking all over for you and Edward." Her eyes twinkled. "Of course, we knew where you might have been, but thought it best to come seek you out."

"No, Mama," Lucy gasped, finding it difficult to get her words out in her breathlessness. "He is not here. He is gone."

"What?" her mother exclaimed, the color draining from her face. "He has run off?"

"What is this?" her father demanded, suddenly appearing by Lucy's side. "The man has left you?"

Lucy shook her head, clinging desperately to her father's sleeve in an attempt to get him to listen to her. "Lord Hutton, Papa. He was here! I saw him, at the French doors!"

Tears blurred her vision as she saw her father's face pale slightly, his change in demeanor warning her that he had immediately come to the same conclusion as she.

"We must find him, Papa!" Lucy begged, blinking back her tears in an attempt to keep her composure. "I cannot let Lord Hutton—"

"Take your mother to the drawing room," her father interrupted, taking her hand and gently removing it from his sleeve. "I will summon the butler and find Edward's mother. She must know of her son's disappearance." He gritted his teeth. "As the Marquess himself is not here, I must hope she will permit me to take charge."

"You are sure he has gone, Lucy?" her mother asked, taking Lucy's arm. "We should speak to the footmen to ensure that is the case. Perhaps he has simply been caught up in conversation?"

Lucy shook her head. She did not need for the footmen to search for Edward—her heart already knew that something was terribly wrong. He would not have left her sitting there for so long, having promised to only be a few moments. He had been the one to remind her of their first dance together, that she only had a little time to rest. Edward was not about to forget his obligations simply because of a conversation. He was not that kind of man.

"I am sure we will find him very soon," her mother continued as they entered the drawing room. "Lord Hutton can have nothing to do with this, surely!"

Lucy quickly described what Lord Hutton had done to Edward already, speaking in rapid tones as she paced up and down. Her mother's features changed from hopeful to horrified, having been kept in the dark up until that point over Lord Hutton's true nature. By the time Lucy had finished speaking, her mother had been forced to sit down heavily in a wing-backed chair, her eyes wide and staring.

"I must change at once," Lucy continued, relieved to recall that they had brought some clothes with them, given that they would be staying overnight. "I cannot help with the search otherwise."

"Lucy!" her mother gasped, sounding horrified. "You cannot do such a thing! You have responsibilities now—the ball, the guests!"

"My only responsibility is to Edward," Lucy said firmly, battling the overwhelming dread growing in her chest. "I cannot simply pretend all is well at the ball when the man I love is in danger. I will not be long, Mama. Please try to understand."

11

I t did not take long for Lucy to change, having found a maid on her way to her rooms. Her fingers shook as she pulled the pearls from her hair, her hands trembling as she placed them down on the dressing table.

"Is there anything else I can do for you, miss?"

Shaking her head, Lucy dismissed the maid, drawing in one long breath before settling her shoulders and trying to think clearly.

"Edward, where are you?" she whispered under her breath, wandering to the window in an attempt to calm herself before she returned to the drawing room.

Lord Hutton had disappeared through the French doors, but that did not mean that he had remained in the gardens. He could be anywhere by now, but Lucy had not the faintest idea of where to start.

As she looked out of the window, her eyes caught a sudden flicker of movement in the moonlight. Her room overlooked the cobbled paths leading out of the large estate and back towards town, and there appeared to be a carriage approaching. Of course, that was not particularly unusual, although it was a little surprising to see that one of the guests was leaving so soon after the ball had begun. That would be considered quite rude, a slight towards the Marchioness. Lucy's brows rose. That was unthinkable. Surely none of the guests assembled here tonight would do such a thing, which meant...

Lucy's hand was on her bedroom doorknob in a minute, pulling the door open and rushing headlong along the corridor and down the stairs. She had no time to return to the drawing room to explain what she had seen, knowing that every second counted were she to get her dear Edward back safe and sound. That carriage had to be for Lord Hutton, for there was no conceivable way that any of the guests would leave the ball that Lady Blackinstore herself had organized, not without jeopardizing their own reputations.

The front door was opened for her, although the footman gave her something of a bemused look as she passed.

"Find her ladyship. Tell her there is a carriage outside," she said breathlessly, seeing the confusion on his face. "She will know what I mean. Go! Now!"

Without waiting to see whether or not the footman had obeyed her order, Lucy rushed outside, the cool night air hitting her cheeks at once. Glad that she was no longer encumbered by her beautiful yet heavy gown, Lucy lifted her skirts and ran towards the side of the house, where she was sure she had seen the carriage. Her feet crunched on the gravel as she ran, forcing her to slow her steps as she approached. Her heart was hammering so loudly in her chest that Lucy was sure someone would hear it and know of her approach.

Pressing herself against the side of the house, she crept forward, hoping that the shadows would hide her. To her surprise, she found herself gazing at some horses, the carriage closer to her than she had first realized. One of the horses blew out a noisy breath, apparently aware of her presence.

"Hurry," she heard a low voice say, coming from the back of the carriage. "We need to move him before his absence is noticed."

There were some grunts and shuffling steps, followed by a thud that had Lucy wincing. That could not be Edward, could it?

"Do we have everything we need?" came the voice again, now sounding very impatient. "This is to be entirely secret, you understand. I can have nothing traced back to me."

"You won't be involved," came a second voice, more gravely than the first. "You've been at White's all evening. By this stage, the other gentlemen there will be so deeply in their cups that they will not be able to say otherwise. Just ensure you are found there in the morning. I will have his body in the Thames in less than half an hour after you arrive at White's."

Lucy did not need to hear more. Her mind screamed at her to act, to find a way to save Edward from Lord Hutton's clutches, but she simply could not think of what to do. Should she make them aware of her presence, they would most likely overpower her too. It was obvious that Lord Hutton was not working alone, which did not surprise her given both his age and his corpulence, but she also did not think she stood much of a chance against those that he was working with, at least not on her own. At the same time, Lucy could not simply sit and wait for the footman to deliver her message to Lady Blackinstore, for by that time, the carriage would be long gone.

Slowly moving forward, Lucy prayed silently that the horses would not start with surprise when she approached them. Thankfully, although one let out a quiet sound, they soon allowed her to stroke their velvety noses.

"There we go," Lucy whispered, listening hard to the conversation going on at the back of the carriage. "I just have to try and slow them down."

At least Lucy knew about the intricacies of a horse and

carriage. Even in the darkness, it still proved difficult for her to find the buckles that lay just behind the horse's front leg. She did not want to injure the animals in any way, but simply to cause enough of a distraction to allow her time to go in search of Edward, although she was not exactly sure what she would do when she got to him. Slowly, the buckle began to loosen, the horse shifting only a little as she relieved the harness on one side. It did not take her long to do the other side, her confidence growing as her fingers became surer. The second buckle was easier to undo than the first, and relief flooded her as the horses remained silent.

"Hurry up, man!"

Lucy sprang back into the shadows, her hands pressed against her chest, her heart pounding. She managed to see the outline of a man climbing into his seat and lifting the reins, only for a curse to leave his lips.

"Whatever is the matter?" came Hutton's hiss as he leaned out of the carriage window. "We do not have time for this!"

"The harness has come loose," the man replied, jumping down from the step. "If you want to help..."

Lucy waited until Hutton stepped out from the carriage, huffing and puffing as he did so. She did not know what else to do other than to wait for him to go to the front of the carriage. Then she could quietly step over to the open carriage door.

"It won't take long," she heard the first man say. "The buckles have just become slack."

Peering into the gloom of the carriage, Lucy lifted her skirts and pulled herself inside, desperately hoping that she would not be seen. It appeared that Lord Hutton and his man were too busy frantically getting the horses ready for them to notice her and, for once, she was grateful for her soft slippers.

"Edward?" she whispered, her hands reaching across to the form she saw lying across the seats. "Edward, is that you?"

Her fingers reached out and tentatively brushed his brow, feeling his skin cool and clammy. Fear wrapped itself around her heart, and she desperately felt for a pulse, praying that he still lived.

Thankfully, a small warm breath puffed across her hand while she ran her fingers over his face, sagging with relief as she realized he was still alive. Apparently unconscious, however.

What am I to do? Lucy thought to herself, growing a little frantic with worry. She could hear Lord Hutton's voice growing closer, the horses' harness apparently fixed.

"Edward," she hissed, patting his face with her hand. "Edward!" There was no response, and with a sudden lurch of fear, Lucy realized that Lord Hutton was almost upon them.

12

"Go, man!" Lord Hutton exclaimed, pulling the carriage door open. "What are you waiting for?"

Lucy held her breath as the carriage slowly began to move, with Lord Hutton pulling himself up into the carriage at exactly the same time. Lord Hutton was wasting no time in getting away, apparently fully aware that every second they lingered was a second closer to them being discovered.

"Wh...what?" he spluttered, the carriage door still open behind him. Lucy saw his eyes narrow, only for a slow, malevolent smile to spread across his face. "Well, this has worked out better than I expected."

Lucy saw the threat in his eyes, heard the menace in his voice, and did the only thing she could think to do in that situation.

Launching herself at him, she pushed hard against Hutton's large bulk, her hands hitting him roundly in the stomach. The man's breath left his body with a whoosh, and with the force of her strike, he fell backward, completely out of the carriage door. A dull thud told her that his body hit the ground, fear crawling up her throat as she looked out after him.

Was he dead? Had she inadvertently killed him?

To her very great relief, Lucy saw the man's bulky form turn over, attempting to push himself onto his hands and knees. No shout came from him, no cries to alert his driver that something was amiss. The carriage clattered out of the gates and into the London streets, evidently heading towards White's. That was where Lord Hutton had said the carriage was going, although she did not want to think what the driver intended to do with Edward once Lord Hutton was gone.

Lucy pulled the carriage door shut with trembling fingers, wishing that Edward would wake. She had no idea where she had found the strength to push Lord Hutton from the carriage, hoping that someone from the house might find him before he could make his escape. She had been given no time to think and, as such, had acted instinctively. At least, for the moment, Edward was safe, but unless he awoke, she could not think about how to get him home.

Moving carefully over to him again, Lucy knelt in between the carriage seats, ignoring how uncomfortable she was as she took in his closed eyes. The lamp lighters had been hard at work, allowing her to see his face in a little more detail and helping her to find the deep gash on his forehead.

Stifling a gasp, Lucy leaned forward and studied it as best she could, and she noticed that it was still oozing blood.

"It is no wonder you are unconscious," she murmured softly. "Whatever am I to do, Edward?"

The only thing she could think of to do was stop the bleeding. Tearing a large strip from the bottom of her skirts—and praying that her mother would understand why she had done it —Lucy wadded up one strip and placed it gently against the wound before using a second strip to hold it in place. To her utter delight, Edward groaned slightly as she gently placed his head down again, the bandage now firmly secured.

"Edward?" she whispered, tenderly brushing his cheek. "Are you awake?"

He groaned again, but she pressed a finger to his lips.

"Please, we must be silent," she begged, hoping he would listen to her. "You are in Lord Hutton's carriage. He is not here, but his driver does not know that. Please, stay quiet."

"What happened?" Edward murmured, his eyes opening just a little as he attempted to focus on her face. "I only remember going to fetch you a glass of ratafia."

Lucy answered him, trying not to let her concern over him show on her face. "You were quite right to suspect that Lord Hutton had deadly intentions towards you. It appears he almost had you, too!"

Edward winced when he tried to sit up, the pain he felt evident on his features as he grimaced.

"Careful," Lucy murmured, rising so she might sit opposite him. "How are you feeling?"

"Sore," Edward mumbled, his eyes now tightly closed. "We must return to the house, Lucy. Lord Hutton cannot be allowed to escape." Cracking open one eye, he tried to smile before leaning his head back against the squabs. "Unfortunately, I do not think I will be of much use, my love. I can barely see straight and certainly cannot stand without assistance!"

Lucy swallowed hard. She was still alone, even with Edward now conscious. His injury was severe, meaning that he would not be able to assist her in any particular way.

"What are we to do?" she asked, half to herself. Her mind worked furiously, knowing that she could not remove Edward from the carriage anytime soon, for he would not be able to take a step on his own. That meant that, somehow, Lucy was going to have to drive this carriage back to the house by herself.

"We are headed towards White's," she murmured. "Although he will stop a street or so away. Perhaps then..."

The responsibility weighed heavily on her shoulders as the carriage began to slow. She only had minutes to think—minutes to make a decision about what she needed to do.

"There may be shotguns," Edward said softly. "This is Lord Hutton's carriage, is it not? He might have hidden some around the carriage so that I would not attempt—or be able to —escape."

Lucy nodded, fully aware that Lord Hutton could have hidden a shotgun with the intention of shooting Edward dead before flinging him in the Thames. She did not need to tell Edward that, of course, so she frantically began searching the carriage, her fingers seeking the feeling of cool metal instead of plush materials or wooden boards. The carriage had now come to a complete stop, and Lucy could hear the driver murmuring something to the horses.

Hurry, her mind screamed as she felt up above the window. *Find something. Anything!*

"Hutton?" came the voice. "Aren't you getting out?"

Lucy said nothing, praying that Edward, too, would remain silent. His eyes were still closed, although he did not look to be unconscious again.

"Looking for me to open the carriage door, are you?" came the voice again, this time fraught with tension and a trace of mockery. "Or is it because your bulk will not allow you to exit without the steps?" A harsh laugh echoed through the air, making Lucy's skin crawl.

She could not find a gun, could not find any sort of weapon that would allow her to take control of the situation.

She could not give up, not now.

Suddenly, an idea hit Lucy full force. It was incredibly dangerous, but it was the only solution she could think of.

"Trust me, Edward," she whispered, leaning forward to press a kiss to his cool cheek. "And stay here."

Knowing that the driver would be placing the foldable carriage steps to the door on her left, Lucy pushed open the right-hand side carriage door and peered out.

There was no sight nor sound of anyone, and, with trepidation, she slowly lowered herself to the ground, hoping her slippers would make very little noise. Holding her breath, she waited until she heard the driver muttering from the other side of the carriage with the sound of the portable steps being put in place.

"There, Hutton," the driver sneered. "Hurry up, man! Didn't you say we…"

His voice trailed off, and Lucy fled to the front of the carriage at once, hauling herself up into the driver's seat as best as she could. Sweat trickled down her back as she maneuvered herself in, grasping the reins and startling the horses. The driver's shout told her that he had opened the door and discovered Lord Hutton's absence, giving her the impetus she needed to tug hard on the reins. The horses jumped into action at once, and she flicked the reins once, twice, until they were moving swiftly away.

Lucy did not know where she was going, trying her best to maneuver the carriage along the streets of London in a desperate attempt to lose the driver, who, she assumed, would be chasing them on foot. She could not tell how Edward fared, nor whether the driver was close behind them or not, turning the horses as best she could down one street and then another.

"Left!"

Startled, Lucy visibly jumped, only to realize that Edward was shouting directions at her from inside the carriage.

"Turn left, Lucy!"

With hands gripping the reins in an almost deathly grip, Lucy turned the horses left and then right, following Edward's directions. Relief flooded her as she saw the entrance to his home, and she turned the horses back into the gate. Mustering the last of her energy, she pushed the tired horses a little faster until, finally, they arrived back at the front of the house.

13

A n array of footmen met them at the entrance, followed by Lucy's terrified mother and Lady Blackinstore.

"Lucy!" her mother exclaimed, her eyes wide with fright. "Where have you been? Where is Edward? What on earth is going on?"

"I am well," came Edward's thin voice from within the carriage. He had opened the door to make himself visible to his mother. "Although I think I might need some assistance to come inside."

Lucy could not move, could not speak, her hands frozen to the reins as she sat up in the driving seat, her heart slowly calming its frantic pace. She had made it back safely with Edward. She was not about to lose him, nor was she in mortal danger. That realization filled her with relief, although her body was growing colder by the minute.

"Come down, Lucy!" her mother exclaimed, reaching up for her. "Come in, you must come in!"

"I—" Lucy opened her mouth to try to explain that she could not do as her mother asked, only for her mother to grasp her skirts and tug gently at them. It was the fear and worry on her mother's face that finally allowed Lucy to let go of the reins and make her way down from the carriage, sagging against her mother the moment her feet touched the ground.

"Oh, my dear," Lady Withington whispered, pulling Lucy into a tight embrace. "You had me so terribly worried."

Lucy did not know what to say, slowly realizing that her mother truly did care for her. All this time, Lucy had thought her mother only really cared about one thing: for Lucy to marry. But it appeared that she was, in truth, deeply concerned over her daughter.

"I did not know what to think," her mother continued, her voice wavering. "The footman appeared to tell us that you had seen a carriage. Your father immediately raced after him, leaving myself and Lady Blackinstore to follow behind."

"Where is Papa?" Lucy asked, pulling back from her mother's arms in search of her father. "He is safe, I hope?"

"I cannot say," her mother replied, glancing around as though he might appear out of the gloom somewhere.

Lucy leaned heavily against the carriage for a moment, drinking in the fact that she was safe and well. Two footmen helped Edward out of the carriage, and although he was leaning heavily on one of them, he opened his free arm towards her. Lucy did not hesitate to move towards him as quickly as she could, exhaustion flooding her.

"My wonderful Lucy," he whispered, wrapping an arm around her waist as she rested her head on his shoulder, with one hand wrapping itself around his neck. "I cannot believe what you did. Incredible, wise, brave Lucy. I would have been at the bottom of the Thames if it had not been for your quick thinking and courage."

"The bottom of the Thames?" Lady Blackinstore repeated, her voice growing faint. "Whatever are talking about, Edward?"

Lucy could not reply and neither, it seemed, could Edward. Instead, they remained as they were for a good few minutes, simply clinging to one another as though they needed reassurance that they were truly still alive, still together. Lucy felt tears clog her throat as she looked up into his face, seeing the makeshift bandage still in place. What horrors had Hutton planned for him?

"None of that," he whispered, apparently able to read her thoughts. "I can tell from your face that you are worrying about Lord Hutton. Do not fear him. Come, we must go inside and rest."

"And the guests," his mother interrupted, drawing herself up tall. "What of them?"

Edward retorted, shaking his head at his mother. "After what we have been through this evening, I cannot think of festivities, nor do I have the strength to even stand for one dance!"

"But what shall we tell them?"

Lucy, keeping her arm around Edward's waist, began to walk with him towards the house.

"Why not tell them the truth, my lady?" she suggested. "That way, your ball will be the talk of the town for weeks and months to come, and since this one was so rudely interrupted by Lord Hutton attempting to dispose of your son, I should think that you might throw another one in its place!"

Lady Blackinstore opened her mouth to reply, but slowly closed it, her eyes growing thoughtful. One more glance at Edward and her mind was settled.

"You are right," she said, walking with them back towards the house. "It was rude of me to consider the guests before your own well-being, Edward—and yours too, my dear Lucy. You must forgive an old woman's foibles."

"Of course," Lucy replied as Edward said just the same thing.

"I shall speak to our guests and return to you in the drawing room as soon as I am able," she finished, giving them both a quick smile before rushing ahead back into the house.

"Are you sure you can manage, my dear?"

Lucy smiled and nodded to her mother, knowing that the footman was taking most of Edward's weight but unable to physically separate herself from him. The memory of how she had first seen him—lying across the carriage seats, his skin so cool and damp to the touch—reminded her of just how close she had come to losing him forever.

"Almost there," Edward murmured as the door to the drawing room was held open and he was gently placed down into one of the seats. Lucy took her seat next to him at once, still troubled by his weakness.

"I am sure I shall be quite all right," Edward reassured her while Lucy's mother gave rapid instructions to one of the footmen. "In truth, I am only a little dizzy, my love. Do not look so frightened."

"I am not frightened," Lucy replied, a little more loudly than she had intended. "I am tired, that is all, and worried about you."

"Come here," Edward mumbled, pulling her towards him. Despite the presence of her mother, Lucy leaned into him and rested her head on his shoulder whilst he kept one hand around her shoulders. Lucy saw her mother glance at them, but to her surprise, there was only a small smile and a softness in her features that told Lucy she did not mind in the least.

ONE HOUR LATER, the doctor had only just left Edward's side, having cleaned the wound and giving him something to help him sleep, although Edward declared he would not drink a drop of it.

Lucy had been refreshed with tea and cakes, and Lady Blackinstore came in to announce that the news had thrown everyone into a whirlwind of excitement and that she expected the rumors to continue for weeks. She seemed quite happy at this news, too, although her smile faded slightly on seeing Edward's wounded head.

"I am well, Mama," Edward insisted, catching her hand. "You do not need to worry. Just a small concussion."

Lucy's father, who had entered some time ago with a look of satisfaction on his face, cleared his throat loudly.

"I thought we had better discuss what occurred this evening," he said once everyone's attention had been caught. "I do not even know what happened to Lucy, nor Edward, although I am glad to see you both back safely."

Lucy looked to Edward, feeling tiredness seep into her muscles and down into her bones. "Lord Hutton was to blame, Papa."

Edward squeezed her hand gently. "I have been a little concerned over Lord Hutton of late, I must confess, but I had stationed the footmen to ensure he did not set foot on the grounds. However, he somehow managed to make his way inside, and with the help of one of the ruffians he has under his control, he took me by surprise. That is all I remember..."

"I did wonder where you had gone when you did not return," Lucy added, glancing at him.

"It was Lucy who sounded the alarm," Lady Blackinstore interrupted, smiling fondly at her. "And it was she who told the footman that she had seen the carriage."

Lucy felt herself blush at the admiration in Lady Blackinstore's voice. "I did think it was strange for someone to be leaving the ball so soon, and I could not waste time in returning to the drawing room to fetch Papa."

"It is just as well you chose to come at once," Edward replied.

"Although I am still not quite sure how you managed to end up in the carriage?"

Every eye was suddenly on her and Lucy's cheeks grew even hotter. Briefly, she sketched out the details of what had happened and the decisions she'd made, hearing her mother gasp on occasion as she continued with the description. "I do not know what happened with Lord Hutton," she finished heavily. "When I pushed him from the carriage, I saw him attempt to rise, but he may well have escaped."

To her surprise, her father let out a guffaw. "He was trying to, that oaf, but he twisted an ankle and, given his excessive weight, could do nothing but crawl."

A spiral of hope rushed through Lucy. "You mean, you found him?"

"He is with the constable as we speak," her father replied, looking more than a little satisfied. "He will feel the full extent of the law, have no doubt about that." His mouth drew into a thin line. "I will make sure of it."

Lucy swallowed the sudden lump in her throat, relief sending tears to the corners of her eyes. "Thank you, Papa," she whispered, hardly able to speak.

He shook his head. "I should never have pushed him towards you," he said quietly. "I am sorry, both to you and to Edward. I can see now that you are well-suited for one another. Your thirst for knowledge helped you tonight, I can see that now. In truth, my dear, I consider you quite remarkable."

"She is unlike any other woman of my acquaintance," Edward added, his thumb rubbing the back of Lucy's hand. "I know that might seem like a bad quality to some, but to me, it is more than I have ever hoped for. I cannot wait to make Lucy my wife. Without her, I might not have returned home tonight. She has proven her strength and courage, her mettle and fortitude. I could not be prouder of her, nor love her more."

Lucy could hardly breathe. As she looked up into Edward's eyes, the rest of the room faded away, leaving only her and her betrothed. How much she loved him, how much her heart yearned for him when he was apart from her. Smiling through her tears of relief and joy, Lucy leaned up and pressed her lips lightly to his, not caring that others were present.

"I love you with all of my heart, Edward," she breathed, seeing the answering love resonate in his eyes. "I could not bear to see you harmed. I swear that I will always stay by your side, support you and love you in all that you do." Remembering how they had first met, she gave a slight shake of her head. "After all, you saved me from Lord Hutton once, and now it was my turn to save you."

Edward lifted her hand to his lips and brushed a kiss against it, shooting sparks of heat up her arm. "I did not know how lucky I would be when I made such a promise to you, Lucy," he murmured gently, so only Lucy could hear. "That night in the arbor, I considered it simply an easy solution for us both, but look how quickly I fell for you. No one in the world can compare to you, and I consider myself the luckiest gentleman in England to have you by my side. Our wedding cannot come soon enough."

Lucy's heart burst with happiness. As she settled herself against Edward's side, her eyes closed with a combination of contentedness and exhaustion. She had never imagined that the man she had met that night in the arbor would turn out to be the answer to all her prayers, the man who would love her as much as she loved him.

"I love you, Edward," she whispered, safe by Edward's side.

THE END

MARRIED TO A MARQUESS

By Joyce Alec

1

L ondon 1837
   Miss Alice Henstridge stood silently at the back of the church, feeling woefully unprepared for the step she was about to take. The church welcomed a dozen guests, she had been told, but Alice was sure she did not know any of them other than her parents.

Most of them were friends and acquaintances of her husband-to-be, William Bexley, the Marquess of Worthington. The quick wedding had been as much of a surprise to her as it had been to the guests, having been quite unprepared for her mother and father to announce her betrothal in the societal papers before discussing such a thing with her.

Then again, Alice was well used to doing exactly as her parents requested, going along with whatever notion they thought was best. She had done so her entire life, and when they had told her that she would be marrying William in three short weeks, she had accepted her betrothal with just the correct amount of delight and thankfulness.

Now, however, she was not so certain that this was the best course of action. 'Wedding jitters' her mother had called it, and

Alice attempted to believe that this was all it was. After all, did not many couples marry for life without knowing much about the other?

Alice lifted her chin and hoped that she looked well enough, even though she had heard from one of the many, many guests who had called upon her since her betrothal that her groom to be was less than pleased about the wedding.

She had simply smiled and brushed off the comments, pretending they did not slam into her heart with a twinge of pain. Even though she had accepted the situation with gratefulness, Alice did not want to marry a man who was disinclined with the very idea of matrimony. That could not be a strong foundation on which to build a marriage, could it?

So troubled had she been, that Alice had sought out her father on one occasion. Timidly, she had laid out her concerns, trying to ignore the deep frown on her father's face as she spoke.

"Why has he agreed to marry me if he does not care for matrimony in the slightest?"

"Because he wishes to do so," her father had replied, firmly. "Before his father died, he made a great many stipulations in his will. In short, his father made sure that the man does not receive any of his funds until he is wed. His mother, Lady Worthington, is thrilled about the match because of the dowry you bring and has made it clear to her son what his expectations are. He will be there to wed you, have no doubt. Lord Worthington is looking forward to the union."

Alice had not had the strength to reply, to question the decision further. Instead, she had meekly thanked her father for explaining things to her and retired back to her rooms. The thoughts troubled her still, but she had been forced to press them to the back of her mind.

The truth was that Alice did not feel like she was likely to wed. At seventeen, she had already had two seasons with very little interest from the gentlemen of society, given that she was a little plain and very shy. No amount of cajoling from her mother had brought her attempts at conversation to any sort of fruition. In short, Alice was a quiet little mouse who was pushed to the shadows.

It had seemed that this marriage was the best solution to her parents' concerns over her future as well as fulfilling her own dreams. Of course, Alice wanted a husband and family, a home of her own, and to marry the Marquess of Worthington was an honor she simply could not turn down.

Not that she knew very much of him, of course. There had been once or twice when she spotted the man, finding him loud and certainly attractive, but never once speaking to him. To discover that he was being forced into matrimony in many respects did not sit well with her, but to refuse would bring shame and scandal to her own family as well as on her own head, and Alice simply could not allow that to happen.

The music began, pulling Alice from her thoughts. It was time. The door opened, and every single head turned towards her. It was overwhelming, and Alice's stomach immediately began to churn with nerves. She was thankful for the heavy veil that covered her face, sure that she would be pale should anyone have seen her. Taking slow steps forward, she focused on the man at the front of the church waiting for her. It was just as her father had said. He was there, just as her father had promised. Her groom. Her husband to be. Her marquess.

The problem was, however, that whilst her groom might be present, he was clearly quite disinterested. He gave her only a cursory glance as she approached, turning back to face the clergyman almost at once. In fact, as Alice approached his side, she noticed that he smelled of whisky, and given how he swayed slightly, she realized he must have had a lot to drink.

Her heart dropped like a stone. This was not what she had anticipated.

Finally standing next to Lord Worthington, Alice dared a glance up at her groom but discovered, to her consternation, that he was not even looking at her. Instead, he had something of a ribald grin on his face and gave someone just to her left a hearty wink. She heard someone gasp, evidently shocked at his behavior, which made her cheeks burn with both shame and frustration. Her future husband, apparently, was something of a rake.

A loud buzzing rose in her ears as the clergyman began his service, his bland tones not even catching the slightest bit of her interest. When her father had stated that William was, at least, willing to marry her, she had not thought that he would be so obviously disinterested in her.

To be making eyes at another woman on his own wedding day was utterly scandalous! Of course, she had been aware that William was known to be something of a flirt, having captured many young ladies' eyes, but her father had reassured her that this was all simply an act and that he would settle down the moment they were married. As she had always done, Alice had believed her father entirely.

The clergyman was staring pointedly at her, but Alice felt completely frozen from the inside out. This was not what she had wanted, not what she had been led to believe. She could not marry a man like this, could she?

A sudden clearing of a throat behind her reminded her that her father, mother, and a great many guests were all waiting for her. To turn and run now would be devastating, not just for her but for her family in general. After what her parents had done in fixing this match for her, despite her lack of beauty, she could not back out now.

"I do," she whispered, barely able to get the words out through lips that refused to move.

A sigh of relief rippled around the church from behind her, as though they had expected her to refuse. Evidently, the guests were more than aware that this was an arranged marriage.

Her body still completely cold, Alice closed her eyes and heard her groom mutter the same words as she, sighing heavily after he had done so. Hot tears pricked at the corner of her eyes, but she refused to let even a single one fall. She had just tied herself to this man for life, and already he appeared to be regretting it.

Kneeling when she was told, she heard the clergyman pronounce the blessing before finally announcing to the church that they were now husband and wife. Reaching for her husband's arm to steady herself as she rose, Alice realized that he was already standing, not giving her even the scantest bit of attention. Her legs trembled as she turned to exit the church, knowing that she should have her hand on her husband's arm. He walked slightly ahead of her, taking his time so that he would not stagger given how much liquor he had apparently imbibed.

Her face burned with shame, and she was fully aware that her husband had not yet lifted her veil. Alice walked behind him, grateful that she was not called upon to acknowledge the guests at this time. She would have to make it outside with dignity intact, not letting anyone know just how fragile she felt.

"Well, good day to you, wife," her husband said, as they reached the door of the church. "I have given my steward instructions on how to care for you. I do not know when I shall see you next, but I am sure you will be quite content on your own. Good day."

And, so saying, he climbed into a waiting carriage and, within seconds, was hurtling down the road away from her.

2

Alice wrote the date in her beautiful, swirling handwriting before continuing her letter to her mother. All was well at Wren Park, the estate her husband had packed her off to some three years ago. She ignored the stab of pain in her heart, fully aware that today was, in fact, her third wedding anniversary and, as yet, she had still not seen her husband since their fateful wedding day.

Finishing her letter, Alice scanned it carefully before sealing it and ringing for the butler. It had become her habit to write to her mother on a regular basis, usually once a week, and her mother would be expecting to receive her correspondence.

There was not usually much to write about, except the state of the gardens or the visits she had been blessed with, but still, Alice always managed to fill a page or so with her news. Never once did they mention Lord Worthington nor his absence, although in the times her parents had visited her home, there was always concern written all over her mother's face.

Only once had her mother spoken to her of her regret in allowing Alice's father to push for the marriage, promising her daughter that she had not had the slightest inkling that the marquess would treat her so. Even her father had grunted that it was not seemly for a husband to leave his wife alone for so long. It had been a balm to Alice's wounded heart, even if it did not quite cover the shame of being a forgotten wife.

However, she had finished this letter with a request, which was noticeably different from the other occasions on which she had written to her mother. In it, she requested the use of her parents' London townhouse, arriving sometime next week. She reminded her mother that Lord Worthington had never given her permission to use his properties in town, meaning that she was trapped at Wren Park unless her mother could spare her the use of the townhouse. She then went on to state that the carriage was already being prepared, so that her mother would not have any temptation to write back and refuse.

Alice was more than aware that her mother's gentle heart would not allow Alice to arrive in London, only to find her parents' townhouse closed up tightly. It was a little cruel to be manipulating her mother's affections so, but Alice needed to escape the confines of the estate. Three years was more than enough.

Handing the letter to the butler, a kindly-faced older man who treated her more like a daughter than the lady of the house, she asked for tea to be sent to the library, intending to curl up with a good book. He nodded and smiled before leaving the room.

Sighing to herself, Alice made her way to the library, thinking that at least her husband had shown her a kindness in depositing her in a beautiful home with a full complement of staff. They had become her companions, in many ways, for often Alice would find herself in the kitchen having tea with the housekeeper and, on occasion, the cook.

It was unseemly, of course, for a mistress of her standing never fraternized with their staff, but Alice was quite done with convention for the time being. Principles and propriety were what had driven her into her terrible marriage, so she had decided she was done with all the formalities. If her husband was to abandon her entirely, then he had nothing to say about how she spent her free time.

Not that he cared, however. His actions made that more than apparent. She had not seen him in these long three years, although she had received a note each Christmas wishing her well. She had gone through sadness, despair, anger, and frustration until a plan had slowly begun to form. No longer was she going to be the quiet little mouse that did as she was bid, nor was she going to stand for being left alone to wither away quietly for as many years as her husband chose until he decided to plant a babe in her belly and then, most likely, ride off again. The thought caused her to shiver, knowing that, as his wife, she had very little rights. He could treat her as he wished, and no one, not even her, could say anything against him.

Of course, Alice realized that the only reason she was in this situation was because of her inability to do or say anything about what she felt or thought. It was true, was it not? She had simply obeyed her father and she was fully expected to obey her husband in much the same way. It was what had been expected of her, or, at least, that was what she had thought.

In behaving in such a way, Alice had come to realize that she had become something of a doormat — and look where it had got her. She had agreed to marry a man she had never met only for him to treat her with apparent disdain the very moment their marriage was declared. She had lived at his country estate for three years without him, apparently expected to simply accept her fate with gratitude.

The tea tray at her elbow and her book forgotten, Alice contemplated her future. She had already made a decision that was going to change her future in some way, although she was not quite sure yet as to what would happen. Alice grimaced as she picked up her china cup. She was not about to be stuck here for the next however many years, nor was she going to be the obedient wife that simply waited for her husband to show only the slightest bit of interest. Things were going to change.

Already, she had visited the seamstress in the small village next to the estate, having access to some funds. Her husband had deigned himself to send her a small amount each and every month – although, having very little to spend her coffers on, Alice had simply saved it, which meant that she was now able to order an almost entirely new wardrobe.

The seamstress, who had been completely overwhelmed with delight at Alice's request for new gowns in the latest styles, had been more than willing to oblige, utterly thrilled by Alice's interest in her work. She had been for numerous fittings, and the gowns were to be with her the following day.

Frowning, Alice did a quick calculation in regard to how quickly her letter would reach her mother. If she left two days from now, she would arrive in London in four days hence. By then, her mother should have been able to make all the arrangements, provided there was no refusal from her father. Alice did not think there would be, however, for she had seen first-hand how unsettled her father was over Alice's absent husband.

Surely, he would agree that his daughter needed a little joy in her life and that returning to London to enjoy the season was entirely proper.

However, that was not Alice's true intention.

Three years had changed her appearance somewhat, but not to the point that she was entirely unrecognizable. However, deep down, Alice was sure that her husband would not have any idea what his wife truly looked like. In fact, she did not think that he would recognize her at all.

She intended to take on a false name and enjoy the season as she ought to have done when she was still in her father's house. Back then, she had been a quiet wallflower, barely able to pluck up the courage to speak to anyone and knowing full well that she was not the most beautiful of young ladies either.

However, in three years, Alice had grown a little taller and had taken up gardening, bringing a slight bloom to her normally pale face. In addition, her skin had cleared — the cook promised that it was because of the fresh air — and her hair had both lengthened and brightened in the sunshine, for Alice refused to wear a bonnet whenever she was outside in the gardens.

However, it was her confidence that shone through, which she hoped would lead to an ability to stand tall and consider herself an equal when she was in the midst of a London ball.

Smiling softly to herself, Alice wondered what her husband would think when he saw her, but it would not matter. He probably would not recognize her. She hoped that she might shame him into realizing what he had done in leaving his wife alone for three years, although she was not yet sure how to go about it.

At least she would have her dear friend Madeline, who was now Lady Astor, to assist her in the upcoming weeks. It would be wonderful just to see her dear friend again, having not laid eyes on her since Alice had been sent to the country estate.

Sighing to herself, Alice refilled her teacup and sat back in her chair, allowing her thoughts to run wild. A mixture of nerves and excitement coiled in her belly, making her look forward to the next stage of her life.

3

"**M**adeline!"

Alice could not keep from weeping. She embraced her friend as soon as Madeline was announced, realizing just how much she had missed Madeline's company.

Alice's parents had allowed her to use their townhouse, and Madeline called as soon as she received Alice's request for a visit.

The two women had been very close in their girlhood, although Madeline had always been much more outgoing and often grew frustrated with Alice's decision to cling to the walls whenever they attended a ball or soiree.

"Now, now," Madeline said, her own voice betraying her emotion. "None of that. No tears." Her smile wobbled, and she laughed. "Even though I am overjoyed to see you."

"And I you," Alice responded, taking her friend's hand and leading her to a chair. "Please, be seated. There is so much I want to ask you."

Madeline sat as Alice rang for tea, her eyes contemplative.

"Has it been just terrible?" she asked softly. "Being at that estate all alone?"

Alice sat down carefully so that she would not crumple the back of her new gown. "It was terrible for the first year, I will admit, but I have since come to terms with it — although I do not intend to simply go on as I have been any longer." Her jaw set, she looked across at Madeline, who was regarding her carefully.

"Your hair is more of a golden brown," Madeline said quietly. "Although your eyes are as green as ever. I do not know what your husband will make of your appearance."

"I do not think my husband will know me," Alice replied, firmly, seeing Madeline's raised eyebrows. "Why should he? He barely looked at me during our wedding ceremony and did not, if I remember correctly, even lift my veil!" Anger rose in her chest at the thought, although she pushed it down again by sheer force of will. "No, Madeline, he will not recognize me."

Madeline said nothing but frowned slightly. A brief silence ensued as the tea tray was brought in and placed between them, and Alice waited until the maid had left before continuing.

"I am not quite sure how I shall react when I see my husband again," she said, softly. "That is why I shall need your help, Madeline. I shall need someone's support and, besides that, I have no idea as to how to gain entrance into society's whirlwind."

Laughing, Madeline accepted a cup of tea from Alice, a quick smile on her face. "I might be able to help you there. It appears that our dear friend Catherine is to have a ball in her honor."

"Oh?" Alice's heart lifted at the mention of her friend, thinking that she had not seen her in as many years. "It has been so long since I have seen her."

"Of course," Madeline replied sensibly. "Regardless, her

father is hosting a masquerade ball in two days' time. I am sure you will be welcomed."

"Oh, but Catherine will not wish to help me in my pretense," Alice said worriedly. "Once she discovers that I am not giving my true name, she will not like it."

"I will help her understand," Madeline responded calmly. "It is not as if you are in search of a husband or anything devious. You simply want your husband to take responsibility for his treatment of you. Besides, it is not Catherine we must worry about. Other members of the ton will of course question who you are. When you are asked about your family, we will explain that you are my distant cousin. Now, have you decided what name you are going to take on?"

A swirl of nerves in her belly, Alice nodded. "I think I shall be Lady Emma Taylor."

"A good, strong name," Madeline agreed at once, adding a cube of sugar to her teacup. "You shall be quite in demand, I am sure." A slight frown crossed her brow. "But what if one of your old acquaintances recognizes you?"

Prior to her marriage, Alice had never been a bubbly and vivacious sort, capturing all kinds of attention. She had faded into obscurity, which at least, would help her now to re-enter society without difficulty. "You forget that I was not exactly a diamond of the first water," she reminded Madeline, a trifle sadly. "Quiet and unassuming — and entirely unnoticed."

Madeline's frown disappeared. "And your appearance is somewhat changed," she murmured, her eyes studying Alice's features.

"I am even more plain?" Alice asked, trying to inject laughter into her voice, but failing miserably.

"Tosh!" came Madeline's reply, surprising Alice with the amount of vehemence in her expression. "You have never been plain, Alice. Your mother simply did not know what colors and styles suited you best." She tipped her head. "And you certainly never complained about what she put you in."

Alice sighed, knowing that her friend was right. "In truth, I thought it best to do as she asked," she said heavily. "And look where that has got me."

Madeline cleared her throat, dragging Alice from her melancholy. "You are not plain, Alice, you have never been. Whoever your seamstress is, she has done a wonderful job. The colors of your dress suit your complexion perfectly, and the hint of green brings out the color of your eyes." She laughed softly. "You have truly blossomed, Alice. The years have been good you. You are lovely! Now that I think on it, I do not believe anyone will recognize you in the least, although I must say I believe you will catch a great number of gentlemen's attentions."

"There is only one man's attention I wish to catch," Alice muttered under her breath, wishing she could grasp her husband by the collar and scream at him everything she had been keeping in her heart for so long. "Although once I have it, I am not quite sure what to do with it." In fact, Alice realized, she knew very little about her husband.

"Tell me, Madeline," she began, her interest piqued. "You have been in London for the last few years, have you not?"

"I have," Madeline replied, a little warily. "My husband has a country estate, of course, where we retire in the winter, but I much prefer the business of town."

Nodding quietly, Alice regarded her friend. "Then you must have seen my husband."

Madeline's eyes widened slightly. "You do not know anything about him, do you?"

"Of course I do not!" Alice exclaimed, her tea slopping dangerously to one side as she gestured wildly. "So, you must tell me what he is like. What am I to expect?"

When Madeline frowned, Alice leaned a little forward in her chair.

"This is to help me, Madeline, so keep nothing from me. I do not want to be so surprised that I am unable to speak to the man." In her mind's eye, she could still see him as he had been on their wedding day — unsteady on his feet, winking at some other woman behind Alice's back. Had he changed in these last three years?

Shifting a little in her chair, Madeline regarded Alice carefully. "You are aware, of course, that on the day of his wedding, his entire fortune was released, as per his father's will."

"Yes," Alice said, slowly. "I understood that he had his own reasons for marrying me and that the fortune was one of those reasons. Not to mention, he also received a very generous dowry from my father."

Madeline glanced towards the open windows before looking back at Alice. "He then proceeded to send his mother to the dower house, even though he had no intention of living in this father's main estate just outside of London. He has stayed in his townhouse here, although I believe he returns to his estate in the winter months."

When he could have stayed with me in Wren Park, Alice thought to herself, her heart sinking slowly in her chest. "I see."

"His mother is distraught over his behavior, I promise you," Madeline continued, quickly. "She has wanted to see you, but I believe she was never told where you resided. The man sent her to the dower house almost the moment you were married!" Shaking her head, Madeline sighed heavily. "I do not believe that your husband is either a kind or a good man, my dear. I am sorry to say."

A heavy weight settled in Alice's chest. "You mean, he has had affairs and the like?"

She expected Madeline to agree at once and was surprised to

see her friend frown heavily. Was Lord Worthington not entirely as she had expected?

"He is something of a flirt, that is for certain," Madeline said, eventually, as though choosing her words with the greatest of care. "But I have to admit that neither myself nor Lord Astor has heard of any kind of affair. He does not keep a mistress, I believe, although many women have tried — and failed — to put themselves in that position."

Alice drew in one long breath, her body shaking slightly as she let it out. This was not as bad as she had feared, for she had thought her husband a notorious rake who would have left a trail of discarded women behind him.

"I see," she said, softly. "I will confess that is something of a surprise."

"He will flirt with you, that I am sure of," Madeline responded, firmly. "But it appears nothing ever comes of his flirtations." Tipping her head slightly, she studied Alice. "What is it you intend to do with him, Alice? Are you going to reveal yourself at once?"

Shaking her head fervently, Alice put her cup down. "No, I will keep myself as Lady Emma Taylor for the time being and, once I have met my husband, perhaps some kind of plan will form in my mind. My main intention is to shame him with the realization of how terribly he has treated me. I long to hear him apologize for what he has done to me these last three years and to beg for my forgiveness."

A coldness wrapped around her heart as she gave her friend a grim smile. She was not about to be affected by her husband's flirtations, no matter how good a flirt he might be.

"Then I hope you achieve what you wish, my dear," Madeline said quietly.

4

A lice could not help the trembling in her soul as she walked into the grand entrance of the house, although she looked forward to seeing Catherine again. Apparently, the invitation had been almost instant once Madeline had mentioned to Catherine exactly what Alice was intending, which came as something of a surprise to Alice.

Catherine had always been straight-laced, so she was amazed to learn that her friend was perfectly content with her pretense. Then again, perhaps Catherine had changed in the three years Alice had been away.

The grand affair was a masquerade ball, so Alice was positive that her husband would not recognize her. Making sure that her mask was securely in place, tied with a silk ribbon, Alice greeted her hosts, pressing Catherine's hand gently so that she might know who she was.

"Ah!" Catherine exclaimed, her eyes bright behind her mask. "It is so good to see you again, my dear Lady Emma."

Relieved that her friend had remembered her faux name, Alice gave her a quick smile. "And I am delighted to see you also.

I am sure you have a great many more guests to greet, so mayhap we can speak again later, once the ball is in full swing?"

"Of course," Catherine replied, letting go of Alice's hand. "I do believe we have had some particular guests arrive already, however. You will find Lady Astor and *some* others already in the ballroom."

Alice swallowed hard, fully aware of what her friend was attempting to impress upon her.

Her husband was here.

NOT QUITE MANAGING the easy smile she attempted, Alice walked away from Catherine and made her way down the steps into the ballroom. There was a great crowd of guests already, but, to her very great relief, she saw a masked lady, who she presumed to be Madeline, walk towards her. She had evidently been keeping a watch out for her.

"You have arrived, then," Madeline smiled, looping her arm through Alice's.

"Indeed," Alice murmured, attempting to smile. "I must thank you for the loan of your carriage. I did not put you out, I hope?"

"Think nothing of it," Madeline assured her. "We have two, and Lord Astor did not mind either way. It would do no good for you to appear in your husband's carriage now, would it?"

"It certainly would give the game away somewhat," Alice murmured, still looking around the room. "Is he here, perchance?"

Madeline paused. "Yes, I believe so. To your left, my dear."

Alice turned, dropping Madeline's arm so that she might look across the room.

Her eyes alighted on him almost at once, forcing a sharp

intake of breath. He was just as she remembered him, with dark blonde hair, his eyes — brown, if she recalled correctly — flashed with humor as he talked to one of the young ladies that surrounded him. He wore the smallest of masks, a white creation that covered only one eye and a small part of his nose before tailing away at his cheek. Apparently, he did not want to remain hidden; he wanted people to be fully aware of his presence. His clothes fit him perfectly, his cravat without even the slightest imperfection. All in all, he was a handsome gentleman.

A rush of anger flooded her, her hands curling into fists. Did society know that he was married, or had they all forgotten? Did they think nothing of him leaving his wife to rot in some distant country estate whilst he enjoyed all the fun and frivolities of the season?

"Careful," Madeline murmured, putting a calming hand on Alice's arm. "Do not give yourself away, my dear. He shall know you at once, for even I can see your anger. It is practically coming off you in waves."

"How dare he?" Alice whispered, loudly, shaking off her friend's hand. "Standing there as though he is an unattached gentleman."

"Is this not what you expected?" Madeline asked, gently. "Did you expect to find him holed up in a corner somewhere, refusing to speak to even a single lady?"

The slight note of mischief in Madeline's voice made common sense calm Alice's anger.

"You are right, of course," she was forced to admit. "I had every expectation of seeing him in such a situation, but now that it is before my eyes, I find myself furious."

"Then it is just as well you are wearing a mask," Madeline said, lightly. "For you will need to calm yourself before you speak to him."

Alice turned back to her friend, shaking her head. "I have no intention of speaking to him, my dear."

Looping her hand through Madeline's, Alice felt her friend stiffen as she turned her eyes back behind her. "It appears as though you will have no choice, for he is coming this way. Apparently, you have caught his eye."

Snorting indelicately, Alice lifted her chin. "He has not been introduced."

Madeline laughed and squeezed Alice's arm. "It is a masquerade, my dear. We do not hold to such conventions at a masquerade. In short, there will be no introductions of any kind, not until the unmasking in a good few hours." She looked over at Alice, her eyes glinting behind her mask. "You might even dance with him, and he will never know who you are."

It was on the tip of Alice's tongue to say that she would never stoop so low as to dance with the man she hated, only for him to appear by her side, rounding on them both so that they were forced to stop in their tracks.

He bowed, and Alice had every intention of refusing to follow suit, but it was the increasing pressure on her arm from Madeline that forced her into doing so. Still, she allowed herself only the tiniest curtsy, finding it difficult to even look directly at the man. All of a sudden, her heart was hammering in her chest, her breath coming quickly as she battled for control.

Her husband, the man she had married, was standing directly in front of her. Had he recognized her after all? Was this why he had approached them so quickly? Swallowing the ache in her throat, Alice lifted her eyes and looked directly at him, suddenly afraid that he was going to take her by the arm and drag her from the room before railing at her in seething tones.

When her gaze finally met his, she discovered that he was smiling at her warmly, no anger in his eyes.

"Now," he began, jovially. "There is no need for introductions tonight — not yet at least — but I simply must have a dance with both of you ladies. Are your dance cards full?"

Alice found that she could not speak, staring at him numbly. He had not recognized her after all. Yet now, he wanted to dance with her. Alice found that she could not refuse, for her dance card was entirely empty, having only just arrived.

"I shall not put my real title, of course," he said, catching her dance card in his hand and scrutinizing it, even though she had not given him permission to do so. "I shall simply be 'Lord W' so as not to give the game away."

He scribbled something down and gave her a hearty wink before turning to Madeline, who held out her wrist so that he might write his name in one of her spaces.

"All done," he grinned, giving them both a jaunty bow. "I shall look forward to taking my turn with you both on the floor later this evening."

Alice watched him walk away, realizing that she had not said a single word and now, to her horror, saw that she was engaged to dance with him twice.

"But only the once with me," Madeline murmured, lifting her eyebrows. "It appears that he has something of an interest in you, my dear. How...awkward."

"It is more than awkward," Alice hissed, not wanting to dance with him in the least. "It is downright despicable. He should not be showing any woman any kind of preference."

"And yet, he has," Madeline replied, firmly. "And you are going to have to dance with him, Alice, otherwise you will make yourself even more of an object of interest. Besides, it would be terribly rude."

Alice shook her head, her jaw clenched. She would not dance with her husband. She could not. It would be too frustrating, too mortifying, even though she would be the only one who would know of her shame.

"I will not dance with him," she grated.

Madeline put a soft hand on her arm, drawing her attention away from Lord Worthington for just a moment.

"Think calmly, my dear. I know this moment has been overwhelming, but to refuse to dance with a man who has signed your dance card will bring more difficulties than it is worth. He will want to know why, and society at large will question who you are and why you refused him. Dance with him, Alice, and then simply move on."

"I cannot move on," Alice said, sadly, as a ball of misery settled in her stomach. "I am trapped. There is nowhere else for me to go other than back to his estate, to his lands, to spend his money."

"Then perhaps you should show him that you are a strong woman, Alice. Show him that you are not about to be swayed by a gentleman's dictates and rules, that you know your own mind and your own heart. That you will not put up with being treated in such a disgraceful manner."

"And what good will that do?"

Madeline smiled. "Show him all of that first, Alice. And then reveal the truth."

"My lord."

Giving one last glance towards Madeline, Alice allowed herself to be led onto the floor, despite every bone in her body screaming that she should not allow such a thing. It was no good, of course, for Lord Worthington had appeared by her side the moment the last dance had finished, ready to lead her onto the floor.

"Are you in town for long?" he asked, as they began to dance. "I am aware that these masks hide our true features, but

I am quite sure I have not seen you at such an event before now."

"I have only just arrived," Alice replied, coolly. She was relieved that her voice had not failed her, although she struggled to keep any trace of anger or upset from it. "I am not quite sure how long I shall stay."

"I see," he responded, giving her an assessing glance. "Then I shall have to make the most of your company while I can."

He grinned at her, but Alice felt nothing but distaste.

"And you, my lord," Alice began, remembering Madeline's advice. "You spend much time here in town, I hear?"

His grin widened. "Indeed."

"Hiding from something, are you?"

His grin vanished at once, replaced with a look of astonishment which he swiftly covered with a look of nonchalance. "Not at all, my lady. Where such a story has come from, I am not sure."

Alice sniffed delicately, waiting until she returned to his side before continuing. "I have heard all about you, Lord Worthington."

"Ah, so you know me then," he chuckled, apparently attempting to get back to their airy discussion. "And I thought my mask hid my face quite well."

"Nonsense," Alice declared, recalling how Madeline had encouraged her to show Lord Worthington that she was not like the other flighty ladies of his acquaintance, ready to accept whatever nonsense he spouted. "You chose that mask so that people would know who you were — the ladies, I presume, especially."

The cheerfulness was slowly wiped from his face as he continued with his dance steps, looking at her in a slightly puzzled manner. "You are not afraid to say what you think, my lady."

Alice let out a quiet laugh. "I was not always so, my lord, but I have come to learn that hiding away in the shadows, simply agreeing with whatever it is a gentleman might say, is unhealthy."

"Oh?" His raised eyebrow told her that he was waiting for her to explain herself a little more.

"To do so allows oneself to be trampled by those who believe they have a higher position within society — or a higher position than you, at least." She gave a slight shake of her head. "No, I shall no longer allow myself to be told what to do and how to speak or what to wear. I am my own person, my lord, so do not expect me to fall at your feet in regard for your good looks or charm. I can see straight through them."

She saw him swallow, his mouth set in something of a thin line. "I see," he muttered, looking away from her.

"I am more than aware of who you are," she continued, enjoying the way he was becoming so discomfited. "And I find your flirtations both childish and inappropriate. You may have hordes of young ladies at your beck and call, but you will not find me amongst them, my lord. I am sorry to say so, but there it is."

The dance, mercifully, came to a close, and he released her almost at once and bowed quickly.

"I can see my own way back to my friend," Alice said, lifting her chin a little as she stepped away from him. "I thank you for the dance, my lord, and shall look forward to our next one."

He did not say anything, but his eyes rested on her for a long moment before he stepped away.

Feeling more than satisfied, Alice walked gracefully back towards Madeline, who was being led off the floor by her husband. Alice greeted them both, laughing to herself as Madeline sent her husband off in search of something to drink, evidently eager to discover how Alice had done.

"Well?"

Alice chuckled. "I do not think he will be returning for his second dance," she laughed, feeling proud of herself. "I made it clear that I do not appreciate nor want any of his flirtations."

Madeline looked shocked. "You did not say that?"

"I did," Alice declared, smiling. "And you should have seen the look on his face. I think he must consider me a persona non grata to him now."

"Goodness," Madeline murmured, as another gentleman came to claim Alice's hand for the next dance. "I suppose that is very well done, Alice."

THE SENSE of triumph in Alice's chest brought her a great deal of happiness that spread throughout the rest of the evening. She was not sure whether or not Lord Worthington would ever seek her out again, but if he did not, she would find him and continue their conversation until she was satisfied. Madeline was right. She had to prove to him — and even to herself — that she was a strong woman, who would not bend to a gentleman's demands any longer. She had lived that life for too long, and it was time for things to change.

In her mind's eye, Alice could see herself railing at him for leaving his wife in such a terrible circumstance, for not even being aware of who she was. The guilt he would feel would be almost overwhelming, crushing him before her. Then, when it was as if he could take it no more, she would reveal herself and her conquest would be complete. He would be so astonished, so guilt-ridden, so humiliated in front of society by what she had been forced to do, that he would try to make things up to her for a long time to come. Perhaps for the duration of their marriage.

However, that illusion was shattered the moment he

returned to her side, ready to take her to the floor for their second dance.

Wilting a little, she walked onto the floor and, aware that this was a waltz, tentatively put her hand on his shoulder and clasped his hand.

"You dance wonderfully," he murmured, a quiet smile on his face. "What a shame I do not know your name."

"I doubt you need it," Alice replied crisply. "Are there not many other ladies here this evening who are entirely envious of me? I am sure you may lavish your attentions on them, and they will be more than delighted with it."

He frowned. "You intrigue me, my lady."

"Is that so?"

Nodding, he continued to regard her from behind his mask. "No lady of my acquaintance has ever spoken to me in the way you do. I find it quite... refreshing."

"Regardless, do not think that I wish for your company to be focused on me," Alice responded, her heart beginning to hammer in her chest.

This was not at all going the way she had intended.

"You have another?" he asked, softly.

That question forced her to look at him, her eyes narrowing. "Do you?"

An uncomfortable look came over his face, evidently unsettling him. He opened his mouth to answer, only for the music to come to an abrupt stop and the announcement that the unmasking was upon them.

"Wonderful!" Lord Worthington exclaimed, grinning at her. "Finally, I shall look upon your face, my lady. You shall not be able to hide your identity from me then, I am sure!"

Alice felt her heart begin to race as she lifted her hands to untie the silk ribbon, suddenly terrified that her husband would remember her face from their wedding, even though he had not lifted her veil. The mask slipped from her face, and she caught it in one hand before looking up at him.

There was not even a flicker of recognition.

"It seems you are new to town," he said, heavily. "For I do not recognize you in the least."

He caught her hand, his gloved fingers twining with hers.

"Please, do not leave without telling me your name. For whatever reason, I simply cannot leave here this evening without it."

The hint of desperation in his voice gave her no joy, her heartbeat slowly settling as she saw that he did not know her in the slightest. It was unsurprising, but nevertheless, a heavy weight sank into her chest.

"I am Lady Emma Taylor," she murmured, giving him a quick curtsy and turning to leave the floor.

5

Over the next sennight, Alice saw her husband very often, but treated him with the same cool disregard she had done that very first night. However, instead of putting him off, it only seemed to encourage him.

She would find his name on the same two dances at each and every ball she attended, for he always made sure to waltz with her, no matter how much she tried to remove herself from his presence. His attempts to engage her in conversation never brought her any kind of pleasure, for she found his manner entirely inappropriate for a married gentleman.

Despite herself, she would watch him as he took other ladies on to the floor, her eyes unable to leave him. It was true that he was a handsome man, but that did not make up for his lack of character. In truth, she was both disappointed and hurt. Hurt that he was not the kind of man she would ever have sought for a husband and disappointed that the last three years had taught him nothing. Apparently, he had not changed.

"You are watching him a little too often, Alice," Catherine murmured one night when they were at yet another ball. What with it being the high point of the season, Alice had found herself at a ball almost every night, thanks to either Catherine or Madeline's friendship.

"You will give yourself away," Catherine warned, pressing a gentle hand to Alice's arm. "Come now, distract yourself."

Sighing heavily, Alice turned her back on the dancing guests and tried to smile. "You are very wise, Catherine. What would I do without you and Madeline to help me pick my way through this delicate situation?"

Catherine smiled but said nothing, greeting one of the gentlemen talking to Lady Astor and her husband. Alice forced herself to remain steadfast, trying to listen to the conversation flowing around her but finding her thoughts entirely caught up with her husband.

"And how are you this evening?"

Madeline's sympathetic smile told Alice that her friend was not unaware of the difficulties she was currently working through.

"I am well, I thank you," Alice replied, aware that there were other gentlemen and ladies in their company.

"Have you danced very often?"

It was a veiled question, and Alice tried her best not to grimace. Her friend wished to know whether or not Lord Worthington had signed her dance card as he usually did, and, unfortunately, Alice had to admit that yes, he had.

"Quite often," she answered, managing a quick roll of her eyes. "I believe all my dances but one are taken."

Madeline's eyes flashed with indignation for her friend.

"I have company for the supper dance also," Alice continued, her heart sinking into her stomach. "So, you need not worry that I will be lonely."

Her friend's smile became fixed. "No, indeed. I am glad to hear it."

Alice sighed inwardly, wondering whether or not she would,

somehow, be able to escape before the supper dance took place. Of course, Lord Worthington had signed his name to it almost at once, whilst she had been caught up talking to another gentleman.

Any other lady might have colored and laughingly rebuked him from catching her off guard, but her reaction was quite the opposite. It had taken everything in her not to wrench her dance card from his grip and stalk away in the opposite direction, giving him the cut direct, but sense had forced her to remain where she was.

Were she to turn away from him, then society would wonder why she was treating him so, and she did not want to garner any further attentions. Thankfully, thus far, she had been accepted into London society with barely a question. No one appeared to recognize her, something that had always given her a slight amount of worry, but evidently, she had changed in her three years away.

The music began once more, and Alice smiled as Madeline took her husband's proffered arm, evidently delighted to be dancing in the arms of her husband. It was a happy marriage, and Alice was more than pleased for Madeline, even if she could not stop herself from feeling a hint of jealousy over the wonderful husband her friend had been blessed with. How different life could have been had Lord Worthington been even remotely like Lord Astor.

"My dear Lady Emma, I believe this is our dance."

Alice's smile froze as she heard her husband's familiar voice, turning to face him with trepidation in her heart.

"Are you not weary of dancing?" she asked, attempting to sound nonchalant. "You have danced almost every dance, I believe."

"Watching me, were you?" he laughed, his eyes twinkling with mischief. "My lady, I confess that I have had nothing more than this moment in mind, for the entirety of the ball. To have the pleasure of your company not only for the dance but also for supper." He put his hand over his heart and sighed heavily, a wide smile on his face. "Wonderful."

Alice was not taken in. No blush crept into her cheeks, no soft smile tugged at the corners of her mouth. She was entirely unaffected, and she could detect the frisson of doubt that crept into his features as he continued to smile at her.

"Shall we?" he asked, eventually, when she simply did not respond. "Come now, Lady Emma! Are we not friends yet? Have we not spent enough time in each other's company to find one another tolerable at least?"

Keeping her mouth closed, Alice tried to concentrate on the steps of the dance instead of on her husband.

"Still, you do not speak to me," he sighed, looking sad. "Can you not see that I only wish to get to know you better?"

"I am sure you do," Alice responded, keeping her eyes averted from his face. "Sadly, I cannot say the same."

A faint line of annoyance crossed his face, which he wiped away quickly, covering it with a slight laugh. "You wound me, my dear Lady Emma."

It took everything Alice had not to respond, but she clamped her mouth shut and prayed that the dance would soon end. The supper dance meant that she would have to endure his company for a little longer, but at least there might be others that would join them.

His close proximity was something of a strain at the moment and, in spite of her indifference to him, Alice discovered that she did, for whatever reason, find him more than a little attractive. It was not a realization she wished to dwell on in the least, angry with herself for being as shallow as the rest of the ladies he pressed his attentions on.

"You are determined then to remain a mystery to me?" he asked, breaking into her thoughts. "But why so, Lady Emma?"

"It is not deliberate, Lord Worthington," she said, tightly. "Merely that I do not feel it necessary to give you all the details about myself and my life when we are hardly more than acquaintances."

He looked nonplussed for a moment before the bright smile was back on his face once more, although it now appeared to be somewhat strained.

"I do wish to know you better," he said, as the dance came to an end. "Is that such a terrible thing?"

Alice stopped dead, forgetting to curtsy as the couples began to move from the floor. "Why do you wish to know me better, my lord?"

Surprised, he stared at her as though no one had ever asked him such a question before. In fact, she was sure that no one ever had, since everyone seemed delighted to accept his attentions whenever he gave it.

"Walk with me," he murmured, leading her from the floor. "And I shall tell you."

Alice found herself borne away, tension running through her body. Shaking off his grip, no matter how appropriate, she turned to face him the moment they reached a quieter corner of the ballroom.

With all the other guests now turning to go into the supper room, they were left to have a somewhat private conversation. Alice glared at him, wondering how he was to answer her question. When would he realize that she was not like all the other ladies of his acquaintance? When would he stop hounding her?

"You asked me why I seek a further acquaintance with you," he murmured, quietly. "Can you not tell, Lady Emma? Must I make my interest in you so obvious?"

His words did nothing to calm her. "You are trying to tell me that you find me somewhat attractive?"

He grinned jauntily. "In short, yes."

"And I should be delighted with this, I presume?"

The grin slowly slid from his face. "It is a compliment, is it not?"

She snorted and turned away, desperately seeking some place of refuge. The doors were open, and she stepped out on to the terrace, allowing the cool air to calm her hot cheeks.

"You are quite impossible, Lady Emma," came his voice as he stepped out beside her. "I am only trying to please you."

Shaking her head, Alice turned her head away from him and stared out into the darkness. "You can please me by pressing your attentions onto a woman who desires them. Now, please excuse me, Lord Worthington. I believe I require a few minutes alone."

All was quiet for a few minutes, making Alice believe that Lord Worthington had done as she asked, but when she turned her head, she saw him still standing there, studying her intently.

"Please," she repeated, standing a little taller. "I have no wish for company at the present moment."

"You mean you have no wish for *my* company," he responded, with such a serious expression on his face that she was slightly taken aback. "Might I ask, Lady Emma, why you seem to dislike me so on such a short acquaintance?"

Alice could not tell him the truth, for fear that he would discover the truth about who she was. "I simply do not have time for rogues and rakes, my lord."

He made a surprised sound in the back of his throat. "And you believe me to be such a thing?"

She looked at him steadily, refusing to answer but making her response more than plain. To her very great surprise, he appeared quite affronted, his brows knitting together in a deep frown.

"A rake, my lady, suggests that I toy with young ladies, stealing kisses here and there, and promising them things that I never intend to give." His jaw clenched, and he paused for a brief moment. "I am not that kind of man."

"You are an incorrigible flirt."

"And what of it?" he retorted, sounding somewhat annoyed. "That has done no harm, has it? It is just a game, a distraction, from the difficulties of my life."

She spun on her heel and stared at him, her fingers itching to slap him across the face. "Difficulties?" she ground out, her jaw clenching. "And what difficulties might a man of your standing have, pray tell? From what I have been told, the only difficulties you have are how to safely return to your home when you have imbibed so much that you cannot even stand up."

His brow furrowed, his eyes darkening in the gloom as he stared back at her. "I am simply distracting myself from what I have done," he said, quietly. "From what I have allowed others to force me into. Is that so terrible?"

Alice raised her chin, forcing herself to think before she spoke. She desired more than anything to tell him who she really was so that he might wilt before her eyes, aware that she knew precisely of what he spoke and found the idea that he considered her a 'difficulty' to be more than insulting.

Yet, if she did that now, she would never bring the shame on him that she had planned. It would simply remain between him and her, instead of all of society becoming aware of exactly what he had done to her. She was aware that there were a great many in society who were not quite sure whether Lord Worthington was bound in matrimony or, if he had, whether or not his wife still lived. Given that he lived as a man who was completely unattached, Alice could not blame those who saw him for suggesting such things.

"I believe that distracting oneself is a cowardly attempt to pretend you do not truly have any kind of responsibilities," she said, slowly, thinking out each sentence before she said it. "It is a pretense that you have not acted in a certain way in the past and a continued charade that you are not bound by those actions." Looking straight into his eyes, she settled her shoulders and lifted her chin a notch. "You can understand, then, why I do not wish for your attentions."

To her surprise, he let out a harsh laugh. "But you are equally pretending, Lady Emma."

"I certainly am not," she blustered, knowing full well that he was speaking the truth, although he was not aware of it.

"You are, my dear lady," he continued, ignoring her protest. "I have seen your eyes on me as I escorted other ladies to the dance floor. I have caught you watching me, although you always just look away before my eyes meet yours." He stepped closer, and Alice instinctively moved back, feeling her back pressed against the railing of the terrace.

"Tell me the truth, Lady Emma," he murmured, reaching up to catch her chin with his hand. "Tell me honestly that you do not want my attentions."

"I do not want your attentions," Alice responded, immediately, her skin prickling under his touch. "If you must know, the only reason I have been watching you is because I have been entirely horrified with what I have heard of you and wanted to see whether or not it was true." She closed her eyes briefly and swallowed hard, before looking back up at him. "And now I have seen that it is exactly as everyone says."

No matter how hard she glared at him, he did not drop his hand from her chin, instead letting his fingers trail up over her jawline and towards her ear, where he caught a stray curl and ran it through his fingers. Alice battled against the sudden urge to respond to him, knowing that he was simply attempting to make his point. He wanted to show her that she truly did want his attentions on her, that, in watching him, she was jealous of the time he gave to the other ladies. If only he knew the truth of who she was.

"You must not believe everything you hear, Lady Emma," he murmured, moving a fraction closer to her and putting one hand on the railing behind her. He was so close to her that there was simply no means of escape, not unless she pushed at him hard and, for whatever reason, Alice was struggling to even think clearly. His breath tickled her cheek as he lowered his head, his other hand capturing her chin once more and tilting it towards him.

"I am a terrible flirt, that I will admit to," he promised her, his eyes searching hers. "But I swear to you that I do not steal kisses from young ladies or put them in any kind of compromising position."

Alice took a breath, trying to steady herself. "Then what exactly do you call this, Lord Worthington?"

He laughed softly, rubbing his thumb lightly over her bottom lip. "I call it a game, Lady Emma. You intrigue me."

She wanted the game to be over. She longed for a husband who cared about her and wanted to be with her. For just a moment, her guard came down. She closed her eyes and leaned into his hand as he cupped her cheek, and she placed her own hand over his. Her heart rate quickened, responding to his touch. She opened her eyes to see him staring back at her with a look of fondness, and he smirked as if he knew he could win her affection.

Quickly, she regained her composure. He would not win this game. Without warning, she pushed past him, staggering forward as he stumbled back.

"How dare you?" she exclaimed, horrified to find that her eyes were filling with tears. "How dare you press your attentions on me when I have not given you permission to do so! By keeping me out here, you *have* put me in a compromising position. You know how important it is to ladies that our reputations remain pristine."

The satisfied smile on his face heated her anger all the more and, raising her hand, she slapped him soundly across the face, shocking him entirely.

"I am not some pawn in your chess game, Lord Worthington!" she cried, feeling moisture drip from her lashes onto her cheeks. She was completely and utterly ashamed of how easily she had slipped under his spell, her mask slipped away almost entirely. "And to think that I had hoped the rumors would not be true."

Wiping her cheeks, she stalked past into the ballroom, her back ramrod straight but her self-esteem in tatters at her feet.

6

Thankfully for Alice, most of the other guests had already gone through to supper when she had left the ball. She had not spoken to a single other soul, except for the surprised footman who had called for her carriage at once. She had asked him to pass on a message to her host and was back home within an hour of leaving Lord Worthington.

From there, she had attempted to put every thought of him from her mind but, even now, when dawn was beginning to break, Alice still found herself tossing and turning. She could not get his behavior towards her from her mind, could not forget how her heart raced when he had touched her.

Tears soaked the pillow as she wept, crying over her own foolishness and her lack of sense. He had sworn to her that he was not a man who stole kisses from ladies, but it seemed that his actions were moving in that direction - and he had called it 'a game.' That insult pierced the very heart of her, bringing her more pain that she had ever thought possible. Her own husband, the biggest flirt London had ever seen by all accounts, had made his interest in her apparent. He did not know she was his wife.

Why had she responded to him so? She had been unable to stop herself from reacting to his nearness, recalling the way he had rubbed his thumb over her bottom lip. She had come alive in that moment, his actions sparking feelings she had never before experienced. Was this what desire felt like?

If that was what she felt, Alice despised it all the more. She did not want to have any kind of affection or desire for the man she called husband. The memory of his touch and the affection in his eyes brought her only sadness, completely ashamed over how she had responded to his attentions. Her facade had been entirely lost, for now, he would not see her as the strong, dispassionate lady who cared nothing for him, rather he would see her as a conquest. He had managed to force her to respond to him, proving to them both that she was not as unaffected by him as she appeared.

"You do look pale this morning, my lady," the maid said, worriedly, handing Alice her breakfast tray of a cup of chocolate and some hot, buttered toast. "Should I send for the doctor?"

Alice gave her a wan smile. "I am just tired, that is all."

The maid nodded, although the frown did not leave her face. "Perhaps you might rest for a while longer?"

"I think I shall," Alice murmured, quietly. "Although I am to visit Lady Astor tomorrow afternoon."

"Then you should certainly make sure to rest today," the maid replied, patting Alice's hand. "Just ring if you need anything, my lady."

Alice nodded, picking up a piece of toast in an attempt to eat. "I shall, I thank you."

The maid left, unaware of just how much of a balm she had been to Alice's soul. It was just as well that her parents' townhouse retained a skeleton staff whom Alice had known for some time, for they were more than willing to go along with any and all plans that she had. They were kind to her, apparently aware of what circumstances she had been left in, and Alice knew that she could trust no rumors about her true identity would make their way from this house. At least, here, she could hide from her husband in peace.

"Alice!"

Madeline's face was filled with concern as Alice entered the room, rising to her feet to catch Alice's hands. "Are you well? I have not heard from you for two days!"

Alice managed a smile. "It is hardly two days, Madeline. I saw you at the ball two nights ago."

"And it is now two days since then," Madeline retorted, searching Alice's face. "What has happened to you, my dear?"

Desperately hoping that she would not cry, Alice shook her head. "I am too ashamed to tell you."

Madeline's shoulders slumped. "Ah. It is to do with that husband of yours, is it not?" She pulled the bell for tea and guided Alice to sit down beside the fire. "What did he do?"

"Did you not see him after supper?" Alice asked, a little surprised that he had not been crowing with delight for the remainder of the evening.

Shaking her head, Madeline studied Alice curiously. "No, I did not. He took his leave soon after supper."

"Oh." Frowning, Alice wondered what had possessed Lord Worthington to leave so hastily. "Perhaps my slap damaged his perfectly presented face somewhat."

Madeline's gasp met her ears, although her eyes came alive with interest. "You slapped him? Whatever for?"

Knowing that she would have to tell her friend, and thinking that perhaps it might lift some of her burdens, Alice quickly sketched out the details, the words tumbling from her mouth.

"How did you respond when he touched you?" Madeline asked, sounding quite astonished. "Did you slap him then?"

Heat poured into Alice's face. "Not at first, and that is something I truly regret. It took me a few moments to realize what it was he had said to me. In truth, I became a little lost and fell to his charms. Then, when I realized he did not I was his wife, I slapped him. How could he do that?"

Madeline's face took on a knowing look, and she grasped Alice's hand. "Do not torment yourself over this, Alice. It is to be expected."

"Expected?" Alice exclaimed, angry with herself all over again. "The man I despise took his fondness for me too far, and I responded like some flighty young miss who is overawed by his attentions. I truly believe that he was going to try to kiss me!" She wrung her hands. "You should have seen the look on his face when I pushed him away." She swallowed hard, hating the memory of it. "He was laughing at me."

"Oh, Alice," Madeline murmured, softly. "I am sorry that he did such a thing."

"I cannot see him again," Alice said, brokenly. "He has won, Madeline."

Madeline's wrath was immediate. "Don't be ridiculous, Alice! You cannot simply return to the country and give up on your plans just because it seems as if he was going to kiss you!"

"How can I not?" Alice returned, miserably. "I am no longer the strong, aloof lady that is unaffected by his advances. My facade has failed entirely."

"Nonsense," Madeline said loudly, forcing Alice's attention. "You cannot give up now, Alice. I will not have it! I have seen you blossom under this 'facade' as you call it — although I am quite sure that this is simply someone you are becoming instead of someone you pretend to be."

Sniffing indelicately, Alice looked at her friend. "What do you mean?"

Madeline's gaze was resolute. "You state that you are merely pretending to be Lady Emma, who is both a strong and self-reliant lady, refusing to be swayed by a charming smile or flattering words." Her expression softened as she smiled. "Can you not see that this is no longer a pretense, Alice? You *are* Lady Emma Taylor."

Still a little confused, Alice frowned. "That is just a mask, Madeline."

"No, it is not," Madeline returned at once. "You are strong. You are self-reliant. Think of it, Alice. You have grown weary of your husband's inattention and have returned to London of your own accord, having found and arranged both travel and lodgings, albeit your parents' townhouse. You have attended balls and soirees and never once given a girlish smile to any young gentleman who might seek to flatter you."

"That is because I find such things entirely void of both truth and meaning," Alice murmured quietly. "I know that some gentlemen have an interest in me, which is the only reason for their attentions. I am not here to find a husband!" Heat crept into her cheeks at speaking so plainly, but Madeline only nodded.

"You see, my dear?" she said, happily. "You are the kind of person you have always wanted to be. In taking on the characteristics of Lady Emma, which you considered only a disguise, you have, in short, become such a lady yourself." She leaned forward and touched Alice's hand. "Which means that you cannot allow Lord Worthington, the rogue that he is, to affect your strength and dignity."

Alice sighed, her lips trembling as she struggled to respond to Madeline. Finally, she understood what her friend was saying, but still could not see a way ahead. Thankfully, the arrival of the tea tray gave her some minutes to compose herself.

"I know you are worried that he will think of you as a conquest," Madeline continued, sitting back in her seat as the maid left the room. "But you must have given him something of a resounding setback for him to have left the ball so early. For him to depart a gathering without even taking in supper is unheard of, I assure you."

Alice bit her lip and thought hard. She realized now that leaving London and returning to the country estate was simply a desire to run away from what she had started, finding it almost too much to bear.

"I do not like that I responded to him so," she admitted as Madeline poured the tea. "I should have pushed him away at once."

Madeline gave a slight shrug, as though what Alice had said was not at all perturbing. "You are attracted to your husband, Alice. What does that matter?"

"I do not want to be."

Laughing, Madeline shook her head. "I am afraid we do not always have a choice when it comes to matters of the heart. You shall simply have to fight that inward battle on your own."

It was a relief to be able to share her torment with her friend, Alice admitted to herself, finally relaxing a little in her chair.

"So, shall you stay?" Madeline asked, looking at her from over the top of her teacup.

Alice frowned. "I shall take a few days to gather my wits about me once more, but yes, I believe I shall stay and see this thing through to the end."

Madeline raised her teacup slightly, in a small toast. "I am delighted to hear it."

7

Over the next three days, Alice rested both her mind and her body, staying abed longer than she ought and refusing to go out into society at all. Invitations were declined, politely of course, whilst Alice considered what she might do the next time she saw her husband.

Madeline, on the whole, left her alone, although she did send a note to say that Lord Worthington had been at a musical evening she had attended and had appeared perturbed to discover Lady Emma's absence. She then wrote again the following day to announce that Lord Worthington had sought her out again the previous evening at a coming out ball for a Miss Mary Dewley.

Apparently, he had been most keen to discover whether or not Lady Emma was present and had frowned for a good few minutes on discovering her absent once again.

Such notes did not bring any kind of peace to Alice's spirits, finding herself even more confused over her husband. Surely, now that he had proven to them both that she was not as unaffected as she appeared, he would consider his task completed. So why was he still seeking out her company? Why did he seem so disconcerted to discover her absent? It made very little sense. For her own self, she was finding it impossible to remove him from her thoughts despite her own deep humiliation.

It was distasteful to her to admit that she found her own husband an attractive man, even worse to say that she did catch herself, on occasion, recalling his touch. She put it down to having never experienced such a thing before, even though in her heart, she knew it was more than that. After all, he was her husband, even though he did not act as a married man ought.

And so, after three days, Alice found herself more than ready to leave her townhouse and find the company of her friends. Madeline and Catherine, both of whom were, apparently, concerned for her, had invited her to join them for afternoon tea, and Alice was keen to join them. After all, leaving the safety of her home and making her way to Madeline's townhouse was not going to put her in any danger of seeing Lord Worthington now, was it?

Her friends greeted her with enthusiasm and delight, which was a comfort to Alice's soul. Neither of them held any kind of reproach in their gaze, pressing her hands and encouraging her to sit down so that they might discuss all the goings on of late.

"How have you been, my dear?" Madeline asked, the moment Alice seated herself. "I have been worried about you."

"I am quite well, I assure you," Alice promised, smiling at her friend.

"So long as you have not been tormenting yourself with thoughts of regret and frustration," Catherine added, reminding Alice that she had allowed Madeline to tell Catherine of what had happened. "You should not allow such a thing to fill you with remorse."

Alice sighed. "I know I shall have to see him again, but I confess that I do not feel ready for it."

Madeline's eyes lit with a sudden interest. "He seems distressed over your ongoing absence, Alice."

Alice frowned. "I cannot give reason to that, I admit. Why should he be chasing my company when he has already achieved his purpose?"

"His purpose?" Catherine asked, looking confused.

Nodding, Alice set down her tea cup gently. "His purpose was to prove that I was not as unaffected towards him as I thought. Now that he has achieved that aim, I cannot understand why he still seeks me out, unless he wishes to add to my humiliation."

Catherine's lips twisted. "I cannot say, my dear. I had not thought of that before."

Alice could not help but sigh. "He swore to me that he was not the kind of man to steal kisses from any young lady he wanted, but now I realize that such words were just a pretense to make me think better of him." Her lips trembled, but she pressed them together and forced her tears away. "Now I realize that he is just as I suspected. Goodness knows how many other young ladies he has kissed!"

To her very great surprise, Madeline shook her head. "I must disagree with you there, Alice. Of course, you must never repeat this, but servants talk, and I have been privy to the gossip. I have made some very discreet inquiries and have discovered, to the best of my knowledge, that the man has never once kissed another lady or had a mistress. It seems as if he enjoys the attention from other young ladies, but never acts on them."

Alice did not know what to say, her heart clenching for a moment.

"That does not detract from his misdeed, however," Catherine said softly. "He should not have been alone with you and made his affection for you so obvious. He does not know you are his wife."

"Quite," Alice murmured, her thoughts whirling. "He knows he is wed, does he not? Although, I am more than aware that many gentlemen take mistresses, so perhaps I should not surprise myself that he has done only a very small by touching me in such a familiar fashion."

Madeline's expression softened. "There is something about his behavior towards you that is very different from how he has acted before, Alice. I am sure he is not as disaffected as he appears. He may surprise you the next time you meet. Perhaps he regrets taking such liberties!"

"Or he may wish to laugh in my face," Alice muttered, shaking her head. "I can hardly bear the thought of seeing him again, yet I know I must. I will continue to be Lady Emma, refusing to engage with his flirtations until, finally, I reveal the truth of who I am to him in front of all society." Her heart began to pound at the thought.

Catherine's face grew anxious. "I do hope this all works out as you hope, Alice. I am sorry for how he has treated you as his wife, but I cannot help but worry about what he will do once the truth is out."

"Who knows what he will do to me after such a humiliation?" she continued, giving her friends a half smile. "He may very well pack me off to Scotland or some other faraway place, but at least my heart will be glad in the knowledge that he has been shamed before all society, that everyone will know that he is wed and how he has treated me thus far."

There was a brief silence as the three ladies considered Alice's plans.

"Well, if you are sent to Scotland, then I swear I shall visit you regardless," Madeline chirped, breaking the tense silence. "You have my unwavering support in this matter, Alice."

"And mine," Catherine added, rising to her feet. "Now, I must go, for I have an engagement with Mama that I must keep."

Pressing her cheek to Alice's for a moment, Catherine smiled. "You are one of the bravest ladies of my acquaintance," she said, straightening. "I shall see you tomorrow evening."

"Tomorrow," Alice replied, knowing that she had already accepted the invitation to Lord and Lady Dalrymple's ball.

Her heart lifted at Catherine's sentiment, growing a little more relaxed within herself.

"You shall simply have to ensure that he does not get a hold of your dance card," Madeline said, the moment Catherine had left. "Although, how you are to manage that, I am not sure."

Alice laughed softly. "Yes, that would aid my cause somewhat. If he is not on my dance card, then I need not spend more than a moment in his presence."

Madeline grinned, her eyes sparkling with mischief. "Then I shall be your guard," she replied, a plan evidently forming in her mind. "Should I see him, then I shall direct your attention elsewhere, for we must seek to have your dance card filled as quickly as possible." Her smile softened. "That will not prove to be too difficult, my dear. You are in demand, it seems."

Shaking her head a little, Alice gave her friend a wry smile. "Imagine if I had been as accepted during my come out, Madeline. How different my life might have been." Her thoughts drifted to an imagined life, one where she was wed to a man who, at the very least, held her in some affection, instead of to one who did not seem to care whether she existed or not. A lump began to form in her throat, and with an effort, she pushed such thoughts away. "Dreams such as these are not helpful, however," she finished, with only a slight wobble to her voice. "I must make the best of my situation."

Madeline's face was lined with sympathy, although her tone was brisk. "Quite, my dear friend. However, that does not mean that you cannot change your circumstances, as you are doing.

Who knows what this might bring for your future? Perhaps you might, one day, have the life you dream of."

Alice, thinking that such a thing was most improbable, gave a slight shake of her head, before turning the conversation to what Madeline intended to wear the following evening. The idea of Lord Worthington ever coming to love her or to hold her in any kind of affection was almost laughable, although Alice appreciated Madeline's attempt to console her. Setting her thoughts to the ball, she attempted to forget about her husband, relieving herself of the anxiety she felt — at least, for the time being.

ALICE TRIED to stop herself from trembling, hiding her face behind her fan as she drew in a steady breath. The ball was already in full swing, and having made a late entrance, Alice hoped that she might put Lord Worthington at even more of a disadvantage. However, she would have to face him still, and that made her quake despite her attempts at bravery.

Madeline, at least, was ready and waiting for her, having promised to watch for her entrance. She was by her side in a moment, drawing her away from the hosts and towards the group of acquaintances she had been talking to only a moment ago.

"I am sure most of you know my dear friend, Lady Emma Taylor," she smiled, squeezing Alice's arm briefly. "However, I will be more than delighted to introduce her to those of you who have not had the pleasure of making her acquaintance."

There were a few laughs of good humor, and Alice found herself introduced to a few gentlemen and ladies she had not had the opportunity to meet thus far as well as greeting a few old acquaintances. So caught up was she in the conversation, that she only just heard Madeline clear her throat, a signal that Lord Worthington was nearby.

"And are you inclined to dance, Lady Emma?" one of the gentlemen asked, his eyes lingering on the dance card that dangled from her wrist. "I do hope I might secure one or two?"

Alice smiled, holding her wrist up for his inspection. "I am late, I must confess, but I would be delighted to dance with you, Lord Barnes."

Lord Barnes made an exclamation of delight and quickly signed his name to two dances, only for three other gentlemen to follow suit. That left only a few dances remaining, and, from the slight widening of Madeline's eyes, Alice made the assumption that her husband was drawing near.

"Lord Barnes," she said, quickly. "Is that not our dance? Shall we go?" It was most unusual for a lady to prompt a gentleman in such a manner, but Alice found that she could not bear the thought of being caught in conversation with Lord Worthington. Thankfully, Lord Barnes beamed at her and held out his arm, which she took at once — only to come face to face with her husband.

"Lord Worthington," Lord Barnes said, bowing quickly as Alice gave him a quick curtsy, refusing to meet his gaze, and, instead turned her attention towards Lord Barnes.

"Are you dancing, Lady Emma?" came Lord Worthington's voice, a slight twinge of humor intertwined with his words. "I do hope you have saved a space for me."

Alice was not about to let him check her card and, stepping past him, gave a brief wave of her hand. "Unfortunately not, my lord," she murmured, still directing her gaze towards Lord Barnes. "I do not think we shall see much of each other this evening."

"How disappointing," she heard him murmur, as she and Lord Barnes stepped out onto the floor, joining a set already formed. Satisfaction filled her as she began to dance, her wide smile bestowed on Lord Barnes, who seemed altogether dazzled. The rest of the evening went smoothly; the moment she stepped off the floor with Lord Barnes, she found her dance card filled by various other gentlemen. She was sure she had Madeline to thank for this behavior, seeing her friend give her a quick nod and smile from the side of the ballroom. Alice stepped out for every dance, exhausting herself in the process but finding that she had barely a moment to ever think of her husband.

However, that did not mean that she was not aware of him. She was more than aware of him; his deep scowl caught her gaze no matter where she was in the room. That gave her pause, but she refused to give him more than a cursory glance, certainly nothing that he could consider as an affectionate smile. Why he seemed so affected by her dancing, she could not understand, for had not the man proven his point already? Why, then, did he still want to seek out her company? Why did he seem so put out with being unable to put his name down for one of the evening's dances?

The supper dance gave Alice a little respite, although she could not help but think of the last supper dance she had attempted to enjoy. At least, this time, her partner was more than polite, securing her a chair beside Lady Astor before leaving her side in order to bring her back a plate filled with delicacies.

"And all is going well?" Madeline murmured, her eyes flickering back and forth across the room in search of Lord Worthington. "He has not attempted to throw one of your gentlemen aside so as to claim the dance for himself?"

"No, indeed!" Alice declared, a little taken aback by the suggestion. "I do not think that he is that desirous of my company."

Madeline did not either agree or disagree, her expression

contemplative. By this time, her partner had returned with a wonderful array of delicacies, just as Lord Astor appeared by Madeline's side. Their conversation turned to various other topics and stayed well away from the matter of Lord Worthington.

By the time the ball was drawing to a close, Alice's plan to leave early had gone up in smoke. She found herself quite enjoying the evening, truth be told, for she was constantly dancing and given very little time to rest. She did not remember when she had ever enjoyed herself so much. Perhaps it was because she had now managed to push her husband from her thoughts almost entirely, allowing her to focus on the enjoyment of the ball. How she wished she would have had so much confidence when she was younger and unattached.

She enjoyed the evening so much that it was almost dawn by the time she decided to leave. She was almost one of the last few guests present, and Lord Worthington was nowhere to be seen. Giving her farewells to Madeline, she promised that she would call upon her come the afternoon before making her way to collect her cloak and hat — only for a gentleman to step out of the shadows and catch her wrist. Alice let out a soft scream, finding herself now in a small room just off the hallway where she had only just been walking.

"Come now," said a familiar voice, filled with mirth. "You cannot be so coy with me, my dear."

"How dare you?" Alice breathed, her cheeks flushing with color as she realized who it was next to her. "I have made my feelings clear, Lord Worthington, have I not? Or do you not remember the pain I inflicted last time?"

She glared at him in the candlelight, seeing the humor on his face slowly die away.

"You think I did not mean it, that you have somehow proved to us both that I am, somehow, deeply in love with you, but that is simply your arrogance that makes you believe such a thing," she stated, her hands managing to find the door handle.

He frowned then. "You have been avoiding me, Lady Emma."

Letting out a harsh laugh, she shook her head at him, realizing the truth. "And you believe that I am, somehow, playing games with you? That I am trying to 'play coy' as you put it?" She tossed her head. "Nothing could be further from the truth."

For the first time since she had set eyes on him, her husband actually looked entirely on edge. His demeanor changed entirely, his body tensing as he struggled to know where to look.

"The truth is, my lord, that I have particularly enjoyed this evening because I have not had any kind of attention from you. After what you felt so eager to bestow on me the last time we spoke, is it any wonder that I wished to remove myself from your presence?"

"I had not thought...." he murmured, trailing off as he struggled to know what to say. "I mean, that I—"

"You believed that, deep down, I was just the same as any other young lady here," she said, firmly. "I hope now that you can see this is not the case."

Pulling open the door, she gave him one final glare before stepping back out into the hallway and shutting the door firmly behind her.

8

B y the time Alice rose from her bed, it was already early afternoon, which did not give her long to prepare to visit Madeline. Thankfully, she had slept well, sinking into an exhausted sleep almost the moment her head hit the pillow. She had found herself satisfied with how she had spoken to her husband, glad that she had managed to, finally, make her point clear to him.

However, as she dressed with the help of her maid, Alice could not get rid of the unsettling feeling that Lord Worthington was not going to be so easily dismissed. For whatever reason, he seemed determined to have some kind of affection from her, even though she had assured him that she felt nothing for the man. At least now she could admit that he was a handsome man, but, thankfully, that did not increase any kind of good thoughts towards him.

After a small repast, Alice made her way to Madeline's townhouse, finding that Madeline was quite ready to receive her, although she did admit to having something of a headache, so Alice endeavored to remain quiet.

"A little too much of that watered wine, I think," Madeline

said, grumpily. "But what else is there to drink when you are standing up for almost every dance?"

Alice made a noise of sympathy, smiling at her friend as she slowly got up from her chair to ring the bell. "I can return home if you wish it?"

"Nonsense," Madeline replied, stoutly. "I wish to hear all about what happened during the rest of the ball. After the supper dance, I barely saw you."

Alice shrugged. "There is not much to tell, I'm afraid. I danced almost every set, which I am sure only happened because of you, and then made my way home." A slight frown drew a line between her eyebrows, making Madeline narrow her gaze.

"What else?"

Knowing that her friend knew her too well to hide the truth, Alice sighed and told her exactly what Lord Worthington had done as she had attempted to leave.

"So, he is still besotted with you, then," Madeline murmured, looking surprised. "He has not behaved this way with anyone before, I am sure of it. Perhaps that is a good thing."

Shaking her head, Alice frowned. "No, it is not a good thing, Madeline. Whilst I do not quite agree with the idea that he is infatuated with me, I will state that he should not be besotted with anyone, considering he is already married."

"To you," Madeline replied.

"Yes, I know that," Alice said, sighing. "But, regardless, he believes me to be Lady Emma and not his wife. He should not be pursuing me when he is not free."

"He pursues you for his own ego, you believe," Madeline said quietly. "He wants you to behave like every other lady of his acquaintance."

"And when I do not, he continues to try and force me into either changing my opinion or, at least, my behavior regarding him." Alice shook her head. "He is quite ridiculous in some ways."

Nodding slowly, Madeline's frown deepened. "Has he said anything to you about... well, you — about his wife, I mean?"

"No." That has been one of the greatest pains she had been forced to endure these last weeks. Never once had he said anything about being wed, although he had more than one opportunity to tell her such a thing.

Madeline's lips twisted. "I am sorry, Alice."

Alice shook her head, finding herself unable to speak for a moment.

"It does not come as a surprise to me, I will admit to that," Madeline continued, after a moment. "Society as a whole is confused over his current matrimonial state, for, as you say, he does not behave as a man who has a wife at home." Madeline rolled her eyes disdainfully. "Many other men are seemingly happy to declare their married state, whilst pursuing other ladies for other inappropriate liaisons. However, it seems that your husband is not one of those men."

"Then why not declare that he is wed?" Alice asked, numbly. "Why did he pack me off to the country and never again lay eyes on me these last three years?" Her eyes smarted with hot tears. "Our marriage is not even consummated, which leaves him open to annulling our union."

"He will not do such a thing, particularly not after three years of marriage," Madeline refuted calmly. "You need not fear such a disgrace, Alice, although I am sorry for the way he has treated you — both in the country and here in London."

"Do not be." Alice forced a cheerful expression, trying to smile at her friend. "This will all fall on his own head. He is doing nothing other than causing his own downfall." A slight twist caught her by surprise as the image of his horrified expression came to mind.

"You look a little discomfited by the idea," Madeline murmured quietly. "Are you all right?"

Alice drew in a deep breath, settling her shoulders. "Yes, I am well. It is just the game I am playing, Madeline. At times, it grows wearisome."

"I can understand that," Madeline answered, her eyes smiling at Alice. "But it will all come to fruition, I am sure. Your husband will learn not to treat you in such a poor way again. This will be the biggest lesson of his life."

Hoping that what Madeline said was true, Alice drank the rest of her tea quietly, her mind working over the next stage in her plan. When and how she would reveal herself was yet to be established, although there was a large party soon at Vauxhall, one of the highlights of the social season. Perhaps there, she might reveal the truth to Lord Worthington? News would spread quickly until almost all of London would know of his treatment of her. In fact, Alice was sure it would be in society papers come the very next morning.

"You are looking a little more satisfied," Madeline commented shrewdly. "Your plan is taking shape, then?"

"It is," Alice confirmed and began to sketch out the details for her friend. Unfortunately, she was interrupted by a quiet knock on the door.

Madeline, frowning, took the calling card from the butler, muttering something about not having any arranged visits today. Alice refilled her tea cup, watching her friend out of the corner of her eye. Madeline's eyes widened slightly as she read the card, sending a worried glance towards Alice.

"What is it?"

Madeline handed the card back to the butler, her lips thin. "Apparently, Lord Worthington is here."

Alice's mouth fell open. "Here?" Her heart slammed into her chest, her eyes staring at the calling card in the butler's hand as though she didn't quite believe the name written there.

"He has obviously sought you out," Madeline said, quietly. "You have refused to tell him anything about yourself other than your name, but your friendship with me could not be hidden. Apparently, he has come calling in the hope that you are here."

"Then I must go," Alice said at once, getting to her feet. "He must not see me."

She could not bear the thought of seeing her husband again, not so soon after last evening. He would be all politeness, with the occasional flirtatious comment as he looked at her with those brown eyes of his that seemed to be filled with warmth every time he let himself linger on her countenance. Alice did not think she could bear it.

"He is just outside the door, my lady," the butler murmured, looking askance. "He refused to wait in the hallway."

Alice was forced to sink back down into her chair, relieved that, at least, the heavy wooden doors had kept her words from reaching Lord Worthington's ears.

"Apparently, I am not to escape him," she muttered, trying not to panic. "What a wretched man he is."

"I agree," Madeline said, calmly. "Are you sure about this, Alice? I can send him away."

Alice shook her head. "No, you cannot, and I know that as well as you. To refuse him entry would only cause all kinds of talk."

"I can plead a headache."

Closing her eyes briefly, Alice lifted her chin and set her shoulders. "Pray, do not lie on my account. I can manage, Madeline, I promise you."

Her friend studied her for one more moment before nodding. "Then you had best let him in," Madeline said to the butler, once Alice had rearranged her skirts. "We will be brief, Alice. I promise you that."

The moment Lord Worthington walked in, Alice's stomach began to churn. She did not want to see him, but he had forced himself into her presence, as he had done so already on previous occasions. He was becoming a somewhat overbearing presence, and her struggles with her own feelings only added to her difficulty. Still, she was forced, only by good manners and expectation, to rise and curtsy to him, allowing him to kiss her hand, where his lips lingered a moment too long.

She tugged her hand away almost at once, her skin heating as she sat back down, feeling as though she had been doused in flames. Not only was his gesture entirely inappropriate, but it spoke of an affection that he should not have for her, not when she was Lady Emma and certainly not after their discussion last evening. It should not come as a surprise to her that he continued to refuse to accept her dislike of him, apparently certain that he could work his way into her good graces as she was sure he had done with many a lady before her. A ball of frustration pushed itself into her heart as Madeline began a polite conversation.

"Let me ring the bell for tea," Alice murmured, excusing herself and walking to the other side of the room to ring the bell.

They needed a fresh tray, of course, but she herself was desperate for a few minutes to calm herself, thinking she might either scream at him or burst into hot, furious tears, such was her anger. The imprint of his lips upon her hand burned still, reminding her of his pressing affections only a few days earlier.

How dare he do such a thing, when she had made it more than clear that she did not want any of his flirtations bestowed on her? It seemed that her husband was dogged in his own desires and goals, refusing to accede defeat and accept her refusal to become any more acquainted with him.

What he did not know was that she was aware that he was a married gentleman and, as such, should not be pursuing any lady of his acquaintance. Up until this point, she had believed what Madeline had said about Lord Worthington, that he flirted terribly but had not taken a mistress. Could she really continue to believe that now when she had received such attentions?

Wandering to the window, and uncaring about how rude she must be appearing, Alice looked out across the streets of London, trying her best to calm her frantically beating heart. Turning her back towards her husband and Madeline, Alice closed her eyes and concentrated on calming the boiling anger in her veins.

Slowly, she managed to regain some control, her fists slowly beginning to uncurl as she took in long, slow breaths.

You are not the same girl he married, she reminded herself. *You are not under his control. Do not allow his behavior to affect you in such a way.*

"You are quiet this afternoon," said a voice in her ear, making her jump.

"Lord Worthington," she murmured, turning to face him but taking a small step backward so that he was not standing too close. "How are you today?" She kept her tone cool, and no smile lingered on her lips.

Behind him, she saw Madeline shake her head, her eyes full of apology. Alice was sure her friend had tried her best to keep Lord Worthington from interrupting Alice's solitude, but had apparently failed. That did not come as a surprise to Alice, well aware that her husband was not easily put off from his intentions.

"All the better for seeing you," he replied, giving her a jaunty smile which quickly began to fade when she did not immediately respond. "Are you unwell?"

"No," Alice replied, immediately. "I am just not interested in your flirtations, Lord Worthington, as I have stated more than once."

"Ah." He glanced away, looking slightly repentant. "I see. You are right. I should not have done such a thing."

"No," Alice confirmed, thinking that he was either talking of this afternoon's improper greeting or the previous evening's attempt. "You should not be taking such liberties with me when I have made it more than plain that I do not want them."

"I confess I was just overwhelmed with seeing you again," he said, quickly, still smiling at her. "Despite everything, you are still something of a mystery and one that I am inclined to solve. You have not told me anything about yourself other than your name, so I was forced to observe you. I saw your friendship with Lady Astor, and was told you are a distant cousin. I had to hope that you might be visiting her with some regularity. How fortunate that I should find you here."

Turning to face him more directly, Alice kept her face firm and ignored the sparkle in his eyes. Clearly, he still believed that she was going to change in her demeanor towards him at any moment were he charming enough. When would the man learn?

"Lady Astor has become something of a firm friend, my lord," she said, searching his face for any sign of anxiety. "And she has told me a great deal about you."

"Is that so?" he replied, throwing a quick glance back towards Madeline. "But I thought you already knew me well."

Alice spat out a harsh laugh. "Indeed, my lord, but she is able to tell me of all the rumors that follow you wherever you go and, as yet, I have not decided which ones I will believe." She watched him closely and saw him shift a little as though growing slightly uncomfortable. "In addition, my lord, I should think it more than evident that I do not need her advice to tell me that I should keep myself from becoming a close acquaintance with you. From your past behaviors, your refusal to respect my wishes, and your insistence on chasing me when I do not wish to even speak to you, it is plain that you are not a man whom I would consider honorable in any sense."

The look on his face told her that her words had cut deeply, although there was a faint line of anger around his mouth. "I see," he said, crisply. "You have outdone yourself this time, Lady Emma. Your bluntness does you credit. You are quite right. I am not an honorable man."

Alice lifted her chin, refusing to back down or apologize for her words. "Then why are you so insistent on forcing me to accept you?"

His jaw tightened. "You are a challenge, Lady Emma, even now."

"Ask yourself, Lord Worthington, why any lady of sense would wish to spend time in your company?" she stated, her voice growing louder. "I have heard the rumors and do not know what to believe, and I have seen your behavior, in very close quarters I might add, and have observed that you are not a man of principle." Her eyes flashed. "And I do not care to spend time in the company of such a gentleman."

"But a man can change, can he not?" he continued, a little more quietly although his eyes remained sharp. "I swore to you that I did not steal kisses from any lady, nor take on a mistress. That is not the kind of man I am."

Alice rolled her eyes, unable to stop herself. "Yet, you seemed as if you were going to kiss me if I had not stopped it, which means that I have no reason to believe any of your words."

"I was not going to kiss you," he said tight-lipped, his eyes flashing with a fierce anger. "I have my own reasons not to kiss you. Never before have I done such a thing, although I have been offered that — and more — a great many times. I had to prove to you that you were not as disinclined to me as you thought."

"And since you have achieved that goal," Alice asked, feeling heat creep into her face, "why do you insist on chasing after me? Surely, you are not seeking marriage."

He bit his lip and, to her surprise, paused and stared out of the window, taking his gaze from her. Silence bloomed between them until all that Alice could hear was the thumping of her heart. She saw that Madeline had exited the room, although she did not know when her friend had left. Apparently, Madeline had thought it best to give them the space to talk, although the door remained ajar.

Lord Worthington took a deep breath, placed his hands behind his back, and turned back to face her. "You have asked a question I am not sure I can answer, my lady," he said, quietly. "You are correct; I am not seeking marriage or even a courtship. The only thing I can say is that you have captured my attention in a way that I have never experienced before."

"That is something I cannot believe," Alice replied, at once. She tilted her head and regarded him carefully. "Is it your ego that forces you to continue with such actions? Do you enjoy the other women's smiles and fluttering of their lashes so much that you simply cannot help yourself?"

Lord Worthington stared at her as though she had suddenly grown a second head, only to frown heavily. "I had not considered that," he muttered, running one hand through his hair and roughing it up entirely. "You are unsettling me greatly, my lady, I must confess."

Alice's angry reply died in her throat as she saw, to her surprise, that her husband appeared truly discomfited by what she laid at his feet. Was he sincere? Could he truly be struggling with the questions she had put to him?

"It is true that I enjoy a lady's attentions, but I cannot see that as a bad thing, Lady Emma. A gentleman always enjoys the attentions of a lady." He looked at her earnestly, as though waiting for her to confirm that he was not in the wrong.

Thinking for a few seconds, Alice gave him her reply. "A true gentleman seeks out the attentions of perhaps one particular lady," she said, firmly. "With hopes to wed, mayhap. They look to the future and think calmly and clearly about what lies ahead instead of losing themselves in current enjoyments and their own pleasures." She tossed her head and turned to look out of the window, unable to keep her gaze on him any longer as the pain of knowing what her husband had done grew. "That is an honorable gentleman, my lord, and he is removed from you."

For a few minutes, there was complete silence, which grew with both tension and gravitas as the seconds ticked by. Alice's heart began to thunder in her chest once more as her husband neither spoke nor moved.

"You must excuse me," Lord Worthington said, eventually, sounding broken. "You have given me much to think on, Lady Emma."

Alice did not speak, did not even turn to wish him farewell. Instead, she listened to his footsteps as they walked towards the door, waiting until the door closed firmly behind him before dissolving into tears.

9

M adeline ensured that she kept Alice's arm looped through hers as they made their way into the ballroom, having been invited to Lord and Lady Benson's ball. It was, by all accounts, one of the highlights of the season, but Alice barely noticed any of the decorations or enchanting small touches that highlighted the room. She was far too anxious.

Ever since their heated discussion some days ago, Alice had not seen Lord Worthington again. It should not matter to her, of course, but she realized that she had wounded him with her words, even if they were the truth.

Madeline had asked her repeatedly why she was so concerned over his absence from society, but Alice had been unable to give a truthful answer. She had told Madeline that she was worried that her husband would return to his country estate, where she was meant to be, only to discover her absent – but that was not the truth at all.

She simply could not get the look on his face from her mind. It haunted her. It told her that she had done him damage, had caused him pain. One part of her tried to be satisfied with that, tried to remind her what pain he had caused her, but the other part told her that she should not have been so cruel.

Why do I care? Alice asked herself over and over. *It is not as though I owe him anything.*

Her dance card was filled almost at once, but, to her surprise, Lord Worthington did not appear. This was now the fourth event he had been absent from. She had attended something every evening since she had spoken to him, but had not seen him since. It was most unusual.

For the most part, Alice enjoyed the evening, allowing herself to take part in the dancing and conversation. It was only when another gentleman commented on Lord Worthington's absence that her heart sank in her chest.

"Quite strange for him to miss out on such occasions," said one gentleman, thoughtfully. "In fact, I cannot remember him absenting himself from such things ever before. At least not in the last few years."

Alice stopped herself from asking any questions and kept her smile fixed.

"Mayhap he is ill," said the other gentleman, shrugging slightly. "Now, my dear Lady Emma. I believe it is our turn on the dance floor."

Smiling, Alice took his arm and began the dance, trying her best to push Lord Worthington from her mind, but finding she could not.

Was his absence her doing? Had she really pushed him to consider his own behavior, given that she had called him dishonorable? Then surely, that was a good thing, was it not? So then, she should not be worrying about him.

However, no matter how hard she tried, Alice found that she could not remove him from her mind. As the night wore on, Alice found herself growing weary, tired of trying to stop her thoughts. As she had brought her own carriage, Alice made her farewells to Madeline before moving to thank the hosts for their generosity in inviting her.

"Oh, Lady Emma!" Lady Benson exclaimed as she began to walk away. "I forgot. One of the footmen has a note for you."

Alice frowned. "A note?"

"Yes, I believe it arrived earlier this evening, but as you could not be found in the crush of guests, I instructed the footman to hold it for you." Lady Benson walked with Alice towards the entrance of the house, gesturing to one of the footmen who produced a silver tray with a note held on it.

"A mysterious note, to be sure," Lady Benson chuckled, curiosity written all over her face. "Who is it from?"

Holding the letter in her hand, Alice glanced down at the seal, her heart turning over. "I am not sure," she lied, not wanting to give the older lady gossip fodder. "Excuse me, please, and thank you for a wonderful evening."

Lady Benson looked more than a little disappointed not to discover who the letter was from, but managed a graceful curtsy before walking back in towards the ballroom.

Alice mounted the carriage steps and sat back against the squabs, the letter practically burning through her glove and searing her fingers. Her husband's seal was unmistakable, given that she used the same one herself on her own correspondence. Why had he written to her and delivered it to Lady Benson's house? Could he be aware of her true identity?

The darkness of the carriage did not allow Alice the liberty of opening and reading the letter, so she attempted to stop her whirling thoughts and, instead, consider the situation practically. William had sent the letter to Lady Benson's home, evidently in the hope that she would be there — even though he had been invited to the ball but had, for whatever reason, chosen not to attend. That meant that he was still not aware of where she was staying. If he was aware of her true identity, then it would not have taken much for him to work out that she was residing in her parents' townhouse. That meant that she was still Lady Emma Taylor to him.

A sigh of relief escaped her lips as Alice slowly began to relax, the tension draining out of her as the carriage drew up to her townhouse. Within a few minutes, she was sitting beside the fire in her bedchamber, already dressed in her nightgown. The cook had sent up a tray with a few small pastries and some chamomile tea, but Alice wanted nothing other than to read her husband's letter. Dismissing the maid for the night, she waited until the door clicked shut before picking up the letter and breaking the seal.

Despite knowing that William could not possibly know of her identity, it did not stop her hands from shaking slightly as she unfolded the parchment, wondering what he had to say.

"My dear Lady Emma Taylor," she read aloud. "I am forever in your debt for revealing to me the depths of my own ungentlemanly behavior and I must also apologize for the way our last conversation ended. Be assured, whilst your words cut to my core, they were much needed. I have found myself unable to attend social events as I have considered what you said, realizing that I am exactly what you said of me.

"Lady Emma, I must beg an audience with you once more, for you speak to me in ways that no other women of my acquaintance ever has. I value your wisdom and insight. As you will not tell me where you reside, might I call upon you at Lady Astor's house come the morrow? Perhaps a short walk in Hyde Park? Should you be absent when I call, I will take it that you have no wish of my company, which I can well understand.

"Yours, Lord Worthington."

The letter slipped from her fingers, landing on the small end table as Alice sat back in her seat, stunned beyond measure. She could not take in what it was she had read, and was entirely unsure as to whether or not his words could be trusted. Was this just some ploy to work his way back into her favors?

She shook her head to herself, sitting up a little straighter and picking up the letter once more. Her eyes ran over the handwritten lines again, finding that there was an honesty there she had not expected. That only left her with one question: would she meet with him?

"What harm can it do?" she asked herself, pouring a cup of chamomile tea. "If it is only to talk, then there is very little wrong with that."

What Alice did not want to admit was that there was a slight fluttering in her stomach at the thought of walking with her husband, of having his sole attention. But then, the realization that they would be seen out together by others in society brought a heavy weight back to her stomach.

Was this what he was seeking? A chance to show society that he had some kind of penchant for her company? Confused beyond measure, Alice threw back her head and groaned. This was not what she had intended. She had never expected to be the one struggling with confusion and doubt, yet that was exactly what had occurred. By his letter and his attentions towards her, he was confusing her entirely, forcing her to wonder what he intended. Was he simply wishing to discover more of what she thought of him? Or was this some kind of feeble attempt to place himself in her good graces?

The more she thought of him, the more confused she became until her head began to grow heavy with all the thoughts captured within. A slight ache forced her to retire to bed, hoping that the quiet darkness would welcome her into its embrace and allow her a few hours of dreamless slumber before she had to face Lord Worthington again.

∾

MADELINE'S EYES widened as she finished reading the letter, handing it back to Alice without a single word.

"Well?" Alice asked, a little impatiently. "What does he mean by it?"

Lifting her teacup to her lips, Madeline took a long sip before setting it down again. "I am not sure," she said, eventually. "This behavior is out of the ordinary."

"You do not believe that he is honest, do you?" Alice asked, lifting one eyebrow. "Surely this is simply some ploy to win over the one woman in society who does not care for his behavior." This was the conclusion she had reached in the early hours of the morning, when sleep would not come — and had been the only thing that had allowed her to finally close her eyes. "It is a ruse, of course."

Madeline shook her head, frowning slightly. "I confess, I am not sure."

Alice sighed. "I felt the same, at first, but then I recalled everything he has attempted before now. His advances towards me were rebuffed," she continued as a ripple of heat crept up her neck. "I believe he thought that, after that, I would realize that I was in the wrong for pushing him away and would become just as every other lady. When I did not, he attempted to speak to me alone, pulling me from the hallway into a private room."

Drawing in a long breath, Madeline's frown deepened. "But you did not respond to that either."

"So he arrived here and a war of words began," Alice finished, settling her hands in her lap. "Now he must play the contrite gentleman in order to win me over."

A short silence told her that Madeline was thinking things through carefully. "I am inclined to believe he is genuine in his words, Alice."

"You cannot read that from a letter," Alice retorted a little haughtily. "I am inclined to think the worst of him."

"And that is understandable," Madeline replied, calmly. "But bear in mind that I have known him longer than you, Alice, and be assured that I have never once seen him behave this way." She held up a hand to stop Alice's answer, smiling gently. "Yes, you have been wed to him, but he has remained here in town these three years, for the most part. I have seen him very often, and I can assure you that he has never once appeared in the least bit contrite over anything he has done."

"That means very little," Alice said in response. "For he has had many ladies falling at his feet. I doubt the man has been rebuffed once." She shook her head, her shoulders slumping. "He promises me that he has never kissed another lady before, nor taken a mistress, but I cannot tell whether or not to believe him."

Madeline's expression grew sympathetic. "I could tell you the same, but I doubt that would make much of a difference. There have never been any obvious associations between him and another lady, nor even rumors of them. That is usually the proof that there are no liaisons, for such things do not remain hidden for long."

"Society would think very little of it if he were to take a mistress, I suppose," Alice said heavily. "It is the way of things."

"Unfortunately so," Madeline agreed, her eyes dimming a little. "Thankfully, my own dear husband has promised he will do no such thing, and I must hope that he keeps his word."

Alice smiled at her friend, aware that Madeline was deeply in love with her husband. "I am sure he will."

Giving herself a slight shake, Madeline set her shoulders and grinned. "So, now that you are here, Alice, I presume you are going to meet with Lord Worthington?"

Now it was Alice's turn to frown. "What do you mean?"

Madeline lifted one delicate shoulder. "You could have

refused to meet him, could have stayed away from my home, but instead you have decided to come and see him. Deep down, you wish to know whether what he's said is true or not."

Alice rubbed at her forehead, unsure she liked that her friend was so perceptive.

"Oh, my dear," Madeline sighed, settling back in her chair. "You are mixed up over the man, are you not?"

Refusing to answer, Alice lifted her teacup to her lips, catching Madeline's slight laugh. She was right, of course; Alice was entirely confused over her husband and his behavior, despising the knowledge that she still found herself attracted to him.

"You are going to have to remind yourself of what he has done to you," Madeline finished just as there was a quiet rap on the door. "Do not lose your heart so easily, Alice."

Her warning complete, Madeline rose to greet Lord Worthington, leaving Alice to follow suit.

Alice rose and curtsied, more than aware that he was studying her with a look of gratitude on his face. Her cheeks warmed despite herself, attempting to retain her poise as she sat back down as gracefully as she could.

"Might I ring for tea, Lord Worthington?" Madeline asked, a slight smile on her face. "Or were you planning an outing of some kind?" A light twinkle of mischief lit both her words and her eyes, making Lord Worthington laugh.

"I see you have been in cahoots with Lady Emma," he replied, his eyes darting towards Alice. "You are quite right, Lady Astor. I was hoping that perhaps, I might ask Lady Emma to accompany me on a short walk? Perhaps Hyde Park?"

"It is soon to be the fashionable hour," Alice said, quickly. "I am not to be put on display, Lord Worthington, if that is what you intend."

His brows furrowed. "I had not thought of that," he

muttered, appearing perturbed. "No, Lady Emma, you are right. I do not wish to show you off, although I am sure any gentleman would be grateful for your attentions to them."

The corner of his mouth lifted slightly, as though he struggled not to fall back into his old way of speaking. Alice kept her face impassive, although her heart began to quicken its pace just a little.

"You might still walk in the park if you keep to the smaller paths," Madeline suggested, helpfully.

Lord Worthington's smile grew. "Of course, that would be just the solution!" he exclaimed, turning back to Alice. The smile left his face. "That is, if you wish to accompany me, Lady Emma?"

The eagerness of his expression, the hope in his eyes, made Alice squirm in her seat. She was disinclined to believe him, knowing that he was able to put on whatever facade he chose, but in truth, she did want to discover what it was he wished to talk to her about and chose to incline her head.

"Fantastic," Lord Worthington got to his feet at once, a sudden look of relief etched on his features. "Shall we go?"

Surprised at how quickly he wished to be in her company alone, Alice shot a quick glance at Madeline before rising to her feet.

"Of course, Lord Worthington," she mumbled, only just catching Madeline's quick grin out of the corner of her eye. "You do not mind, do you, Lady Astor?"

"Not in the least," Madeline declared, waving them off. "I shall see you once you return. You are staying for dinner, are you not?"

Knowing that Madeline would want to hear every little thing that Alice had discussed with Lord Worthington, Alice accepted at once before walking from the room with Lord Worthington close behind.

10

They walked in silence for a few moments, with Lord Worthington clasping both his hands behind his back. Alice felt the tension grow between them with every step, struggling to know what to say.

"You have been absent from society of late," she murmured when the tension grew too much to bear. "Have you been ill?"

He let out a harsh laugh, surprising her. "Not ill, no. Melancholy...perhaps." He glanced at her, his dark brown eyes intense. "And I lay that blame solely at your feet."

Feeling a little off balance, Alice held his gaze for a moment. "I am not quite sure what you mean."

"Did I not say as much in my letter?" he asked, quietly. "You have spoken to me in a way that no one else has ever done. Your blunt words cut into my very soul, forcing me to look back on my last few years with fresh eyes."

"Oh." Alice did not know what else to say, discovering that her heart very much wished to believe him, but finding that her mind refused to accept it.

"You do not believe my words, of course."

"No," Alice replied, frankly. "I do not."

He nodded but did not laugh nor smile. "It is as I should expect."

Alice glanced at him, aware for the first time of the heavy bags under his eyes, the purple smears that showed just how truly tired he was. Had he not been sleeping? And, if he had not, was it really because of what she had said, or was it merely too many nights spent at the exclusive gentlemen's club, White's?

"I have not been in society very much since you last spoke to me," he said quietly. "I must confess that I tried to push your words from my mind, but I have discovered that I am unable to do so."

"I see," Alice replied, primly, as they approached Hyde Park. Surely now she would be able to see whether or not he had truly meant to keep their conversation quiet, for if he turned her towards where the many carriages would be, then she would know that he was not in the least in earnest.

As they turned into Hyde Park, just as he had promised, he kept to the quieter paths.

"After the way I have behaved towards you, I owe you a great deal of gratitude for even being willing to come out walking with me," Lord Worthington said heavily, clasping his hands behind his back as they walked. "No, I do not blame you in the least for being entirely unsure about my words and my intentions," he continued, sounding fervent. "If you can believe me, then I will confess that I owe you a great debt, Lady Emma."

"A debt?" Alice could not stop herself from questioning what he meant, struggling with her astonishment at seeing him so changed in both demeanor and in speech.

He nodded, his countenance taking on something of a despondent look. "If only I had met you some years ago," he muttered, quietly. "Then perhaps I might have been a very different man."

It was on the tip of Alice's tongue to say that he had met her some years ago, at *their* wedding, but she bit her lip and said nothing.

"I have made some very poor choices," he continued when she did not reply. "Now that I look back on my life, I realize that I have been living for entirely my own pleasures, pushing away my responsibilities because I despised the way I was forced into them."

Alice stopped dead, wondering if she was one of the responsibilities he was talking about. After all, he had been cajoled into matrimony by his father's last will and testament. She had always considered that he had simply been urged into doing so, but now that he spoke of force, she began to think that it might have been more than that. "And you are laying this change at my feet?"

He turned to face her, spreading his hands. "You are the only lady who has ever rebuffed me on so many occasions," he said softly. "I know you might still be disinclined to believe my words, but I cannot help but tell you the truth: I have never felt as lost as I do now."

She shook her head, keeping her hands clasped together so that he would not see her tremble. "I cannot believe that my continued snubbing of your advances has brought about this change, my lord."

"But in truth, it has," he responded, at once. "For years, I have lived my life in perfect contentment, pushing away all thoughts about my responsibilities and my future so that I can live the way I please. For a long time, I was unable to do so, having had particular expectations and requirements from both my father and then my mother, who used my fortune as a way to force me to do as they wished." He pressed a hand to his eyes for a moment, as though quite overcome with memories. "I realize now that this has made me into the worst kind of man."

Alice found that anything she wished to say remained stuck

in her throat, finding him altered but still finding it difficult to trust that he was speaking the truth.

His head lifted, and he caught her gaze.

"What is it about you that helps me to speak so openly?" he murmured, quietly. "You are quite unique, Lady Emma. Had you not come into my life, then I think that I would never have reached this state of true discernment."

She managed to smile, thinking back on her three years of almost solitary confinement. Was he now regretting treating her in such a way? It was not as though she was simply going to trust that he was now a changed man, tell him the truth of her identity, and forgive him at once. One meeting, one conversation, was not enough to prove his change of heart to her.

"One final thing, Lady Emma," he said, stepping closer and capturing her with his gaze. "I wish to sincerely declare my apologies for my behavior. It was both ungentlemanly and entirely inappropriate. I was pushing you to respond to me in the way that all other ladies of my acquaintance have done, and it was only because you did not do as I expected that my attentions became more fervent." His eyes dropped from her face, a look of shame in his expression. "It was wrong of me, and I humbly beg your forgiveness."

Finding that his words appeared more than genuine, Alice struggled to sort out her jumbled thoughts. Her heart beat frantically in her chest as he looked up at her again, earnestly. Could she so easily give him the assurance he was looking for when she still did not believe every word he said? Could a man so easily — and so quickly — change his entire being?

"I thank you for your apology," she said slowly. "But, in truth, I shall wait until I see that you are truly in earnest, Lord Worthington. I do not give my forgiveness easily, and I am not so quickly swayed."

A brief flash of hurt crossed his face, only for him to bow

slightly. "I understand," he said, firmly. "Were I in your situation, I would feel much the same way, I am sure." Holding out his arm to her, his smile returned. "I have every intention of proving to you — and to all of society, I might add — that I am much changed." A faraway expression came over his face, his gaze drifting away. "I shall remain for the final part of the season, and then I shall leave London, perhaps for good. There are many things I need to rectify, but I shall have to take some time to work out how best to go about them."

Her hand reached for his arm almost automatically, as Alice discovered that she truly did wish to believe him so changed. Her touch seemed to startle him, for he jumped a little before smiling at her again.

"I should return you to Lady Astor," he murmured, before turning them both around and taking the path to exit Hyde Park.

11

A sennight later, Alice felt as though she were sinking deeper and deeper into a quagmire. Things were not going as she had planned.

Her husband had appeared to change entirely, like a caterpillar entering its metamorphosis, except this time, the beautiful butterfly was slowly wilting back into its duller, rounder form.

Lord Worthington was very rarely in society these days, and almost everyone was commenting on it. On the rare times she had seen him, he had greeted her with graciousness and candor and had shaken himself from the young ladies that began to flutter around him. It was as if he truly did not wish for their company, that he realized just how ingenuine they were — and how false his life really was.

Alice had noticed, in addition to all of this, that he had not danced even one single dance with anyone of note, choosing instead to take to the shadows. As ladies did not ask gentlemen to dance, it meant that he was able to take himself away from such festivities, although there were a great many disappointed ladies that attempted to cajole him into taking part.

Alice had initially been very dismissive of his behavior, but as the days passed, she could not help but notice just how much he was alienating himself from those he had once considered to be greatly important to his acquaintance. The ladies that had crowded him now gave him a frown and turned their backs.

It would take a great deal of recompense to work himself back into their favors, but he appeared not to care one jot. That knowledge greatly unsettled Alice, for it meant that she was forced to consider that her words had truly brought about a change in his behavior and in his character, despite how much she was disinclined to believe it.

It also meant that she had been forced to consider her own heart, surprised to find that there was a slight ache that grew with each day she did not see him. That was a feeling she detested; she did not wish to have any kind of affection for the man she was forced to call her husband, yet it simply would not disappear, no matter how hard she tried.

"Can you see him?" Madeline murmured in her ear as they walked into the drawing room. The musical evening was bound to be a wonderful event, and with a small number of guests, Alice found herself wondering whether her husband had been amongst the invited guests and, if so, whether he would make an appearance.

Alice gave a tiny shake of her head, her eyes roving around the room. "No, I cannot see him. He may not have been invited."

"I believe he has been invited," Madeline replied with a knowing look.

Smiling, Alice chuckled. "Servants' whispers again?"

Her friend did not give any note to that comment, tossing her head. "All I will say is I am sure he will be here," Madeline murmured, greeting a few friends with a nod and a smile. "Whatever are you going to do about him, Alice?"

That was very much the difficulty. It appeared that her plan to publicly shame her husband was now in doubt because how could she shame him if he were not present? In addition, at the times she had seen him, he had appeared as much changed as he had been in Hyde Park. It was becoming more and more difficult to believe that he was not as altered as he had promised, that it was, in truth, a genuine change as opposed to a façade.

"There!" Madeline clutched at her arm, her smile wide. "He has just entered."

"Pray keep your voice down," Alice murmured, trying to avert her gaze. "There is no need to appear to be interested in him." In truth, however, Alice felt her heart beginning to beat a little faster as Lord Worthington drew nearer.

"My dear Lady Astor," he said, bowing deeply. "And Lady Emma. How lovely to see you both again."

Alice curtsied but said nothing. There was no flirtatious smile, no wink of the eye. Nothing that would make her think that he was, in any way, interested in gaining her attentions. That did not mean, of course, that there were not the usual young ladies swooping in for his attentions, however, her smile faltering slightly as a rather large older lady with her daughter in tow stepped in, directly in front of Alice and Madeline. It was more than a little rude, of course, and Alice felt a dart of anger pierce her heart.

"Lady Harris," came her husband's mumble.

"Lord Worthington," she heard Lady Harris gush loudly. "I am so delighted to see you! You have been absent of late, and we have all been worried."

Stepping back, Alice felt her face burn with embarrassment at having been so easily dismissed by the older lady. Apparently, she was easily discarded when Lord Worthington was in the room.

Lady Harris must not know he is married or she would not be forcing her daughter on him. Do people not remember that he married? How can so many people not even know I exist?

"You are to sit with my darling girl now, Lord Worthington," Lady Harris said, as though it were already decided. "I believe the first performance is about to begin."

"As much as I would be delighted to sit with Lady Annabelle, I am already engaged," Lord Worthington said, a trifle loudly. "I must give my apologies, Lady Annabelle, and Lady Harris. Do excuse me."

To Alice's surprise, Lord Worthington came to stand by her side, offering his arm. "Shall we sit, my dear Lady Emma?"

Suspicion needled at her mind, but she accepted nonetheless and, with a nod of encouragement from Madeline, came to sit with Lord Worthington in the row of chairs that faced towards the piano. From behind her, she heard Lady Harris' gasp of outrage followed by loud whispers, but she lifted her chin and ignored it all. There was something about being on her husband's arm that brought her a sense of pride, as though she alone was the one who had captured his affections.

That awareness was a douse of icy water, making her shiver as he seated her in one of the chairs.

"You are cold, Lady Emma?"

She glanced up at him, seeing his dark eyes filled with concern.

"No, not in the least, I assure you," she said, firmly. "I was just lost in thought for a moment."

"Nothing too troubling, I hope," he said, quickly.

She shook her head and returned her attention to the piano, seeing that a Miss Denton was about to play. As the music filled the room, Alice tried to give herself a stern talking to. There was no reason that she should wish to have Lord Worthington's affections, not when he did not know who she truly was and especially when he had abandoned her for three long years.

The man might have attempted to change his character, but a sennight of such a change did not merit any kind of fondness from her, nor should it create any kind of desire for his affections. Why then, had she felt such pride in his proclivity towards her company instead of that of Lady Annabelle?

"You have saved me, you know," Lord Worthington whispered, shattering her thoughts.

She glanced at him, trying to ignore the strange swirls deep in her belly as she looked into his eyes. "Saved you?" she repeated, trying to sound nonchalant. "What can you mean?"

He shook his head, glancing back at the pianist. "Lady Harris has been particularly insistent that I spend time in the company of her daughter."

"But you enjoy the attention," Alice protested, seeing the pain in his eyes and wondering at it. "Do you not?"

She saw his jaw clench, his eyes glazing over for a moment. The piano music drifted between them, and yet he still did not answer.

Eventually, he let out a heavy sigh and turned his eyes back to her. "Perhaps I did, once," he admitted. "But now I have had a chance to reflect, all thanks to you, I might add. I realize that I have been using it to simply play a part. To hide the parts of my life that I do not want to consider, hiding it even from myself." His smile was pained, his mouth tight. "It is as though I have lost myself, but deliberately so. Can you understand even a modicum of what I am trying to say? Or am I rambling utter nonsense?"

Alice could see the look in his eyes as he tried to smile, aware that, for the very first time, she believed everything that he was saying.

"I do understand, I believe," she murmured, quietly.

"Although I confess that I do not know everything of which you are speaking."

His smile became somewhat grim. "Of course, you would not, for, as I said, I have hidden it from everyone, even from myself. Society thinks of me as a well-meaning rogue, but that is not the truth of who I am."

Alice found herself desperate to know more of what her husband spoke of, realizing just how little she knew of him. With a sharp shock, she realized that the only true things she knew about her husband were that of his title, his family, and his behavior towards her. She knew nothing of what truly troubled him, of what he thought, of what he hoped, of what he dreamed...and the worst of it was, Alice wanted to know such things.

"Alas, I believe I have shared too much with you," he continued, patting her hand for a moment. "You are quite too good to listen to me, Lady Emma, especially after what I have put you through."

"Think nothing of it," Alice said, quickly. "I will admit that I am a little more inclined to believe your words now, Lord Worthington."

He chuckled, as the performance came to an end. "I am glad of that at the very least." As the applause rang out, he kept her gaze, a thoughtful look in his eyes. "Might you honor me with your company tomorrow, Lady Emma? I shall call on you at Lady Astor's home, of course, if you are agreeable? I am in need of some advice."

"And you think I am best placed to give it?"

"I can think of no one else," he exclaimed as the second pianist struck up a merry tune. "But only if you wish it, my lady. I should not like to impose."

Alice found herself agreeing to his plan almost at once, surprised that her heart squeezed with pleasure at his delighted smile. For the remainder of the evening, Alice found that she could not keep her eyes from searching the room for her husband, nor stop thinking about their walk tomorrow. What was it he wanted her advice on? Could it be about his wife? His responsibilities? And if the opportunity presented itself to reveal the truth of who she was, would she take it?

12

"Alice, I cannot understand why you are so vexed," Madeline said with a sigh. "The man has changed, has he not?"

"It seems that way."

"And you now believe him to be genuine?"

Alice struggled to answer. The truth of the matter was that she did not want to believe him, but all of society was now remarking on the change in Lord Worthington, and his snub of Lady Harris had made a lot of the women most upset with him. Having discussed the matter at length with Madeline, Alice was presented with the truth of the matter: her husband was no longer behaving as he once had been.

"I suppose I must," she said, the words almost dragged from her reluctant lips.

Madeline smiled, a look of satisfaction on her face. "Then you must decide how to continue, safe in the knowledge that the man you wed is no longer that same man."

"But he is," Alice protested, remembering her cold winters when she had cried many tears over him. "He left me there, alone, for three long years!"

Madeline's expression did not change. "Yes, he did, and you might as well ask him about it, Alice. If he is truly as changed as he appears, then he does not need to hide the fact that he is wed. Perhaps you will discover the reasons behind what he did."

Alice snorted. "He left me there because he wanted to play the rogue here in town."

As she spoke, however, the words Lord Worthington had confessed to her only a few hours previously haunted her memory. The derision left her face, her eyebrows furrowing as she considered what he had said.

"All you are doing is talking to him," Madeline continued quietly. "Do not frown so. You shall get wrinkles, and then what will become of you?"

Hearing the mischief in her friend's voice, Alice had to laugh, the anxiety she felt lessening somewhat. "My heart, Madeline, is more than fickle."

A knowing look appeared on Madeline's face. "Ah, so that is the long and the short of it, then. You find your husband somewhat agreeable now?"

Alice sighed. "I confess that I do. I do not wish it, of course."

"It is a good thing to be attracted to one's husband, let me assure you," Madeline said calmly. "But as things stand, I can understand your very great predicament."

Thinking quickly, Alice's lips twisted. "Perhaps the time has come to reveal the truth about myself. It shall not be the public humiliation that I have hoped for, but I believe that he will still feel the shame of knowing that I have seen every last bit of his rakish behavior."

Madeline rose from her seat and grasped Alice's hands. "He may not respond in the way you wish, Alice. What if he is angry with you?"

Alice shrugged, growing tired of the whole façade. "I have to tell him the truth, Madeline. But only once he has sought my advice, for I would know what it is that is troubling him so."

"You must be careful, Alice," Madeline cautioned, her eyes filled with worry. "This could cause a great deal of heartache for you both, not just at this moment but for years to come."

Accepting Madeline's caution gracefully, Alice nodded and bade her friend goodbye. "I will not be long," she assured her. "And then I shall tell you all, I swear it."

ALICE DID NOT HAVE to wait long for Lord Worthington to arrive and soon found herself walking in Hyde Park with him once more, again keeping to the quieter paths. It was a little too early for the fashionable hour, which Alice was grateful for. She did not want to be the subject of rumors, nor did she want anyone else to know what she was about to discuss with her husband.

Lord Worthington, however, was quiet. In fact, he barely said more than twenty words to her as they entered Hyde Park, his face etched with a deep struggle that Alice could not help but inquire about.

"You look somewhat sorrowful today, Lord Worthington," she began, carefully. "Are you well?"

Lord Worthington gave something of a harsh laugh, his eyes fixing on the path ahead instead of towards her. "You are most perceptive, Lady Emma. In truth, I have struggled not to wear my jovial face, in a manner of speaking. I have become quite accomplished at hiding my difficulties from others, and, in that way, from myself." Finally, his eyes met hers. "But not with you, I dare say."

"No," Alice responded, firmly. "You know that I can easily see through your facade now."

"I am sure you can," he replied with a quick smile. "In truth, I should not have met with you this afternoon."

"Oh?" Alice's heart sank into her boots, looking up into his face. "I am sorry to hear it. I can return home if you wish it?"

He shook his head and grasped her hand, placing it into the crook of his elbow. "You misunderstand me, my lady. It is you that I struggle with, for you seem to know me better than any other of my acquaintances. I need your words, your truths, for they clear the fog in my mind and help me to see clearly."

Alice's heart began to pound in her chest as she stopped, looking up into his face with confusion. "I do not understand what the struggle is, then, my lord."

For a moment, he looked down at her, his face tight with emotion. His fingers reached up and touched the curve of her cheek, and her entire being came alive at once. She found that she could not breathe as he looked deeply into her eyes.

"It is because of how much I feel for you, Lady Emma," he replied, heavily, shaking his head and beginning to walk once more. "I cannot help my heart, and I have struggled to hide it from myself, and from you, but still it yearns for you."

Alice did not know what to say, her mind whirling with a thousand different thoughts.

"I told myself that I wanted your affection because I did not like being treated in such a way," he continued when she said nothing. "But in truth, I found you one of the most beautiful ladies of my acquaintance, in both character and in face." His arm tightened under her arm. "I should never sought you out the way I did, but I confess that even now I do not regret it, for I know such a thing can never happen again."

Alice cleared her throat, trying not think clearly. "I am surprised at your words, my lord."

"I am ashamed of myself, I admit," he replied, quietly. "If I were free, I would confess my affection for you and seek to court you, should you have me. However, I now know that I must be true to my responsibilities and put aside my feelings."

"Were you free?" Alice asked, trying to sound offhand. "What are you speaking of, Lord Worthington?"

There was a brief pause, and, as Alice glanced at him, she saw how he hung his head, unable to look at her.

"I am not free because I am a married man, Lady Emma," he replied, heavily. "I am wed, and I have treated my wife despicably."

13

A silent scream lodged itself in Alice's throat as she stared at her husband, hardly able to believe what he had said.

"You are shocked, of course," he continued, his voice so quiet that she struggled to hear him. "I can return you to Lady Astor, should you wish to exclude yourself from my company immediately." Finally, he looked over at her, his expression filled with shame and grief. "Although I confess that I am still in need of your advice."

Alice bit her lip, her emotions whirling through her and making it difficult for her to think clearly. He had just confessed the truth to her, sharing his regret and sadness over what he had done. Did he realize just how much that meant to her? However, questions still remained in her mind: Why had he done such a thing? Why had he abandoned her these three years?

Thinking that should she continue the conversation for a few more minutes, she might discover the truth, Alice decided that she would remain silent on the issue of her identity for the moment.

"I shall remain with you, Lord Worthington," she said,

quietly. "I will confess that I am completely stunned by your revelations, for why would a married man keep the truth of his matrimonial state a secret?"

"That is a fair question," he replied, sounding relieved that she would stay with him. "I shall tell you all if you wish to hear it. Then I shall seek your advice on how to progress from the lowly position I have left myself in."

Alice nodded, her eyes taking in every expression on her husband's face.

He looked relieved, a sigh leaving his lips. "I have just come from visiting my mother. I was there late last night and spoke with her this morning before returning to London."

"I hear she lives in the dower house, but two hours from London."

He nodded, but did not smile. There was no delight in his eyes as he spoke of her, as though their relationship was somewhat strained.

"And did you find her well?" Alice did not know what his mother had to do with her situation, but something told her to listen carefully to what her husband had to say.

Lord Worthington's lips twisted. "In a way. She is never pleased with me, you see."

"I see," Alice mumbled, thinking that his mother might have every right to be disappointed in him, given his behavior.

He laughed. "I presume you think that she must be justified in her criticism of me, and you might well be right. However, the lady has never been an affectionate one. Even as a boy, I could never please her." His lips thinned. "It was she who persuaded my father to set stipulations in his will."

Alice remembered, only just in time, that she was meant to have no knowledge of such things. "Stipulations?" she asked, knowing full well what had been asked of him.

He set his shoulders and shook his head. "My father wrote in his last will and testament that I must marry before his fortune, in its entirety, was released to me."

Alice nodded. "That must have been difficult for you."

To her very great surprise, Lord Worthington shook his head, stopping in his walk so that he might face her. "No, indeed. I did not consider it a burden in any way."

"No?" Alice could not believe that, given how much in his cups her husband had been on his wedding day.

"No, of course not. I looked forward to choosing my own bride, for I never wished to marry without love or affection at the very least." He smiled at her, looking a little self-conscious. "You may believe me to be quite ridiculous in such an expectation, given that very few gentlemen consider it, but I found that I could not marry for anything less."

This certainly did not make sense to Alice, for she had only set eyes on her husband on the day of their wedding. She could not help but frown, her eyes piercing him. He did not look in the least disturbed by her perusal, simply meeting her gaze with a despondent look.

"When my mother insisted I marry right away, I chose a woman whom I thought could make me happy. I did not love her, but she was tolerable, and I believed my affections for her could grow. However, my mother did not see things as I did. She arranged my betrothal, and my subsequent marriage, without so much as asking me. As I said, I did not love the woman I chose, and upon reflection, I would have not been happy with her. However, I was upset that my mother stole that choice from me. She had no right, but what could I do?"

Alice stopped dead, feeling as though she were about to be blown over by the wind. The air was pulled from her lungs, the emotions she felt almost choking her. Had her husband been manipulated into wedding her? She had been told that he had come to the ceremony willingly, that he truly did wish to marry her, but now it appeared that it had all been a lie.

"Are you all right?" Lord Worthington asked, looking increasingly worried. "I have not shocked you too greatly, I hope?"

Alice could only make her way to a small bench, sitting down heavily and drawing in long, deep breaths. So this was why her husband had been so badly behaved at his wedding and why she had been sent to live alone for three years... He had not had a choice in the marriage. He had not wanted to marry her.

Lord Worthington took one of her hands and chafed it, his eyes searching her face. He did not understand what the matter was with her, for he did not know the truth of her identity.

"I am quite well, I assure you," Alice croaked, feeling some warmth come back into her fingers. "I do apologize."

His eyes did not leave hers, filled with concern. "I am sorry if what I said has caused you such distress. It was not my intention."

Swallowing, Alice let out her breath slowly, trying hard to focus on her husband. "No, I am well, I promise you. I am surprised to hear that you are wed, for there is no mention of your wife in any regard. There are whispers, of course."

"And I am a truly terrible man for treating my wife in such a way," he replied, coming to sit next to her. "In truth, despite my regard for you, I must seek your advice on how to approach my wife for I have no one else to ask." The agony in his expression intensified as he let go of her hand. "How am I to make amends to her when I have treated her in such a terrible way?"

Alice looked into his face, keeping her gaze steady. She did not see a single ounce of dishonesty there, for he was returning her gaze with an eager expression, as though desperate to hear what she had to say.

"I believe you may simply be honest with her," she replied, slowly. "Honesty can go a long way to healing someone's broken heart."

"She will never forgive me," he replied, dropping his head into his hands. "I have left her there for three years and have forbidden my mother — my conniving, manipulative mother — from visiting her, knowing that it would do the lady more harm than good. I have rarely written and have not returned to my estate since depositing her there." He glanced up at her, his face drawn. "So, you see, I am quite the wretch and deserve every bit of wrath she places on my head."

Alice nodded, finding that she simply could not speak. The desire to tell him who she was grew with every moment, to relieve him of some of his pain. This had never been the path she had intended to walk when she had first come to town, but her husband had changed right before her very eyes to the point that she could no longer bring herself to disgrace him in front of all society.

There was more to his story and to his treatment of her than she had first realized, discovering that she could, somehow, begin to understand why he had left her so alone, although that did not make up for it, of course.

"You are right when you say that you deserve every last bit of wrath I might place on your head," she began softly, feeling a trembling in her soul begin to take hold. "But perhaps, I might somehow be able to find a way to forgive you. What do you think, William?"

14

"William?" he repeated, slowly, his eyes taking her in as though looking at her for the first time.

Alice lifted her chin and did not remove her gaze from his, although she was now aware that she trembled all over. She had revealed the truth of her identity to her husband and was unsure as to how he would respond. Would he be angry with her? Ashamed? Utterly astonished?

As she watched, his expression changed from one of surprise to one of shock, his face draining of color as he pushed himself a little away from her, his hands grasping the bench for support.

"You are not my wife," he breathed, not even blinking as he stared at her. "You are Lady Emma Taylor."

"A false name, I'm afraid, my lord," she replied, sounding much more assured than she felt. "It was necessary so I could see exactly the kind of man I had married."

He pressed his lips together as though holding back an exclamation of some kind.

"I grew tired of being kept up in your estate for three long years with no company to speak of and no husband at my side," she continued, her voice cracking with emotion. "I came here with the intention of shaming you before all of society, hoping that it would be the thing you needed to do as you ought and return to me." Her vision blurred as she struggled to contain her emotions. "It appears, however, that my plan has gone awry, thanks to your sudden change of character."

"Lady Emma," he whispered, shaking his head. "I mean, Lady... Worthington."

"Alice," she stated calmly. "My name is Alice."

To her very great surprise, the man got to his feet and stumbled away from her. She stared at him as he began to pace in front of the bench, his eyes never leaving her. She saw the way his hands shook, realizing that she had shocked him beyond measure.

"Forgive me, but I must leave you," he said, hoarsely. "This is all too much. I am too ashamed."

"William!" she exclaimed, rising to her feet. "You cannot simply leave me here in the park, not after all that has been revealed! There is much we need to talk about."

"I cannot," he said, bowing deeply. "I must ask you to forgive me again, my lady. Do excuse me."

MADELINE PUT her arm around Alice's shaking shoulders as she wept, holding her friend close.

"I am so sorry, Alice," she murmured, gently. "I cannot imagine what you must be going through."

"He looked at me as though I were a wraith," Alice whispered, through her tears. "A fearsome beast come from the past come back to remind him of all his sins."

Madeline's smile was sad. "You are, in a way," she replied softly. "Now, you must stay overnight with me. I absolutely insist."

Alice shook her head. "No, I must return home."

"You cannot!" Madeline protested. "I will not allow you to be alone at a time such as this, Alice. You will need friends about you and, although Catherine is very busy with the season, I am sure she will wish to see you."

Swallowing her tears, Alice patted her cheeks dry with her lace handkerchief and tried to think clearly. All she wanted was to run away, far away, to seek refuge away from her husband. Then again, if she returned home to her country estate, to her prison, there was no reason why her husband should not seek her out there. The walls slowly began to close in on her, making her break down in tears once more.

"You will stay, I insist upon it," Madeline said firmly. "I am sure things will be clearer by the morning."

However, come the morning, Alice still felt as dull and as lost as she had done the previous day. Having spent a night tossing and turning in bed, she was both pale and wane, her eyes smudged with exhaustion. She had lingered in bed for some of the morning hours, finally falling into a restless sleep that brought her, for at least some time, a little peace.

"My dear Alice," Madeline exclaimed, the moment Alice walked into the drawing room. "How are you?" She rose at once and took Alice's hand, her eyes searching Alice's face.

Alice did not know what to say, not able to find the words to express the numbness in her soul, the grief, and pain that were mingled with despair. She had not thought that her husband would simply turn his back and leave her, as he had done those three years previously. She had thought that his change of character would force him to remain, to talk with her about what he had done. Now, it appeared that her hopes had been in vain.

Had he railed at her, that would have been a better reaction than simply leaving her standing alone.

"You are exhausted," Madeline said when Alice did not answer. "Come and sit down."

Alice shook her head. "I will return to my parents' townhouse," she said quietly. "That is the only place I can think of where I will feel secure." She had thought on her dilemma of where to go for some hours, realizing with relief that Lord Worthington did not know her address here in town. "If he does seek me out, can you send me a note of some kind? I feel as though I need a few days to simply hide away, to come to terms with what has occurred."

A flash of discomfiture crossed Madeline's face but was gone in an instant, making Alice frown slightly. Was she putting Madeline in an awkward position by asking her to act as a go-between? She did not have anyone else that she could turn to.

"Of course," Madeline said at once, lifting Alice's unease. "But are you sure you will not stay, Alice? I do hate to see you go when you are clearly still upset."

Alice shook her head. "I am grateful to you, Madeline, but I need my solitude."

"I am sorry for what happened," her friend replied quietly. "But perhaps your husband simply needed time to overcome the sheer amount of shame and mortification he felt at your revelation."

"Or perhaps I have been taken in once more," Alice responded at once. "In truth, Madeline, I am not sure of the man at all anymore. He is a man with many faces, I think, and I have simply become confused over which one he is wearing."

To her surprise, Madeline did not agree, putting her hand on Alice's arm and shaking her head. "I believe there is more to him than you realize, Alice. Of course, there is much that you need to discuss, for the last three years cannot simply be blown away, but I trust that there will be healing for you both. In time."

Alice was not sure what made Madeline sound so certain over such things but accepted her friend's words regardless.

"You mean to go now?"

Alice nodded and attempted to smile. "Yes, I do. I have already called for the carriage. I will see you again soon, Madeline."

Her friend pressed a kiss to Alice's cheek and squeezed her hands, her eyes glittering with moisture. Alice, appreciating her friend's sympathy, managed a watery smile before she left the room.

ALICE SAT QUIETLY in her carriage, not even noticing the twists and turns of the road as it wound its way back home. Nor did she notice the slight smile on her butler's face as she handed him her bonnet and gloves, her mind still weighed down with all that had occurred. Her future was now dull, laying out as barren and as bleak as it had been when she had lived those three years alone. She did not know what Lord Worthington meant to do with her, nor what he would say when they next had to meet. All she could see was the way he had looked at her, the paleness of his features as he had turned around and left her alone in Hyde Park.

A sudden scent caught her nose, making her frown. Turning to the butler, who was standing quietly to her left, she lifted one eyebrow.

"A gift of flowers, my lady," he said, anticipating her question. "I have put them in the drawing room."

Thinking that they must be from Catherine, whom Madeline had written to only yesterday, Alice felt her heart lift a little. "Lovely, thank you. I think I shall take tea there."

"Of course," the butler murmured, bowing slightly and walking away. Alice made her way to the drawing room, wondering what on earth was making such a wonderful scent. Catherine must have sent a large number of blooms for the beautiful smell to make its way through the house!

Pushing open the drawing-room door, Alice took one step in, only to be completely and utterly shocked. The entire room, it seemed, was filled with flowers. They were everywhere. They adorned the tables, the mantelpiece, and, as she took another small step inside, the floor. Vases were everywhere, although where such a great number had come from, she could not tell. The scent of the blooms wafted around her, making her heart bloom with delight and happiness.

"Who has sent all these?" she breathed to herself, picking up one delicate bloom and lifting it to her nose.

"These are all the flowers I should have sent you, these three years past."

The flower dropped from her fingers as she stumbled back, seeing Lord Worthington, her husband, stepping into her line of vision from the corner of the room. "Lord Worthington," she breathed, her eyes widening. "How—"

"I confess that Lady Astor told me of where you were staying," he said, looking more than a little guilty. "It took a great deal of convincing, but she believes me to be genuine in my affection and regard for you."

Alice could not breathe, pressing one hand to her stomach as she saw her husband slowly advance towards her, his eyes lingering on her.

"I believe I have a great many apologies to make," he said, now only a few steps away from her. "Not only for how I have treated you since our wedding day, but in leaving you only yesterday all over again." He closed his eyes, as though the memory of what he had done was painful to him. "I am truly sorry, my dear."

Her entire being was alive, her heart squeezing almost painfully in her chest as she held onto the back of a chair for support.

"I will admit that I was truly stunned by your revelation," he continued when she did not reply. "My shame was so great that I found myself almost running away from you." He dropped his head for a moment, before looking back at her. "How can you ever forgive me?" His voice broke, his eyes glazing over with emotion as he regarded her with an almost desperate look.

Still clinging to the chair, Alice felt fresh tears fill her eyes as they traveled over the many, many flowers he had sent her. "It will take some time for us to fully heal," she said brokenly. "But you have changed, Lord Worthington and, even now, I believe that change to be ongoing."

He put his head in his hands, as though he could not take in what she was saying.

"I should never have left you," he said, his voice muffled through his hands. "You should never have been left there alone. It was as though I were punishing you for what my mother forced me to do."

"I did not know that you were in such a difficult predicament," Alice replied truthfully. "My father did not tell me anything of the kind."

His brown eyes looked into her green ones as though he were seeing her for the very first time. "I do not deserve a woman like you," he said softly. "Not after the rogue I have been."

"But you are not that man any longer," she replied, managing to loosen her grip on the chair and step closer.

"I swear I shall never do such a thing again," he promised,

holding out his hand to her. "You must know that I was never unfaithful to you." He looked deep into her eyes. "Will you honor this blackguard with your trust, even though I know I do not deserve it?"

Alice studied him for a moment, thinking just how changed he was from the man she had first met. He was broken and entirely vulnerable, laying himself open for her regard. She found that she did not wish to punish him and discovered that she could, at the very least, begin to give him the trust he craved.

"I will," she said, softly, taking his proffered hand.

For a long moment, he did not speak, simply looking down at the hand that held his. Alice did not know whether she wanted to laugh or cry, her heart so full that she felt it might burst from her chest.

"You have captured my heart. Who would have guessed that the woman I had such affection for would prove to be my wife?" he said eventually, lifting his head so that he might meet her gaze. "How will we explain this to society?" he laughed half-heartedly. "I will take all the blame of course."

"I confess that I have found myself drawn to you," Alice admitted, seeing the sudden spark in his eyes. "I did not wish to be, of course."

He took a small step closer so that they were only inches apart. "Do you think you might come to love me in time?" he asked almost breathlessly. "I believe that I have already lost my heart to you, for you have captured me like no other."

Alice considered this, allowing one of her hands to drape over his shoulder, finding that she reacted strongly to the touch of his skin against hers. "I believe the first stirrings of love are already within my heart," she murmured, looking up into his face. "So long as you do not abandon me again, William, then I do not think that it shall be long before these small shoots blossom into something beautiful."

"I swear to you, I shall never leave your side again," he promised, putting both arms around her waist and making her tremble inside. "Never."

Alice pressed her lips to his, feeling her shattered heart slowly begin to mend as he returned her kiss. It appeared her trip to town had been entirely successful.

THE END

A VISCOUNT'S SECOND CHANCE

By Joyce Alec

1

London 1838

"I am not quite sure about this," Eleanor murmured as she stepped out of the carriage and looked up at her new home.

"Now, now," came the reply, as her companion, Miss Wiltshire, stepped out beside her. An older cousin of Eleanor's, she had come to live with her almost as soon as Eleanor had wed. She had stayed by Eleanor's side since the death of her husband a little over a year ago and had been nothing but a support to her. "It is quite proper for you to return to society now that your year of mourning is over."

"I know," Eleanor replied, with a heavy sigh. "But I feel as though every eye is on me. I am quite sure I shall be in tomorrow's papers or some such thing."

Miss Wiltshire chuckled and grasped Eleanor's arm, so as to hurry her indoors. "You will be just fine, I assure you. After all, it is not as though you were wed to the man for long. To have to mourn him a year is quite ridiculous."

But expected, Eleanor thought to herself, as she stepped inside her townhouse, letting the memories flood her.

She had been there only once before, in the days after their wedding. Her husband, the Earl of Brooke, had been a kind man and twenty years her senior. He had chosen to reside at the townhouse with her for a few days before returning to his country estate.

Handing her hat and gloves to the waiting butler, Eleanor allowed her mind to run back over the time of her marriage. It had all been set up and agreed to by her father, and Eleanor had not been allowed to even murmur a complaint. It had not mattered that she did not love the earl, nor that she found his age in comparison to hers quite distasteful. All that mattered was that she married well and, being her father's only child, Eleanor had found herself quite forced into the matter. It was as though she were merely a pawn in her father's chess game, knowing that he only truly cared about wealth as opposed to her wellbeing. Eleanor was sure that her father had done quite well in the bargain, for the Earl of Brooke had not been a poor man. In fact, he had been quite rich and, having had no children nor any other relatives to speak of, Eleanor now found herself to be something of a wealthy woman.

However, living in the country, albeit with the company of Miss Wiltshire, had been something of a burden. She had taken her mourning year as she ought, spending her days quietly, but slowly began dreaming of her return to town and of meeting dear friends and acquaintances once more. The Season was only just beginning, and Eleanor hoped that she might begin to allow herself some enjoyment, although she was inclined to worry what society might think of her return to London.

"Tea in the drawing room, your ladyship?"

Drawn from her thoughts, Eleanor looked up at her butler and nodded, smiling warmly at him. "Thank you, you are very thoughtful," she said, seeing his perfectly expressionless face flicker for just a moment. "That would be wonderful."

"At once, my lady," he replied, clicking his heels together and walking away.

"Your husband employed wonderful staff," Miss Wiltshire commented, as they walked together towards the drawing room. "They seem to know what you wish before you even ask it."

Eleanor nodded. "Indeed, they were all very loyal to him, and I have decided to keep each one in their positions for the time being."

Miss Wiltshire preceded her into the drawing room, murmuring something about the warm fire already burning brightly in the grate. It was not the warmest of days, and Eleanor was grateful for the warmth, rubbing her hands together for a moment before seating herself down beside the fire. She had not much memory of this place, other than the few days she had lived there with the earl, although the recollection of her wedding night was one she would rather forget.

The earl had spent most of his time up in the country out riding, for that was his one passion. Unfortunately, that passion had been his death. She could still remember the day that the groom had been permitted to see her, twisting his cap in his hands. He had been completely drenched by the rain, dripping puddles on the floor, telling her that her husband had been found with a broken neck, the horse standing nearby.

Apparently, they presumed that he had attempted to jump a hedge, but had not quite managed to keep his seat. There had been talk of doing away with the animal, but Eleanor had forbidden it immediately, aware that it was not the creature's fault that her husband was now cold in his grave.

To her shame, she had not felt a great deal of sorrow over the earl's death. She had never really known him, for they had not often spent time in one another's company, nor had they conversed together often. She had been grateful he had allowed her to have the company of Miss Wiltshire, an older, distant cousin, for her life would have been quite lonely without her. Eleanor had confessed to Miss Wiltshire her guilt over her lack of grief, but the older lady had reassured her on more than one occasion, that it was quite to be expected. After all, it was not as though Eleanor was mourning someone she had grown close to, someone she had loved, but rather someone who had been more of a stranger than a husband. Still, Eleanor could not rid herself of the deep feeling of guilt over her lack of sadness. She did not dislike the earl; she just did not know him.

"This is a very fine room," Miss Wiltshire said, interrupting her flow of thoughts. "Were it not so wet outside, I am quite sure that beautiful sunshine would stream in through these windows."

Smiling at Miss Wiltshire, Eleanor let herself relax, the tension draining away. She did not have to worry about her husband any longer, given that she had already had her year of mourning. There was no scandal or any such thing. She would simply return to society as a wealthy widow, and, whilst that would bring whispers enough, she would not have anyone look down on her for her lack of love for her first husband. Nobody knew what went on behind closed doors. Besides, she was still young at only twenty-two years old.

"When do you intend to walk in Hyde Park?" Miss Wiltshire asked, giving Eleanor something of a knowing look.

Eleanor shook her head. "Not today, that is for certain. It is raining quite heavily, and I doubt anyone should see me, even if I were to venture out."

The only reason Eleanor would walk in Hyde Park was to allow those from society to become aware of her presence in town, for walking during the fashionable hour would bring a great deal of interest from others. In addition, she hoped to rekindle some friendships and acquaintances, which would bring a great deal of joy to her life.

Company had been something Eleanor had greatly missed, but she was quite sure that in a week or two, she would be throwing herself into all the delights society had to offer. How wonderful it would be to hear an orchestra striking up a waltz, to be dancing across the floor in a gentleman's arms.

A small sigh of expected happiness left her lips.

"You are going to have to be careful, Eleanor," Miss Wiltshire warned, as though she had read Eleanor's thoughts. "You are a wealthy widow now."

Frowning, Eleanor considered what Miss Wiltshire meant. "You believe I shall have gentlemen seeking my company simply because I have wealth?"

"Of course!" Miss Wiltshire exclaimed. "And there are plenty of such gentlemen too, believe me."

Eleanor shook her head. "I do not think any such gentlemen will be at the events I attend, Miss Wiltshire."

"Ah, but they will," Miss Wiltshire warned, with a gleam in her eye. "You are young and handsome, and with wealth to match, there will be a great many gentlemen practically lying at your feet. You shall have to watch that you do not lose your heart, Eleanor, for I know how much it calls for love."

Knowing that Miss Wiltshire was right, Eleanor tried not to blush, but found it almost impossible. She and Miss Wiltshire were quite in one another's confidence, and Eleanor had confessed, on more than one occasion, that she often wished her father had not forced her into such a loveless union. Miss Wiltshire had surmised from this, quite rightly of course, that Eleanor did intend to marry again one day, but only if the gentleman in question loved her truly.

"I do admit that I wish for such a thing, but I am in no hurry," Eleanor protested, weakly. "I have only just come out of my mourning year, and now that I have more than enough to care for us both for the remainder of our lives, I do not think that I shall marry hastily."

"Be careful, my dear," Miss Wiltshire said again. "There are many scoundrels and rogues underneath the façade of love. Gentlemen know what a lady wishes for, and they will use that to their advantage. Men who have no more than a few shillings to rub together, having thrown away their wealth at the gambling table, are more than inclined to say or do anything in order to achieve their status once more."

Her words made Eleanor's heart sink. How was she to know which gentlemen were such rogues should they begin to pay close attentions to her?

"I will help you, of course," Miss Wiltshire continued, as the tea tray arrived. "You may count on my assistance to guide you."

Eleanor waited until the maid had left before thanking Miss Wiltshire. "I do want to thank you for your presence here, Miss Wiltshire. I do not know what I would have done without you."

The older lady smiled, her blue eyes warming and cheeks dimpling. In truth, Miss Wiltshire was not too old a lady, even with her graying hair. She did not have a great many wrinkles, and her figure was still trim. Eleanor, at times, wondered why Miss Wiltshire had never married, for she was as fine a lady as ever there could be, even with her lack of title. Miss Wiltshire was, in that regard, quite guarded about the past, and Eleanor knew not to pry.

"I do hope that you will find some enjoyment here in town," Eleanor continued, pouring the tea. "I would not have you run around after me. You must find something to entertain you."

"Oh, I believe I shall be highly entertained," Miss Wiltshire responded with a laugh. "For who else is to discover the truth about the many gentlemen that will seek your hand? No, indeed, I shall be both useful and discreet, although I will greatly enjoy listening to the orchestra or taking the air at the park, I am quite sure."

Eleanor handed Miss Wiltshire her cup and smiled, feeling a little more settled than when she had first arrived. Perhaps things would work out just as they ought and they would both have an enjoyable Season, unhindered by rakish gentlemen who only cared for her fortune and not her heart.

2

Henry, Viscount Armitage, laughed as he took the last few sovereigns off the table, pocketing them with delight. "It appears that I will increase my fortune this evening, instead of depleting it."

Lord Thornley grunted, throwing himself back in his chair. "It seems I am going to have to give you a vowel, Armitage."

The smile left Henry's face immediately. Lord Thornley was well known for writing out vowels, but never paying what he owed.

"I know you must despise me for being forced to do so, but in truth, I have very little choice," Thornley wheedled, looking quite forlorn.

Henry was not in the least bit taken in, knowing that this was all an act Thornley put on to garner sympathy for others. However, such a façade was wearing thin.

"If you had nothing to play with, then you should not have sat down at the table," Henry said, gruffly. "I do not like vowels, Thornley, least of all from you."

The other gentlemen left the table, evidently unwilling to be caught up in a war of words between the two gentlemen. Henry watched them go, seeing Thornley sigh dramatically once more.

"I enjoy the game, you see," he said, softly. "I enjoy it too much."

Henry shook his head. "Then you must get better control of yourself."

"You are most understanding," Thornley droned, looking entirely bored. "In truth, my fortunes are so changed that it appears I am going to be forced to marry a lady of wealth."

Only just managing to stop his snort of derision, Henry rose from the table, accepting Thornley's vowel with disapprobation. "I wish you luck, then," he muttered, intending to walk away from Thornley. "I believe you will need it."

Unfortunately, Thornley dogged his footsteps, his loud whining voice continuing to drone towards Henry's ears. "You do not think me capable of finding such a wife, then?"

Gritting his teeth, Henry took a breath and tried to calm his growing frustration. "I care very little of what you do, Thornley, just so long as you pay me what you owe."

"You think I shall be quite unable to do what I intend," Thornley continued, his voice growing louder with every word. "How rude you are!"

Henry, now tired of Thornley's presence, rounded on the man, making every attempt to keep his own voice low. "Thornley, I doubt you will be able to find a lady with a great fortune to marry you, yes. Once they are aware of your lack of fortune and your inability to keep a hold on your gambling habits, then what on earth could coerce them into matrimony?"

Thornley smiled a slow lazy smile that told Henry he had allowed the man to push him into incivility, which appeared to be the reaction Thornley desired.

"Love," Thornley said, confidently.

"Love?" Henry scoffed, his temper flying loose. "Do be serious, Thornley."

"I am quite serious," the man replied, calmly. "By the end of the Season, I intend to be betrothed, if not wed, to a woman of great fortune. I should say it will take all of six weeks."

Henry did not know how to respond, finding the man's confidence entirely inexplicable.

"If I am successful, you will release me from my debt, and pay me twice what I owed," Thornley continued, his voice now quiet and firm. To Henry's surprise, he grasped the arm of a passing gentleman, calling on him to bear witness to the gentleman's agreement.

"And if you fail?"

"Then I shall pay you thrice what I already owe," Thornley said, with the air of someone who was more than confident in what he had planned.

Growing tired of the man's conversation and ridiculous ideas, Henry shrugged. "Very well, Thornley, if it will put an end to this conversation, then I agree. You have six weeks."

He shook Thornley's hand and made to turn away, only for the man to grip his hand harder, refusing to release him.

"And you are not to speak to the lady of what I am about," Thornley responded, carefully. "Should you do so, then the agreement is forfeit, and you will not only release me from my debt but give me four times as much as what I owe. Your reputation will suffer, even more, than it already has."

"I am a gentleman," Henry stated, hotly. "A gentleman does not deliberately manipulate a situation for his advantage."

Thornley grinned, his eyes narrowing just a little and making Henry feel as though Thornley somehow had the upper hand. Releasing Henry's hand, Thornley stepped back and bowed, seeing Sir Thomas—an older man with slightly graying hair—mutter something about the matter being settled, before leaving the conversation directly.

Henry was about to turn away when his stomach twisted with a sudden thought. "Do you have your eye on anyone in particular?" he asked, abruptly, taking a step closer to Thornley. "Tell me it is not some old decrepit heiress, someone who will marry you only to die in a few months' time."

"No, it is not," Thornley said sharply, as though somehow offended by the suggestion. "I do have someone I am considering, however." A wicked gleam came into his eye, making Henry frown all the more. "A Lady Brooke? She is quite new to town, I believe."

A white-hot jolt rushed straight through Henry's frame pinning him to the floor. He had not heard that Lady Eleanor had returned to town—although she was now Lady Brooke, of course. He had seen her on more than a few occasions a little over two years ago, and he had always thought her quite lovely, although he never plucked up the courage to be introduced to her.

In truth, he had even imagined courting her, only to hear that she had become betrothed to Lord Brooke. His frustration over his inaction, in regards to the lady, had driven him into a course of action he now regretted, although he had never spoken of his regard for the lady to another living soul. Neither had he known that she had returned to town, his heart clenching at the thought.

"Lord Brooke died last year, I am quite sure you heard of it," Thornley continued, airily. "She is now one of the richest widows in all of England, I am quite sure. I shall have no difficulty convincing her that I am greatly in love with her."

"Not if I can do so first," Henry said, fiercely, surprising even himself with his own vehemence. The thought of the lovely

Lady Brooke caught up in Thornley's conniving grip was more than he could bear.

Thornley chuckled, shaking his head. "You cannot speak a word to her of this, Armitage, nor to any other gentleman save Sir Thomas, who is our witness."

"I do not need to," Henry answered, firmly. "For there is nothing in our agreement that states I cannot try to draw her towards me instead of you."

Thornley rolled his eyes. "You? I doubt it, Armitage. With your damaged reputation, you struggle to find even a single lady willing to have your name on her dance card. I am in no danger. Attempt to take her as your own if you will, for I am quite sure I shall be triumphant. Good evening to you, Armitage."

Henry gritted his teeth as Thornley walked away, the shame over his reputation creeping up through his chest and sending heat into his face. He had attempted to re-enter society after a year away and had thought that things were going as well as could be expected. However, Thornley seemed more than a little keen to remind him that he was still persona non-grata to a great many eligible young ladies of the ton.

When Lord Brooke had announced his engagement to Lady Eleanor Dawson, two Seasons previously, it had taken all of the joy from Henry's life in one, unforgettable moment. He had never even been introduced to the lady, but had always admired her from a distance. His profound shyness had always caused him to struggle when it came to being introduced to eligible young ladies, and even more so to those he found particularly lovely.

Lady Eleanor Dawson had always seemed poised and collected, gentle and serene, with a smile and a word for almost everyone. How many times had he watched her take to the floor, imagining that he was the one who held her in his arms? On more than one occasion, he had attempted to draw near to her, only to find his tongue sticking to the roof of his mouth, his palms sweating and his composure utterly shredded.

The day of her announced betrothal, Henry had become both frustrated and irritated with his own lack of action, angry with his shy nature and quiet speech. He had done what he had never done before—become rip-roaring drunk down at White's, the exclusive gentlemen's club of the ton. The other gentlemen there had thought it a hilarious spectacle, encouraging him to continue to drink yet more liquor to the point that Henry had become completely unconscious. When he awoke, he found that he was still unable to rid himself of the image of her, and so had ordered yet more whisky.

Being titled and wealthy, it had made no difference to him how much coin he spent on liquor and, having very few close friends, had no one to encourage him to stop. Henry could only recall waking up two days later, discovering himself in a strange room with no idea how he had got there—nor whose bed it was.

Rough hands had shaken him awake, and he had found himself staring into the eyes of a furious gentleman who asked him what it was he thought he was doing.

Henry could never forget the shame of that moment.

Apparently, he had somehow managed to climb into an open window of a townhouse, using both the ivy and the nearby tree branches to gain entry. For whatever reason, he had then climbed into a bed—which he had been told, was the bed of the eligible Lady Annabelle Harrington, daughter of the Earl of Marchmont.

He had been immediately thrown from the house, with barely enough time to pull on his pantaloons. His undressed state and subsequent condemnation by the earl himself had forced Henry from society for a time, his reputation completely and utterly ruined.

After almost a year away, hiding in his country home, his

dear friend, Lord Tressel, paid a long overdue visit. Having only just been married himself and then, subsequently, on his honeymoon trip, he had been unable to call on Henry until that point, but had both berated him and encouraged him in that one visit.

Henry had not gone into specifics as to what had driven him to such an inebriated state, but had told Lord Tressel—who had stated his surprise at hearing of Henry's behavior—that it would certainly not happen again.

On hearing this, Lord Tressel had encouraged Henry back into society, telling him that all was not lost. Rumors had died down, gossip had moved onto their next piece of meat, and that, should he be quite sensible, he believed that Henry would be accepted by society once more.

It had taken everything Henry had to come back to London, determined that his shyness was not about to render him quite useless, forcing him to stay hidden in the country like some kind of recluse. In his heart, Henry did not want to be alone for the rest of his days; he knew that he did want someone by his side. That would mean that he would have to find a wife, and in order to do that, he would have to court. And that meant a return to society.

Lord Tressel had been more than helpful in encouraging Henry to leave his shy nature behind and to command the room, showing those who still recalled his behavior that he was not in the least bit intimidated by them—even though, in truth, it was not something he could easily ignore.

Lord Tressel had told him, in no uncertain terms, that should he remain in the shadows, he would never achieve his desire of a wife and family of his own. Henry had to admit that he was a little jealous of the happy state that Lord Tressel now found himself in, clearly missing his wife. He was not quite sure whether Lord Tressel had found love, but he certainly gave the appearance of it.

Henry did not want to wed another simply out of duty, hoping that he might, at the very least, have some kind of affection between himself and his future wife but, given his reputation, he might have to settle for the former. Affection could grow with time, could it not? The last thing he wanted to do was wed a lady who would grow to despise him, who had only married him for his title. Whether he would find such a lady, he was not sure at all, desperately hoping that the ton would accept his re-entry into society with no great attention.

However, they had not been as welcoming as he had hoped. A year was not long enough to wipe society's memory of his behavior. Of late, a few of the wallflowers had allowed him to take them onto the floor, which was better than none at all, but progress was certainly slow. He did not need to be reminded of his past indiscretions, for the consequences of them were more than obvious, and he certainly did not need to be ridiculed by Thornley, who was now making his way towards the ballroom, apparently keen to take Lady Brooke out onto the dance floor should he manage to catch her attention.

Henry let out a long, slow breath, attempting to dampen down his anger. His fingernails still bit into his palms as he thought of Thornley dancing with Lady Brooke. It was not to be borne, but without an introduction to the lady, he could do very little to stop Thornley from pressing his attentions onto her. What was he to do, when he could not even speak to the lady?

3

"The man is not getting to you, I hope?"

Looking to his left, Henry saw Lord Caldwell approach, his eyes firmly fixed on Thornley's retreating back.

"He is always inclined to rile me," Henry said, frustrated with his reaction to the man. He had played Thornley at cards often enough and had always thought him a whining, boring sort of man. Thornley was the kind of man who got on Henry's nerves when he was in his company for too long, but he had never considered him to be a conniving, clever sort of fellow. "I confess that I have never thought him a serious threat before, however."

Caldwell lifted his eyebrows. "And he is now?"

Letting out a regretful sigh, Henry shook his head. "Not to me, in particular, but to the eligible young ladies of the ton. But, then again, society thinks that I am more of a danger than he."

Chuckling, Caldwell shook his head. "The man is going to attempt to wed, then? He has long been saying that he needs to find a bride but has never seemed to make any attempt to court any eligible ladies."

Knowing that he could not say more, for he would not risk nor break the agreement between himself and Thornley, Henry simply nodded. He could feel Caldwell's eyes on him for some time, but he pressed his lips together all the harder, refusing to speak a single word.

"And how are you, Armitage? It is good to see you back with us again."

There was sympathy in the man's voice, which both grated on Henry, but was also appreciated.

"I am well. I thank you."

"Making a return to society?"

Henry laughed wryly. "I am attempting to, at the very least."

"They will forget soon enough," Caldwell said, slapping Henry on the back. "A youth's folly, was it not?"

"It was," Henry replied, even though it was not all that long ago. "Unfortunately, it appears that the ton has long memories and are quite unwilling to wipe my indiscretions from their mind."

"I see," Caldwell muttered, shaking his head. "Will no one dance with you?"

"Not unless they are utterly desperate," Henry muttered, passing a hand over his eyes. "Or new to town and, even then, they are warned away soon enough."

"That is most unfair," Caldwell said sympathetically. "Men have been forgiven for much worse. It was not as if you pressed your intentions on Lady Annabelle; you simply wanted to fall asleep."

Henry was grateful for the very forgiving way Caldwell relayed the events of that evening. "I do not even remember it," Henry responded with shame. "I am embarrassed to admit I was in something of a state."

Caldwell nodded, his eyes drifting away for a moment. "I am quite sure my cousin would dance with you, should I speak to her?" Caldwell murmured. "She is quite the thing at the moment. Her acceptance of you should help smooth the waters."

Surprised at the kindness of a man who was merely an acquaintance, Henry stared at Caldwell for a moment before thanking him profusely.

"I should not like to soil your cousin's reputation, however," he continued, slowly, wondering who it was that Caldwell was talking of. "Particularly if she is in search of a husband."

"You are quite all right on that count," Caldwell answered, beginning to walk towards the door of the card room. "She is widowed, unfortunately, but has now come into a substantial amount of wealth. So, you see, her reputation will not be blemished in the least with a dance from you, given that most of the ton are eager to make her acquaintance."

"Then I would be greatly appreciative of her kind regard," Henry said quickly. "What did you say her name was?"

"Lady Brooke," Caldwell responded over his shoulder. "Or, Lady Eleanor Dawson, as she was formerly known. Perhaps you remember her."

Henry stumbled, struggling to regain his footing as he attempted to find his poise once more. Thankfully for him, Caldwell did not turn around, sparing Henry any embarrassment. Her name went around and around his head, his heart slamming into his chest as he followed Caldwell from the card room. Finally, after all these years, he was going to meet the lady he had so admired from a distance, so long ago.

"Ah!" Caldwell exclaimed as they made their way into the ballroom. "There she is. The dance is almost an end, and then we shall garner her attention."

Henry waited impatiently, going hot all over as he saw Lord Thornley twirl Lady Brooke across the floor. She appeared to be having a wonderful time, for she was both laughing and smiling with Thornley, which only made Henry grit his teeth. Thankfully, the dance was over after only a few more minutes, and Henry breathed a heavy sigh of relief as Lord Thornley led Lady Brooke off the floor, although he did not miss the glare that Thornley sent his way.

"Good evening, fair cousin," Lord Caldwell called, catching Lady Brooke's attention. "I see you are quite the belle of the ball already. And this only your second ball, I believe."

Henry could not speak as Lady Brooke drew near, her eyes sparkling with delight as she saw Caldwell, greeting him warmly.

"It is good to see you again, cousin," she replied, smiling. "And how is your lovely wife? Is she present this evening?" she asked, her gaze flickering to Henry for a moment.

"She is indisposed at the moment," Caldwell said, leaning forward slightly. "With child, I believe."

Henry saw the way Lady Brooke's face lit up with joy, clasping Edward's arm as though it was the most wonderful of news.

"It is to be kept quiet for the moment," Caldwell continued, smiling with happiness.

"Oh, of course, I will not breathe a word until you are quite sure," Lady Brooke responded, still evidently thrilled with his news.

"Nor will I," Henry managed to say, reminding Caldwell of his presence. He stood as tall as he could, attempting a smile. "Upon my honor, I swear it. I must congratulate you both, however. That is a wonderful blessing."

Caldwell smiled and clapped Henry on the shoulder. "I do thank you, Armitage. Now, let me introduce you to my fair cousin, Lady Brooke. Eleanor, this is Lord Armitage."

Henry bowed at once, giving himself a moment to collect himself before standing up once more to look into her eyes. He found that she was considering him carefully, her blue eyes careful and warm. Her mahogany hair was swept up into an elegant style, and her gown seemed to shimmer in the candlelight. However, there was a vibrancy about her features that sent swirls of nervous anticipation into his stomach, making him clear his throat more than once before speaking.

"I am delighted to make your acquaintance, Lady Brooke," he said, relieved that he did not sound in the least bit gruff. "Although I will say that I am sorry for the loss of your husband."

She smiled at him, and his world seemed to grow brighter. "I thank you, my lord, that is most kind of you."

"Are you glad to be back in town?" he asked, growing more confident with every word. "I understand that you lived some distance away, at your late husband's country estate."

"Indeed, I did," came the reply, although there was a slight lift of her eyebrows that betrayed her surprise at his knowledge of her. "It was very agreeable there, but I must confess that I am glad to be back in London once more. The country can be somewhat lonely at times."

Henry nodded, understanding completely. "Of course, I quite understand."

"You do?" she asked, glancing at Caldwell and then back at Henry.

Henry was at a loss about how to answer this, realizing that she had not yet heard a single rumor or piece of gossip about him.

Thankfully, Caldwell chuckled and shook his head. "You will hear a great many things about Lord Armitage, but it is as many things are—he made a mistake of youth and is now continuing to be punished for that one indiscretion, even though it is some time after the event."

Lady Brooke turned bright eyes on Henry, and, despite

himself, he felt a rush of shame creep up his neck. Dropping his head a little, he took his eyes from her face, feeling almost unworthy to look at her.

"I see," he heard her say.

"I assured him that you would show him some kindness," Caldwell continued, blithely, apparently oblivious to Henry's growing embarrassment. "After all, one mistake—over which the man had deeply repented of—should not be held against him. Do you agree?"

There was a brief pause, and Henry felt almost sick with nerves. Was she about to refuse him, not wishing to besmirch her own reputation? He could not blame her if that were the case.

"Should you like to dance, Lord Armitage?"

Her soft voice was as much of a surprise as a balm to his soul, his head shooting up of its own accord so that he might look her in the face, desperate to see whether she was being entirely serious. To his complete and utter relief, she was looking at him quite earnestly, although there was a slight twinkle in her eyes that told him she found his disbelief a little amusing.

"I had hoped to secure a dance with you," he replied, his voice hoarse with sudden emotion. "But I was quite sure you would not have a single space remaining on your dance card."

"Nor do I," Lady Brooke replied. "All but the supper dance, I believe, are taken."

"The supper dance?" Henry repeated, hardly believing his luck. "Should you permit me, I would greatly delight in writing my name there."

Henry hated that his hands trembled as he held her dance card, but soon his name was there, written clearly for all to see.

"I am surprised that you have no name there already, my lady," he murmured, as he let her card drop. "That is the most favored of all the dances, and you are doing me a great honor in allowing me to escort you."

She laughed, and Henry found himself smiling in return.

"I will confess that I used my fair cousin as an excuse to refuse any gentleman who asked," she said, sending a smile up towards Caldwell before returning her bright eyes back towards Henry. "In truth, I have an older companion who is here with me this evening, and I fully intended to sit with her during supper." Her expression softened. "She has done me a great deal of good, and I would not wish her to be slighted in any way. I do hope you will not mind if she joins us?"

"Of course not," Henry responded, fervently. "Just being able to dance with you is a gift in itself."

Her smile softened, as though she were quite aware of the struggles that faced him. "Then I am very glad to offer it to you."

Henry nodded and bowed before taking his leave, promising to see her again very soon. His heart lifted as he made through the crowd, thinking to himself that the gazes of those around him were somewhat softer than what they had been before. He could hardly wait to have Lady Brooke in his arms.

4

"Good gracious."

Eleanor laughed aloud as Miss Wiltshire walked into the drawing room, stopping short at the sight of the abundance of flowers that adorned almost every available space.

"I see that you made something of an impression last evening," Miss Wiltshire murmured after a few more moments of astonishment. "This is quite an assortment."

"I just rang for tea," Eleanor said, as her companion sat down carefully. "Although if you would care for something a little more substantial, I can send down for it?"

"No, no," Miss Wiltshire answered, with a wave of her hand. "I rose late this morning, I confess, but it is only because last evening's entertainment was so wonderful that I was lost in dreams for a good long while."

"I am glad to hear it," Eleanor replied, smiling softly. "I was worried that you would not enjoy yourself."

Miss Wiltshire shook her head. "I had a wonderful time, I thank you, although I will say that I was not entirely enamored with some of your dancing partners last evening."

"Oh?" Eleanor saw the way that Miss Wiltshire frowned slightly, her concern evident. "Did you discover something about them?"

Miss Wiltshire smiled, her eyes lit with a sudden interest. "Indeed, I did. I have discovered that being a companion means that I am privy to all the goings-on of polite society, whether I wish to know it or not. The other companions, thrown together as we were last evening, are more than willing to discuss the latest gossip and on-dits and, although I confess that I was not immediately willing to listen, I realized that their chatter gave me something of an insight."

The arrival of the tea tray meant that Eleanor had to wait for a few moments before Miss Wiltshire could continue, discovering that she was quite eager to hear whatever it was Miss Wiltshire had to say. Of course, Eleanor was not in the least bit interested in marrying, so it did not matter whether the gentlemen she danced with turned out to be rogues or not.

"Well," Miss Wiltshire began, as the door closed. "Lord Collingham, who I believe you danced with first, is looking for nothing more than a mistress, and Lord Guarder has barely two pennies to rub together, despite his ridiculous outfits making us believe otherwise."

Eleanor could not help but giggle, for Lord Guarder had been one of the most ridiculously dressed gentlemen there, with strong colors and patterns across almost his entire outfit. It had almost made her eyes water.

"I am glad to see you were not taken in by him," Miss Wiltshire said, with a smile. "There was another gentleman I was warned about too, a Lord Armitage?"

"Yes, he was the gentleman who escorted us both to supper," Eleanor reminded her, seeing her companion's expression clearing.

"I do not know the specifics," Miss Wiltshire said, slowly, evidently struggling to remember what had been said. "But they said something about some past recklessness that had pushed him from society."

Eleanor nodded. "My cousin introduced us both and told me very clearly that Lord Armitage had made something of a mistake some time ago, and that no one had, as yet, forgiven him for whatever he did. It seems a shame that, although he has tried to make recompense and even been away from society for a time, that they are still so unfriendly towards him."

Miss Wiltshire frowned, a line forming between her brows. "And how do you know such details?"

"My cousin, Lord Caldwell," Eleanor said, lifting her cup to her lips.

"And you trust him?"

Smiling, Eleanor nodded. "I do."

When she had first been introduced to Lord Armitage, she had been surprised at the sudden jolt that had gone through her, for she had met many handsome gentlemen already and none had made quite the same impact. She had brushed it off, however, and smiled kindly at the gentleman, feeling a slight stab of sympathy for him—although she could not help but wonder what terrible indiscretion he had done.

"He was quite handsome, was he not?" Miss Wiltshire murmured, as though privy to her thoughts.

"He was, yes," Eleanor replied, firmly. "But that is of no matter, Miss Wiltshire. I am not intending to marry. If I ever marry again, it will be for love. I do not need to marry to have my future secure."

Miss Wiltshire said nothing, but regarded Eleanor carefully for a moment longer, before picking up her own china cup. Eleanor let her gaze drift across the many beautiful flowers in her drawing room, appreciative of each one. It had been a wonderful welcome into society; that was for certain.

She smiled as she thought about the previous evening, remembering each and every dance partner. She had appreciated every one, although not every gentleman was to her particular taste. It had also been quite lovely to see her cousin again, and even more of a delight to learn that he was soon to be a father. All in all, her return to London was exactly what she had hoped.

And so, for the next sennight, Eleanor flung herself headlong into all that society offered, enjoying herself thoroughly. There were balls and musicals, parties and more, and, as a wealthy widow, she was almost always included on the guest lists.

However, as the sennight went on, she discovered that the same gentleman was almost always at her elbow, almost always desperate to seek her out for a dance. It was as though she could not escape him, and to her surprise, Eleanor found herself growing slightly wary of the man. She had thought that she might appreciate the man's kindness and attentions towards her, but it appeared that Miss Wiltshire's warnings had done their job.

"Is he still after you?" Miss Wiltshire asked, one morning, as they met together for tea in the drawing room.

Eleanor sighed and nodded, pouring the tea for them both. "I cannot take myself from him, no matter how hard I try." She glanced up at Miss Wiltshire and saw the sympathy on her face. "Have you discovered much about him?"

Miss Wiltshire shook her head. "No, I have not, although I understand he is not much liked."

"I wonder why that is," Eleanor murmured, lifting her cup to her lips.

In truth, Lord Thornley had become something of a thorn in

her side, and she found herself shirking from him whenever he drew near. Perhaps it was because he was too keen in his attentions, too desperate to be close to her. She found him cloying, as though he were a strong perfume that she simply could not rid herself of.

"I should be able to find out more in the coming weeks," Miss Wiltshire continued. "Being one of the newest additions to society means that not everyone is willing to discuss the gentlemen with me. Indeed, I have never found them to be as talkative as that first ball we attended."

Without warning, Eleanor found her thoughts going to Lord Armitage, remembering how delighted he had been to get her attentions. She had not seen him since, except for one previous occasion earlier that week, when she had spotted him from across the room. Their eyes had met for the briefest of moments before someone had stepped into their path, severing their connection. Then she had been caught up in the whirlwind of the ball and had quite forgotten that moment, only recalling it as Miss Wiltshire spoke.

"You had best be careful of him," Miss Wiltshire said, quietly.

Growing a little exasperated, Eleanor nodded, throwing her companion a slightly frustrated glance. "As I have said, on numerous occasions, I have no intention of wedding, Miss Wiltshire. Even Lord Thornley, as attentive as he is, holds nothing for me."

Miss Wiltshire smiled, although the glitter in her eyes did not quite disappear entirely. "I do think it best if you can manage to refuse him for whatever reason," she said, as though it were quite easy to excuse yourself from a gentleman's dance. "Let him see—and let society see—that you are not in the least bit enamored with him. Something about the way he looks at you disconcerts me."

"I shall," Eleanor promised, thinking that Miss Wiltshire's warnings were often on the very same tangent. "Please, do not worry yourself."

Miss Wiltshire's smile was a little more relaxed as Eleanor refilled both their china cups. "I must confess that I am looking forward to the next ball, for I have heard wonderful things about Lord and Lady Valliant's occasions."

"As have I," Eleanor said, with a smile. "I have heard it said that it is one of the most sought-after events of the Season. I am quite looking forward to it."

"And," Miss Wiltshire continued, as though she had not heard Eleanor. "It is said that Lady Valliant displays the jewels that were handed down to her from generation to generation. They are without price, it is said, and are guarded heavily."

"It is very kind of her to allow us to look upon them," Eleanor replied, holding back the urge to roll her eyes. "Or perhaps, it is very brave of her to do so."

Miss Wiltshire did not notice Eleanor's distaste, and chuckled, her eyes sparkling. "Indeed. Regardless, I am looking forward to seeing them. A necklace, bracelet, and other smaller pieces, I believe. They will be quite exquisite."

Eleanor looked to change the subject, thinking that there was nothing gaudier than displaying one's wealth in such a way, although she would not say such a thing to Miss Wiltshire for fear of offending her. No, she might not even look upon them, thinking that she would much prefer to spend her time dancing or enjoying conversation with her new acquaintances.

Silently, she wondered whether Lord Armitage might be there, aware that the invitations to the Valliant event were many and widespread. She wondered at the part of her that wished to see him again, although she told herself it was merely for sympathy's sake that she wished to see him once more. She might even dance with him in the seemingly vain attempt to encourage society to welcome him back into the fold.

A slight smile played about her lips as she thought of the upcoming ball. It would be a wonderful event; she was quite sure of it.

5

Henry smiled as Lady Brooke walked towards him, a wide smile of greeting on her face. His own heart lifted, although he would not betray such an emotion to the lady, thinking just how beautiful she looked.

"My dear Lady Brooke," he murmured, bowing and reaching for her hand. "May I say you look lovely this evening."

"You may," she said, her eyes alight with happiness. "It is good to see you again, Lord Armitage. I have missed your company these last two weeks."

Henry blinked, a little taken aback by her candor, which, from the expression on her face, had surprised her also. He pressed a brief kiss to the back of her gloved hand before releasing it, giving him a few seconds with which to think of a response.

"I must confess that society has not, as yet, welcomed me back as I had hoped," he said, by way of explanation for his absence. "Although I will say invitations have been a little more frequent these last few days."

"I am very glad to hear it," she said, warmly. "I have heard that the ton can be quite unforgiving, but I have been fortunate to never require forgiveness from them for any misdeeds." There was a twinkle in her eyes and a lift to her eyebrows that made him aware that she was, as yet, unaware of what he had done, but he shook his head in response.

"There will be a great many gossip mongers who will tell you the truth of it, and then even more, should you wish to hear it. In short, I disgraced myself by drinking far more than I should have and ended up in someone else's home..." His cheeks heated as he tried to finish the sentence, knowing that it was best she heard the truth from him and not the gossip which added heads and tails to the story. "And, unfortunately, in someone else's bed."

He saw her expression change and held his breath. This would be the moment that would decide the furthering of their acquaintance, for, if she decided to reject him—as well she might—then there could be no hope for him, no hope of even a friendship with her. His stomach tensed, and his palms began to sweat as she continued to regard him, her expression serious.

"Are you often inclined to drink?" she asked, softly. "Or had something driven you to it?"

He swallowed hard, knowing that he could not tell her the truth, that it had been the unrequited love in his heart for the lady before him that had pushed him to do what he should not. "Without going into the matter, yes, something I considered to be quite horrifying had pushed me towards White's. That was very uncharacteristic of my behavior, for I confess that I have no recollection of what I did or why. It was the most humiliating circumstance I could have ever found myself in, and not something that I ever intend to do again."

"I can see why you were pushed from society," she said, slowly, after regarding him for a few more moments, "but you will find that I am not as unforgiving as them." Her serious expression lightened just a little, a small smile on her face. "Thank you for telling me the truth."

Henry wanted to crumple at her feet; such was the relief he felt. He could hardly believe that she had heard the truth of his wrongdoings and had chosen to overlook them, to get to know the man he was now as opposed to who he had been back then. A huge sigh of relief left his lips, his shoulders slumping as he tried to smile back at her.

"I can tell you are not used to such a sentiment," she said, softly. "Ah, come now, sign my dance card, Lord Armitage. I can see a gentleman approach, and I would rather, without being indiscreet, have my attention entirely taken up."

Surprised at her request, but not unwilling, Henry took her proffered dance card and saw that there were only three slots remaining. "I shall sign my name to two if you will permit me?"

A slightly arrested look came over her face, as she looked just past his left shoulder. "How many dances remain, should you take two?"

"One," he replied, quietly. "But one cannot be so bad, for only one gentleman?"

She swallowed and looked back at him, her throat working for a moment. "I know this is terribly unorthodox, but might you sign your name to all three?" A blush stained her cheeks. "We shall ignore the third if you prefer, for I would not wish anyone to suspect—"

"I should be delighted," Henry interrupted, calmly signing his name on the third space. "Have no fear, Lady Brooke. I am more than delighted to come to your rescue."

He heard the sudden sigh from her lips, realizing that she was, truly, relieved by his action. He had just released her dance card when none other than Lord Thornley appeared by his side, giving him a hard glare before turning to Lady Brooke and bestowing on her a simpering smile.

Realizing that this was the gentleman Lady Brooke did not wish to dance with gave Henry the greatest amount of happiness, and he could not prevent himself from grinning in response to Thornley's glare, quite disconcerting the man.

"Ah, Lady Brooke," Thornley murmured, dropping his head for a moment. "You are looking positively regal this evening."

"I thank you, Lord Thornley," she said, curtsying briefly. "How are you this evening?"

"Very well, very well," he said, standing tall and completely ignoring Henry. "Although I come to solicit you for a dance, my dear lady. I cannot do without one."

Lady Brooke took on a stricken expression, her eyes widening slightly. "Oh, I am terribly sorry, Lord Thornley, but my card is full." She dangled it in front of his face for a moment, so that he could see she was telling the truth, but unable to read any of the names written there. "I shall be sorry to miss you."

Thornley bit his lip, his gaze turning angry. "I presume Lord Armitage has managed to procure a dance?" he asked, still refusing to look at Henry. "How unfortunate I was too late."

"Indeed," Lady Brooke replied quietly. "However, I am sure we shall meet again at another event very soon."

Thornley opened his mouth to continue the conversation, but Lady Brooke had stepped away, leaving only him and Henry standing together.

"What a shame," Henry commented drily. "She is quite a popular lady, I see. You shall have to be quicker next time, Thornley, particularly as we are almost three weeks into your allotted six."

Thoroughly aggravated, Thornley rounded on Henry, his eyes burning with rage. "You think that you can pull her from me just like that? You, who have a reputation so soiled that you can barely make an appearance with someone whispering about you?"

"Some members of society are ready to forgive a single trans-gression," Henry replied, mildly. "Lady Brooke is one of them. Your grasping fingers and whining tones will do nothing to win her, Thornley. Your failure is almost guaranteed."

Thornley took a step closer, looking as though he wanted to beat Henry where he stood. Henry held his ground, raising his chin and looking directly into Thornley's eyes, completely unafraid. The man was a coward, deep down, and Henry was not about to start showing fear, no matter what the man did.

"You will lose, Armitage," Thornley whispered, his words barely distinct as he spoke through his clenched teeth. "This lady, and your wealth, will be mine."

Henry wanted to say that even with paying Thornley three times as much as he owed was not about to render Henry a pauper, but chose wisely not to say anything of the sort. Aware that there were those around him beginning to listen to their conversation—which was not in the least surprising given Thornley's demeanor—Henry stepped away and inclined his head, before turning his back and walking away.

He walked blindly to the opposite end of the room, to where the wonderful display of the expensive jewels and beautiful pieces were displayed, courtesy of their hosts. He had no partic-ular wish to see them, but, given that it took him as far away from Thornley as possible, Henry felt himself almost driven there. His first dance with Lady Brooke was not for some time and, so, he allowed himself to linger there for a moment, hearing the excited chatter of those around him who thought the display wonderful.

Seeing a small arbor to his left, Henry chose to sit there quietly, observing the crowd and keeping most of his thoughts to himself. He was a little frustrated with Thornley's behavior, whilst being thoroughly delighted to have three dances with Lady Brooke—not that he could dance the three of course, for then that would show partiality, and he did not wish to do that to her, especially when he had only written his name there so that Thornley would not. He could hardly wait to have her in his arms once more, smiling delightedly to himself at the thought.

Hearing the music begin to strike up once more, he watched the crowd that surrounded the jewel display begin to disperse, leaving only a few wallflowers and older companions regarding them carefully. One, he noticed, lingered longer than the others, her eyes falling on the jewels only for her nose to wrinkle, as though a little put off by the display. She did not seem to be too old a companion either, and Henry wondered who she might belong to. She looked very familiar.

Out of the corner of his eye, he saw a footman step forward and ask the lady to leave, only for his gloved finger to take hold of one of the jewels and slip it into his pocket just as the lady turned away. Before Henry could react, the footman called out in horror, catching the attention of almost everyone present.

"One of the jewels has been stolen!" the footman called, his face a mask of horror. "Stop that lady!"

Henry launched himself to his feet at once, intending to grasp the footman's arm and pull the stone from his pocket—only to find himself swamped by the sudden crowd. The companion was now loudly protesting her innocence, whilst the footman stated that she had been the last one at the display and nothing had been missing since then. Their host, Lord Valliant, was blowing and blustering, whilst Lady Valliant suddenly swooned, causing the crowd to gasp as one.

Struggling to make his way through the crowd, Henry watched the footman melt away at the precise moment Lady Valliant fainted. He was a servant, after all, and servants were more than capable of being indiscreet and, in some cases, almost invisible. With horrified eyes, Henry saw the man bump directly into Lord Thornley, almost as though their passing knock together had been an accident, but the brief pause, and the nod of Thornley's head told him otherwise.

Rage burst through his soul as he heard Lady Brooke's voice, calling for a Miss Wiltshire. He realized, at once, exactly what Thornley had done, although why he had done it was yet to be seen. And he remembered the companion as Lady Brooke's, as she had joined them for supper at a previous occasion.

"I must speak to our host," he called, pushing himself through the crowd in desperation. "Please, Lord Valliant. I saw everything."

"This way, please," the older man roared, his eyes narrowing as they landed on Henry. "And do not let that woman get away."

"I am not trying to escape," said the older lady, almost primly, although her face was white with fright.

Henry took her arm and, with his head held high, followed Lord Valliant across the floor.

6

E leanor could not stop herself from shaking as she sat down next to Miss Wiltshire, one hand holding that of Miss Wiltshire's. At this point, she was entirely unsure as to what exactly had gone on, but anyone suspicious of Miss Wiltshire was quite in the wrong.

She glanced over at Lord Armitage and saw him glare fiercely at Lord Valliant, who was already pacing the floor. She remained silent, although everything in her wanted to shout about Miss Wiltshire's innocence, being quite sure that the lady could not have done anything untoward.

"Your name?"

Eleanor jumped as Lord Valliant spoke, realizing that he was directing his questions to her companion.

"Miss Wiltshire," the older lady replied calmly.

"She is my companion," Eleanor added, unable to keep silent.

Lord Valliant raised his brows. "And you are?"

"That is Lady Brooke," Lord Armitage interrupted, loudly, evidently angry over Lord Valliant's rude demeanor. "Widow of the Earl of Brooke."

Lord Valliant paused in his steps for a moment, regarding Eleanor with something like surprise. "My apologies," he murmured, after a moment, continuing his pacing. "I did not recognize you at first."

"Not at all," Eleanor replied coolly. "You have a great many guests, but that is hardly the issue at the moment."

"Indeed." Lord Valliant continued to pace, his eyes landing on Miss Wiltshire with almost every turn of the foot. "It appears you have stolen something of mine, Miss Wiltshire."

"I have not," Miss Wiltshire answered with only a faint trace of anger. "The footman who accused me is wrong."

Lord Valliant shook his head. "My staff is loyal to me, and I believe that you were the last one near the display of jewels before the ruby was seen to be missing."

There was a slight pause. "A ruby, you say?" Miss Wiltshire murmured, softly. "You see, my lord, I have not even the slightest knowledge about what jewel was taken, for, if I am to be truthful, I was not much enamored with the display."

Eleanor drew in a sharp breath, wondering if Miss Wiltshire's brutal honesty was not, perhaps, the best tactic for the situation. Lord Valliant seemed to swell in front of her eyes, his face growing red as he stopped pacing and glared at Miss Wiltshire.

"I can vouch for that," Lord Armitage interrupted, just as Lord Valliant began to bluster. "Miss Wiltshire did not touch a single piece on that table, Lord Valliant."

"Lord Armitage," Valliant sniffed, turning away. "What exactly were you doing watching the table, may I ask?"

Eleanor could see the anger that crossed Lord Armitage's expression as he saw the way Valliant dismissed him, evidently still holding his past indiscretions against him.

"I was taking a few moments to gather myself," Lord

Armitage responded, carefully. "And I saw your footman take the jewel before handing it to Lord Thornley."

A gasp left her mouth before she could stop it, her gloved finger covering her lips.

"I am sorry, Miss Wiltshire, Lady Brooke," Lord Armitage continued, ignoring Lord Valliant's snort of disbelief. "This is my fault."

"Your fault?" Miss Wiltshire echoed, sounding quite confused. "Whatever can you mean?"

Eleanor saw him frown, dropping his head into his hands for a moment before looking back up at them both, shaking his head. "There is too much to reveal at this precise moment, but Lord Thornley is looking to win you for himself, Lady Brooke. I do not like to admit that I may have riled him somewhat, even mocked him for his lack of success. He is now trying his best to force your hand."

"I cannot believe it," Eleanor found herself saying quietly. "What is it that Lord Thornley believes he can do to force my hand into matrimony?" The whole idea seemed quite impossible and, for a moment, Eleanor was quite lost in confusion.

"I believe that if he has the jewel, he will be able to return it whenever he pleases and clear Miss Wiltshire's name," Lord Armitage said slowly, evidently thinking hard. "If you do not wed him, then she will carry the shame of being accused of theft for the rest of her days."

"You are quite out of your head!" Lord Valliant exclaimed, just as Eleanor was about to reply. "Lord Thornley has nothing to do with this, and I am surprised that you would accuse another gentleman of high standing when he was nowhere near the display of jewels."

"I saw him with the footman," Lord Armitage said hotly. "You are making a mistake in accusing Lady Brooke's companion, Valliant."

Lord Valliant's mouth curled. "I do not think I am, Armitage. I know better than to believe anything from a man like you, whereas Thornley has nothing but an impeccable reputation."

"I made one mistake!" Lord Armitage retorted, throwing himself to his feet. "Grievous, yes, but that does not mean that every word from my mouth is a lie."

Eleanor got to her feet and cleared her throat, afraid that the men might start throwing punches at one another, should she not intervene. "Miss Wiltshire did not steal your ruby, Lord Valliant. To accuse her without cause is unfair."

"It is not without cause, Lady Brooke," Lord Valliant replied loudly. "The jewel is gone, and my footman saw her take it."

"I do not have it!" Miss Wiltshire exclaimed, her face now burning red. "I shall submit myself to a search if I have to in order to prove my innocence."

Lord Armitage nodded, throwing Eleanor a stiff smile, encouraging her to remain firm.

"Lord Valliant, you cannot accuse the lady on the word of a footman, however loyal he may be. You do her reputation no good by such falsehoods."

"Pah!" Lord Valliant cried, disregarding him immediately. "She is nothing more than a companion."

"Then this will damage Lady Brooke's reputation," Miss Wiltshire said, firmly, ignoring the slight entirely. "As I stated, I have not touched any of your jewels. Lady Brooke is a generous and kind soul, and I lack for nothing. I have no need of your ruby."

Eleanor held her breath as Lord Valliant paused, evidently thinking things through. He was upset over the loss of the jewel, although he had more than enough on the table as it was. But surely, he would listen to Lord Armitage, despite his reputation, aware that he could not easily accuse Miss Wiltshire when he had no evidence of her theft.

"I will look into the matter," Lord Valliant said, eventually.

"Then you will tell the ton that Miss Wiltshire did not steal it?" Eleanor asked, wishing she had made it sound more like a statement than a question. "You cannot surely—"

"I will say nothing of the sort," Lord Valliant interrupted, his eyes flashing. "I am nowhere near convinced that Miss Wiltshire is not the thief, despite Lord Armitage's 'evidence' to the contrary." He turned his face away and walked towards the door, ignoring them all.

"You cannot do such a thing," Eleanor protested, following after him at once. "Miss Wiltshire does not deserve to be condemned by the ton when she has done nothing wrong!"

"I shall state that the jewel is missing and that an investigation is underway," Lord Valliant said crisply. "Now, good day, Lady Brooke."

Eleanor watched helplessly as Lord Valliant opened the door, stepped through it, and began to address the assembled crowd.

She shut the door behind him, feeling like some kind of caged animal, for to leave now would have every eye on both her and Miss Wiltshire. She did not want that for her dear friend, not when she had already endured so much.

"I cannot believe he would continue to leave her culpability in question," Lord Armitage muttered as Eleanor came to sit next to her friend. "I am sorry I could not convince him otherwise."

"It is not your fault," Miss Wiltshire assured him, her voice hoarse with emotion. "My dear Eleanor, I do believe that it is best that I leave your side for a time."

"Whatever are you talking about?" Eleanor gasped, as Miss Wiltshire brushed a tear from her cheek. "I shall not be without you, Miss Wiltshire, so do not even ask me to consider it."

"But you must." Now that Lord Valliant had left, it appeared that Miss Wiltshire was unable to hide her true feelings any longer, her voice breaking as she spoke. "Your reputation will suffer needlessly should I remain in your house. It is best that I go elsewhere so that you will not be stained by the situation."

Eleanor shook her head, firmly, reaching to clasp Miss Wiltshire's hand. "I absolutely refuse your request, Miss Wiltshire. You are to stay with me, just as you ought. You are not in the least bit guilty, and I refuse to allow anyone to think so. If I were to turn you out, that would suggest that I believe you to have stolen the jewel, when you know I think precisely the opposite. No, do not ask it of me. You will remain just as you are, and we shall continue as we are. This is not your fault."

For a moment, Miss Wiltshire held her gaze, her eyes glistening with moisture, and Eleanor thought she might argue her point once more. Instead, the older lady sighed, her shoulders slumping.

"You are too good to me, Eleanor," she mumbled, shaking her head. "I cannot thank you for your kindness."

Eleanor smiled softly and squeezed her hand lightly. "You are my family," she replied softly, "as well as my friend. What sort of lady would I be if I did not show unwavering loyalty to those I love?"

Lord Armitage cleared his throat, interrupting them both.

"I will help you if I can. As I said, I believe Lord Thornley is behind this. I am quite sure that I saw him take the jewel from the footman. He has set things up in order to trap you into matrimony."

"I will not bend," Eleanor retorted, feeling heat rising into her cheeks. "I have no intention of marrying and certainly will not be manipulated into doing so." She was quite sure she saw a sudden flash of disappointment cross Lord Armitage's face as he got to his feet, but disregarded it almost immediately. Now was not the time to consider Lord Armitage. She had to consider what Miss Wiltshire was to do.

Lord Armitage walked to the window, his head bowed and hands linked behind his back. He was evidently deep in thought, considering the situation.

"You said that there was something between you and Lord Thornley," Eleanor said suddenly, remembering his previous statement in front of Lord Valliant. "What was it, may I ask?"

Lord Armitage turned back towards her, a guilt-stricken look on his face. "I very much hate to tell you this, but I have been engaged in a gamble with him."

"A gamble?" Eleanor repeated. "You mean, a bet?"

"Of sorts," Lord Armitage said, shaking his head. "Lord Thornley owes me a great deal of money, and, as he has not much to rub together, was unable to pay me. Therefore, he came up with a proposition which, much to my chagrin, I agreed to."

Miss Wiltshire raised her head, her emotions now evidently under control. "What was the bet about, may I ask?"

Lord Armitage cleared his throat again, with one finger tugging at his cravat. "Lord Thornley swore he could be betrothed by the end of six weeks and placed his debt on the table. Were he to succeed, then I would clear his debt and pay him some more in kind. If he were to fail, then his debt would increase."

A sickening feeling made Eleanor's stomach clench, her eyes staring at Lord Armitage as though not quite able to accept what it was he was saying.

"Unfortunately, Lord Thornley has decided that you are to be his conquest, Lady Brooke. I am terribly sorry."

7

E leanor felt as though all of her breath left her body in one fell swoop, her hand clutching her middle as she tried to draw breath.

"I may have mocked him for his lack of success," Lord Armitage continued, each word burning her soul. "And so, determined as he is to defeat me, he has chosen unscrupulous methods to attempt to win. As it stands, I shall speak to him at once and hand him back his vowels without question. I had no idea that he could be so despicable. In truth, in speaking to you of this, I have now some of my own fortune to give him. Had I thought he would do such a thing, I would have done as much beforehand."

Breathing hard, Eleanor clutched at Miss Wiltshire's hand, her stomach churning. So this was why Lord Thornley had been so attentive, why he had been so pushy. She had been a mere pawn in a gentleman's game, a trophy that Lord Thornley was intent on winning.

"I am sure you must think less of me now, knowing what I have done," Lord Armitage finished, sounding quite miserable. "But it is no less than I think of myself. I should have refused

Thornley the moment he suggested such a thing, but my frustrations with him pushed me to accept. I do beg your forgiveness."

There was too much to consider, too much to take in. Eleanor got to her feet a little unsteadily, Miss Wiltshire rising with her.

"We should return home," she said softly, suddenly unable to look at Lord Armitage. "Come, Miss Wiltshire."

"Please," Lord Armitage interrupted, coming closer to them. "Do not rush from me so. I know there is a great deal that has occurred this evening, but I cannot let you leave when you are both so affected."

Eleanor drew herself up to her full height and drew in a shaky breath, managing to look at him sternly. "I am quite able to take care of myself, Lord Armitage. I am well aware that the ton will be waiting to look us up and down as we emerge, but I will not shy away from that. Miss Wiltshire is entirely innocent, and I will not be treated as a mere stake at the card table. It is utterly despicable. Good evening, Lord Armitage."

Still clutching Miss Wiltshire's hand, Eleanor opened the door and walked swiftly along the corridor, ignoring the many stares that followed her. The music was still playing and dancing continuing below, but she could not help but hear the whispers of the many ladies present as she made her way towards the door.

"Ah, Lady Brooke."

Lord Thornley stepped into view, blocking her path completely. Eleanor wanted to slap him firmly across the face, but Miss Wiltshire placed her hand through Eleanor's arm, ensuring that she could not do such a thing.

"You are not leaving, I hope?"

"I am, Lord Thornley," Eleanor replied through tight lips. "Please excuse me."

"I shall call upon you tomorrow, of course," Lord Thornley

continued, as though he had not heard her. "There has been a great deal for you to endure this evening, and I should not wish to distress you further, but I believe that there are things we need to discuss."

"Discuss?" Eleanor's gaze shot to him, seeing the slight smirk on his face. "So, what Lord Armitage says is true, then?"

An ugly look crossed Lord Thornley's face, but he did not deny it.

"I have nothing to say to you, Lord Thornley," Eleanor whispered, her fingers itching to strike him. "You are not welcome at my home. Besides, I believe, having spoken to me of your game, the bet is now over."

His hand snaked out and caught her arm, dragging her closer to him, despite Miss Wiltshire's protests. "You would do well not to refuse me, Lady Brooke," he grated, his voice filled with malice. "I could bring the earth to shatter around you if you are not careful. I do not care for Lord Armitage's wealth. I want more than he has to offer. In short, I want your fortune. I want you, and I will have you."

"I will not be intimidated," Eleanor answered with more firmness than she felt. "Do not think that you can somehow threaten me, Lord Thornley. I care very little for my wealth. Even were I to give you half—which I am not inclined to do in the least—I would have more than enough to keep me in good comfort until my last days."

He did not, however, seem in the least bit put off. Still holding her tightly and ignoring Miss Wiltshire's protests, he glared at her. "You think that wealth is the only thing I can take away?" His eyes shot to Miss Wiltshire for a moment, before looking back at her. Her blood froze like ice in her veins. "I will win this wager by any means, Lady Brooke, and you will not prevent it. I will have the entirety of your wealth, and you will submit to me. Have no doubt of my success."

Releasing her, he stepped back and bowed elegantly, a bright smile on his face. "Until tomorrow, then."

Eleanor felt Miss Wiltshire almost drag her along towards the entrance, her limbs refusing to move without help. She was not quite sure what Lord Thornley meant, but his threats against Miss Wiltshire were clear. He would do whatever it took to win the wager, he had said, so she should not expect that this one threat over Miss Wiltshire's reputation was the only thing he would do. She could hardly believe that she was now in such a dire situation, having come to the ball that evening with such happiness.

"Come, Eleanor," she heard Miss Wiltshire say, pushing Eleanor's shawl around her shoulders. "Keep yourself calm until we are away from this place. Do not let anyone see that he has unsettled you—or that you are influenced by their whispers. Come now."

Eleanor was forced to give herself a slight shake, the glazed expression disappearing from her face as she focused on Miss Wiltshire and the approaching carriage. As usual, Miss Wiltshire was quite right. She could not allow the ton to see that she was flustered or ashamed. Holding her head high, she linked arms with Miss Wiltshire once more and walked down the steps to the awaiting carriage.

Once back in their townhouse, Eleanor let herself cry for a moment, as Miss Wiltshire went down below to fetch a tea tray for them both. The servants had all gone to bed, as Eleanor had instructed, and Miss Wiltshire seemed to understand her need to remain awake for some time yet, to go over all that had occurred.

Eleanor did not know what she was most upset about. There had been the terrible accusation against Miss Wiltshire, followed by the revelation that Lord Thornley and Lord Armitage were locked in a wager over her. Then, when she barely had time to take in what had happened, Lord Valliant had left the room without any promise of taking the suggestion of Miss Wiltshire's involvement in the missing jewel away, and then she had been forced to battle with Lord Thornley on their way out from the ball. Tears dripped from her cheeks as she leaned heavily against the wall, lifting her face to the ceiling in an attempt to stop the rivers that ran from her eyes.

She had not thought that Lord Armitage would be involved in any way with Lord Thornley, thinking him something of a kind and honorable gentleman despite his past behavior. Her cousin would not have introduced him to her if he had not been well regarded by him.

In truth, Eleanor had found herself missing his company over the last sennight, although she had surprised herself by telling him that exact thing. How devastating to see that he had been secretly hoping that Lord Thornley would fail in his address to her so that he might add to his wealth at Thornley's expense.

Miss Wiltshire would chide her, should she discover Eleanor's feelings, for had not Eleanor said, on more than one occasion, that she did not wish to marry? Now, it appeared as though she would have very little opportunity to find a suitable gentleman, even if she did want such a thing, for by now the ton would be whispering about her and Miss Wiltshire. Eleanor knew that, by standing by her companion, she would be both ridiculed and rejected by society until the jewel was returned and the blame put squarely on someone else's shoulders. Then the ton would welcome her back almost at once. She could almost hear the witterings of the ladies in her ears, promising her over and over that they had never even dreamed that Miss Wiltshire was the guilty party.

It was just the kind of sycophantic, insincere behavior that Eleanor despised. Wiping her cheeks with her fingers, she brushed the last of her tears away and set her jaw. It was time for her to be quite determined in her actions. She would show the ton, and Lord Thornley if she had to, that she was not about to be run over roughshod by them.

Sitting down beside the fire, Eleanor reflected for a moment on what Lord Thornley had whispered in her ear as he had grasped her arm so roughly. The trembling in her soul from that moment had not quite left her, for the threats he had made had shaken her utterly, although she had done her best not to show her fright. Whatever his reasons, he was quite determined to marry her and was doing everything in his power to do such a thing. Perhaps he had very little coin and could not afford to lose to Lord Armitage, but that did not mean that his lack of fortune was a burden she had to carry.

Biting her lip, Eleanor wondered how she could extract herself entirely from his grip so that he would leave both her and Miss Wiltshire alone. Of course, she could leave town entirely and return to the country, but then that would give the appearance of guilt, would it not? She did not want Miss Wilt-shire to have such an accusation hanging over her head for the remainder of her life. Miss Wiltshire was not particularly old and might yet marry should the right gentleman come along, but that chance was severely decreased by the accusation of theft. Eleanor shook her head to herself, knowing that she could not leave town without Miss Wiltshire's name being cleared. That meant that she would have to think of another way to remove herself from Lord Thornley's licentious intentions.

"I could offer him money," she murmured, unaware of Miss Wiltshire's presence. "More than he needs. Enough to restore his fortune."

"Are you talking of Lord Thornley?"

Jerking in her seat, Eleanor saw Miss Wiltshire studying her with a slight frown. "I apologize; I was lost in thought," Eleanor responded, trying to smile. "Yes, it was Thornley."

"You cannot simply offer him wealth, Eleanor," Miss Wiltshire said practically. "What is to stop him from keeping coming to you to ask for more and more and more, until you have nothing left to live on?"

Eleanor frowned, her heart slowly sinking in her chest. "I had not thought of that," she mumbled, pressing her fingers lightly against her temples. He would end up wealthy and she the pauper.

"He is not an honorable gentleman, Eleanor," Miss Wiltshire said, heavily. "I do not think you can offer him money without him resuming his threats each time he requires more."

"Then what can I do?" Eleanor asked, helplessly. "You saw how he spoke to me, how he grabbed my arm without caution. His threats are murderous, and I cannot think of how to stop him."

Miss Wiltshire nodded, her gaze drifting towards the fire for a moment. "You must speak to Lord Armitage," she said, her eyes now back on Eleanor's face. "Do not protest, my dear, for I know you do not wish to see him so soon, but I believe he might be our only ally. Perhaps he, who knows Thornley better than I, might know what to do. I think he might be our only hope."

8

U nfortunately for Lord Armitage, Eleanor was still not
particularly enamored with him when he came to
call the following afternoon, still quite despondent
and upset over all that had happened. She received him with a
cool demeanor and could tell from the way he could not quite
meet her eyes that he was more than a little ashamed of himself.

"I do thank you for coming to call on us," Miss Wiltshire said
warmly, as he sat down. "You are most kind."

"And yet, I believe, I am not truly welcome," Lord Armitage
murmured, shooting a glance at Eleanor. "Which is quite understandable, truly. I must beg your forgiveness once more, Lady
Brooke, for entering into such a ridiculous agreement with Lord
Thornley. I had no expectation that he would go to such lengths
to secure you."

Eleanor clasped her hands in her lap and sighed heavily, ice
shooting through her veins as she recalled how Lord Thornley had
grasped her arm so tightly, pinning her in place. "No, I am quite
sure you did not have the smallest expectation of his behavior," she
murmured, glancing at Miss Wiltshire and seeing her give a small
nod of agreement. "And I should not hold Lord Thornley's behavior

against you." She knew in her heart that it was true and saw the look of relief in his expression as he bowed his head to her for a moment.

"I will do everything I can to assist you, I swear it," he replied quietly. "If you will permit me, of course."

Eleanor wanted to refuse, to tell him that she could manage quite well without him, but the truth of the matter was that she could simply could not. She had tossed and turned almost all night trying to find a solution to their current predicament but had failed entirely.

"I believe we would both be grateful for your help, Lord Armitage," she replied, albeit with a small amount of reluctance. "I do not think we have any other particular acquaintances who would consider even calling upon us at this present time."

"You have seen the papers, then?"

A jolt hit her at his question, and she shook her head.

"It is best that you do not read them," he replied at once, seeing her abject curiosity. "They are more lies than truth, and Lord Valliant has done very little to suggest that Miss Wiltshire is not the main suspect, much to my frustration. It is all around town, of course."

"We have had a few invitations rescinded," Miss Wiltshire added, making Eleanor's eyebrows lift once more.

She had not known about this, but evidently, Miss Wiltshire had thought she had enough to deal with already.

"There might well be more," Lord Armitage said heavily. "Although some of the ladies and gentlemen who are too sensible to believe such gossip might yet continue to seek your company."

A scratch at the door announced the arrival of the tea tray, and Eleanor waited until the maid had set down the tea tray before continuing the conversation.

"Lord Thornley is to be one of those continuing to pursue

me," she said quietly. "He has not given up his intent to marry me, as you rightly suspected."

"Oh?" Lord Armitage gazed at her steadily, and Eleanor felt a deep reassurance settle over her. She could tell this man almost anything, and, in that regard, it was probably best that she did not hide any of what Lord Thornley had said to her.

"Lord Thornley threatened to do Miss Wiltshire harm if I do not agree to wed him," Eleanor said, slowly, hearing Miss Wiltshire's gasp of dismay. She had not revealed the entirety of what Thornley had said to her, which accounted for Miss Wiltshire's shock.

"I see," Lord Armitage replied, his expression one of horror. "And how did he come to make this threat?"

"I refused to allow him to call on me," Eleanor explained, her hands clenching in her lap. "I told him that I was aware of what he had done in regards to Miss Wiltshire, and I confess that I mentioned your name, Lord Armitage."

He shook his head at once. "No matter. I know he saw me when Lord Valliant was creating such a commotion."

A little relieved, Eleanor drew in a quick breath in an attempt to settle her anxiety before continuing. "As for Thornley, I told him that I was aware of what he had done in an attempt to force my hand, but that did not seem to sway him from his attempt. In short, he only increased the threat, so that I might know the extent he would be willing to go to in order to have me wed him."

"I can offer him the money I owe by breaking the agreement," Lord Armitage said slowly, but Eleanor shook her head.

"He will not have it," she replied, her voice wane. "He wants my entire fortune and to have me as his wife."

Miss Wiltshire began to serve the tea, although her hands shook somewhat. "I must go, Eleanor," she said, handing her a china cup and saucer. "If I am not present, then I cannot be used as a pawn in Thornley's game."

"No," Eleanor replied, firmly, aware of the lady's fright. "To send you away would only show the ton that I consider you quite capable of doing what you have been accused of, and I will not that allow that to happen, particularly when it could affect you for the rest of your life."

"And there is no guarantee that Thornley could not find you," Lord Armitage added, quietly. "Not to alarm you, but it appears that he is a man intent on getting what he wants. I do not think that retiring to the country is a solution."

"Nor is paying him off," Eleanor added hopelessly. "I had considered that, you see, but Miss Wiltshire reminded me that he might then use that to his advantage."

Lord Armitage nodded gravely. There was silence for a few minutes as the three of them sat together, considering what they might do.

Just then, the butler walked into the room, closing the door firmly behind him.

"A Lord Thornley, my lady?"

9

Before Eleanor could react, Lord Armitage got to his feet, holding one hand out to the butler.

"It is best he does not know I am here," he said, softly. "Where can I go?"

Eleanor widened her eyes for a moment, her mind refusing to find the answer he required. It was as though the knowledge of Lord Thornley's presence had stupefied her.

"Give us a moment, please," Miss Wiltshire said to the butler, getting to her feet and taking charge of the situation. "It is vital that Lord Thornley does not know Lord Armitage is here with us. Do you understand that?"

"Yes, of course," the butler replied, his normally blank face holding a modicum of curiosity. "Shall I wait for five minutes?"

"Five minutes," Miss Wiltshire confirmed, quickly turning to Eleanor as the butler left the room. "Now, Eleanor, you must quieten your anxiety and show Thornley no ounce of fear. He will feed upon it."

"Miss Wiltshire is quite right," Lord Armitage agreed, sounding a little urgent. "But I would not leave you both here alone with him. What room is next to this?"

Giving herself a slight shake, Eleanor pushed aside her feelings of worry and tried to think clearly. "There is a smaller morning room to the left," she said, quietly. "The door is just over there." She pointed across to the room to the other door that was adjacent to the one the butler had just closed, and Lord Armitage nodded, his gaze flickering towards Miss Wiltshire for a moment.

"I presume I can exit into the hallway from the morning room?" he asked, evidently worried about Thornley's presence. "I shall stand directly outside so that I can hear all. I do not want Thornley to hurt you."

"I will ask the butler to leave the door open slightly," Eleanor said, her voice a little softer than she intended. "You should hurry."

He paused for a moment, looking into her eyes and bringing her a reassurance that she had not expected. When he touched her arm, however, in a gesture of friendliness, she winced and sucked in a breath. His gentle touch made her bruised flesh scream, although she knew he did not intend to hurt her.

"Have you hurt yourself?" he asked, even though Eleanor wanted to urge him away. "Tell me that was not..."

He drifted off as Eleanor met his gaze, seeing the anger flash into his eyes almost at once.

"I should remain," he bit out, his expression now furious. "How dare he touch you!"

Eleanor shook her head and caught his hand, walking with him towards the door. "You must not," she responded, quietly. "It is best that he speaks freely, and he will not do so if you are present. He must believe us to be without friends, without hope. My courage is buoyed knowing you will be just a few steps away. Now hurry, please."

Dropping his hand and ignoring the warmth that was

burning its way towards her heart, Eleanor opened the door for him and waited for him to step into the other room.

"I will be just outside the door," he promised, his eyes still holding a lingering fury. "Thornley will not get away with this, Lady Brooke. I swear it."

Eleanor held his gaze for a moment longer, only to hear Miss Wiltshire hiss loudly. She quickly shut the door and half ran back to her chair, picking up her tea cup just as the door opened.

"Lord Thornley to see you, my lady," the butler said, quietly, just as Lord Thornley brushed past him and walked into the room, a look of gleeful delight on his face.

"I am delighted to see you both again," he said loudly, giving the impression that he was nothing other than a well-meaning gentleman. "And how are you both, after the ball yesterday evening?"

Eleanor rose to her feet and curtsied as she ought, seeing Miss Wiltshire's quick glance towards her as the butler made to leave.

"Keep the door open, will you?" she called, ignoring Thornley entirely. "The room has grown a little stuffy." She sat back down and tried to calm her frantically beating heart. She would do exactly as Miss Wiltshire had suggested and refuse to show Thornley any kind of fear.

"Leaving the door ajar, my dear?" Thornley asked, sounding surprised. "Anyone might think you were afraid of my company."

"Your company is unwelcome," Eleanor replied, crisply, lifting her chin. "As well you know."

"And yet, see how little that affects me," he said at once, sitting back in his chair. "Now, are you not about to ring for a fresh tea tray? And is your companion not going to leave us in peace?" He threw a withering glance towards Miss Wiltshire, who stiffened at once.

"Miss Wiltshire is not going anywhere," Eleanor retorted, as a spiral of anger began to grow in her chest. "This is not your home, and we are not your possessions. You cannot order us around as you please."

Thornley's grin only widened, his eyes running over her form and making her shrink inside.

"Ah, but you soon will be mine, Lady Brooke," he replied, silkily. "I have come with the intention of setting a wedding date."

Miss Wiltshire snorted, turning her face away from him. "A wedding date indeed. Lady Brooke will not marry you, not for anything."

"Oh, but I think she will," Lord Thornley said calmly, as though he had not just been badly insulted. "When someone's life is on the line, then what choice does she have?"

Eleanor's mind was working as fast as it could, trying to find any way to persuade Thornley that she would not do as he asked, her stomach rolling with growing nausea.

"You can try as hard as you like to find a way out, my dear," he continued, as if able to read her thoughts. "But I can assure you that there is none."

Trying to keep her head, Eleanor gripped the arms of her chair and settled her gaze on the odious man. "I do not understand why you are so desperate to wed me, Lord Thornley. Surely a marriage by force cannot be a happy one?"

He chuckled, and the hairs on the back of Eleanor's neck rose. "It shall be a happy one for me, my dear. Our wedding day will bring me great fortune."

"So that is it," Eleanor replied, disdainfully. "You have no wealth of your own, so you wish to claim mine."

Thornley shrugged, evidently uncaring. "I enjoy the card

table but, as you will no doubt hear, I am not particularly well favored by luck. Unfortunately, that means that any ladies of substance—in particular, heiresses—refuse to even acknowledge me. Thus, I am driven to seek another way to restore my fortunes."

His smile was disagreeable, and Eleanor felt her very soul shake within her. She could not see a way out.

Miss Wiltshire shook her head, her voice shrill. "You are a degenerate gambler and have lost the wealth you have. No wonder you can find no one to wed you."

Thornley reacted at once, getting to his feet and grasping Miss Wiltshire by the arm so forcefully that she was lifted bodily out of her chair.

"I do not want to hear another word from your mouth," he hissed, as he dragged her to the opposite end of the room. "You forget that you will soon be favored by my kindness and my kindness alone."

"After you have used me to get what you want," Miss Wiltshire said, her voice a little unsteady as Thornley released her arm.

"Precisely," Thornley retorted, bringing his face close to hers. "Now remain here whilst I continue to speak to my betrothed."

Eleanor could not help but tremble, seeing Miss Wiltshire's face paling as Thornley returned to his seat. She shook her head at Eleanor as if to say she was quite all right and not to continue to frustrate Lord Thornley, but Eleanor did not know what else to do. She gazed over Lord Thornley's shoulder, seeing a slight movement at the door. Lord Armitage appeared, his shoulder and head visible only as he looked over at her. His gaze was steady, although his jaw was set. Just looking at him gave her strength, and slowly, Eleanor's trembling diminished. She saw his eyes search for Miss Wiltshire, and, out of the corner of her eye, saw Miss Wiltshire give a tiny shake of her head, warning him not to enter. How brave she was.

"Now," Lord Thornley continued, firmly, his face now red with anger. "The banns are to be called this week and then two weeks hence. I shall make all the arrangements."

"I do not agree," Eleanor whispered, her vision blurring with a sudden sheen of tears which she blinked back hastily. "I will not marry you, Lord Thornley."

There was a brief pause.

"Yes, you will," he replied, his voice dangerously low. "You know what I will do if you continue to refuse." His eyes glanced over at Miss Wiltshire, who was staring back at him in utter defiance. "So, the banns are to be called this Sunday hence. I shall make an announcement in the paper tomorrow so that society shall know of our betrothal. They shall think me quite the brave soul, considering marrying a lady whose companion is nothing more than a common thief." His eyes took on something of wistful look, his mouth curving into a cruel smile. "How fortunate I am that Lord Armitage was so willing to take on my bet. Who knew that it would lead to this?"

Eleanor's blood ran cold, her entire body frozen in place as he reached for her hand, kissing it firmly. He lingered there for a long moment, looking over her as though she was a prize he knew he had already won. She refused to look at him, her hand dropping back into her lap as her skin prickled with fear. His gaze ran over her again and again until, finally, he appeared to have had enough.

"Indeed, I shall have a great deal of fun being married to you," he murmured, stepping away. "Prepare yourself, Lady Brooke. I have no intention of dying so soon after our wedding, as your first husband did. I believe I shall live a long life, and you shall be by my side almost every minute of it."

Eleanor did not see him leave, nor hear the door close

behind him. She felt as though she was spinning completely out of control, unable to stop herself from being used by Lord Thornley in whatever way he chose. A loud roar seemed to encircle her as invisible chains tightened around her chest. Once they were married, she would be, by law, his property, and he could treat her as he chose. The thought scared her more than anything.

Her hands were being chafed by two warm ones, and slowly, the buzzing in her ears decreased until she finally looked down at Lord Armitage, who was kneeling before her and gazing into her eyes with concern. Miss Wiltshire was standing next to him, murmuring quiet, soothing words.

An idea, albeit a ridiculous one, hit her full force.

"Lord Armitage," she whispered, grasping his hands. "You must marry me."

His hands loosened on hers, his expression shocked.

"It is the only way!" she exclaimed, looking up at Miss Wiltshire and seeing the astonishment on her face. "You must marry me, Lord Armitage. Before Lord Thornley does."

10

"Lord Armitage is here."

Eleanor rose at once, quickly tying her bonnet under her chin. It had been three days since her request to Lord Armitage, and, as yet, he had not given her an answer. He had declared that she was too overcome with shock to think clearly, although he had promised, at the very least, to consider the idea.

Miss Wiltshire shooed her out of the room, hurrying Eleanor along. At the very least, Miss Wiltshire had not thought the idea too preposterous, although she had not entirely agreed with Eleanor's plan. She had been quite put out for at least half an hour, after Lord Thornley had left, evidently more angry and upset than she was afraid. Eleanor was greatly in awe of Miss Wiltshire.

However, she thought that there might yet be another way to put Lord Thornley on the back foot, although, she confessed, she could not think of anything particular.

"Mayhap when I return, I shall be betrothed," Eleanor murmured, kissing Miss Wiltshire's cheek.

"You are already betrothed," Miss Wiltshire replied drily. "Or did you not read the papers this morning?"

Eleanor rolled her eyes and chuckled, glad that at least Miss Wiltshire could find some humor in the situation. "You know very well what I mean."

Miss Wiltshire smiled. "I do, but remember that you do not know Lord Armitage particularly well either. Take care, my dear, that you do not rush into something hasty."

Aware that Miss Wiltshire's advice was always well thought out, Eleanor nodded solemnly and promised she would be careful before walking to the front door.

Lord Armitage was standing waiting for her, although he seemed not to hear her approach, his eyes roving over the paintings in the hallway. It gave her a moment or two to study him, thinking to herself that he did cut quite a handsome figure. His light brown hair was neat, his outfit impeccable. He gave the impression of being quite the gentleman, and Eleanor felt a swirl of warmth in her belly.

"Ah, Lady Brooke," Lord Armitage exclaimed, his cheeks taking on a faint tinge of color as he realized he had not seen her approach. "I was just taking in the paintings you have displayed here. They are quite wonderful."

"My late husband's taste," Eleanor explained, smiling. "I do not know much about art, I confess, although I attempt to paint watercolors from time to time."

His green eyes turned back to hers, and Eleanor saw a warmth that she had not expected. Her smile grew as he offered her his arm and, taking it, they exited the house and walked down the steps to begin their walk.

"Hyde Park is some distance away," he said, after a moment. "Although perhaps it might be best if we continued our walk along the streets, given the hour."

Knowing he was talking about the fashionable hour, Eleanor

agreed at once. "Yes, of course. There are some shops nearby, and I do love to browse the bookshop when I have the time."

His smile was immediate. "In truth, Lady Brooke, so do I. I should be delighted to take you there."

"I just hope Lord Thornley does not see us," Eleanor said, softly. "His anger and vehemence can be quite frightening."

She felt Lord Armitage's arm tense under her hand.

"I never did ask you what he had done to hurt you," he said, quietly. "Your arm, I believe?"

Eleanor felt her face burn, for she had hoped he had forgotten about that. "It was only some bruises, Lord Armitage. Lord Thornley simply did not want me to leave his presence on the night of the ball."

"He should not have laid a finger on you," Lord Armitage replied, his voice harsh. "Nor on Miss Wiltshire. It is quite despicable that he would do such a thing."

"Then are you considering my proposal?" Eleanor asked, looking up at him. "Or have you thought of another way out?"

He paused in his steps and turned so that he might see her better. His expression was serious, his eyes grave, and Eleanor felt her heart sink into her toes. He was about to refuse her; she could tell.

"I have considered it," he said slowly, "and I must confess that, whilst I am more than willing to do what you ask, I am not sure that you would thank me for it."

"Oh, but I would!" Eleanor exclaimed, putting her hand on his arm. "You would be forever saving me from Lord Thornley."

"But you know very little about me," Lord Armitage protested. "I might be as bad as he, on closer acquaintance."

Eleanor shook her head, knowing that he could not be anything like the man. "I do not believe it, Lord Armitage. You are nothing like Lord Thornley."

"Even with my past behavior?"

Nodding, Eleanor put her hand on his arm. "I understand that everyone makes mistakes, Lord Armitage."

"And I have wronged you already," he replied, as though attempting to put her off the idea. "Had I not entered into this bet, then Lord Thornley would not have sought you." Shame crept into his features, his gaze averted from her.

Eleanor moved closer, ignoring those who passed by them in the street. "Lord Armitage, you are quite right that you bear some responsibility, but a man who is sorry for what he has done always seeks to make amends—just as you are doing. You have shown me that you are truly repentant and that you are willing to do anything you can to help myself and Miss Wiltshire. I cannot ask for more. I trust you, truly. I know you would make a fine husband, should you but accept."

"I want to accept," he replied, with a sudden fervor. "I have been dreaming of this for so long, but now to have it set before me in such a way..." He trailed off and turned away, beginning to resume his walk.

Eleanor stood for a moment, entirely stunned by what he had just, inadvertently, revealed. He had been dreaming of marrying her for a long time? For how long? It could not be the few weeks she had been in town, for that was barely long enough to make an acquaintance. So what was it he was speaking of?

Hurrying her steps to catch him, Eleanor saw him stop at the doorway to a shop, holding it open for her. Seeing it was a bookshop, she stepped inside, but refused to be put off from her questions. If that was what he hoped to achieve in taking her in here, he was about to be disappointed.

Grasping his arm, Eleanor walked purposefully through the shelves and tables filled with books, finding a quiet corner where she might be able to speak to him. Lord Armitage came without comment, evidently aware that he was not going to get away without explaining what he had meant.

Eleanor felt her breath catch in her chest as she studied him, seeing his suddenly awkward expression. What was it that he was hiding from her?

"You said you have been dreaming of marrying me for some time," she began, her voice barely louder than a whisper. "What did you mean by that? Our acquaintance has been only of a short duration."

He shook his head. "It was a slip of the tongue only. Please, let us forget about it; it is of no consequence."

Boldly, Eleanor put one gloved hand on his chest, her gaze steady. "I wish to know the truth, Lord Armitage."

He sighed heavily, briefly closing his eyes. Eleanor waited patiently for him to speak, completely determined to get the truth from him.

"You are quite right when you say our acquaintance has been of a short duration, but you perhaps do not recall seeing me prior to your return to London."

Heat rippled up her neck. "I have met you before?"

"We were never introduced," he said. "And you were not Lady Brooke then. I had every intention of being introduced to you, but my...my regard for you held me back."

He looked away, the stumble in his words telling her everything. He had some kind of affection for her from long before but had never had the courage to speak to her.

"I have always been something of a quiet man," he continued, still unable to look at her. "I was unnoticed by you, of course, which I do not hold against you by any means. However, when your engagement was announced, I left that shy man behind and did something quite rash."

Eleanor gasped her hand at her mouth.

Lord Armitage shook his head. "I can see that you understand what I mean. I am sorry for what I did, of course, but I was angry and frustrated with my own lack of action. When Lord Thornley told me that it was you who was the one he intended as his bride, I could not help but try to stop him." His eyes met hers, his expression somewhat relieved. "And now you know all, Lady Brooke. I am sorry for my part in your troubles."

Eleanor did not know what to say, the shock of what he had confessed freezing her limbs in place. Lord Armitage had held her in such a great affection for so long? It was almost unbelievable.

Without knowing exactly what she was doing, Eleanor gave in to the urge she felt and, standing on tiptoe, pressed her mouth to his. Heat seared her at once, but Lord Armitage pulled back almost immediately, his eyes wide as he stared down at her.

She continued to look at him for another moment, before his mouth came back to hers once more, no longer held back. His arms encircled her waist, as her own came to rest on his shoulders. There was something sweet in their kiss, feeling a sudden passion that she had never experienced before.

He broke it after a few more moments had passed, although his arms did not release her from his embrace. She smiled as he blinked furiously, clearly trying to work out whether what had occurred had, in fact, truly occurred.

"I believe you shall have to marry me now, Lord Armitage," she said, softly, stepping back from him.

A quiet chuckle came from him, his mouth finally curving into a smile. "I shall do my very best to be the kind of husband you deserve, Lady Brooke."

"Eleanor, please."

He gave her a half bow, his eyes alight with happiness. "Then you must call me Henry."

Eleanor could not help but smile, even though butterflies filled her stomach. Finally, she could see a way through the dark cloud that had settled around her ever since Lord Thornley's appearance in her life. There was a chance for love in her marriage, a chance for a family and for all she had ever hoped for.

"However, I cannot wed you, not when the banns are already being called."

"Then we shall elope," Eleanor replied, quickly. "Scotland is far away, but I would rather suffer a horrible few days in a carriage as opposed to standing up in church beside Thornley."

He nodded, but his expression was still grave. "However, none of this brings Miss Wiltshire's name into the clear. You might very well be saved from his grasp, but that does mean that Miss Wiltshire will continue to be regarded as a thief."

"Oh." Eleanor's happiness evaporated in a moment. "I had not thought of that."

Shame filled her as she realized how caught up she had been with her own difficulties, somehow managing to forget about Miss Wiltshire's predicament.

"I have a suggestion," Lord Armitage continued, making a sudden hope spark in her chest. "You must continue with the charade of going along with Thornley's suggestion."

"What?" Eleanor gasped, her entire being recoiling at the idea. "You cannot be serious."

"I am," he said with a slight smile. "Perhaps, it might even be best if you were to appear quietly acquiescing, so that he is not in the least bit suspicious when you search for the jewel."

Eleanor stared at him for a moment, confusion on her face. "Search for the jewel?" she repeated, still struggling to understand. "What can you mean?"

Henry sighed, his lips thinning. "As much as I hate to say it, I believe the only way to clear Miss Wiltshire's name from the theft of the jewel is to find it and, somehow, reveal to the rest of polite society that it was, in fact, him who took it from Lord Valliant."

"And I have to be the one to find it?" Eleanor continued, slowly, the idea already taking hold. "But then that will remove the need for me to marry if we are successful."

To her surprise, she felt a sudden spiral of disappointment at the idea and struggled to keep her emotions from showing on her face.

Henry cleared his throat, looking a little self-conscious. "Perhaps I should be hoping that we do not find the jewel, then," he commented with a wry smile. "Although, should we be successful, I will leave the decision about the future entirely in your hands. Now that I have laid bare my heart, I shall can no longer hide what I truly feel, nor do I want to. However, should you decide to remain unattached, as you currently are, then I shall accept your decision."

"It is not a decision I need to make now," Eleanor replied quickly, aware of how he was looking at her, a desperate hope shining in his eyes. "The most important thing is to find that ruby and clear Miss Wiltshire's name."

He nodded. "Quite." He smiled at her and touched her hand. "Shall we browse for a while? Or should you like to return?"

"I think I should like to browse," Eleanor said, feeling a lot more settled and contented than she had before. "Thank you, Henry. You have been most kind."

He did not reply, but nodded, before taking a few steps away to begin perusing the books. Eleanor followed at once, standing opposite him and trying to look at the titles in front of her.

However, whenever she looked up, she could not help but feel a thrill of delight to see him looking back at her. Her future was quite safe with Henry by her side. All she had to do was convince Lord Thornley that she was willing to go along with his plans with the sole intention of bringing him to ruin.

11

"You are going to save me a dance, I hope?"

Eleanor tried to smile and nod, but her mouth refused to move. Instead of a smile, she scowled up at Lord Thornley who was standing in front of her with a wide grin on his face.

"I think three should do it."

"What a shame," Eleanor answered, holding up her dance card. "I only have one dance remaining."

Lord Thornley's grin vanished at once, grasping the card so quickly that Eleanor's arm was almost pulled from its socket. He frowned angrily, his eyes piercing her as he looked at her again.

"You did this deliberately."

Eleanor lifted her chin a fraction. "I did no such thing, my lord. I cannot help if I am beset with gentlemen wishing for a dance with me—and when you are the last in line, can you really place the blame at my feet?"

"You will excuse yourself from these gentlemen," Thornley bit out, his face growing red with anger. "And you will dance with me."

Eleanor wrenched back her dance card with an effort. "No, I will not. It would be unseemly, and I am quite sure you wish your betrothed to be all propriety, do you not?"

He paused and took a step back. "You have decided to go along with this, then?"

Sighing, Eleanor let her gaze travel over Thornley's left shoulder, her own shoulders slumping as she took on the manner of one who had been defeated. "I can see that I must."

He snorted. "Your love for that companion of yours does you no credit, Eleanor, although it is much to my benefit, I can assure you. Most other ladies would have tossed her aside, but I knew that your compassionate heart would not allow you to do such a thing. It has been your downfall."

Biting her tongue, Eleanor stopped herself from shooting the harsh retort towards Lord Thornley, remembering what Henry had said. She must appear to be willing to wed him in order to save Miss Wiltshire's life.

"You will dine with me," Thornley continued, seemingly forgetting about the dances. "Miss Wiltshire is not welcome. I shall make it a dinner party so that you might show the ton just how much you care for me." He lifted one eyebrow, his gaze direct. "You will do nothing to embarrass me, Eleanor. I warn you now."

"I will do no such thing," Eleanor said, even though her stomach turned over at his words. "When is this dinner to be?"

"Three days' time," he said. "I must sort the details at once."

He left her side almost immediately, allowing Eleanor to breathe a sigh of relief. She did not want to go to the dinner party, but it appeared that she had very little choice. Besides, that might allow her the opportunity to search for the ruby, although she had very little idea about the layout of Thornley's property. The thought of searching his home had a trickle of

sweat making its way down her back, suddenly terrified about
what he might do should he catch her in the act.

"I believe it is my dance, Lady Brooke."

Henry's hand was on the small of her back as he smiled
down at her, although concern radiated from his features.

"Ah, yes," she mumbled, her breath coming a little easier as
she walked onto the floor with Henry. "I do apologize, I was a
little distracted."

"I saw Thornley talking with you," Henry replied quietly, as
they took their places. "I do hope you are all right?"

The concern in his eyes made her smile, the tension
draining away from her as they began to dance. "I am quite well,
I thank you. I somehow managed to distract him from his irritation over having been refused a dance."

"And how did you do that?"

Eleanor gave a wry smile. "I did as you suggested, and said I
was willing to acquiesce to his demands. He practically laughed
in my face, however, stating that my concern for Miss Wiltshire
was my weakest point."

"It is not," he said, firmly. "It is one of the most beautiful
character traits you have. I would not see you without it."

The warmth in his voice shot straight to her heart, making
her cheeks flush with pleasure. "I thank you," she murmured,
catching his gaze for a moment. "It appears I am to attend a
dinner in three days' time." She looked over his shoulder once
more, unable to keep his gaze any longer; such was the intensity
of his regard. "I shall try to find the jewel."

He nodded, his face a mixture of concern and relief. "I am
glad, but you must be careful. Remember, that if you find it, you
must simply leave it where it is."

She frowned, looking at him again. "Why is that?"

"He must not know that you have found it," he replied

quickly. "And if it was you who was to discover it, then he could easily claim that you had put it on his person, in order to lift the blame from Miss Wiltshire."

"Then how are we to reveal the truth of his guilt?" Eleanor asked, growing more confused by the moment.

Henry lifted one shoulder and smiled. "You will tell me, and together, we will think of something. Do not fear. The first hurdle is simply finding it, and that is to be difficult enough."

Eleanor nodded, a swirl of anxiety sudden rolling around her belly.

"You can do this, my dear," Henry murmured, evidently seeing her worry. "Do not allow your worry to show. You will defeat him, I promise you."

THREE DAYS LATER, and Eleanor found herself sitting amongst the other guests, trying her best to appear in good spirits. She had been given no opportunity to leave Lord Thornley's presence, and even over dinner, he had insisted that she be escorted by one of the maids to the retiring room. It was as though he suspected she might to attempt something untoward, fully aware that she knew he was the one who had taken the jewel and was, therefore, taking no chances. The men had only been at their port for a few minutes before joining the ladies in the drawing room, otherwise, she would have used the time to begin her search.

Lord Thornley smiled at her, his eyes dark, and Eleanor found that she simply could not smile back. His smile was snake-like, aware that he had her in his tight grip and that she was unable to wriggle free. As one of the ladies began to strike up a tune on the pianoforte, a few couples stood up to dance, and Eleanor saw Lord Thornley move towards her swiftly. Sick to the stomach of her sycophantic behavior, Eleanor quickly moved away, praying that another lady might prevent him from catching her.

"Eleanor."

His voice was loud, and Eleanor cringed on hearing him. She had no other choice but to turn and face him, seeing the way his eyes practically pinned her to the floor.

"Yes?"

"You will dance with me."

It was a statement, not a question.

"Alas, I cannot," Eleanor said, pressing a hand to her head. "A headache has come on unexpectedly."

His grip on her arm tightened. "Do not play with me, my dear," he bit out, his voice low and threatening. "You know what is expected."

"And I have done everything you have asked," Eleanor replied quietly, wrenching her arm away. "Do not push me, Lord Thornley."

He glared at her and was about to speak again, when Eleanor spotted a young Miss Blackthorn sitting alone, looking longingly at the other couples on the dance floor.

"I am quite sure that Miss Blackthorn will dance with you, however," she said, in a loud enough voice for the lady to hear her. "Can you see? She has no partner."

She lifted her chin and ignored the trembling in her soul, seeing how much he hated her for the manipulation. He could very easily hurt her, as he had done before, but certainly would not do so in public.

"I would be quite delighted," Miss Blackthorn interrupted, rising to her feet and giving Lord Thornley a questioning look.

"I have the headache, I am afraid," Eleanor said, shaking her head sadly. "In fact, I believe I might have to return home. I shall call my carriage."

"I should escort you," Lord Thornley replied, firmly, but Eleanor only laughed and shook her head.

"I would not pull you away from your guests," she answered, aware that he could not threaten her when Miss Blackthorn was present. She was playing a very risky game, but her future was at stake, and that was a greater threat than the anger on Lord Thornley's face.

"I shall call upon you in the morning," he said, his face now a mottled red as his jaw worked. "I do hope your feel better, my dear."

She nodded and smiled, waiting for him to escort Miss Blackthorn to where the other couples were waiting. Ignoring his glare as he glanced at her over his shoulder, Eleanor slipped from the room and drew in a deep breath. This was the only opportunity she was going to have, for she was quite sure Lord Thornley would not allow her to walk about his home unattended ever again. She had very little idea about the layout of Lord Thornley's home, but that would not put her off.

Walking to the front door, she asked for her carriage to be brought around and pulled her dark cloak snugly around her. The carriage did not take long to arrive and, once it was there, she quickly stepped inside. It was only when the carriage rounded the corner that she rapped on the roof and, once more, stepped out into the cold, dark night.

Eleanor's teeth chattered as she made her way to the back of Lord Thornley's home, more from nerves than the cold. The carriage was waiting for her still, and she could quite easily return to it and leave her pursuit, should she choose to. She could run to Henry and ask to flee to Scotland this very moment, and she was quite sure he would do as she asked, but then the face of Miss Wiltshire floated into her mind, and Eleanor knew she had to continue her quest.

"I will not let you down," she murmured to herself, as she opened the door to the servant's entrance and peered inside.

There was no sign of anyone.

Breathing quickly, Eleanor pulled her cloak's hood over her head, hoping it would provide her with some kind of cover. She kept to the shadows and crept up the old wooden staircase, wincing with every squeak and groan that came from them.

Once she reached the top, Eleanor found a corner in which to hide herself and attempted to calm her shallow breathing. She was quite terrified, aware that Lord Thornley could bring a great deal of punishment should he discover what it was she was doing.

Hopefully, he would be satisfied to learn that she had already left, although Eleanor knew he would still be angry over her refusal to dance. Drawing in one long breath after another, she looked about her and tried her best to think calmly. There were a great many rooms, although the hallway itself was sparsely furnished. She knew where the drawing room and dining room were, already able to hear distant sounds of music drifting towards her. That meant that the study was, most likely, another of the rooms along the hallway, whilst Lord Thornley's bedchamber would be upstairs. Eleanor scrunched up her nose at the thought of having to enter such a room, although she would not allow her distaste to put her off her task. Fear raced through her veins as she inched along the wall towards another room, her heart beating so loudly she was quite sure the sound was echoing along the hallway.

Turning the handle of the first door she came to, Eleanor stepped inside and looked about her. No one was within, although it was well lit by a great many tallow candles. It appeared to be Lord Thornley's study, although it was also sparsely decorated. Perhaps this was the proof of just how badly he fared in his gambling habits.

Eleanor did not really know where to begin her search, but made her way to the desk regardless, looking about her with sharp eyes. Biting her lip, she began to leaf through his papers, desperate to see a glint of red.

After a good few minutes, Eleanor had to admit to herself that the jewel was not there. Replacing everything as best as she could, she made her way to the door and, pulling it open just a little, listened hard. No footsteps and no echoing voices drew near her. Stepping out of the relative safety of the study, Eleanor moved quickly to the next room, attempting to be as quiet as possible.

As the hours passed, Eleanor's fear began to leave her. She was no longer afraid of being discovered, given that Lord Thornley seemed quite taken with his guests. His servants were not about either, having apparently already gone to bed— although Eleanor did wonder whether his staff was as scant as his belongings. Each room was in a poor state of decoration, although it was obvious he kept his dining room and drawing room in good order, for the sake of any guests that might call. It certainly had made her search easier, for she had been able to look in almost every nook and cranny although, as yet, had not found the ruby.

This meant that Eleanor was now forced to go to the one room she had been dreading—Lord Thornley's bedchamber. It was upstairs, and Eleanor had forced herself to ensure that every other room had been searched before she chose to enter it.

Lord Thornley did not appear to lock any of his rooms, much to her relief, although what he would do if he found her presence in his room did not bear thinking about. Her stomach rolling with a mixture of anxiety and revulsion, Eleanor took a breath and stepped inside.

The room was dark, save for the large fire burning in the grate. Eleanor took a few moments to ensure that no one else was present, before hurrying towards it, picking up a candle from the mantlepiece. The guests would soon be leaving, for it was already well past midnight, and she could not predict what Lord Thornley would do once they had gone. She had to make haste.

The room was as thinly decorated as the others, and Eleanor began her search quickly. The tallow candle gave her nothing more than a dim light, but, placing it on the side table, Eleanor looked through some papers sitting next to it, but found nothing. The chest of drawers to her left was her next target, but, again, she came up empty.

A sickening feeling began to rise in her chest, as she the dawning realization that she was not about to find the item began to take over her mind. If she did not find it, then, whilst her future with Henry might be secure, Miss Wiltshire would never be free from the disgrace hanging over her head. The thought made her quite sick.

"Help me to find it," she whispered, praying that she would discover where Lord Thornley had placed the red ruby. "It must be here, I know it must."

At that very moment, her eyes landed on a small box, hidden away at the back of one of the drawers. Eleanor drew in a sharp breath, wondering if her prayers had, suddenly, been answered. With a shaking hand, she lifted the box from its hiding place and, setting it down on the table, lifted the lid.

A bright red ruby lay, nestled there, making Eleanor's heart leap for joy in her chest. Picking it up, she held it in her hand, the source of all her trouble.

Remember to put it back.

Henry's words echoed in her mind, and, just as she was

about to do so, the sound of footsteps began to echo along the hallway.

Eleanor's mouth opened in a silent scream as she stood, frozen, for a moment. Then, placing the lid back on the box, she placed it back where it belonged and shoved the drawer closed. With no time to spare, Eleanor threw herself on the floor and scurried under Lord Thornley's bed, her heart pounding in her chest. It was only as the door opened and Lord Thornley made his way inside that Eleanor realized she still clutched the ruby.

12

"Whatever is a candle doing over there?"

Hearing the key turn in the lock, Eleanor placed her hand over her mouth and bit down on her finger, hard. She would not scream, no matter how much the fear coursing through her demanded release. The man was slurring, which meant he had drunk a substantial amount of liquor.

"That stupid maid," Lord Thornley muttered, blowing the candle out. "I shall see to her in the morning."

Hardly daring to breathe, Eleanor held onto the ruby tightly, glancing about her to ensure that she was, in fact, entirely hidden. Her cloak was tight about her, bringing warmth to her suddenly frozen limbs. What was she to do?

She had to wait.

The thought of leaving Lord Thornley's bedchamber brought a fresh frisson of fear to her heart, but it was not as though she could remain there until the morning. Her carriage was waiting along with the coachman and footmen. Although she had told them neither to ask questions nor to worry—with a hefty financial bonus for their silence and patience of course—they were bound to grow concerned her absence at some point.

Besides, leaving Lord Thornley's household in the morning light brought much more danger. She could easily be spotted by one of the servants, or even Lord Thornley himself were he an early riser. Eleanor held her breath as Lord Thornley climbed into bed, practically throwing himself onto the pillows. The bed creaked loudly, but, within minutes, loud snores emanated from his person.

Still, Eleanor did not move.

In fact, she waited for a prolonged amount of time before daring to move, hoping that Lord Thornley was, in fact, truly asleep, and not putting on some kind of act in an attempt to lure her from her hiding place.

He believes you left, she told herself, firmly, *beginning to move towards the edge of the bed. Now hurry!*

Giving herself something of a firm talking to, Eleanor continued to slide her way towards the foot of the bed, her slippers giving her a good enough grip to move without making a sound. Her breathing was quick and shallow, her entire body alive with tension. The ruby was still in her hand, and, despite what Henry had asked her, Eleanor knew she could not return it now. It was far too much of a risk. She would simply have to give it to Henry and beg him to help her think of a way to return it.

Thinking of Henry seemed to calm her, so Eleanor kept her thoughts fixed on him as she slowly pulled herself to her feet, grasping her cloak with one hand to hold it tightly over her dress. Lord Thornley's snores did not stop, and Eleanor crept towards the door, desperately hoping that he had left the key in the lock. To her very great relief, she felt the cool metal brush against her hand and, pressing herself against it so as to muffle the sound, turned it quickly.

The click of the key turning seemed as loud as a thunderbolt and, to Eleanor's horror, Lord Thornley's snores suddenly stopped. She kept herself facing the door, hoping her dark cloak would make her appear nothing more than a shadow as Lord Thornley tossed and turned in his bed. The seconds ticked by with an agonizing slowness as Eleanor waited for Lord Thornley to return to slumber.

Her shoulders slumped with relief as the sound met her ears once more. She turned the door handle, and it opened at once. Her brain screamed at her to slam it closed and run to her freedom, but she forced herself to move slowly and carefully until, finally, she stood on the other side of Lord Thornley's door.

She could not lock the bedchamber again, but perhaps he might believe that he had been too much in his cups to lock his door. Letting out a long breath of relief, Eleanor rested her head against the door for a moment, allowing her breathing to return to a more sedate pace.

Moving through the silent and dark house was no easy feat, but Eleanor took her time and managed to make her way back down the stairs and out of the servants' door. Racing across the gardens, she ignored the worried look on her coachman's face as he helped her inside, her limbs growing weak with relief.

"I know it is late, but I must go to see Lord Armitage," she said breathlessly, just as the coachman made to shut the door.

He nodded and did not say a single word of complaint, evidently aware that something serious was going on. As the carriage rolled away, Eleanor looked down at the ruby in her hand, her fingers slowly releasing their tight grip on the jewel. She had to hope that Henry would know what to do and that he would forgive her for calling on him at such a late hour.

Her heart was still pounded in her chest as Eleanor made her way up the steps towards Henry's townhouse, rapping quietly on the door so as not to use the knocker. Unfortunately, there was no answer and, now terrified that Lord Thornley might somehow appear at any moment, Eleanor was forced to lift the knocker and let it fall.

To her very great relief, the door opened, and Henry himself stood framed in the doorway, looking quite disheveled as though he had only just awoken. His shirt was untucked and open at the neck, with no cravat to be seen. His hair was tousled, and there were no shoes on his feet. Eleanor could not have been happier to see him.

"Goodness!" he exclaimed, staring at her as though she was some kind of apparition. "Eleanor?"

"Oh, thank goodness," Eleanor gasped, stepping forward and flinging her arms around him. He returned her embrace after a moment, and Eleanor found herself sobbing into his neck, the relief of what she had endured overwhelming her entirely.

"Come in," Henry murmured, his arms tightening around her waist. "Come now, you cannot stay outside on the step. Someone could see you."

Eleanor did not let him go. "It will simply add to the scandals that already surround me," she replied, with a hiccupping sob.

"Come," Henry said again, rubbing her back gently. "Please, come in."

Taking a deep breath, Eleanor steadied herself and turned to wave her carriage away, having already instructed them that she would get a hackney back home. She did not want her servants to have to wait any longer for her, given that she had already asked so much of them.

"I am so sorry to intrude on you like this," she said breathlessly, as the front door closed behind them both. "I know it is quite untoward and entirely inappropriate, but I had to see you."

"I have been worried about you," he admitted, running a hand through his hair and making it stick up even more. "Have you only just returned from Lord Thornley's dinner?"

"I have," Eleanor answered, taking off her cloak and handing it to him. "I...I could not do as you wished."

"Whatever do you mean?" he asked, hanging up her cloak.
Eleanor opened her hand and showed him the jewel within,
seeing him frown.

"I am sorry," she said, almost desperately. "He came into the
room just as I found it, and it was all I could do to not be
discovered."

He gazed at her for a moment, his face filled with concern. "I
cannot imagine what you have endured," he said, after a
moment, putting one arm around her waist and drawing her
into his chest. "You have done very well, my dear. Come now, if
you do not mind going to the kitchens, then I can attempt to
rustle up some tea and cake, if that will soothe your nerves?"

Eleanor breathed him in for a moment longer, her relief at
finally being safe in his arms and in his home calming her
entirely. He had been the one she had thought to run to, the one
she knew she could depend on. Just the thought of him had
been enough to calm her when she had been making her way
from Thornley's house. Her affection for this man was growing
steadily, and Eleanor knew she could not pretend she felt
nothing for him.

"You are quite wonderful, Henry," she murmured, finally
stepping back from him. "I cannot tell you how much I am in
your debt."

His eyes caught hers, the flickering candlelight seeming to
put an almost ethereal glow around him. Eleanor's breath
caught in her throat as Henry's fingers brushed her chin, the
gentle touch of his fingers sending a sweeping heat straight
through her.

She closed her eyes as his lips touched hers, the briefest of
kisses, but enough to make her heart come to a standstill for a
moment. When she opened her eyes once more, Henry was
smiling at her, his eyes alight with the deepest of emotions.

"Tea," he said, taking her hand in his. "And I insist that you tell me everything that has happened."

Eleanor followed at once, her whole being settled at being in Henry's presence once more. The ruby still lay, enclosed, in her palm, but with Henry's calm assurance that all would be well, Eleanor felt herself grow quiet once more.

The only question was, now that she had discovered the jewel, would they be able to find a way to lay the blame squarely at Thornley's feet? And, if they did, what would Eleanor choose to do? Would she continue to live as she had, with Miss Wiltshire as her companion? Or would she listen to her heart and choose to marry the man who was now making his way around the kitchen, attempting to make her a fresh pot of tea?

Eleanor smiled as he set down a tray in front of her, having absolutely no qualms over sitting at the servants' table. He touched her hand briefly, smiling at her in the candlelight.

"Have as much as you want," he said, indicating the tray filled with a variety of repasts. "And, when you are finished, tell me everything that has happened."

13

The following afternoon, Eleanor was seated quietly in the drawing room, awaiting the wrath of Lord Thornley that was soon to be upon her. She had no concern over his anger, however, knowing that Henry was soon to be arriving. Smiling gently to herself, Eleanor recalled how he had reassured her only a few hours earlier when she had been seated across from him at the servants' table.

"You were late arriving home last evening," Miss Wiltshire commented, not looking at Eleanor and, instead, focusing on her embroidery. "I do hope everything is all right?"

"Everything is perfectly fine," Eleanor said carefully. "Were you awake?"

"I was," Miss Wiltshire answered quietly. "You are my dearest friend, and I was worried about how Lord Thornley would treat you last evening."

Eleanor smiled. "You need not worry, my dear. Lord Armitage and I intend to come up with a plan that will prove your innocence and remove Lord Thornley from us forever."

Miss Wiltshire looked up with surprise. "Truly?"

"Truly," Eleanor replied, with a chuckle. "You see? You will have a life free of scandal very soon."

Her companion studied her carefully. "And Lord Armitage is to help you?"

"He is," Eleanor said, quietly. "He has suggested that, should things go awry, we might marry." She glanced at Miss Wiltshire, expecting her to be appalled at such a suggestion, given her previous comment, but to her surprise, her companion said nothing of the sort.

"Lord Armitage is a good man," Miss Wiltshire said quietly. "Despite his past indiscretions."

Well aware of the reasons behind Lord Armitage's imprudence, Eleanor felt her cheeks color. "Everyone makes mistakes, I suppose."

Miss Wiltshire nodded approvingly. "Quite. Despite that, he appears to be very helpful in our current predicament."

"You believe that he would not be a bad choice as regards a husband, then?"

A small smile appeared on Miss Wiltshire's face. "I thought you declared that you would not marry, Eleanor." She lifted one eyebrow and regarded Eleanor carefully.

Eleanor's cheeks, already warm, grew hot. "I had thought that I would not, for I swore that I would never marry again without having some kind of affection for the gentleman in question..."

"I see," Miss Wiltshire murmured, looking away from Eleanor. "Then I am quite glad for you, my dear."

"I shall not ask you to leave me, of course," Eleanor replied firmly. "You are to stay with me without question. I insist upon it."

Miss Wiltshire smiled, covering her look of relief. "Thank you."

"Although I am sure you might, one day, find such a man of

your own," Eleanor murmured quietly. "Once all of this business is over, you shall have no need to worry about carrying any kind of scandal with you."

Miss Wiltshire opened her mouth to reply, only for something of a loud commotion to catch her attention. The butler pushed through the door, his face drawn and angry—an expression Eleanor had never before seen on his face.

"Lord Thornley, my lady."

Before the words had left his mouth, Lord Thornley pushed past him and stormed into the room, his eyes glittering with malice. A sudden fear pushed into her heart, a fear that he had known of her presence last evening and had come for retribution.

"Eleanor," he gritted out, standing before her.

Eleanor lifted her eyes to meet his but did not stand. She had no need to show deference to him, not now. His end was nigh, although he did not know it.

"Lord Thornley," she murmured, indicating a seat next to her. "How good of you to come and see me today."

He glared at her.

"I trust you had a pleasant dinner last evening," Miss Wiltshire interrupted, as though drawing his attention to her presence.

Thorney spun on his heel and faced Miss Wiltshire. "It must have been something of a surprise to you that Eleanor returned so early." He lifted one eyebrow, as though demanding that she admit that Eleanor had not returned home as she had said.

Miss Wiltshire did not bat an eyelid, nor throw even the smallest glance towards Eleanor. "Indeed," she replied calmly. "I was abed, of course, but I admit that I did not close my eyes until I heard Eleanor's return."

"And I went straight to bed, of course," Eleanor continued quickly. "My headache has gone this morning, which is something of a relief." Well aware that she had not had the opportunity to explain to Miss Wiltshire the excuse she had given for her hasty departure, Eleanor shot her companion a glance and saw at once that her friend understood.

"You are dismissed, Miss Wiltshire," Lord Thornley demanded.

Miss Wiltshire's eyebrows rose, but she did not make a move to obey Thornley's words.

"I said," Thornley grated, his eyes now narrowed slits, "you are dismissed, Miss Wiltshire."

"I do not believe that is your place, my lord," Miss Wiltshire responded quietly, refusing to back down. "I shall remain here."

"I insist you remain, Miss Wiltshire," Eleanor added, getting to her feet and looking Lord Thornley straight in the eye. "We are not wed yet, Lord Thornley. Be careful."

"Who are you to threaten me?" he retorted, grasping her arm and dragging Eleanor forward. "Do you not remember what it is I hold over you? How dare you—"

"I suggest you unhand the lady."

Wrenching her arm from Thornley's grip, Eleanor watched as Henry walked into the room, his face filled with anger. His lips pressed tightly together as he waited for Thornley to step away from Eleanor, the whiteness around his mouth betraying just how furious he was.

Thornley's hands curled into fists. "How fortuitous that you are here, Armitage," he bit out, each word spiked with malice. "Come to save Lady Brooke, have you?"

"Lady Brooke can take care of herself without my intervention," Henry said, mildly. "But if my presence can stop you from using your strength against her, then I will always be by her side."

Lord Thornley laughed, a harsh sound emanating from his

lips. "Your time by her side grows short, my lord. She will be wed soon, and then what will you do?"

Eleanor watched as Henry pressed his lips even more firmly together, as though attempting to prevent himself from making a retort he might come to regret.

"I have come to tell you that you are to join me at Lord Whittaker's ball tomorrow evening," Thornley continued, turning to face Eleanor. "You have received an invitation, I think?"

"I have, but I have not yet replied."

"Then reply," he said, firmly. "I have also come to notify you that our wedding has drawn closer."

"Closer?" Eleanor repeated, feeling suddenly a little wane. "What do you mean?"

"I mean that our wedding date is now three days hence," Thornley said, his tone brooking no argument. "You are too flighty, too conniving, for me to wait much longer. Attempting to keep Lord Armitage as your hero and protector has only proven to me that you are best wed as soon as possible. Then you shall be mine and mine alone."

"You cannot be serious," Eleanor spluttered, suddenly aghast at the thought. "Our banns have not yet been called for the three required weeks."

"You will be amazed at what can be done when certain suggestions are made," Thornley murmured, his eyes running over the length of Eleanor's body. "The clergy would much rather a lady keep her respectability than lose it, especially when they are meant to be an example to the other young ladies in society."

Horrified, Eleanor stared at Thornley, her mind spinning with what he might have said to have managed such a thing.

"What did you say, Thornley?" Henry asked, his voice low and face now burning with ire.

Thornley chuckled mirthlessly and waved a hand, as though

it were not of any great concern. "You need not worry about that, Armitage, given that she is not your concern. I shall see you tomorrow, Eleanor." He moved closer, and Eleanor forced herself not to shrink back from him. "And should you even put a toe out of line, you will not know what has hit you. I warn you now."

Eleanor waited until the man had left the room before collapsing on the sofa behind her.

"Tea, I think," Miss Wiltshire said, practically getting to her feet. "I will fetch it myself, shall I?"

She did not wait to answer, but left the room, although the door remained slightly ajar. Henry was beside Eleanor at once, his hands chafing her cold ones.

"Are you all right? Has he hurt you?"

Eleanor shuddered. "That odious man, coming here to threaten me yet again." She looked up into Henry's face, suddenly overcome with fright. "I know I should not let his words get to me, but I cannot help it. What has he said, do you think?"

She saw the struggle on his face, clearly torn between telling her what he thought and the pain it might bring her. Pulling her hand from his grip, she captured his face between her two palms and looked into his face.

"Please," she whispered.

Henry sighed, catching her hand and pressing a kiss to her palm. "He will suggest you are with child, I believe."

"With child?" Eleanor repeated, her breath catching in her chest. "How dare he?"

"It is the only suggestion that might push the clergy into acting more swiftly," Henry said, softly. "I had not expected this."

Eleanor searched his face. "Then, shall we have to go to Scotland?" she asked, worried that their plan would no longer come to fruition.

He shook his head slowly. "No, I believe we can use the ball to our own ends."

"How?" she asked, suddenly desperate to see the way out. "How are we meant to have him pull out the missing jewel in front of all to see? It sounds quite impossible, especially when we have the ruby in our possession."

"I will think of something," he replied firmly. "Can you trust me, my dear Eleanor?"

She smiled then, despite her ongoing worry. "Of course I trust you, Henry. You should know that by now. You are the only one I could turn to at a time like this. Your unwavering commitment and dedication to me and to my cause has been almost overwhelming. I am quite grateful to you."

He smiled back, although it did not quite reach his eyes. "I hope you know that I still care for you as much as I ever have, Eleanor. You grow dearer to me every day."

Her heart warmed at his words, and without realizing what she was doing, Eleanor brought her hands back to his face and leaned in to kiss him. He responded at once, his arms encircling her waist as they sat together on the sofa, setting his mouth a little more firmly against hers.

Eleanor could almost feel the way he bridled his passions, holding them back firmly, so as not to overwhelm her. She let her hands fall to his shoulders, her fingers delving into his hair as he angled his head to deepen their kiss. Time slowed around them, as Eleanor's heart began to quicken with a passion she had never experienced before.

The sound of approaching footsteps broke them apart. Miss Wiltshire took her time to enter the room with the tea tray, giving Henry enough time to take his seat once more, although his gaze never left Eleanor.

"Come up with a plan, then, have we?" Miss Wiltshire asked, setting the tea tray down and giving Eleanor a look that told her

Miss Wiltshire was well aware Eleanor and Henry had not been talking. "The ball is tomorrow, so we must have something in mind."

"Are you to come, Miss Wiltshire?" Henry asked, his voice a little hoarse.

"Of course," Miss Wiltshire said firmly. "I am always at Eleanor's side, despite the rumors and scandal that insist on following me wherever I go."

"At least we have been invited," Eleanor murmured, well aware that her invitations to such events had been slightly sparse of late. "Unless Thornley insisted upon the invitation, which would not surprise me."

"And you still have the jewel?" Miss Wiltshire asked, directing her question at Henry.

He nodded. "Tomorrow, this whole situation will be over. Come now, let us put our heads together and come up with a plan. Together, I am sure we will find a way to reveal to the world who Thornley really is."

14

E leanor could not help but clutch Miss Wiltshire's hand as they entered the ballroom, joining the line to greet their hosts.

"You are shaking," Miss Wiltshire murmured, squeezing Eleanor's hand lightly. "Try not to be so afraid."

"This must work," Eleanor whispered, so as not to draw the attention of the other guests. "If it does not...then I shall have to run to Scotland with Henry, and you shall be left to forever carry the scandal of being a thief. The thought of you bearing that burden brings me such sorrow."

"And it would not be as bad as you imagine," Miss Wiltshire replied calmly. "I am but a companion, Eleanor, although I am glad to be yours, I must say." Her expression grew serious. "You cannot think that I should mind that burden too much."

Eleanor shook her head. "No, I cannot have that for you. You are not even ten years older than I, and might yet marry—but that opportunity will disappear entirely should this be left to ruin."

To her surprise, Miss Wiltshire's eyes filled with a sudden sheen of tears.

"I am sorry," Eleanor said, quickly. "I had not meant to upset you."

Miss Wiltshire smiled tightly and blinked back the moisture from her lashes. "You have not," she said, so quietly that Eleanor had to strain to hear her. "You have dreams for me that I will not allow myself to hold and, whilst that is kind of you, you cannot hold onto them. I come from a practically destitute family, with almost nothing to my name. It was only your good and kind heart that allowed me to retain something of my former status. I can hope for nothing more."

Eleanor shook her head. "No, Miss Wiltshire. What if there is a clergyman or the like looking for a wife? Once I am wed, you are to stay with me of course, but I do not want you to put off your own life to simply be by my side for the remainder of my years. A clergyman would do quite nicely for you, I am sure, but only if we can remove this scandal from your shoulders."

"I confess that I have never allowed myself to hope for as much," Miss Wiltshire said. "Neither has there been the time. Your marriage to your first husband was of such a short duration that I barely got my surroundings before we had to enter into our year of mourning. And now we have come to town, only to be faced with another strenuous situation."

"You see," Eleanor said, patting Miss Wiltshire's hand. "Once Henry and I are settled and back to the country, there will be ample time for you to find someone worthy of you. But that can only happen if there is not even a hint of scandal surrounding either myself or you. That is why this plan has to succeed."

Miss Wiltshire's expression grew somber, although there was a new light in her eyes, which Eleanor hoped meant that she finally was able to see the life she could have once all this was settled. It was Eleanor's dearest wish to see Miss Wiltshire happy, given just how good she had been to her.

"I am sure all will be well," Miss Wiltshire replied after a moment, regaining her usual firmness. "That Lord Armitage of yours is quite quick-witted and vastly intelligent. I am sure he has thought of everything."

Eleanor smiled at Miss Wiltshire's words but had no time to respond as she was next in line to greet their hosts. Thankfully, there was not much said, for their hosts were clearly eager to greet all their guests and then continue with their entertainments, so Eleanor and Miss Wiltshire were practically rushed through. Upon nearing the steps, Eleanor felt a wave of dizziness overtake her, aware of what must be done.

"Courage," Miss Wiltshire murmured, pressing the small of Eleanor's back. "Lord Armitage is here, as he said he would be. Just do what he said, and all will be well."

"Where are you going to sit?" Eleanor asked as they slowly made their way down the staircase that led to the ballroom floor. "Remember that Henry said that you must be seen at all times so that no one can say you were anywhere near Lord Thornley."

Miss Wiltshire nodded. "Yes, of course. I shall sit with the rest of the companions, but I believe I shall sit close to Miss Henstridge."

"Oh?"

Miss Wiltshire chuckled. "She is quite the chatterbox, but she is sure to keep my attention, and I will keep hers. There will be no suggestion that I have ever left my seat or that I have gone anywhere near Lord Thornley. Miss Henstridge might bring me something of a headache, but she will be, at least, a wonderful alibi."

Eleanor tried to laugh, but the sound stuck in her throat. She smiled, at least, as Miss Wiltshire walked over towards the other companions. Eleanor watched as she sat gracefully next to another woman, whom Eleanor guessed to be Miss Henstridge, given the way that she struck up a conversation with Miss Wiltshire almost immediately. Relieved that Miss Wiltshire was well placed, Eleanor continued her foray into the ballroom, aware of the many guests in attendance. Couples were already beginning to make their way onto the floor, so Eleanor chose to step to one side, close to the wall so that she might survey the proceedings. It was a dark and shadowy corner, giving her space from the other guests. Eleanor took the opportunity to gather herself, drawing in one long breath.

"Nervous?"

The voice in her ear made her jump, her skin prickling as she realized that it was Henry who stood behind her. Turning to glance at him, she saw that he was dressed almost all in black, save for his snowy white shirt and dark blue cravat.

"Keeping to the shadows, are we?" she murmured lightly, trying to stop the loud thumping of her heart.

He chuckled quietly, and Eleanor felt ripples of heat rush down the length of her body. He was so close to her, the urge to touch him, to be close to him, almost driving her to turn around right there and lean into his embrace.

"Put your hands behind your back," he said softly, and, as she did so, she felt a soft material touch her hands. Clasping it carefully, knowing that the ruby was within, she brought her hands around to the front once more before sending a cautious glance down towards her hands.

"I cannot hide it all in one hand," she whispered, urgently. "He will see it."

There was no answer, and, for a moment, Eleanor wondered if Henry had left.

"You will manage this, Eleanor," came his sudden, reassuring whisper. "I will take care of the rest."

Eleanor could not help but gasp as his lips brushed her neck, but when she turned to look, he was gone.

It took Eleanor a few minutes to collect herself, the weight of the ruby in her hand making her anxiety rise like a cresting wave. She had to, somehow, get this into her betrothed's pocket without him becoming aware of what she had done. Henry had suggested doing it while they danced, and had even rehearsed with her a few times, but she had not been as nervous then as she was now.

Thankfully her gloves were the same shade of cream as the kerchief, which hid it somewhat, but she was going to have to be very careful not to drop the item. At least she had been able to get the ruby into Henry's coat pocket without too much trouble, for the last thing she wanted was to have to attempt to place the ruby into Lord Thornley's breeches. Biting her lip, Eleanor took a breath and stepped forward, into the light, knowing that Lord Thornley would be looking for her.

She did not have to wait long. The man was by her side almost at once, his eyes narrowing as he glared at her.

"I have saved you three dances," Eleanor said, quickly, before he had a chance to open his mouth. "One being the supper dance."

His gaze narrowed. "Are you attempting to toy with me again, Eleanor?"

"No," she said, attempting to sound hurt. "You have given me fair warning. I do not wish for anyone to be hurt."

His eyes did not leave her, nor did they lower in their intensity. Eleanor bowed her head and let her hand grasp the ruby a little more tightly. He had to believe that she was afraid of him, afraid of his threats.

Thornley cleared his throat. "And when is our first dance to be?"

"Now, I believe," she replied, allowing her eyes to meet his with an almost meek look. "Should you wish to dance with me, that is."

He grasped her arm at once, giving her no choice but to be led across the floor. It was a possessive move, and one she was expecting, but the humiliation she felt hit her nonetheless. Glancing to her right, she saw Miss Wiltshire sitting next to Miss Henstridge still, although her eyes glistened with anger. Eleanor felt sweat trickle down her back as she took her place opposite Lord Thornley, relieved that it was not the waltz or another intimate dance. She curtsied, and soon was out on the floor, turning this way and that, only meeting Thornley now and again as the dance progressed. They very rarely held hands, and, given that the dance was something of a slow one, Eleanor could see no opportunity to place the ruby on him.

Unfortunately, one of the gentlemen in their set had already had too much to drink, which meant he swayed and stumbled, making Eleanor wrinkle her nose in distaste whenever she was partnered with him. He even belched at one point, before laughing uproariously. Praying that the dance would soon be over, Eleanor turned to face Lord Thornley once more, only for the drunk gentleman behind her to knock into her.

She was flung forward headlong, her free hand flailing. Thrown bodily into Thornley, she slammed straight into him, her breath knocked from her body.

"What do you think you are doing, Bartholomew?" Thornley roared, attempting to right himself and Eleanor. "Go sit down, man."

Eleanor, still a little dazed from what had occurred, blinked rapidly, only to remember what she was to do. Thornley's coat pocket was close to her, and, without hesitating, Eleanor pushed the ruby and the kerchief into his pocket, just as Thornley grasped her upper arms and pushed her away from himself.

"I am all right," Eleanor murmured, smoothing one hand over her hair.

Thornley scowled, making Eleanor aware that he had not actually asked her how she was.

"And you?" she asked, with every appearance of timidity.

His eyebrows furrowed together, his expression dark. "You have caused something of a display, Eleanor. This is not what I expect from my wife to be."

Eleanor opened her mouth to retort that it was not her fault, but closed it again with a snap. It would not do to argue with Thornley, not when she had managed to achieve her part of the task. She had to continue with her appearance of being on a tight rein.

"Perhaps I should sit down," she murmured, as Thornley continued to bluster. "I feel quite shaken."

Lord Thornley snorted in derision and turned away from her, marching across the floor. Eleanor made her own way back to the side of the ballroom, moving back towards the corner where she had initially hidden herself.

She was there for a few minutes, alone, trying to bring her breathing back to normal. The next part was up to Henry.

"It is done," she murmured, as he idly walked by her, giving her nothing more than a cursory glance. "Coat pocket."

He gave her the briefest of nods, his eyes smiling. The nightmare was almost over.

15

E leanor had to endure another dance with Thornley before Henry chose to enact the next part of his plan. In fact, she had to wait for a few hours before anything else happened. She had remained close to Miss Wiltshire when Lord Thornley did not require her company.

Given what scandal lay over Miss Wiltshire, very few members of society wished to talk to Eleanor, which she did not particularly mind. The ton was a changeable creature, and Eleanor was quite sure that, as soon as blame was lifted from Miss Wiltshire's shoulders, Eleanor would be welcomed back into society with open arms. It made her quite despondent at times, as she realized what it was like to be pushed aside by the ton. Everything she had once loved had lost its sheen, until Eleanor had begun to long for a quiet life back in the country—with Henry by her side, of course.

∽

HENRY, too, was thinking in much the same way. He admired Eleanor for her fortitude and for her love for Miss Wiltshire, hardly believing that she seemed so enamored with him. All that he had once hoped for, he was in touching distance of attaining. How blessed he was.

"Ah, Miss Blackthorn," Henry smiled, seeing the young lady in question rise to greet him. "I believe this is to be our dance."

Miss Blackthorn, whom Henry knew from a prior acquaintance, was a quiet sort of girl—more of a wallflower than a diamond of the first water, but pretty nonetheless. Eleanor had mentioned her previously, and Henry had hit upon an idea.

"I feel quite ready for this," Miss Blackthorn whispered as they walked towards the dance floor. "Although I admit that I feel as though I am a spy, involved in undercover espionage or the like."

Henry chuckled. "Nothing of the sort, but you will be clearing Miss Wiltshire's name, which I know Lady Brooke will be most grateful for. In fact, she has offered to assist you with the remainder of the Season, should you wish it."

Miss Blackthorn blinked, her eyes widening slightly. "I would be delighted to accept," she replied breathlessly. "Her kindness to me would not go unnoticed." She looked away, her cheeks pinking slightly. "As you may know, I am a little shy, which does not particularly enamor me to others."

Henry smiled and patted her hand. "Lady Brooke will be restored to society, and you will be her particular friend. You shall be wed very soon, I am quite sure of it."

Miss Blackthorn's cheeks grew red, which improved her appearance even further, as she took her place across from Henry. Feeling a little nervous, Henry gave her a reassuring nod, aware that Thornley was not only in his set but, in fact, very close to him. Eleanor was sitting beside Miss Wiltshire, who was in conversation with Miss Henstridge. It was all set up just as he had planned.

The dance began. Miss Blackthorn danced very well,

although Henry himself felt like a wooden puppet, so stiff were his motions. His nervousness increased with almost every second that passed, aware that Miss Blackthorn had to play her part perfectly so that Thornley would be revealed as the jewel thief.

Miss Blackthorn caught his gaze and gave the smallest of nods and, as Henry turned to face his next partner, he saw her cross the floor to where she was meant to meet her next partner, just as Thornley made to meet his. Miss Blackthorn stumbled, just as their paths crossed, letting out a sharp cry of pain.

"My ankle!"

Henry saw her go down in a flurry of skirts, whilst Thornley stared at her, apparently utterly confused about what had happened. That was Henry's cue.

"You trod on her foot, you big oaf!" Henry spluttered, giving him something of a hard shove as he walked towards where Miss Blackthorn sat. "You ridiculous lout. Apologize to the lady."

Henry saw the way Thornley glared at him, his face burning red almost immediately, but given that they were now surrounded by various ladies and other gentlemen, he had no choice. In addition, the orchestra had stopped playing so that Miss Blackthorn might be looked after.

"Here, lean on me," Henry murmured, as Miss Blackthorn managed to right herself, being helped to her feet by two other gentlemen. "I believe Thornley has something to say to you."

Thornley's jaw clenched, but he swept into a bow regardless.

"I do apologize," he muttered, clearly wanting to escape from this situation as soon as I could. "In truth, I do not know precisely what happened, but I am told it was of my doing."

"Can you not see the lady is crying in pain?" Henry blustered, quite amazed at the performance Miss Blackthorn was putting on. "Have you no handkerchief you can offer her?"

It was the moment he had been waiting for. Henry felt

Eleanor's eyes on him as Thornley began patting his pockets, eventually finding the handkerchief that Eleanor had placed there earlier, and, pulling it from his pocket with a flourish, handed it to Miss Blackthorn.

Something red, something sparkling, fell from the handkerchief onto the floor and, with a small sound, rested there, plain for all to see.

"What is that?" Miss Blackthorn asked, sounding quite innocent. "Lord Thornley? Is that yours?"

Henry tried desperately not to grin as Thornley's gaze fixed upon the jewel on the floor, the redness of his cheeks slowly beginning to fade.

"That is the missing ruby," said a lady from behind Henry's shoulder. "That is Lord Valliant's piece."

"No," Thornley interrupted, shaking his head. "No, it cannot be. That is not mine. Miss Wiltshire, she was the one who took it."

By now, a large crowd had assembled, and Henry could hear the sound of someone calling for Lord Valliant who, evidently, was present.

"Miss Wiltshire is sitting just over there, Thornley," Henry answered loudly. "Are you truly trying to place the blame on someone who has remained seated this entire evening?"

Thornley turned slowly, his face strained and filled with anger. "This was Eleanor's doing," he gritted out, drawing a gasp from the assembled crowd.

"Are you truly suggesting that your betrothed was somehow in on this scheme?" another gentleman asked, sounding horrified.

"You had better just admit it, Thornley," said another. "Some of us know just how badly you are in debt."

Henry felt a touch on his shoulder and knew it to be Eleanor. He whispered thanks to Miss Blackthorn as she was helped away by another gentleman before turning his gaze back towards Thornley. He knew from Thornley's expression that the man was fully aware that Henry and Eleanor were somehow behind this, but that he could not quite put the pieces together. It was just what Henry had hoped.

ELEANOR DREW IN A SWIFT BREATH, feigning astonishment even though happiness was filling her soul. "You took the ruby, Lord Thornley? And then tried to lay the blame at my dear companion's feet? Why would you do such a thing?"

Thornley snarled at her, his hands now forming fists. "This was your doing."

"How dare you!" Eleanor exclaimed at once, and, with a sound that reverberated around the hall, slapped Thornley's cheek which brought a gasp from the assembled crowd.

"Lord Valliant," said one of the gentlemen, who was holding the ruby. "Is this your missing piece?"

Eleanor held her breath instinctively, even though she knew that the jewel did belong to him. Thankfully, Lord Valliant did not take long to recognize it, turning his fierce stare onto Thornley.

"So, it was you," he said, angrily. "How dare you do such a thing?"

"I...I...," mumbled Thornley.

With a whirl of happiness threatening to burst through her chest, Eleanor stepped closer to Thornley who was, by now, an utter mess. He was stammering and stuttering, all bravado gone. There was nowhere he could lay the blame, no way he could get out of this current predicament.

"Our engagement is at an end, Lord Thornley," she said, loud enough for the crowd to hear. "I will not be married to a thief—

especially not one who tried to blame my dear companion, Miss
Wiltshire." Turning away from him, she began to walk away,
only to pause and look over her shoulder. "I shall never think of
you again," she finished, continuing to climb up the steps and
away from the ballroom.

Eleanor did not know where she was walking, only that she
wanted to find a quiet space where she might watch the
continued proceedings without interruption. She could hardly
believe that their nightmare was now at an end and that Miss
Wiltshire's name was clear of any scandal.

A hand suddenly grasped her wrist, and, with a yelp of
surprise, Eleanor found herself pulled into another room, the
door slammed shut behind her.

Hands grasped her shoulders and pressed her against the
wall, just as Henry's lips found hers. Eleanor responded at once,
digging her hands into his hair and returning his kiss with all
the passion and relief she felt. There was no one like her Henry.
No other man could compare to him. He had stood by her side
and helped her through the mire, bringing her safely to the
other side. How long he had loved her. If she had known even a
fraction of what he had felt at the time, how differently her life
might have turned out. However, at least now, they were
together.

"My love for you continues to burn," Henry murmured
against her mouth as he drew in ragged breaths. "I cannot live
without you, Eleanor."

"And finally, I am free of Lord Thornley," Eleanor responded,
looking into his eyes as he moved slightly away from her. "I do
not believe there is any need for us to go to Scotland."

She saw the swift kick of disappointment in his eyes, and,
needing to reassure him at once, laughed softly. "All I meant,
Henry, is that we might be wed here in town, instead of traveling
to Scotland."

Hope flared in his eyes. "You are willing to marry me, then? To become my wife?"

"Henry," Eleanor murmured, letting her fingers run down his cheek. "How can you think that I would not wish to share my life with you? Can you not see how much I feel?" She brought her mouth to his again, but kissed him lightly and sweetly, laughing softly at the sigh that escaped from his lips.

"I did not love my first husband," she continued, remembering the shock it had been to find out she was engaged to him. "And I came to believe that marriage was simply something I would have to endure."

"Not with me," he said, catching her hands and holding them tightly. "You know how much I love you. Our lives together will be something to be enjoyed, with love as our guiding anchor."

Eleanor smiled, the future spread out before her as a bright, shining path. "I swear I will love you for the rest of my days, Henry. You are the best man I know."

Henry wrapped his arms around her, holding her tightly in his embrace. Eleanor sighed happily to herself, feeling the chains that Thornley had held fall free from around her. Finally, she was to be happy, wed to a man she loved. A man who had loved her, even before she had known his name. Her Henry.

EPILOGUE

Eleanor hummed to herself as she walked outside, her face tilted towards the sunshine. It was a beautiful day and she could think of nothing better than taking a walk outdoors in the fresh air.

The air was crisp and clean, and Eleanor drew in a long breath, smiling to herself. How much things had changed in these last few months.

Wandering through the flower-covered gardens, Eleanor thought back to the day she had read of her engagement to Lord Armitage in the society papers. It had brought a rush of pleasure, seeing her name next to his, knowing that they were to be wed soon. She had spent almost every day in his company, growing more and more excited by the day.

Their wedding day had come and she had made her vows before God, knowing that the love she had in her heart for this man was only going to grow as they spent their years together. Henry had made his vows to her, his eyes practically glowing with love, their hands clasped together as the clergyman pronounced them man and wife. She had hardly been able to believe it had finally happened, almost overwhelmed with happiness and delight.

After their honeymoon, Henry had asked Eleanor where she most wished to reside, aware that she found a great deal of delight in town. However, Eleanor had declared that she had quite enough of town for the moment and so, much to Henry's delight, they had come to live in his country estate and had spent a wonderful eight months residing there together. Henry had shown her what it meant to be loved by a man, a man who cherished and loved her for who she was instead of treating her like a possession, like a duty that needed to be fulfilled. It was an entirely new experience and one that Eleanor was beginning to treasure.

"Eleanor!"

Hearing the sound of her husband's voice, Eleanor turned at once and saw Henry walking towards her, a broad smile on his face. He caught her hands and kissed her, hard, as though he had not seen her in a great many days when, in reality, they had awoken together in the same bed only a few hours earlier.

Breathless, Eleanor broke away from him, laughing. "Have you missed me, Henry?"

He chuckled, pressing his lips to her cheek. "More than you know." His hand rubbed across the soft swell of her belly. "And how is our daughter today?"

"Our daughter?" Eleanor asked, lifting one eyebrow. "I thought you were quite convinced it was to be a boy."

Henry shook his head, his eyes dancing as the baby kicked under his hand. "No, I think it is a determined little girl, who shall be just as beautiful and just as intelligent as her mother."

Eleanor's expression softened. "You should not mind if it is not a boy?"

"Mind?" he exclaimed, his eyes widening. "No, indeed. We shall have a great number of children, I am quite sure, but even if they are all girls, I shall be the happiest man in all of England —especially if they all turn out to be like you."

Eleanor could not help but kiss him again, her hands framing his face. "You are always so good to me, Henry."

He smiled at her and linked her arm through his, before walking through the gardens with her again. "Now, would you like to hear my news?"

"News?" Eleanor asked, surprised. "Yes, indeed."

"It is about Miss Wiltshire."

Eleanor stopped at once, looking at him in astonishment. "Miss Wiltshire?" she asked, wondering what this had to do with her cousin. "Whatever is the matter?" Miss Wiltshire had continued to live with them, just as Eleanor had promised, although she did see less of the lady than she once had.

Miss Wiltshire had found two ladies in the nearest village who had a small dress shop that they ran together and had found both company and usefulness there. She often walked there to spend time with them and Eleanor was glad for her, for she had been worried that Miss Wiltshire would feel a little lonely in the changed circumstances.

"It seems Miss Wiltshire has been seen in the vicar's company of late," Henry said, a broad smile on his face.

"Yes, I knew of that," Eleanor replied, not quite understanding the reason for her husband's good humor. "That cannot be of note, surely."

"Ah, but I had the pleasure of the vicar's company this morning. It appears he and Miss Wiltshire make something of a good match."

Again, Eleanor stopped in her tracks, dropping her husband's arm and staring up at him. Her heart beat frantically in her chest, as a burst of happiness exploded in her heart. "You mean, he wishes to marry her?"

Henry nodded. "He came to seek my permission, although I

told him that was not required." He tucked a stray strand of hair behind Eleanor's ear, letting his fingers run down her cheekbone. "Do you think she will accept?"

Eleanor could hardly speak for joy, thrilled that her friend would soon have a home of her own. "I know she will!" she exclaimed, catching Henry's hand. "She has confessed to me that she thinks him a most amiable man."

Chuckling, Henry shook his head. "It is just as you predicted, Eleanor. Did you not say that she would find a worthy clergyman to be her husband?"

"I believe I did," Eleanor laughed, recalling her words. "I am truly glad for her. Everything we went through with Lord Thornley and his dishonorable plans was worth it."

"More than worth it," Henry murmured, his eyes darkening just a fraction. "I do not think I have ever loved you as much as I do today, Eleanor."

Her expression softened, her heart filled with gladness as she reached for her husband again. "And I love you more with each passing day, Henry," she murmured, before reaching up to kiss him once more.

∾

THE END

A DUKE FOR CHRISTMAS

By Joyce Alec

1

L ondon 1838
Charles, Marquess of Sutherland, eldest son to the Duke of Harve, gazed indolently out of his study window, finding life a little dull, to say the least.

"You must marry, and soon," his mother continued, harping on as she had done on more than one occasion. "You are the eldest son, Charles. It is necessary for you to produce the heir to the dukedom."

"Yes, Mama," Charles sighed, ignoring her as best he could, his thoughts wandering as his mother continued her diatribe. This was not the first time his mother had said such a thing, nor was it the first time she had sought to put pressure on him. The truth was that Charles had no inclination to wed, and certainly not to any young lady that his mother thought was suitable.

"You know your father is aging, as am I," the duchess continued, heaping on the emotional weight even further. "We would delight in seeing a grandchild or two."

Having had enough of the discussion, Charles rose to his feet and shook his head. "Mama, we have talked about this repeatedly. You and father are in the most perfect of health and have many years ahead of you, I am sure. I have no desire to wed so soon, and certainly not to anyone you consider to be a good match. Should I find someone to marry, it will be of my own choice."

His mother let out a sigh of exasperation. "You are too stubborn for your own good, Charles."

"I am more than aware of my foibles, mother," he replied calmly. "You have been so kind as to remind me of them on many occasions."

"Then what are you planning to do?" she exclaimed, getting to her feet. "You are not about to go back to the country again, are you?"

Charles chuckled. "Mama, as much as you despise it, yes, I am going to do just as you suspect. London has become boring of late, and I confess to missing my horses."

"But you cannot just up and leave," she cried, now looking horrified. "We have invitations we have already accepted. Should you suddenly disappear, you will appear rude, Charles."

Very aware that his mother had, more than likely, set up the engagements, Charles sighed. "And yet, I find nothing to keep me here. I am going to my country estate and shall spend a fortnight riding, hunting, and whatever else I feel inclined to do. I shall return at the end of the two weeks however, I assure you."

"A fortnight?" the duchess screeched, her expression dire. "You will miss far too many social events, Charles. I cannot allow you to go."

"Unfortunately, Mama, you cannot prevent me," Charles replied in a soothing tone. "I promise I shall return for Christmas Eve, have no doubt about that. Father will have returned from his business in Scotland by then, will he not? You may then impress upon me any women who have not yet been snapped up by the other gentlemen of the ton." He pressed his hand to the small of his mother's back and, enduring her screeches for a little longer, led her towards the door. Charles was forced to listen to her angry speeches for a few minutes more—at the front door no less—before finally, she took her leave and he was left alone.

He thought about returning to his study to go over a few financial matters, but after his mother's reproof, he found he could not focus on business matters. How much he longed to go out riding across the wild grasses of his country estate. It was simply not the same in London. The town was thick with people and animals, and the only freedom he could have was if he rose at the crack of dawn and took a mount to Hyde Park.

Charles longed for the quietness of the country, for the wind in his hair and the rain on his face. It was not that London did not hold other pleasures—for Charles had often imbibed in those—but, over time, even those grew stale. It was time to return home for a short while, although he had promised his mother to return to London for Christmas Eve.

Pouring himself a snifter of brandy in the drawing room, Charles allowed the amber liquid to run around the bottom of the glass for a few moments before taking a sip. What he had not told his mother was that there was a house party planned— a quiet one, of course—made up of three gentlemen and four ladies. He did not have an in-depth knowledge of all those who had been invited, having relied on two of his closest friends to supply him with those who would be good company.

As the memory of his mother's words began to fade away, Charles sighed happily to himself and refilled his brandy glass. This was bound to be an enjoyable fortnight. Many blessings came with being the son of a duke, for not many people could challenge any or all of his behavior.

Not that he made his flirtations and liaisons too obvious, for that would bring too much unwanted attention, but ladies keen for his considerations were not exactly in short supply. Wealthy widows were of particular interest, for they had no wish to marry again and were happy and settled with their own fortunes.

"And Mother thinks I would be interested in matrimony," he muttered, shaking his head to himself. What a fool he would be to give up the life he had now for only one woman. A wife required too much of him and, at the moment, he was not prepared to give what would be asked. No, he would continue to enjoy himself for some years to come until he had to give in to what his birthright duties entailed. Surely by that time, he would have had his fill of this world's pleasures.

Returning to his country estate would give him more than a little respite from his mother's constant haranguing, particularly when both of his parents preferred to spend their time in town these days. Some years ago, his father had bequeathed him a small estate of his own, and Charles had made that his hiding place, a place where he could go to get away from his parents and his responsibilities to wed and produce children. Just being there would be a relief in itself.

A scratch at the door alerted him to the butler's presence and, on being called to enter, the butler opened the door and announced Lord Walton.

"Walton!" Charles exclaimed as his friend walked in. "You are a little early. We are not to leave until tomorrow morning."

"Good afternoon, Sutherland," came the muttered response.

To his surprise, Walton did not look in the least bit happy.

"Whatever is the matter?" Charles asked, frowning. "You look down in the mouth."

Walton sighed and threw himself into a chair. "My father has given me a warning."

"A warning?" Charles repeated, pouring himself a fresh brandy after giving Walton a glass. "What warning is that?"

"I am to stop harassing the governess."

Charles paused for a moment before allowing a slight chuckle to escape. "Walton, surely you were not doing such a thing?"

"I could not help it!" Walton exclaimed. "Is it my fault that my father insists on hiring such a pretty young thing to teach my half brothers and sisters?"

Charles shook his head and sat down opposite his friend. "You are incorrigible, Walton."

"She welcomed the attention," Walton grumbled, throwing back his snifter. "But apparently my attentions were too obvious to my father, and he worried about a possible scandal."

"She did not complain about you, did she?" Charles exclaimed, surprised.

Walton shook his head. "No, of course not. My father actually walked into the room where I was attempting to steal a few kisses."

A rush of anger flooded Charles for a moment, but he kept his temper and simply shrugged. "Walton, you should not be doing such a thing."

"Why not?" Walton whined, getting up to pour himself another brandy. "She was in the household, and I could not help but see her pretty face everywhere I went."

Knowing that Walton had, most likely, sought the governess out, Charles could not agree with him. Walton, being the son of an earl, also had nobility and credence, but he was much too pushy with his desire for a lady's attentions. He went places that Charles would never dream about.

"I know how you feel about governesses and the like," Walton sighed, sitting back down. "But she is not a servant, Sutherland. She is a governess."

"That does not make a difference, Walton," Charles replied firmly. "I would not go near a servant nor a governess, for you know that by your very actions, you could be putting her liveli-hood at risk. It is thoughtless, do you not think?"

Walton studied him for a moment, but did not say anything, merely grunting before turning his attentions back towards his brandy.

"So, what warning has your father issued you, then?"

A growl of complaint left Walton's mouth. "I am to stop pursuing the governess, or any of the pretty maids, and if I do not, then my name shall be rubbed from his will."

Surprised, Charles lifted his eyebrows in astonishment. That was a weighty punishment for something that many gentlemen would see as a trivial matter.

"Apparently, he shares the same opinion as you do," Walton muttered, shaking his head. "Although where you get your deep respect for the lower classes is quite beyond me."

Charles chose not to answer, knowing that Walton would not understand the reasons for his respect.

The truth was, Charles had been blessed with a wonderful governess, albeit a rather unusual one. He had never understood it until he was older, his mother being the one to explain the tale.

Charles' uncle by marriage had taken on the governess—a Miss Docherty—for his own two children, but, finding her beau-tiful, had chosen to press his attentions on her forcibly. It soon was evident that the man had managed to plant a babe in her belly and, according to Charles' mother, her request for his help and support with the child had been brushed aside. The poor woman had been thrown from the house almost the moment Charles' aunt had discovered what had happened. Almost completely destitute, Miss Docherty had made her way to the only other person she thought might help her—the Duke of Harve.

It had been a bold move, but one that had proven to be for

the good of all. The duke had visited his brother-in-law and sister on more than one occasion, and Miss Docherty, aware of where his estate was, had made her way there. She had been weak by the time she had arrived, and Charles' father had not had the heart to discard her.

Charles could still remember the pain on his mother's face as she had talked about how tired and ill Miss Docherty had been. It was just like his mother to show such compassion, and, despite the scandal it might cause, the governess had been taken in and given a position within the household.

"For what fault was it of hers that your uncle would do such a thing?" his mother had said on more than one occasion.

Charles had found that he could not argue.

Miss Docherty had been turned out to be a quiet and kind governess, despite the pain she had gone through, and Charles had come to adore her. The baby had been born six months after the governess had arrived, and Charles could still remember the way he had looked down at the small bundle with wide eyes, not sure what he was seeing.

As an only child, he had come to love that baby, finding Isabella to be a friend and companion as they had grown up together, even with the gap of five years between them. His father had even kept him back from Eton until he was thirteen so that the happiness in their household might continue for a few more years. Of course, Charles had required additional tutors as well as his governess' lessons, but his father had not appeared to mind. Apparently, harmony and happiness in his household was of the greatest importance to him, as well as the fact that being a duke meant he could do as he pleased, without caring a jot for what the beau monde might think.

Leaving for Eton had been difficult. He could still recall how Isabella had wept countless tears, clinging to him as though she would never let him go. She had been eight years of age, and her best friend in all the world was leaving for Eton. Of course, that meant that there was no requirement for Miss Docherty to remain in the household, and Charles had been concerned about what would happen to her.

His father had bequeathed Miss Docherty with a living, and she had left the duke's household with her daughter, settling in the distant north of England somewhere. Of course, Charles had corresponded with his dear friend Isabella for some time—until the delights of life in Eton and all the new experiences that came with it began to eat away at his interest in corresponding with her.

Her letters were still frequent for weeks, maybe even months, but slowly, they began to lessen until none came at all. Charles barely thought of her now, although he did look back on that part of his life with a pleasant outlook. He was sure Isabella and her mother were happily settled somewhere, and he would be eternally grateful for all that he had learned from his dear governess. That was where his respect for governesses and those within his employ came from—not that Walton would ever understand.

"Just leave that governess alone, Walton," Charles sighed, shaking his head at his friend. "I promise you will have more than enough to distract you once we are returned to the country."

Interest lit up Walton's eyes at once. "Truly?"

Chuckling, Charles nodded. "Of course, Walton. Just swear to me you will not lay a finger on that governess."

Satisfied to see his friend nod, Charles drank the rest of his brandy and sat back with a sigh. This was going to be an excellent two weeks; he was sure of it.

2

C harles flung open the door to his house, managing to startle the butler who had been trying to reach the door before Charles to open it for him. Charles, however, had been more than a little eager to reach his country estate and had practically run from his horse towards the house.

"No, no, no apologies needed, Mr. Stubbs," Charles chuckled, as the butler began to stutter. "It is good to be home." His eyes roved around the hallway, appreciating the festive touches his staff had put around his house. "I can see you have been busy."

"It is good to have you back, my lord," the butler said, recovering his composure. "Everything is ready for you."

"Thank you," Charles replied, handing him his coat, hat, and gloves. "My guests should be arriving this evening, although Lord Walton is with me."

The butler nodded, as efficient as ever. "Everything is ready for you, my lord."

"Wonderful," Charles exclaimed, walking towards the drawing room. "I shall have luncheon in the drawing room, I think. A couple of trays will do us well."

The butler nodded and welcomed in Walton, who had been a few minutes behind Charles. He looked harassed at having to ride so quickly, still muttering about wishing they could have taken the carriage on a cold day like this.

"Come now," Charles laughed as they entered the drawing room. "You cannot be that cold."

"I am frozen to the bone," Walton replied, walking straight over to the roaring fire and holding out his hands to the flames. "We have been riding all day."

Charles shrugged. His estate was the best part of two days' ride away from London, and they had changed horses a good number of times, given how cold it had been. The inn they had stayed at had been comfortable and warm, but Charles had been so eager to return home that he had barely slept, rousing Walton in the early hours of the morning.

"The other guests are arriving this evening?"

Charles nodded. "In time for a lively dinner, I hope." Just the thought of it had him smiling. "And then the festivities shall begin."

That, at the very least, made Walton smile. "I do hope you will not keep the ladies all to yourself, Sutherland," he warned, lifting one eyebrow.

"I cannot imagine what you mean," Charles replied a little airily.

Walton snorted and shook his head, finally moving back a little from the fire. "You are in line to be a duke. Some of us do not hold as noble a title." He chuckled. "Ladies seem to be more inclined to press their attentions onto men who hold titles such as yours, as opposed to titles such as mine."

"I am not particularly interested in any ladies who are seeking matrimony, as well you know," Charles replied firmly. "The ladies who will be attending my house party are not interested in it either. You will be at ease, I assure you."

A look of relief flashed across Lord Walton's face, making Charles chuckle.

"I am glad to hear it," he replied quietly. "I find that I am already looking forward to the arrival of the other guests."

THE REMAINDER of the house party guests arrived later that evening, and, having sat down to dinner, Charles allowed himself to look over the party. He had Lady Fitzgerald to his left, who was sitting next to Lord Walton. Lord Walton was already in discussion with Lady Worthing, and then, next to him, came Lord Smythe and Lady Swift. Lord Hollington was the last gentleman, and then, finally, Lady Marchfield.

Charles was acquainted with them all, although not particularly well, but he considered that he had a very fine party present with him. The ladies were all of independent means, having been widowed only a few years into their marriages to very wealthy men. The gentlemen were all unattached, but, from what Charles knew, none of them wished to be. Propriety could be dispensed with for the next two weeks, and Charles was determined to enjoy himself.

"Port?" one of the gentlemen called as the final course was cleared away. "And shall the ladies excuse themselves to the drawing room?"

The ladies rose as one and excused themselves, making Charles chuckle. He was sure that by the end of the week, the gentlemen would not be as keen to have their port alone without the pleasure of the ladies' company. Lady Marchfield pressed her fingers lightly on his shoulder as she passed, the tips of her fingers brushing the hair at the nape of his neck.

"I do hope you will not all be too long," she murmured softly, making Charles' skin prickle with anticipation. "For we cannot dance without gentlemen."

Charles could not help but turn and watch the lady leave, thinking that Lady Marchfield was a lovely creature, despite the thinly veiled arrogance that she carried with her. It came with being a very rich, independent lady who could do what she liked, whenever she liked, without question. Shrugging inwardly, Charles thought that he could easily put that foible aside for the fortnight he was to spend in her company.

The port had only just been served when the butler appeared by his side, looking apologetic.

"What is it, Mr. Stubbs?" Charles sighed, a little frustrated at having been interrupted already when he had only just opened his port. "And can it not wait?"

"I have tried to get her from the house, but she is very insistent," Mr. Stubbs replied, sounding agitated. "I must beg your pardon, my lord, for such an interruption, but she threatened to find you herself if I did not allow her an audience with you."

Thoroughly confused as to who this particular lady might be, Charles sat up a little straighter in his chair and lifted one eyebrow as he regarded his butler. "Of whom are you talking, Mr. Stubbs?" he asked, growing more and more exasperated. "What lady?" For a moment, he wondered with horror as to whether or not this could be his mother demanding an audience, having chased him from London.

"She would not give me her name," the butler said, quietly, shaking his head. "She insisted that you are old friends and that you would receive her once you saw her."

Charles frowned, glancing at the covered drapes. "How did she arrive?" The weather had been somewhat wild that evening, and the darkness would have been thick around the roads.

The butler shook his head. "I do not know. The lady is quite sodden and is dripping all over the floor in the hall. I would not have let her in, of course, but as soon as I opened the door, she stepped inside without a moment's hesitation." Wringing his hands, Mr. Stubbs dropped his gaze to the ground. "I am sorry to have failed you, my lord, when I know you are busy."

Realizing that he was not about to escape from this situation, Charles sighed heavily and pushed his chair away from the table. "The front hall, you say?" he asked, and, seeing the butler nod, dismissed him at once.

"Gentlemen," he began, drawing the attention of his friends. "I must beg you to excuse me for a time. Please, go to the drawing room whenever you wish, and I shall join you there. I do not expect to be long." He bowed, ignoring the chuckles from the gentlemen, and made his way to the door, hiding his frustration long enough to reach the quiet corridor.

His steps were smart and quick, the sound of his footsteps echoing around the hallway as he made his way down the staircase and towards the front door. A frown crossed his face as he made his way towards the figure standing at his door, seeing the small rivers coming from her. Her dress was wet through, her hair hanging around her face. All in all, she made a bedraggled figure.

"Charles!"

The lady practically threw herself at him as he drew nearer, her arms around his neck as she clung to him, sobs shaking her small frame. Her wet clothing began to seep moisture into his own shirt and breeches, and, still having no earthly idea who the lady was, Charles was forced to lift her arms from his neck and step away.

"What is the meaning of this?" he asked, brusquely. "Who are you? What are you doing here?"

The relief on the lady's face died away at once, replaced with a look of hurt and pain. "Do you not remember me, Charles?"

"No," he said, firmly. "I do not. Pray, who are you?"

She reached out and touched his arm, her eyes filling with tears and her body racked with a sudden shudder from the cold. "I am Isabella," she said quietly, her teeth beginning to chatter. "Isabella Docherty. My mother was once your governess."

3

I sabella Docherty had been living, contentedly, in a small cottage by the sea. Her mother had passed away some years ago, which had been an exceedingly difficult time for Isabella, for she had no other family to speak of. Knowing that she had not come about through an act of love, Isabella had no reason to reach out to her father—not that her father would even want to see her.

Her mother had shuddered on occasion when the subject had been raised and had told Isabella that she should never try to find the man responsible. For a long time, she never knew the identity of her father. Although, she did eventually learn his name from a family friend.

Isabella had come to understand that her mother had been forced into relations with the man with whom she worked for, and being suitably horrified at the thought, had never brought the subject to light again. She could not imagine what kind of man would do that to a lady, filled with disgust that she had been the product of such a disgraceful act.

Her mother, on seeing this, had assured her time and time again that she was very much wanted, very much loved, and was the only good thing that had come from a despicable act. That had reassured Isabella in her youth, and in her growing years, she and her mother had spent many happy times together.

That had now all come to an end.

One day, on returning from her daily walk to the forest to collect herbs and fruits to add to her dinner table, she had found a lady at her door. It had been an older lady, one she did not recognize.

Isabella had tried to be gracious and kind, welcoming the stranger as she would anyone who came to her door, wondering whether or not the lady was in need of help.

As it turned out, she did not.

The lady had a servant with her, a man who was at least a head taller than Isabella, and much stronger. The man had held Isabella fast whilst the lady had gone into Isabella's home and had destroyed almost everything within. Isabella had cried and screamed, begging to know why the lady was doing such a thing, but had received no answer.

Her heart had torn as each item broke, even the curtains she had sewn with her mother being ripped apart. The lady had marched from the house with a satisfied smile on her face and had proceeded to pick up a large stick and beat Isabella with it until she was too dazed to stand. Then, and only then, had the man released her, and she had fallen to the grassy earth. The man had then set her home alight, leaving the lady to crow over Isabella as though she had won some great victory.

"Your mother should never have been allowed such a blessing," the lady had sneered in her ear. "I would have had her stand here to see this, were she alive, but it has taken me years to discover your whereabouts." She had then grabbed Isabella's hair and wrenched her head backward so that Isabella was forced to look into her face. "You are a bastard and do not deserve to live," she had whispered, her fingers twisting Isabella's hair cruelly. "You are a stain."

Then, she had spat in Isabella's face, turned on her heel, and left. The servant had not even glanced at Isabella, apparently at ease with what he had helped the lady to achieve.

Isabella had been left destitute. Yes, she had a small allowance, but even that had to be used carefully, and she only had a few coins in her pocket at the present time and no easy way to fetch more. It was twice yearly that she made her way to town to receive more of her funds, and what she had at that time was certainly not enough to allow her to rebuild her home. The cottage was decimated, with only the stone walls remaining. Nothing was left.

Weak and in pain, Isabella had dragged herself to the nearest town, where the townsfolk had been shocked to see her in such a state. Since Isabella and her mother had lived in the same place for a number of years, the townsfolk had become her friends and acquaintances and were only too willing to help her.

One of her dear friends, the old lady Withers, had taken Isabella into her home and tended to her wounds, feeding her broth and bread, even though Isabella knew she did not have much food of her own. After a sennight, Isabella had felt well enough to travel and, even though the townsfolk had begged her to stay, she had no other option but to go to town to beg for some of next year's funds. Whether she would receive them, she could not say, feeling quite disillusioned.

It turned out just as she had thought. The solicitor had refused to give her an advance and certainly had not believed a word of what she had told him about her home. The way he had sniffed at her and looked away told her that he thought very little of her, perhaps believing that she spent her money on things such as liquor or expensive dresses. Lost and entirely without hope, she had only one idea left.

She had to turn to the man who had been so kind to give her mother a home and an allowance in the first place, the Duke of Harve. The solicitor had not been keen to disclose his whereabouts to her, for she was not sure whether he was in his country seat or in London itself. When it became clear to the solicitor she was not going to leave the premises without the duke's current address, he eventually told her where she might find him.

Unfortunately, that too had turned out to be something of a failure. The duke had not been home, and the lady of the house was out at a soiree and would not return until the early hours of the morning. In fact, she had learned that the duke had gone to Scotland to survey an estate there, and was not expected to return before Christmas Eve. She had practically collapsed on the doorstep then, the weakness in her limbs and in her heart too much to bear.

The butler, on seeing this, had not been able to simply leave her on the doorstep, not when it was growing cold and dark. He had ushered her around to the servants' entrance and, taking her into the kitchens, had left her in the care of the cook.

She was grateful for their kindness, not recognizing a single one of the staff. That was not surprising, given how long it had been since she had left the household. In addition, the family was wealthy, and she had no idea just how many houses and how many servants they actually had.

Upon discovering the connection to the family, the cook had advised her to go in search of the young master, murmuring that the lady of the house was not likely to see her any time soon. Isabella had gathered from this that the duchess attended a great many societal events, which did not leave much time for other things. It was the way of the ton, to go from one party to the next with only a few hours of sleep in between. In addition to this, the thought of Charles had brought a warmth to her heart, and she had agreed to go in search of him.

The staff had been most helpful in finding her the address, having told her that the marquess had his own estate in the country and, even though it was some distance away, Isabella had been resolved to reach him. The last of her funds had been spent on traveling to the nearest inn, with only one overnight stop, but when she reached her destination, she realized that she was going to have to walk the last ten miles on her own.

She had no funds left with which to reach his estate either by hackney or on horseback, and so had been forced to trudge her way along many miles of track towards his home. The path had been littered with stones and pebbles, and her feet soon became painful. Halfway there, the heavens had opened and, even with her shawl and cloak around her, she had become soaked to the skin. Her fingers froze, her nose grew red, and every breath was painful.

It had been a huge relief to come in sight of his home and, instead of making her way to the servants' entrance, she had pounded on the front door until it had opened, and then, with the last bit of strength she had, pushed her way past the startled butler to stand inside.

Now she was hanging onto Charles for dear life, having recognized him almost as soon as he descended the stairs. He had not changed too much since she had last seen him, although he was taller and broader than she had imagined. His sandy hair was much the same shade, and she could not forget the warmth in his hazel eyes, although, from the looks of it, he did not recognize her.

She did not blame him, given that she looked as though she had just crawled out of a river, but in her utter relief, she had been unable to stop herself from throwing her arms around him and sobbing into his neck. He had untangled her from him after a minute or so, looking at her with confusion.

It was only when she had stated her name that his confusion slowly began to die away. She could see it in his face, see how he was staring at her as though she was a ghost of some kind, a memory of his past that had come to haunt his future. It was not the welcome she had expected, and the hurt she felt within was surely to be evident on her features, but yet, she could not help it. She was freezing, utterly exhausted, and standing before the man she had once called her closest friend in all the world, only for him to be staring at her without even a hint of welcome in his face. It made her heart tear.

"What are you doing here, Isabella?" he asked, slowly, his eyebrows furrowing.

"I need your help," she replied, her eyes filling with tears at his brusque tone.

"Help?" he repeated, his eyes now darkening. "From what I understood, your mother was left with a home and an allowance that would see you both until the end of your days." He tilted his head a little, regarding her carefully. "Is that not enough for you?"

A streak of anger rushed through her body. "I can assure you, Charles, that we have lived very well for some years."

"You *will* refer to me as 'my lord'."

Isabella felt sick. This was not the Charles she knew. No affection filled his eyes, and he offered no delight upon seeing her again. It was as if she was an inconvenience, a burden that he did not particularly want to shoulder. By giving her such a command, he was reminding her of the vast chasm between their stations in society, and it was as though he had sliced her heart with a sharp blade; such was the pain coursing through her.

"Well, my lord," she replied softly, unable to keep the

sarcasm from her tone. "I shall not detain you from whatever it is I am interrupting. I shall make my way to the kitchens and see if they will let me stand by their fire for a few minutes until I am dried out in the hope that I can be given a small morsel of bread for I have not eaten for some time. I shall be on my way come the morning. I am sorry to have bothered you at what is, apparently, such an inconvenient time."

Tears blurred her vision, but she would not let them fall. Walking past him, although she did not know where she was going, she made her way along the corridor towards the back of the house, chancing upon a surprised maid who showed her the way to the servants' stairs. She did not care what kind of impression she had made upon Charles, nor that she had been particularly rude to him. The only thing she could think about was the disdain in his face and the coldness in his eyes. They tore her very soul apart.

4

Charles stared after the lady, suddenly unable to either move or speak. He had evidently upset her, but surely, she could not expect him to simply welcome her with open arms when he had not laid eyes on her in ten years.

Could she not have written to him, to ask for his assistance in whatever matter it was? Surely, she did not have to simply turn up on his doorstep, looking like some sort of bedraggled cat who had been outside for too long? Huffing to himself, he folded his arms and frowned, frustrated that his plans for a rousing fortnight were already going awry. He did not want to have any kind of issue that would take his attention away from his guests. This was meant to be a time *away* from responsibilities.

That being said, Charles could not help but feel a slight twinge of guilt over how he had treated her. She had been his dear friend as a child, but that had been a long time ago, and he had not once thought of seeking her out. He supposed that the very least he could do would be to allow her to stay, if only for a couple of nights.

The cook could take care of her in terms of food and clothing, and he was sure there would be a bed for her somewhere.

He could spare her some time in a day or two when the festivities required him to rest for an hour or so. In the meantime, he was sure that Isabella could help the cook and the housekeeper in their daily tasks, for he certainly did not want her amongst his guests. They were above her station and, whilst Charles wanted to ensure that she was treated with respect, he certainly did not want to encourage the friendship they had once shared. That was a part of his past, and he did not want to bring that particular relationship back to life.

"What am I do to with her, my lord?" the butler asked, anxiously rubbing his hands together. "I am truly sorry for allowing her entry, but as you have seen, she is tenacious."

Charles nodded gravely. "Yes, she is. However, I would not turn her out. Tell her she can remain here until I have the time to see her. Give her a bed, food, and whatever clothes you can spare, for it does not appear as though she has arrived with anything." Shaking his head, he stopped himself from rolling his eyes, thinking that the girl was quite foolish to not have even prepared for her journey. "Tell her to assist the housekeeper where she can, for it may be a few days until I have the time to spare."

"Of course," the butler agreed, bowing his head. "You are most gracious, my lord."

Frowning, Charles watched the butler walk away, wondering if he had truly heard the slight tinge of sarcasm in the butler's last words. Surely, the man would not speak to him in such a manner. Shaking his head to clear his thoughts, Charles turned on his heel and made his way back up the staircase towards his guests. He *must* have imagined it, for the butler would not have dared speak to him in such a way.

In addition, was he not already being most kind to Miss Docherty in giving her a roof over her head and food to eat until he was able to speak to her? It was not as though he was throwing her back outside into the cold to trudge back towards the inn, which was at least ten miles away.

Feeling more satisfied with himself and his chosen course of action, Charles entered the drawing room once more and threw himself into the festivities, determined to enjoy every moment with his guests.

THE FOLLOWING MORNING, Charles awoke late in the day, his head still spinning from the amount of liquor he had imbibed the night before. It had been a jolly evening, however—what he could remember of it at least. There had been dancing and frivolity. He was sure that this would be a wonderful fortnight.

Groaning quietly, he pushed himself up onto his elbows before shoving his pillows behind him and resting his head back against them. His guests would not be awake yet, he was sure, for he had been the first to retire.

Tugging at the bell pull, he only had to wait for a few minutes until a maid arrived with his breakfast tray. The aroma of warm chocolate made his stomach growl, although his eyes pinched shut when the curtains were thrown back.

"It is a gray day, my lord," the maid murmured as she tied the curtains back. "And the gardener says there is to be snow."

Charles chuckled to himself, thinking that it would not be too much of a bad thing should there be a heavy snowfall which could extend their house party for a few days. Of course, it would mean that he would miss Christmas in town, were that the case, which would bring a great deal of wrath from his mother.

"Are any of my other guests awake yet?" he asked, only for the maid to shake her head. Relaxing against his pillows,

Charles smiled to himself as the maid closed the door, finding himself at ease.

However, he was not about to have his peace for long. To his utter shock, the door slammed open once more, and Isabella Docherty stood, framed in the doorway.

"Whatever is the meaning of this?" Charles spluttered, pushing himself up against the pillows. "You should not be here! Get out at once."

"I will not!" she exclaimed, her eyes burning with fire. "How dare you send the butler with a message for me, as though I am a servant below your regard!"

Charles blinked, finding it difficult to think coherently as he gazed at her, finding her to be something of a beauty. Now that she was clean and dry, her long, fair hair tied up neatly, he could hardly believe that it was the same woman who had appeared on his doorstep the night before.

"You have nothing to say?" the lady screeched, storming closer to him. "I have come to you for aid, in the hope that you might assist me, only for you to inform me that I am to work below stairs for you until you deign yourself enough to meet with me?"

"What did you expect?" Charles stuttered, grasping at the gaping collar of his bed shirt and tugging the material together. "I have not seen you in ten years, Miss Docherty, and from what I remember, you and your mother were given a very handsome living for—"

"For a disgraced governess?" she whispered, her lips growing white with anger. "Was that what you were going to say?"

He shook his head, wondering what it was he had been about to say. "No, indeed. In fact, the way your mother was treated by my uncle was wrong; I know that. I would say, in fact," he continued, a surge of pride filling his chest, "that I treat my servants with more respect than any other gentleman of my acquaintance, and that is all because of your mother."

To his satisfaction, he saw her falter for a moment, the anger in her eyes fading a little.

"I see," she said slowly, her voice quieter than before. "How wonderful to know that your uncle's prevalent behavior means that you will not take such liberties with your own staff, although I would have thought that a gentleman of firm character would know not to do such things regardless." Her eyebrow arched, and Charles felt the sting of her rebuke almost slap him across the face.

"Now, see here," he retorted, growing angry with her. "I am not the same kind of man as my uncle, and he is not even my blood relative. I know how to treat my staff."

"But not those you once called friends," she interrupted, pinning him with her gaze.

Charles stopped speaking at once, his mouth hanging open for a moment before he shut it with a snap. "You do not know of what you speak," he muttered, shaking his head.

"I know how you have treated me," she exclaimed, throwing her hands up in exasperation. "Did you not see how I was last evening? Do you think that I wanted to stand in your hallway, ice cold, and dripping puddles onto your floor? Can you not understand that, out of sheer desperation, I have turned to the only family I thought could help me?"

A cold hand wrapped itself around Charles' heart.

"But you are not interested in what misfortune has befallen me," she continued, her anger now replaced with a deep sadness that was etched across her face. "You returned to your friends without a moment's thought for me."

"I said I would speak to you when I had the time," Charles said lamely, cringing inwardly at his weak words. "I had not completely disregarded you."

She shook her head, rebuke in her eyes. "I had hoped that you would have even a modicum of the kindness and compassion your father showed to my mother, but instead you prove by your indifference that you are only interested in your own pleasures."

Heat rushed up Charles' neck and into his face, sparking his anger. "You do not have the right to speak to me that way!"

"Oh yes," she murmured, completely unfazed by his anger. "I am meant to call you 'my lord' and show you the respect you think you deserve, simply because you have a title and I do not." A slight sneer tugged at her mouth. "You will find my deference extremely lacking, Charles."

Growing more and more enraged with every word that came from her mouth, Charles threw back the bedclothes, flung himself from the bed, and came towards her, anger in his every step. "You go too far, Miss Docherty."

To his complete surprise, she grasped his shirt and pulled him towards her, her blue eyes searching his face. "Do you not see me, Charles?" she cried, her eyes suddenly filling with tears. "I am Isabella! I've always been Isabella to you." Her fingers tightened on his collar and, much to his surprise, Charles felt his anger die away at once like a tide quickly receding from the sandy shore.

"I am in desperate need," she continued, her hands leaving his collar and coming to frame his face. "I have no one and nothing to my name. No one else can help me and so, through the cold wind and pouring rain, I made my way here, hoping that you would be glad to see me." She closed her eyes, and tears fell to her cheeks. "How much you have changed."

Her last words were like a whisper, echoing around his mind and forcing their way into his heart. He stared at her, stunned at how his own frustrations had disappeared the moment she had touched him. Her hands were warm on his cheeks, his heart suddenly thundering in his chest as he looked down into her face, realizing just how close she stood to him.

"I have no other choice but to do what you ask," she continued, dropping her hands from his face and walking towards the door. "I shall cook and clean and do whatever I must until you find the few minutes it will take to talk to me." Her lingering gaze was filled with disappointment, and a sting of shame pushed against Charles' heart. "Good day, my lord."

5

I sabella made her way back below stairs, tears pouring down her cheeks. She had tried to convince herself that the way Charles had treated her was simply due to the fact that he had guests waiting for his company, but when the butler had finally given her his message from Charles, her heart had broken into smithereens.

She was to be treated as a servant, not a friend. There was to be none of the camaraderie she had once experienced, nothing of the closeness they had shared as children. Perhaps it had been nothing more than a dream, to hope that such a thing would still exist between them, but still, the change in him had been a shock.

Her anger had forced her to toss and turn all night, not sure what she should do. The answer had come to her in time—she was simply going to have to do what Charles said. There was nothing else for her to do. She had no home to go to and no money to her name. The solicitor had already refused to help her, and she had placed all of her faith in Charles, trusting that he would assist her.

How disillusioned she had been.

The staff had been more than kind, and even the cook had stayed up late with her, listening to Isabella cry her heart out over what had happened. Isabella was positive that the lady did not understand a word of what she had said, through sobs and sniffles, but it had been enough to have someone just listen to her.

Eventually, the cook had ushered her to bed, where she had been given a nightdress and a clean dress for the morning, which had caused her to cry all over again. Only then had she truly realized the extent of what had happened to her.

Isabella had always prided herself on being strong, but coming to terms with the knowledge that she had lost everything was too much to bear. Tears had soaked her pillow, intermingled with her anger and frustration over Charles until she had fallen into an exhausted sleep. It was a relief to have a warm bed to sleep in again, even though the bed itself was a little more rickety than she was used to.

Come the morning, she had risen early and helped the cook with her preparations for breakfast, learning more about Charles and his honored guests. Her heart had sunk on hearing that Charles had become something of a wastrel, although she was glad to hear that he always treated his staff with respect.

The cook had proved to be a source of information, and it had been the knowledge that he was hosting a house party that had sparked a hot anger deep inside her chest. She was to remain here, awaiting his good pleasure, like a servant before a king? She could understand that her audience with him could be held up if he had important estate business or the like, but to discover that her needs were lower than his own pleasures had upset her greatly. He was too busy enjoying himself to spare a few minutes for her. It was both a grave disappointment and a painful awareness of just how he saw her.

That had been why she had stormed up to his room, having

followed the maid with the morning tray. It had been to no avail, however, for she was still in exactly the same situation as she had been when she had arrived. She had to admit that it had been a relief to say exactly what she thought and felt, and the shock in his eyes had been evident.

Perhaps he was unused to people speaking to him in such a manner, given that he had warned her that she had no right to speak to him so plainly, but of course, she had ignored that entirely. However, as she trudged back down the stairs, Isabella knew her words meant nothing. He would continue as he had intended, and she had probably only made things worse by her outburst. It was not as though he was going to be willing to give her any of his precious time after such a heated exchange.

How much you have changed.

The words she had said rang around her head, adding to her anguish. She had carried an idea of him for so long, believing that he would be just as she remembered him. How foolish she had been. The times they had spent together had been when they were children, and one's character did not always stay fixed as they grew into adulthood.

Charles, when she had known him, had been kind and compassionate. He had always thought of her needs, and they had spent many hours together, talking and laughing. She had been allowed to stay in the schoolroom with him, learning alongside him, and her love for him had grown with every passing day. It was a childlike love, similar to the kind that one might have for a brother or cousin, but it had never left her.

"Well?" the cook asked, her round face glancing up at Isabella as she walked into the kitchen. Evidently, the maid had seen Isabella disappear into Charles' room after she had left and had reported it to the cook. "Did you speak to the master?"

Isabella gave her a tight smile and saw the disappointment flare in the cook's eyes.

"I am sorry," she muttered, shaking her head as she stuck her hands into the dough she was kneading. "What with you both being such good childhood friends, I had thought that he might be willing to talk to you."

"I thought so, too," Isabella whispered, a lump in her throat. Battling tears, she tried to focus on what she could do with herself. There was no use in sitting about crying over his lack of consideration; she could make herself useful until such a time as he decided to speak to her. "Now," she said, a little more briskly. "What can I do?"

"Are you sure you want to help?" the cook asked doubtfully. "You are not of our station and—"

"Nonsense," Isabella declared, thinking that it would be good to have her mind focus on something else instead of how poorly Charles had treated her. "I shall be more than happy to help. I know there are countless chores to be done with the house party, and I am happy to do what I can to help." She gave the cook a wry smile. "Besides, it is what the master has decreed that I do."

The cook chuckled wryly, before suggesting that Isabella begin to help her with the preparation of the main meal for the evening before going in search of the housekeeper. There was the kitchen maid of course, but Isabella was glad to throw herself into the work and assist the cook where she could, finally getting her mind away from Charles.

SOME HOURS LATER, the meal was in the process of being served, and Isabella finally had the opportunity to step aside and allow the rest of the staff to do their work. She had no idea of procedures or the like and was glad to have a few minutes to rest.

Isabella was not sure just how many hours she had spent helping the cook with the dinner preparations, but it had certainly stopped her from thinking about Charles and her own desperate situation. She had found the cook, kitchen maid, and housekeeper all to be of the friendly sort, although the butler did not say much to her at all.

Hard work was never something she had shirked from, finding a joy in it. Although she and her mother had been given a home and a yearly fund, she still had to plant their own vegetables, bake their own bread, and sew their own clothes. It had meant rising with the dawn and laying her head on her pillow often before the sun set, but it had been a life that Isabella had loved. She was grateful that the skills she had learned were now being put to good use whilst she waited for Charles to spare her a few minutes of his time.

"Oh, Isabella, there you are."

Pushing herself up from the table, Isabella saw that the housekeeper looked somewhat frazzled, her expression harassed.

"I must beg a favor from you," the housekeeper continued, tucking a few stray hairs back into her tightly coiled bun. "One of the maids has just now gone to ensure the fires are well lit in the drawing room for after dinner, and has discovered that the bourbon tray and glasses have, somehow, been knocked to the floor. She did not notice it before, apparently, because it is right in the corner. Although, that does make me wonder whether or not she is doing her job properly."

Isabella hid a smile, aware that the maid was probably worried that the housekeeper would think such a thing.

"Do you need me to clean it up?" she asked quietly. "I do not mind in the least, I promise you."

The housekeeper's stern expression broke away as she smiled in relief. "If you could assist the maid in doing so, I would be most grateful. The dinner is almost at an end, and the ladies will soon be exiting to the drawing room, and I would not like to have such a mess still being cleared up when they appear."

Isabella walked away at once, promising that she would come back down to fetch another crystal decanter and glasses once the current situation was dealt with. The housekeeper said that she would leave the tray with the items on the table ready for her to collect, and without hesitation, Isabella continued up the stairs and made her way to the drawing room.

"Oh, Miss Docherty!" the maid exclaimed, as Isabella entered. "I have cleaned up the bourbon, but glass is everywhere."

"Go and fetch another brush, and we shall clear this up in no time," Isabella said, taking the brush from the maid. "Hurry now."

The maid scurried away at once, leaving Isabella to survey the damage. Glass was sparkling all across the floor, and she hurriedly began to sweep it up, knowing that they would need to sweep the floor at least three times before they could declare it safe. Bending down, she carefully swept the brush over the nooks and crannies in the floor, brushing the glass into a pile.

The door creaked open, and just as Isabella was about to get to her feet and encourage the maid to hurry up, she heard the distinct sound of Charles' voice.

"I must return to my guests, Lady Swift," he murmured, his voice light and filled with a warmth that had Isabella's cheeks heating. Isabella crouched as low as she could, hiding herself behind one of the large ornate chairs, desperately hoping that neither Charles or his lady would see her. More murmurings filled the room, making Isabella cringe. This was not something she wanted to hear.

6

Charles had tried his best to ignore any kind of guilt over what Miss Docherty had thrown at him, telling himself repeatedly that she was simply het up over his lack of interest in whatever she had done to put herself in such a desperate situation.

However, the only thing that had got her fiery words from his mind had been the delightful Lady Swift, who seemed more than keen for his attentions. Once his guests had finally arisen, they had spent an enjoyable afternoon together, taking a cold, but sparkling ride across the expanse of gardens and woodland that he could claim as his own. He had been surprised that Lady Swift had chosen to ride a mare, rather than sit in the carriage with the other ladies, but had found her company delightful. They had spent some time in conversation, and he had to confess that her bright eyes and quick smile brought him delight.

Dinner had been a profoundly rousing affair and, although dessert had not yet been served, Lady Swift had suddenly had it in mind to go in search of her shawl, which she believed she had left in the drawing room earlier that day. Charles had been about to suggest that he send one of the servants to fetch it, only to see Lord Walton give the tiniest shake of his head, his eyes widening slightly. It was as if his friend could read his mind and was warning him off his chosen course of action. Realizing that Lady Swift might have other things in mind—and was staking her claim by being so obvious—he followed her at once and left the room, promising to be back before dessert was served.

Lady Swift, it seemed, had not needed directions at all, for she had taken him by the hand and opened the first door she came to, which happened to be the drawing room. A roaring fire blazed in the grate, and candles were lit all about the room. However, there was a stillness about the place that had his every hair stand on end, as though something was begging him not to follow through with his intentions.

Lady Swift's smile became coy as she turned towards him, and Charles found himself bumping into the wall behind him, his heart beginning to hammer in his chest.

"Lady Swift," he murmured, as her hands pressed against his chest. "We are being a little indiscreet, are we not?"

She laughed softly. "I doubt anyone will say anything, and you know as well as I do that I am not looking for a rich husband, so you need have no concern that I will chase an engagement."

Charles drew in a short breath, finding it difficult to fill his lungs. Her nearness made it almost impossible to respond, his eyes going to her lips that were drawing closer and closer to him.

How much you have changed.

Why Miss Docherty's words should enter his mind at this particular moment, Charles could not say, but there they were. He pulled back from Lady Swift, his eyes drifting away from her. A strange sense of shame filled him, as though Miss Docherty was present with them and was giving him something of a disapproving look.

Charles frowned. He did not want to think of Miss Docherty at the present moment, not when Lady Swift was so near to him, so why was he now struggling to get her from his mind?

"You are not hesitating, I hope?" Lady Swift murmured, grasping his hands that lay by his sides and pressing them to her sides. "We had a good time this afternoon, did we not? And I am more than aware of why you invited both myself and the other ladies to your house party. We all have one thing in common: not one of us is in search of a husband."

Charles dropped one hand from Lady Swift's waist and tugged at his cravat, finding it a little too tight. "Yes, well," he muttered, clearing his throat. "That is to say—"

"And I came regardless," she continued with a sudden heat in her eyes. "I am not offended in the least, Lord Sutherland."

Trying to smile, Charles nodded, but glanced away. Something was very wrong. He did not want to kiss Lady Swift, having been excited by the prospect only a few minutes before. *It is only because of what Miss Docherty said to you earlier today*, he reasoned with himself, trying to push his sudden reluctance away. *Do not be so ridiculous, man! Get a hold of yourself!*

"You are right, Lady Swift," he murmured, allowing his hands to tighten a little around her waist.

"I am very glad to hear it," she replied, pressing herself against him a little more firmly. Charles' body responded at once, and, finally, Miss Docherty's words faded from his mind. When Lady Swift's lips touched his, he kissed her immediately, but to his surprise, he felt no swift kick of desire, no sudden thrill racing through his body. He broke their kiss almost at once, blinking furiously in confusion.

"You are playing with me, Lord Sutherland," Lady Swift said calmly, a hard line suddenly appearing around her mouth. "What are you doing?"

Trying to think of an excuse, Charles attempted to smile. "I must return to my guests, Lady Swift." He could not, for the life of him, work out what it was that was wrong with him, but he felt uncomfortable over the situation.

Lady Swift took a small step back and stared at him, her face an expression of shock. "You are turning me down?"

"No, not in the least," he responded, trying to catch her hands. "It is just that my guests are waiting, and I must play host."

"Nonsense!" she exclaimed angrily. "They will not care, Sutherland! You have shown your interest in me all day. If you do not wish for a liaison between us, then you must say so now!"

Charles stammered incoherently for a moment before Lady Swift stamped her foot, turned, and swept past him in a flurry of skirts, evidently angered over his indecision. Charles stayed where he was, leaning heavily against the wall. He could not believe what had just occurred, nor what his own reaction had been.

Foolish! He had been utterly foolish. Turning down a woman such as Lady Swift was incomprehensible. Why had he reacted in such a thoughtless manner?

Putting his head in his hands, Charles groaned aloud. Lady Swift would, no doubt, share her story with the other ladies in the house who would regard him with a little bit of suspicion and possibly some disdain over turning away from Lady Swift.

A sudden sound had him jumping in fright, his eyes roving around the room to discover where it might have come from. Taking a few steps to his left and to his right, he continued to search the room for whatever that noise might have been. To his surprise, he saw none other than Miss Docherty crouching behind one of the chairs, a brush in her hand and shattered glass at her feet. She slowly met his gaze, her cheeks heating with color and, seeing that he had found her out, got to her feet.

Charles did not know what to say, overcome with mortification that she had heard every single word that had passed between him and Lady Swift.

"I did not mean to overhear, if that is what you are thinking," she said firmly, breaking the tension. "The bourbon tray must have been knocked over last evening, and it was not discovered until now. That is the only reason I am in this room."

Seeing the glass at her feet, Charles slowly backed towards the door, sure that his face was burning with heat. "I shall leave you to finish your task, then," he mumbled. "The guests are to be arriving here in a short time, so do be quick." Feeling a little more like himself, he lifted his chin and returned her gaze, seeing the flash of anger in her eyes.

"I am not your skivvy to order about, Charles," she said, brandishing the brush at him as though it was a blade. "I am assisting your staff because I have no other choice. However, I can see that I am going to have to wait on your good pleasure for some time if what I witnessed is what you are filling your hours with." Her eyes narrowed. "Are you to take your pleasure with all the ladies in the house or just one in particular? I only ask because I need to know how long I will be waiting."

The sarcasm in her words stung, and, for once, Charles did not know what to say in response. He was embarrassed by what she had seen and heard, and still, her words rang in his head, refusing to leave him in peace.

"Just see that you do it," he muttered, finding the doorknob and exiting the room at once.

Striding back towards his dining room, Charles passed a maid with another brush in her hand, bringing to mind the way that Miss Docherty had brandished her own brush at him. She obviously thought very little of him, but, he reasoned, that was simply because she did not understand the kind of life he led. How could she? She had never lived in such a way before.

Perhaps, if he allowed her to join his house party, she would see that he was not as bad as she thought.

But why do I care? Charles asked himself, frowning. *Just listen to what she has to say and then send her on her way. Her opinion of you is not important in the least.*

However, no matter how much Charles tried to reason with himself, the words she had said refused to leave him.

"I have not changed too much," he muttered to himself, determined to prove her wrong. "And Miss Docherty is going to see it."

Walking back into the dining room, and avoiding Lady Swift's glare, he seated himself once more and continued on with the meal, a feeling of self-satisfaction settling over him. He would speak to Miss Docherty the following day and would have her join the house party by the afternoon. Then she would see just how wrong she had been in forming such an unfavorable opinion of him.

7

"The master requires you in his study, Miss Docherty."

Isabella looked up from her dough in surprise, fully aware that she had flour everywhere as she made yet another loaf of bread. "Now?"

"Yes, now," came the butler's reply, his expression never changing although Isabella was sure she saw a twinkle in his eye.

"Very well, then," Isabella muttered to herself. "I shall finish the kneading and go up to him."

The butler frowned. "He said—"

"I am aware of what he said," Isabella interrupted, not meaning to be rude, but knowing that she could not leave the dough as it was. "Once the bread is ready to rise, I shall go up to him immediately." She plunged her hands back into the dough and continued with her work, ignoring the huff of disapproval from the butler.

Once the bread was set aside with a warm cloth over the top, Isabella peeled off her apron, washed her hands in freezing cold water, and made her way up the stairs, hoping that she looked presentable, at the very least. Smoothing one hand over her tight bun, she brushed down her dress once more before knocking at the door to his study and walking in.

"I sent for you a half hour ago."

Isabella lifted one eyebrow. "You also charged me with assisting below stairs, and if you wish to have bread with this luncheon, then you will have to forgive my tardiness."

Charles' frown deepened, but he did not comment further. Gesturing her to a small chair in front of his desk, he sighed heavily as she sat down. "You are proving something of a trial, Miss Docherty."

I am glad to hear it, Isabella thought to herself, but, wisely, kept her lips buttoned.

"Your accusation that I have changed since you knew me last has begun to bother me," he continued when she did not reply. "Given that you do not know me in the least, I cannot say why your words have dug their way into my mind as they have done, but, regardless, I think you wrong in your estimation."

"I knew you as a child," Isabella replied hotly. "You were kind and considerate, giving time to anyone who asked it of you. You had no airs and graces, but a determination to find your purpose in life." She paused, giving him a slight shake of her head. "It seems you have not yet found that purpose unless you intend to continue in seeking your own pleasures for the remainder of your life."

"You have very little idea of what my life is like!" Charles exclaimed, his hand thumping down on his desk. He glared at her for a moment before slowly sitting back in his chair, his mouth growing taut. "Had you any idea, then perhaps you might form a very different opinion."

Isabella shook her head. "I can see very well, Charles. Your actions do not require explanation."

How could he not see that the way he had turned from her,

pushing her to one side in favor of his guests, was what had made her realize that he was not the man she once knew?

"Nevertheless," Charles said in a calmer voice, "I am here now to listen to whatever woes you might have."

Isabella closed her eyes, determined not to react to the way he was simply downplaying the tragic nature of events by calling them 'woes'. She took a few long breaths before opening her eyes and beginning.

"My home has been destroyed," she said simply.

He frowned. "What do you mean, destroyed?"

"I mean just that," Isabella replied quietly, as a vision of what had occurred began to race through her mind. "A woman appeared with a large, burly man by her side. I was held by him whilst she destroyed every single thing in my home before setting it alight."

She saw the way his mouth fell open, his face going a shade paler.

"She called me a bastard and a stain," she continued, hating that her voice was shaking a little. "I am not sure who the lady was, but she said something about my mother, and that it had taken her years to find my whereabouts." She shook her head. "It was as though she had been seeking to do this for many years."

"But you have an allowance, do you not?" Charles asked, after a few seconds of silence had passed.

There was no sympathy in his face, no words of compassion, just a cold consideration of her finances.

Isabella bit back her harsh retort, her eyes burning with a sudden lot of unshed tears. "The solicitor would not allow me to take anything from the next half-year," she replied firmly. "The last of my funds for this half-year were spent seeking help, and regardless of whether I could have my additional funds, there is nowhere near enough to rebuild my home. It is truly decimated." Her voice cracked despite her determination to remain calm, although she managed not to cry.

She remained sitting ramrod straight, her eyes never leaving Charles' face. He was her last hope, her only hope. If he did not help her, then she was not sure what she would do. There would be nowhere for her to go.

Charles nodded slowly, his eyes suddenly leaving her face and drifting across her left shoulder. She saw him bite his lip, as though worried about something.

"You say it was a woman who did this?"

"An older woman, yes," Isabella replied, quietly. "I have never seen her before."

"And have you made any assumptions as to who she might be?"

Isabella paused, knowing that what she had to say could hurt him dreadfully. "I had wondered whether she was the wife of the man who..."

"You believe her to be my aunt," he bit out, his eyes dark.

"Not many people know that I am a bastard," Isabella replied quietly. "And she seemed intent on revenge."

Charles did not say anything for a few minutes, his face paler than before, and his brow furrowed. Isabella folded her hands together in her lap and waited patiently, desperately hoping that Charles was not about to turn her out, seeing her as the inconvenience he did not need at this present time.

"Your mother, I presume, has passed away," he said a short time later, not lifting his eyes to meet hers.

"Yes, she did," Isabella replied softly, her mind filled with images of her loving mother. "It was some time ago, however, so the pain and grief have lessened. I am just glad she was not alive to see the terrible wrath of your aunt, if that is who she was." She shook her head, hating that a single tear had fallen from her eye and brushing it away hastily. "Although, of course, I do miss my mother terribly."

"I had not heard," he murmured, half to himself.

Isabella shrugged. "We have not been in touch for many years, Charles. It does not surprise me that you did not know of the loss of my mother."

He sighed, passing one hand over his eyes. "We used to write very often."

The memory of writing letters to her dear friend made Isabella's emotions well up, for it had not been her that had paused in their correspondence, but rather, she had been forced to give up when Charles had not responded to her for over a year. She was about to remind him of it, only to see a sudden confusion and despondency etched across his face, as though she had reminded him of something painful.

"We had a lot of happy days together, did we not?" he said softly, finally meeting her gaze.

"We did," Isabella agreed, the reminders of their time together a somewhat painful memory.

"You were as stubborn back then as you are now," he commented, a little wryly. "No one has spoken to me as you have for some time."

Isabella tilted her head and regarded him. "That is because I find you so changed, Charles. I have never been afraid to speak my mind, and certainly not with you."

Two spots of color appeared in his cheeks and, for a moment, Isabella wondered whether or not he was about to grow angry with her once again, but instead, he settled back in his chair and steepled his fingers together. "I am going to have to find out whether this was my aunt's doing," he said, frowning. "You say you have nowhere else to go?"

Isabella shook her head as a twist of despair wrung her heart. "Where can I go, Charles? I have nowhere and no one. I believe that was your aunt's intention, for she wanted me to be utterly destitute. Although, I think she hoped my mother would still be alive." She lifted one shoulder. "I was the second choice, but she achieved her aim regardless."

"I can add to your coffers," he began, his gaze drifting away from her as he thought hard. "And we shall have to find you a new situation, away from this place."

A slight shiver ran through Isabella. It was not as though she did not appreciate his kindness, but it was still so very cold and calculated. There did not seem to be even a hint of compassion in his words. Telling herself to be grateful for what she was being offered, she tried to smile. "I thank you."

"But not until after Christmas," he continued, as though he had not heard her. "I do not like the circumstances that you have described, and must write to my father to discover what he has heard about my aunt. Also, I will need time to find you a suitable home."

Isabella shuddered, remembering the vehemence in the lady's eyes. "I am not sure her need for revenge is yet satisfied, even though it was not my poor mother's fault for what happened."

Charles' eyebrows rose. "You think she might come after you again?"

"I do not know," Isabella replied truthfully. "But I will confess to being a little afraid. I have never been as scared as I was that day."

His eyes searched her face as he leaned forward, putting his elbows on the desk in front of him. "She did not hurt you, I hope?"

Looking away from him, Isabella did not know what to say. This was his aunt that she was accusing after all, his blood relative.

"Isabella!" His tone was harsh, his voice commanding.

Isabella had no choice but to look at him, hating that her lips trembled with the recollection of how she had been thrashed. "I was beaten," she said, her head dropping to her chest. "I am well now, however."

A long, pronounced silence followed, and Isabella found that she could not lift her head; such were her emotions. It was not like her to cry or give in to any kind of outburst, so she battled with her feelings, refusing to let another drop of moisture fall. She did not know whether Charles believed her story, nor whether he would take the news of her beating seriously. After all, she was just his friend from long ago, whereas the lady who had destroyed her entire life was his relative, his own father's sister. Usually, such misdeeds were simply swept under the rug, never to be mentioned again.

"Then I think it best you stay here," he said quietly. "I shall write to my father today and ask him to talk with his sister. We need to know if this truly was her or if someone else was involved."

Isabella wanted to say that there could be no one else who knew of her connection to his uncle, but kept her mouth closed. Rising to her feet, she thanked him quietly and made her way to the door.

"Oh, and you are to move to one of the guest bedchambers," he said, almost as an afterthought. "The housekeeper will provide you with gowns and the like. Make sure to join us for dinner."

"Dinner?" she repeated, staring at him as though he had lost his mind. "You told me that I should help below stairs, and I assure you that I am more than competent—"

"Nevertheless, it is my wish that you join us for dinner and remain here as one of my guests," he said firmly, his gaze fixed on hers. "And please, no arguments this time, Miss Docherty."

Seeing that she was not to be allowed any rebuttal, Isabella chose to nod, closing the door behind her. She leaned against it for a moment, her breath coming quickly as she tried to deal with everything she thought and felt.

What a relief it was to see that he was, at the very least, willing to listen to her, willing to hear what she had to say. He had not turned his back on her or thrown some coins at her and sent her away once more. It was more than she had hoped for, although she was not sure she looked forward to joining his guests for dinner—not after what she had overheard the previous evening.

8

Charles sat back in his chair, his brow furrowing as he thought about what Isabella had said. Even though he now made sure to refer to her as 'Miss Docherty', she was always going to be Isabella to him. He could hardly take in what she had told him, but something in him knew that he had to believe her.

She had been so bedraggled when she had first arrived on his doorstep, arriving without a single thing to her name, which meant that she was completely dependent on his mercy. He wondered whether she had gone to town in search of his father, remembering that she had said that the solicitor would not help her. *So, she must have been in town*, he thought to himself, angry that the solicitor could be so uncaring.

Father is away, however. Is that why she came here?

His stomach churned as he thought of what she must have endured, growing hot and cold with anger and revulsion over what Lady Johnston, his aunt, had done. He had very little doubt that it was his aunt, for, as Isabella had said, what other person knew that she was a bastard, borne to a mother who had been assaulted by his uncle?

Even the thought brought him a feeling of shame, his features twisting as he thought of how much Isabella's mother had borne, even though her love for Isabella had been evident from the first moment she had been placed in her arms. He was relieved, at least, that his governess had apparently lived a happy and content life for many years after she had left his family, although he found that there was a niggle of guilt in his soul as he thought about how he had chosen to stop correspondence with Isabella.

It had not been intentional at first, for they had been very good friends. In fact, they had corresponded for a few years, but soon the lure of town and all it had to offer a young man had taken up much of his time. It seemed writing to his friend was of very little consequence.

He had become caught up in balls and soirees, in cards and liquor, in ladies and their fine kisses, until Isabella had become nothing more than a memory. He had never felt guilty about such a thing, however, not until the moment he had seen the sadness on her face. Not until this very day.

She had sat in front of him, not lifting her eyes as he had mentioned how often they had used to write, but he had still seen the sharp pain in her expression. She had sent him letters for many weeks, without a single reply, until her letters had stopped coming altogether. Had he been wrong to ignore her? Had he made a mistake in pushing her from his life and from his mind?

Getting up from his desk, Charles wandered to the window and looked out across the estate. His plans for two weeks of jovialities and the like now seemed less likely, although he was still determined to enjoy himself. Not too much was needed of him in order to help Isabella.

The first thing would be to send his steward to find a few small cottages that he might consider purchasing for Isabella—

furnished of course—but this time of year, that might prove a little more difficult. Snow had fallen, and with the icy conditions, sending letters and receiving replies could take longer than normal.

Frowning, Charles leaned his head against the cool glass, closing his eyes for a moment. He would have to write to his father, but whether or not he had returned from his estate business in Scotland yet, he was not sure. The duke was not scheduled to arrive home until it was closer to Christmas Eve.

"I could write to Worthington," he muttered to himself, his mind suddenly coming alive with the thought.

Lord Worthington had been one of his closest friends, although something of a rake and a wastrel; that had to be said. However, in the last few months, Worthington had moved away from London, back to his country estate, declaring himself in love.

Charles had snorted at the thought, but Worthington had turned into a very different man in the weeks before his departure to the country, and, since then, Charles had not seen him more than once or twice in town, when Worthington needed to visit his solicitor. Apparently what Worthington had claimed had been true—he was in love with his wife.

Shaking his head to himself, Charles walked back to his desk and pulled out a fresh piece of parchment, determined to write to his friend immediately. Worthington's estate was not far from where Miss Docherty had lived, if he recalled correctly, and it would be worth finding out whether the state of the cottage was as Isabella had said.

It was not that he did not believe Isabella's story, but rather that he wanted to find out the exact extent of the damage. If there was any hope of restoring it, then he might choose to do that, rather than purchase a new property for Isabella, for she had mentioned that she had been happy living there and had friends within the small village nearby.

However, that would all depend on whether he could get his aunt to leave Isabella alone for good. His jaw clenched as he began to write, anger stirring in the pit of his stomach as he thought about the beating Isabella had been forced to endure. How anyone could lay a finger on her, he could not understand. It was not as though it was Isabella's fault that she had been borne out of wedlock—nor was it her mother's fault.

The responsibility lay with his uncle and his uncle alone. Charles remembered how he had overheard his father say, on more than one occasion, that if the man had been his own flesh and blood, he would have beaten him severely for what he had done to the governess. However, given that he was only in their family by marriage, there was very little that the duke could do, apart from speaking clearly and concisely to the man.

His aunt and uncle never visited the duke's home, not in the entire time Isabella and her mother had lived there, and Charles had never had occasion to wonder how that had affected his aunt. He had simply assumed that she had accepted it without question—although now he wondered if the isolation from her brother and his family had driven her to such desperate measures.

Writing quickly, he wrote first to Worthington and then to his father, before sealing up both notes and ringing for the butler who arrived in a trice.

"These are to be sent straight away," he said, handing the butler the letters. "And Miss Docherty is to be set up in the purple bedchamber. Do ask the housekeeper to find some gowns for her, even if it means going to the village and buying some from the seamstress there. She is not to be in old worn-out things, do you understand?"

"Of course, my lord," the butler replied, his face expressionless. "Is there anything else?"

"Miss Docherty is to dine with us also," Charles remembered. "She is to be treated as one of my guests from this point onwards."

There was only a fraction of a second before the butler replied, his surprise carefully hidden. "But of course, my lord," he murmured.

Charles dismissed him and poured himself a brandy, suddenly weary from all that he had heard.

Sitting before the fire, Charles contemplated what Isabella had told him, slightly pleased that he was to be able to prove to her that he was not as changed as she thought him to be. She would soon see that he was not the harsh, unfeeling gentleman she considered.

However, that did not tell him why he found himself in need of her good opinion. Swirling his brandy in his glass, Charles sighed heavily to himself before draining the glass. Whatever it was, he had to admit that Miss Docherty had a firm hold of him and certainly was not letting him go.

"WE ARE to be joined by a friend of mine," Charles explained as his guests sat down at the dining table. "That is why there is an extra chair." He did not allow himself to frown, although he did wonder why Miss Docherty had not yet arrived. The dinner gong had sounded, and she was yet to make an appearance.

"A friend?" Lord Walton asked, looking a little surprised. "Which one of the fellows have you asked then?" He chuckled, looking around the group. "I do hope it is not Lord Witherton, for he is the most boorish man I have ever met."

The ladies tittered, but Charles did not join in with the

laughter. "No, indeed, it is not Lord Witherton, but Miss Docherty."

The laughter faded at once.

"Miss Docherty?" Walton repeated, looking a little confused. "Wait, is that not the girl who—"

"She is a friend of mine," Charles said loudly, interrupting Walton. He did not want his friend to reveal Miss Docherty's humble beginnings, for then surely the ladies would look down their noses at her. "She is to stay with us until we depart on the twenty-second of December, as planned, and I would be grateful to you all for making her welcome." Pasting a smile on his face, he gave the ladies a slight bow, hoping to encourage their sympathies. "She is, in fact, recovering from a somewhat tragic situation and may be a little quiet, but I am sure she will be delighted with any friendship you might care to offer her."

Murmurs of agreement came from the assembled ladies, although Lady Swift continued to gaze at him with fire in her eyes. Ignoring this, Charles turned his attention towards Walton once more, seeing his frown deepen. Hoping that his friend was not about to launch into a flurry of questions over whether Miss Docherty was, as he suspected, the daughter of Charles' old governess, Charles gave him the tiniest shake of his head, which, to his very great relief, Walton acknowledged.

More than that, he tapped his nose with one finger, making Charles want to sink into the floor in embarrassment. There was no need for Walton to be so obvious but, then again, his friend had never been particularly restrained.

"I just wonder where she is," Charles muttered to himself, thinking that they would soon have to start on the first course. He sat for another minute or two, before nodding to the footmen to serve.

Just as they did so, the door opened and Charles, getting to his feet, turned to see Miss Docherty enter the room, her cheeks red and eyes glancing around the room.

She was absolutely breathtaking, and Charles felt as though he had been backhanded across the room. Trying not to stare at her, he cleared his throat and put on a wide smile, opening his arm to her.

"Ladies and gentlemen," he said, as she drew near him. "Allow me to introduce Miss Docherty, my very dear friend."

9

Isabella had not wanted to dine with the rest of the group, finding it difficult to leave the servants' quarters, even though she had only spent two days or so in their company. The cook had not been as friendly, once she discovered that Isabella was to move to the bedchambers upstairs, although Isabella did manage to make her smile by promising to come back downstairs to make bread in the morning.

It had felt very strange to walk from the servants' quarters to one of the most beautifully furnished rooms she had ever seen. Her breath had caught as she had been shown inside, her eyes roving around the large four-poster bed, the ornate furnishings, and beautifully carved dressing table. The windows were big and let in vast amounts of light, giving the room a delightfully bright appearance.

"New gowns have been purchased for you," the housekeeper had said, as she followed Isabella into the room. "You will find all you need in the wardrobe, although I did have to guess your sizing, so if anything is not right, do let me know, and I shall send a maid to help you alter it."

Isabella had stared at the lady, stunned. "You mean Charles bought me clothing?"

The housekeeper's mouth had twitched, as though she was hiding a smile, but she had simply nodded, excused herself, and left, reminding Isabella that the dinner gong would be sounding in less than an hour.

Isabella had hardly had time to accustom herself with the place before a maid had arrived at the door, ready to help her dress and prepare for dinner. Of course, Isabella was not used to such things, so she had almost refused, but had seen the frightened look in the girl's eyes as she began to decline and had stopped herself at once.

The maid would be the one who got into difficulty if Isabella appeared at the dining table without her hair done just so or her dress slightly askew. She had allowed the girl to assist her, and once she had dismissed her, had spent a good five minutes staring at herself in the mirror.

Her reflection was someone she did not know, and for a moment, she struggled to gather her wits. The thought of having to enter the dining room and greet Charles and his guests was terrifying, for Isabella knew she did not truly belong next to those of such a high class. Indeed, if they found out that she was a child born on the wrong side of the blanket, then their disdain for her would be immediate and obvious.

So late had she sat waiting that she missed the dinner gong entirely, and ended up rushing down the stairs, aware that she was already late. Walking into the dining room, she had felt every eye on her, but had taken her seat without a word, although she had managed to smile at them all.

Now Charles was looking at her as though he had never truly seen her before, his gaze intense and focused. Isabella managed to glance at him once or twice, but chose to turn away from his regard, greeting each of the guests in turn as Lord Walton took it upon himself to introduce each of them.

Isabella tried not to blush as she greeted Lady Swift, more than aware of what she had overheard passing between the lady and Charles. Lady Swift studied her for a moment before turning back to Lord Walton and starting a merry discussion on what Christmas traditions Walton had planned.

Christmas had always been a happy time for Isabella, even though she had only shared it with her mother. It was a day free from chores, free from the harshness of daily living. A day to spend together, to be thankful for all they had. She had loved it. They had brought in pinecones and put them on almost every surface they had, allowing the scent to fill their home.

Isabella smiled to herself, remembering how her mother used to spend hours in search of any kind of greenery to add a special touch to their house. It was usually ivy or holly with their red berries. The townsfolk had all come together to eat, bringing whatever they could to share with one another. It had always been simple fare, but the company was what had warmed her heart. How different this Christmas would be. A sadness crept over her, making her smile fade.

"Is everything all right, Miss Docherty?"

Her gaze shot to Charles' face at once, suddenly aware that she had been lost in thought. "Everything is quite well, I thank you."

"May I say how lovely you look this evening?" he murmured, his gaze running over her. "The color suits you."

Isabella flushed, feeling more irritated than complimented. She was not about to be his Lady Swift if that was what he hoped. However, she could not forget that he had been kind to her in giving her such items in the first place. "I thank you for your generosity," she managed to say before turning her head away to join in the discussion at the other end of the table.

She knew that she was giving him something of a set down by not continuing the discussion, but the last thing she wanted him to think was that she was suddenly open to his attentions. Isabella was not about to engage in flirtations or even stolen kisses. The whole idea turned her stomach and did not change her opinion about Charles and his behavior one bit.

Was that what his intentions were, in forcing her to join him and his guests? Did he want her to think that he was behaving just as other gentlemen would? Hardly listening to the conversation at all, Isabella concentrated on eating her food with as much decorum as she could manage, knowing that there was a standard on how a lady should dine.

She did not belong there, and despite Charles' kindness to her in providing her with clothes and a furnished room, she did not want to join him and his guests.

Once dinner was finished, the port drunk, and the gentlemen back through in the drawing room, Isabella was left to endure an evening of so-called entertainment, finding herself sitting stiffly in a chair and wondering how long she would have to wait before she could retire. There was singing and music, as well as copious amounts of brandy and wine, and Isabella found herself with something of a headache.

Isabella bore their company for an hour before finding that her irritation grew so much that she was practically forced from her seat. However, upon standing, she realized that no one had noticed her in the slightest. Charles was busy singing some ribald song alongside Lady Fitzgerald, whilst the other ladies had found themselves a partner and were dancing together, albeit a little unsteadily. Isabella was well aware that, with her presence, the numbers were now uneven, with five ladies to four gentlemen, but then again, given that she did not wish to engage in any kind of dancing or the like, it probably would not matter.

Making her way to the door, Isabella threw Charles one last

look, seeing the way he looked down at Lady Fitzgerald with a broad smile on his face, his eyes dancing. A jolt of awareness ran straight through her as she grew aware of just how handsome the man was, heat rippling up her spine. His eyes caught hers, and Isabella felt her breath hitch. Hurriedly turning the door handle, Isabella slipped outside into the hallway.

Closing her eyes for a moment, Isabella tried to calm her frantically beating heart, wondering why on earth she was reacting to him in such a way. Just because she had suddenly found him to be a somewhat attractive gentleman did not mean that her heart should go into such a flurry. Frustrated with herself, Isabella balled her hands into fists and gave herself a stern talking to.

Walking quickly along the corridor, Isabella managed to slip downstairs, about to prepare herself a tea tray, only to be shooed back upstairs by the housekeeper, who told her in no uncertain terms that she would bring one to her in her bedchamber. Not quite ready to retire, Isabella requested that it be brought to the library, thinking that she might find herself a good book to curl up with for the evening.

Charles' library was more expansive than anything she had seen before, a wide smile spread across her lips as she walked a little further into the room, her gaze drifting across the countless books that lined the walls.

One of the most precious gifts her mother had given her was teaching her how to read, and it had been a long time since Isabella had been given the opportunity to refresh her mind with a new book. Letting her finger trace gently along the bookshelves, Isabella smiled to herself as she searched the titles, finding not one, but three books that piqued her interest.

The door opened behind her, and thinking that it was the housekeeper, Isabella did not turn around. "Thank you very much," she said absently, as she continued to look through the titles. "Could you place it by the fire?"

"What are you doing in here?"

Startled, Isabella jumped visibly and turned to see Charles standing just inside the door, his expression dark. The housekeeper appeared behind him and brought the tea tray inside, depositing it on the table without a word before disappearing again. Isabella swallowed hard, a little perturbed by the expression on his face. Was she not meant to be in this room?

"Why did you leave?"

Isabella shrugged, refusing to be intimidated. "Such amusements do not interest me."

"Do not interest you?" One eyebrow arched incredulously. "Dancing, music, and fine wine do not interest you?"

Unable to prevent herself from laughing, Isabella shook her head, ignoring how his brows knocked together. "Charles, I am not someone who has grown up with such things, as you should know. I am not interested in dancing with a glass of wine in my hand." Shaking her head, she turned her attention back to her books, although tension raced through her body as he walked towards her. "I much prefer to read, although if you would prefer that I not remain in your library, then I shall leave at once."

He scowled as she picked up her books, walked straight past him, and sat down beside the fire, happiness filling her as she saw the gently steaming teapot. How she had missed the luxury of sitting quietly with a pot of tea and a good book. The fire would give her ample light to read, and Isabella was sure she would have a most enjoyable few hours, provided Charles stopped glaring at her.

"You are the most peculiar creature, Miss Docherty," he muttered, shaking his head at her. "I am not at all pleased that you have left the other guests. It is quite rude to leave without saying a single thing."

Isabella sighed and looked up from her book. "I am not like your other guests, can you not see that? You should not have the same expectations for me as you have for them. Although, I do not wish to be rude. I will be sure to bid your guests farewell if I choose to depart the festivities early tomorrow evening."

He did not say another word, but kept her gaze for a few moments longer before turning on his heel and leaving the room.

10

<hr>

For the next few days, Isabella found herself spending most of her time with the other guests, which left very little time for reading or walks in the gardens. Even though it was bitterly cold, Isabella longed to feel the crisp, cool air on her face. It was as though being part of the house party meant being part of a prison, albeit in a gilded cage.

She certainly did not enjoy the other ladies' company, even though she could feel Charles' eyes on her whenever she entered the room and sat demurely with the others. He seemed intent for her to enjoy herself, but nothing they said or did brought her any kind of happiness.

Every day, the ladies would sit around a tea tray and discuss the latest on-dits, the suggestion and gossip often making Isabella blush. The ladies, she gathered, were all quite alone in the world, but seemed to prefer it for a great many reasons, including the fact that they could shower their attentions on any particular gentlemen they chose.

Today was no different. Lady Swift and Lady Marchfield were chuckling about some young man in town who had attempted to make advances to them both, and Isabella felt her ears burn as they spoke openly about their conquests.

"I thought I saw you cozying up to a certain gentleman here, Lady Swift," Lady Marchfield murmured as the other ladies stopped their discussions and leaned in to hear her response. "Did I not see you leave the room with him a few days ago?"

Lady Swift tossed her head. "I do not think we will suit."

"Oh?" Lady Marchfield questioned, sounding quite surprised. "I had thought—"

Lady Swift interrupted, her dark eyes flashing with a sudden anger that surprised Isabella. "He wanted a long liaison with me, and I told him that I enjoyed my freedom. Naturally, we both came to a mutual agreement that there was very little point in beginning any kind of acquaintance, not when I could not give him what he desired."

Knowing very well that this was not the case, Isabella frowned. Lady Swift was as false as the others, trying to cover her tracks by coming up with a lie about Charles that made it look as though she were the one to bring an end to their possible relationship. Her stomach churned with a sudden nausea, sickened by her current company.

"Please excuse me." Isabella rose without knowing where she was going, her feet taking her towards the door without another thought. All she wanted to do was get away from that room, away from the clammy, dirty air that she was being forced to breathe. She knew that Charles expected her to remain with his guests, and had not been pleased when she had taken herself to the library days before, but she could not stand their company for another minute.

Stumbling up to her room, Isabella pushed open the door and practically threw herself inside, startling the maid within who scrambled to her feet at once with an apology on her lips.

"No need for that," Isabella interrupted, walking over to the wardrobe. "Might you help me find some clothes suitable for walking?"

"Walking, miss?" the maid asked, her gaze glancing over to the window.

Frost had drawn its intricate, beautiful patterns across the pane in the early hours of the morning, but, as yet, the frost had not disappeared. That told Isabella just how cold it was.

"I wish to walk, no matter the chill," Isabella replied stoutly. She had been outdoors almost every day of her life, no matter the weather. There had always been crops to see to, animals to care for, and neighbors to visit. Being stuck in one room for most of the day was almost torture to Isabella's mind.

To her relief, the maid pulled out a pair of boots as well as a warm cloak. Continuing to delve into the depths of Isabella's wardrobe, the maid laid out yet more items of clothing until Isabella was sure she would burn with heat, even with the coldness of the day.

Soon, she was wrapped up warmly and made her way down the stairs, slipping out of the front door without any difficulty. Her lungs filled with the cold air, making a smile spread across her face. How much she had missed the refreshing wind against her face.

As unladylike as it was, Isabella picked up her skirts and ran, headlong, towards the gardens. Her boots were sturdy and warm, and soon her cheeks were red, her nose nipping with the cold. It was heaven.

Isabella wandered around Charles' vast expanse of garden, wondering what was to become of her. It had been a few days since Charles had written to his father, and she was not sure when she could expect an answer. Town was not all that far away, but, as she recalled, the duke was currently in Scotland, unless he had decided to return to town earlier than planned.

Would Charles get a reply soon? And what would it mean for her?

She felt so incredibly lost, even though she tried hard not to allow herself to grow despondent. It was as if she were an island, standing alone in the middle of the vast ocean. Her home was gone, in its entirety. She had nothing with which to rebuild it, and even if she could, Isabella knew it would never be the same again. The curtains she had sewn with her mother, the table-cloths they had embroidered together, were all gone. She would never get those things back. They had been completely without price, and someone had seen fit to take them away from her just because they did not like who she was.

Tears filled her eyes, threatening to fall at any moment. She was angry over what had happened, upset that Charles' aunt, Lady Johnston, had chosen to take her long-held wrath out on her when, in truth, it should have been her husband that she put the blame on. Of course, that was not how Charles' world worked, yet another reason that she did not want to be a part of it.

Her breath frosted in front of her face as Isabella struggled to contain her tears. Her Christmas was going to be very different this year. She was not sure what Charles intended for her, as she knew the house party was to be returning to London by Christmas Eve, although whether she was to go with them, she did not know. Perhaps she could ask him to let her remain at his country estate, for she would much prefer to be with Charles' staff below stairs than in some fancy townhouse in London.

The staff had not quite managed to maintain their friendly relationship with her now that she had been moved upstairs, but Isabella continued to go below stairs every day, insisting on making at least three loaves of bread. It meant rising early, but Isabella had never been one to rest long in bed, and, the truth was, she missed putting her hands in the dough. It was something she had always done, since the first day she and her mother had moved to the cottage in the country.

"Oh, Mama," she whispered, tears beginning to trickle down her cheeks. "I miss you so."

Her words floated away on the breeze as a sudden stab of pain threatened to overwhelm her. Seeing a small wooden bench, Isabella sank down onto it, put her face in her hands, and cried.

She had not meant to allow the tears to fall, but once they began to trickle down her cheeks, they became something of a flood, and Isabella found that she could not stop them. Her shoulders shook as sobs rattled through her, her tears unabated. She cried for the loss of her mother and for the pain she endured upon seeing the house she had shared with her completely destroyed.

She cried for the days she had endured alone, wondering what was to become of her, and she cried for Charles. Charles, the man who had shown her kindness in the end, but who had treated her as a veritable stranger the moment she stepped into his house. Isabella wept over how much he had changed from the young man she had once known, her heart rending as she thought of his inappropriate liaison with Lady Swift.

On top of it all lay the burden of her sudden and inexplicable attraction to him, which had begun the night she left the drawing room for the solace of the library. He was handsome, of course, but she could not explain the way her body suddenly came to life when he smiled at her, although that in itself was not a frequent occurrence.

Isabella did not want to feel that way and certainly did not want to linger on the fact that her foolish heart still yearned for the friendship they had once had, telling herself repeatedly that she was being ridiculous.

"Isabella?"

Turning in her seat, Isabella jerked in surprise to see Charles standing behind her, an inscrutable expression on his face.

"You do not need to follow me everywhere, Charles," she said at once, hastily wiping the tears from her eyes and trying her best to gather her composure. "Do you not have guests that require your attention?"

He did not reply, but came a little closer to her, his feet crunching across the frosty grass.

"If you mean to reprimand me once again, then you may as well go back inside," she continued, thinking he was about to speak to her about why she had left the room so abruptly. "I will not go back, not until I am ready. I need to breathe first. I need to be away from those vile gossips who spend their lives doing nothing but seeing to their own pleasures." Getting to her feet, she backed away from him, shaking her head. "I will not be dragged back into that world when I am not ready. Do not ask it of me."

She saw his jaw clench, his hazel eyes seeming to glow with an intensity she had not seen before.

"You are quite content in your world, Charles, but that I can assure you that it is not for me." Shaking her head, Isabella watched him as he stopped a few steps away from her, looking a little lost. "They have never had to rise early to bake bread or sew their own curtains to keep the sunlight out in the early hours of the morning." She smiled sadly, thinking of her mother once more. "Their life and mine, your life and mine, are so very far apart," she finished with a small sigh. "You cannot expect me to simply slot into your world. It might have happened when we were children, but those days are long gone." Her eyes met his and lingered there, a quiet sadness in her gaze. "I do not think we can ever be the same again."

To her surprise, he did not move away, but instead drew closer, and, reaching for her, caught her hands.

"You were crying," he said softly, concern in his expression. "Am I truly so terrible, Isabella?"

Moisture crept to the edge of her lashes once more as she looked up at him, completely astonished by the tenderness in his voice. What had come over him? "It is not just you," she replied quietly. "I have lost my home and all that I love with no idea what my future might hold." Dropping her head, she battled against her urge to cry once more, hating that she was appearing so weak in front of him. "I am so very alone," she whispered, sniffing.

"I know," he said softly. "I received a letter from my friend, Lord Worthington, confirming that all you said was true. I am very sorry, Isabella."

Before she knew what was happening, Charles' arms had gone around her and, moving closer to her, he held her close, not saying a single word. Isabella wanted to ask him what he was doing, confused by his sudden change in behavior, but she discovered that her tears were, once more, falling like rain, and all she could do was cling onto him.

11

"You have a letter, my lord."

Charles held out his hand, and the butler handed him the sealed parchment at once. Surprised to have received a reply so promptly from London, especially when he believed that his father was still in Scotland, Charles broke the seal at once and scanned the writing.

Charles, the letter began. *I returned early from Scotland due to the large volume of snow that began to fall, and just in time, it seems. I am sorry that Miss Docherty did not find your mother or me at home, although I am glad that she has found her way to you.*

Truthfully, there have been some goings-on with your aunt for many years, which I have kept from you as I did not think them of any great concern to you. Over the last ten years, she has grown more and more enraged over what your uncle did, as well as my insistence on keeping the late Miss Docherty on in my household.

Charles drew in a deep breath, a twist of worry tightening in his stomach.

Her temper has become well-known amongst the staff, and I had heard that they all live in fear of her. Your uncle came to speak to me sometime last year to seek my help with my sister. Together, we came up with a plan to remove her to a small estate of her own, where she has lived for a few months. Your uncle has visited her on occasion, as have I, and I thought she appeared to be doing much better. However, if she was the lady who attacked Miss Docherty's home, then I wonder whether Miss Docherty herself is safe, even within your household. I have written to your uncle to ask about my sister's current state of mind.

In short, Charles, consider your aunt a grave danger to Miss Docherty. I believe her to have gone mad with anger and grief, and destroying Miss Docherty's home, whilst terrible in itself, may not satisfy her. I pray you be on your guard and ensure that Miss Docherty remains safe. I do not know what your intentions are for her, but I ask that you will treat her with the same kindness and consideration we showed her mother. For once, Charles, think of someone else before yourself.

Charles read the letter two times over, before letting the parchment fall from his fingers, seeing it flutter down onto his desk. His father's words, whilst filling him with worry and apprehension, did not concern him as much as the sentiment his father had shared—that Charles was, in fact, a selfish person by nature. His father felt that he had to ask Charles to care for Miss Docherty, encouraging him to think of himself last, instead of first. Was he truly that kind of man?

"For goodness sake!" he exclaimed, rising from his desk in frustration. "I am doing exactly the same thing again." Here he was, reading about his aunt and the danger to Miss Docherty, and the only thing concerning him was what his father had said about his behavior. He was acting selfishly, caught up in his own feelings and emotions.

Groaning aloud, he poured himself a brandy, despite it only being mid-morning. His father had never told him about his aunt's growing anger over Isabella's mother, nor that she had been sent to live in an estate of her own. Was his father right in believing that Lady Johnston had been driven mad by the entire situation?

Frowning, Charles recalled how his uncle and aunt had never had children of their own, although his uncle had children from his first wife who had died during childbirth. Why had his aunt harbored such terrible rage? Was it because his governess had borne a child from her husband, whereas she had never been able to carry one? His heart twisted a little in sympathy for his aunt, despite the harm she had caused.

At the same time, he recalled how Miss Docherty had cried in his arms only two days prior. He had, of course, gone to demand she return to the house for his other guests had found her absence more than a little rude, but instead, he had simply held her as she sobbed. He had been so caught up on the impression Miss Docherty was making on his guests that he had forgotten the trauma she had experienced and was, evidently, still dealing with.

The way she had described his guests had, at first, made him stiffen with anger, before realizing that she had every right to say what she did. All the ladies did was talk about whatever titbits of gossip they had heard, making assumptions and conjectures that, at times, could easily turn into rumor. It had never bothered him before that moment, but standing outside by Miss Docherty, and seeing the disdain on her face, had sent a chill right into his soul.

She was correct when she stated that their worlds were very different, but it had made Charles question what it was he loved about his world so very much. Why did he want Miss Docherty to slot into his world without a second thought? Was it because he thought himself better than her? That she should simply step into his realm with delight and pleasure?

He had asked her if he was truly so terrible, and she had not answered. She did not need to. His hope of changing her opinion about him had failed, for the answer had been in her eyes. His heart had stung with the pain of her silent reproof, pushing question after question into his mind.

"Then what am I to do with you?" he muttered to himself, thinking about what his father had said. Was there any chance that his aunt could discover that she was there? His father did not say where she now lived, but even writing to his uncle could take some time before there was an adequate response. His plans to return to London for Christmas Eve now seemed to shatter before his eyes. Surely the most important thing was now to look out for Miss Docherty, even though he was not sure what to do with her.

His guests needed him, however. There were still days left before they were due to return to London, and he was expected to come up with various entertainments, which would include Isabella. Would it be so terrible to continue with the house party whilst she was present within his home? It would give her company, at least, but then he recalled what she had said about his guests, and his heart sank. She did not belong with these people, and they were looking down their noses at her already, simply because she did not join in the idle gossip that the ladies seemed to enjoy so much.

You could always declare the house party over, said a small voice. *That way you can focus on protecting Isabella.*

The thought struck him, hard, but he tried to dismiss it at once. He could not send his guests home without warning, for then he would become the talk of London. They would have no understanding of why he did so, and certainly would raise their eyebrows at how he had remained behind with Miss Docherty.

Then again, he could ask Lord Walton to remain, so that her reputation would be safe—not that she would care particularly about such things given that her hopes for matrimony would most likely be a cleric, farmer, or a clergyman.

"No," he said to himself, a little more firmly than he had intended. "I cannot send them away; it would not be right. But I shall have to inform Miss Docherty of the present situation and beg her not to do anything rash." That would mean no more walks in the garden without company, and certainly no sudden disappearances from their company. She would dislike it intensely, but Charles simply shrugged at the thought. She would simply have to bear it gracefully.

MISS DOCHERTY WAS NOT ALL that compliant.

"I will not stay in the company of those I dislike," she declared when he had called her to his study and explained all to her. "I shall either stay in my rooms or visit the staff below stairs. The cook is becoming dependent on me making bread for her."

"Nonsense," Charles retorted, horrified by the idea that Miss Docherty was spending time with his servants. "You cannot be so stubborn, Miss Docherty."

"Isabella!"

She did not buckle, but simply glared at him. "I have always been Isabella to you, Charles. Do not start with such nonsense now, I...I cannot bear it." Her voice lost some of its anger, the frustration leaving her gaze.

Charles felt like a stone had settled in his stomach, seeing the expression on her face. "Very well," he said quietly. "Isabella, I must beg of you to do as I ask. I am trying my best to protect you."

"I shall be protected within these four walls, shall I not?" Isabella asked a little more softly. "It does not matter where I go, so long as I remain indoors."

"I know how much you love to be outdoors," Charles said,

with a half-smile. "If you wish it, I should be happy to join you whenever you wish."

Her smile was tight, accompanied by a slight shake of her head. "Only when you are free from your obligations to your guests," she replied so quietly he strained to hear her. "I would not make myself a heavy burden to you, Charles. I shall be content pottering around below stairs or reading quietly. I confess I have become somewhat used to my own company since my mother passed away."

The sadness in her expression made his heart lurch, as his father's words began to roll around his mind once more. He had to protect her, for who else would do so? There was no one in this world she could call family, and the friend she had gone to had turned out to be less than willing to help her. Shame climbed up his spine, spreading warmth through his face. Clearing his throat, he rose from his chair and came around to face her, deftly catching one of her hands in his.

"Isabella, I am sorry for how little I have offered you before now," he said honestly. "My father's letter chimed your words, and I have been forced to consider my actions and even my very character. Believe me when I say that I am trying my best to keep you safe, and even though the future might appear blurry at this moment, I swear to you that you will not face it alone."

The astonishment in her eyes was immediate as she blinked, apparently trying to absorb what he had said.

"I want to trust you," she said quietly. "And I do thank you for your concern. I will remain within these walls. I promise."

"And we shall walk together each afternoon," he promised, catching her smile. "I would not ask you to give that up, not when you love it so very much."

The genuine smile on her face made him sent a surge of warmth into his heart as though, for the very first time, he was finally doing the right thing. Realizing that their hands were still joined, he held onto them a little more tightly, suddenly unwilling to release her. His breath hitched as she lifted her face a little more to look into his eyes, a sudden and sharp urge to bring her closer to him and kiss her soundly overtaking him.

"Isabella," he said hoarsely, moving closer. "I...." He did not know what he was trying to say, unable to think clearly. Her presence, her closeness, was making his head spin as he tried to sort out his flying emotions into some sort of coherent order, but finding that he was entirely unable to do so. One urge kept pushing him, the desire to press his lips to hers growing stronger with each passing second.

Unable to fight it any longer, Charles lowered his head and caught her lips with his, heat searing through him and lights exploding in his head.

Only for a short, sharp pain to ripple through his cheek from where she had slapped him.

12

Throwing herself from her chair, Isabella stumbled back from Charles. "What are you doing?" She hated that heat had rushed through her at his kiss, despising the fact that she had been weak enough to allow it, albeit briefly.

Charles rubbed the side of his face, looking more than a little annoyed. "I think that was obvious, Isabella." To rose to his feet and faced her, his mouth a hard line.

"I am not your conquest!" she exclaimed, her hand stinging from where she had slapped him. "I am not like Lady Swift!"

His expression changed from annoyance to shock. "Surely, you do not think that I would treat you in such a manner, Isabella?"

"Of course I do," she retorted, refusing to believe that he could truly feel anything for her. "You are well used to that, are you not? Used to having ladies fall at your feet, used to stealing kisses from those you choose?" Isabella could feel her cheeks heat as she backed away from him, hating that he had managed to capture her under his spell.

He shook his head, looking as though he was about to

explode in temper, and Isabella felt herself shrink inside, suddenly afraid of his anger.

"Isabella," he said, his voice loud and filled with wrath. "I..."

She stared at him in astonishment as his voice suddenly faded away, the anger in his eyes dimming. The finger he pointed at her dropped to his side, his shoulders slumping. It was as though the fight had gone out of him in one breath.

"You are right to think that of me," he said, in a voice that was filled with misery and contempt for himself. "Oh, Isabella, what have I become?"

The eyes that lifted to hers were ones bright with sadness and shame, and, without warning, Isabella felt her heart wrench with pity for him.

"My father has shown me that you were right to question my integrity," he continued, turning away from her. "I become angry at your assessment of me when you have every right to think as you do."

"Charles," she heard herself say, reaching out one hand to him. "I did not mean to cause you this much suffering."

He glanced at her before slumping down in a seat by the fire. "It is a fire I need to go through," he said quietly. "A fire of refinement. I am a man who cares only for himself and his own pleasures. A man who turned away from his oldest friend because he considered her an inconvenience." His voice broke, and he passed a hand over his eyes.

Isabella was stunned. This was no pretense, no game that he was playing to try and make her bend to his will. It was as though he was being taken apart, piece by piece, right before her very eyes. She had never believed that anything she said would get through to him, but apparently, it had pierced his very soul and now he was being transformed.

"I have brought nothing but misery to my parents," he

continued unhappily. "They are right in their estimation of me, as are you." He shook his head, before looking up at her sharply. "But no longer. My guests must go. You are the priority."

Isabella gasped, her hand going to her mouth. "Oh, no, Charles!" she exclaimed, her breath hitching. "They will despise being sent away early. Did you not have some wonderful entertainments planned?"

He shook his head, a determined look on his face. "And yet, I see now that such things are not important. I would rather be here with you, ensuring your safety and wellbeing than continue with my plans."

Stammering, Isabella tried to protest, but to her shock, Charles seemed quite determined. She could hardly believe that he was genuine in his intentions, given how much she knew he adored all the festivities he had planned, but as he threw himself from his chair and stalked from the room, she was left standing in disbelief, unable to take in the extraordinary events that had just occurred.

Charles had kissed her, then declared what a scoundrel he was, only to leave her standing alone while he went to send his guests packing. She did not know what to do or to think, still frozen to the spot.

However, she could not help but smile just a little, relief suddenly filling her as she wandered to the door. This was the very first hint of the Charles she had once known, the kind, compassionate, and sometimes, impetuous, young man that had been her friend. Could she allow herself to hope that he was truly genuine? That he really was attempting to change?

WANDERING ALONG THE CORRIDOR, Isabella was surprised to hear a sudden crash. Shrieks and shouts erupted from nearby, which made her hair stand on end. To her astonishment, Lady Swift came crashing out of the drawing room and stormed along the hallway towards Isabella, shouting and wailing with every step. Behind her came the other ladies, each one spitting with fury.

Apparently, Charles' swift decision to bring an end to the house party had not gone down well.

"You!" shrieked Lady Swift, stopping dead in her tracks and glaring at Isabella. "This is all your doing!" One long, bony finger prodded Isabella's shoulder as she stared at Lady Swift, not sure what she meant.

"You think you can have him all to yourself, but I assure you that he is not that kind of gentleman. He will have his fill of you soon enough, and then where will you be?"

Isabella opened her mouth to defend herself, entirely bewildered at what was going on, but Lady Swift, having said her piece, turned on her heel and marched away. Each of the other ladies gave Isabella a look that was filled with loathing, as though she had somehow influenced Charles to bring the party to a sudden close.

Letting out a long breath and still feeling bemused, Isabella continued to make her way along the hallway, only to hear Charles' loud voice booming across the hallway, intermingled with two other gentleman's voices. Apparently, Charles was having a bit of a difficult time in encouraging his guests to leave. Isabella had to admit that even she was stunned by his swift decision, and not wanting to be the brunt of any more wrath, hurried up the staircase towards her bedchamber.

It did not take long to push her feet into cozy boots and pull her warm cloak around her shoulders, and after only a few minutes, Isabella found herself outside, her feet crunching over the still frozen ground. The warning Charles had given her rang in her ears for a moment, but she did not heed it for long. She would only be outside a few minutes, needing to get away from the commotion going on within.

Isabella had to admit that whilst she was utterly astonished by all that had just occurred, she could not help but be thrilled with the fact that Charles was showing her such consideration. It made her feel as though she was actually important to him, that their long-standing friendship meant something to him. Whether it would be a lasting transformation, she could not say, but Isabella was determined to trust that, at least for the time being, he wanted to prove that he could change.

The gardens were quiet and still, with barely even a bird song to interrupt the silence. Isabella smiled to herself as she walked, enjoying the sights and sounds of being outside alone on a cold winter's day. The sun was barely visible, even though it was still early afternoon, and a cold grayness wrapped itself around the trees. Despite this, Isabella found a great deal of happiness and contentment in being outdoors, straying a little further than she ought.

"I knew I would find you here."

With a shriek, Isabella spun on her heel to see the same woman who had destroyed her home. It was Lady Johnston. Isabella's heart began to slam repeatedly into her chest, making her gasp for breath.

"Trying to get back into the family, are you?" the lady sneered, walking closer to Isabella, who immediately began to back away. "As soon as I found out you had been at my sister-in-law's door, I knew I had to stop you."

"Stop me?" Isabella repeated, trying to think of a way to get past the lady, but discovering that she had the same brute of a man standing just behind her. He would easily stop Isabella if she tried to run past them. "I came to them for aid. That is all."

She tried to keep her voice calm, even though her mind was screaming in panic. "How did you know I had gone there?"

Lady Johnston laughed wickedly. "Do you not think that I have spies within the walls of my brother's home, as well as my husband's? I know all their goings on. Ever since they decided to banish me from my own home, I have been determined to know everything that goes on in their households."

"I assure you, I mean no harm to your family," Isabella pleaded, her eyes glancing all around her in an attempt to find a way to escape. "I have simply come to them in search of help."

The lady shook her head, her dark eyes glinting with a hint of steel. "No, you intend to get your claws into that nephew of mine."

"I do not, I swear to you," Isabella promised, growing more frightened with each passing second. "Charles has been very good to me and—"

"Charles!" Lady Johnston shrieked, her eyes widening as if with shock. "Charles! You dare to call him Charles when you are nothing, nothing, compared to him. You have no right!"

Isabella allowed the lady to continue her rant as her stomach clenched with fear. The man standing to Lady Johnston's left was wearing a somewhat crooked grin, as though he were enjoying the prospect of bringing Isabella's life to a swift and sudden end.

"No, indeed," Lady Johnston shouted, drawing closer to Isabella. "It will not happen. I will not allow it. Your life, your stain on the world, and on my family, is to come to an end."

Isabella caught sight of a flash of metal and did the only thing she could. Slamming herself hard into Lady Johnston, she knocked her into the burly man and, terror screaming in her mind, she ran past her and further into the woods. No thundering of feet sounded behind her, and no strong hand came out to grasp at her. Although, she could hear Lady Johnston's screams of frustration echoing behind her.

She had no idea where she was going, aware that the light was already starting to fade and that the cold air was nipping at her fingers and nose. It was only then that she felt something warm at her side and, pressing her hand to her gown, discovered that her fingers were bright red with blood.

13

C harles frowned to himself, pausing in his steps as the smallest of sounds met his ears. His guests had created a fuss at being asked to leave, even though he had tried to explain as best he could. It appeared that they were all caught up with just how poorly they were being treated, as opposed to how desperate a situation Isabella was in. The shame of it was that he knew he would have reacted in much the same way before Isabella had shown him the depths of his selfishness.

The sound came again, and Charles felt a ripple of fear run down his neck. Was that a cry?

"My lord."

The butler, on seeing him, rushed towards him with a look of worry etched on his features.

"What is it?" Charles asked, surprised to see his butler in such a state. "Has something happened with one of the guests?"

The butler shook his head. "Miss Docherty, my lord, she was seen out walking in the gardens, going towards the forest."

Charles frowned. "I told her to stay indoors."

"On top of which, there was a lady seen walking in the

grounds," the butler continued. "The gardener was to go after her, but the large gentleman with her gave him something of a beating."

Charles felt his heart begin to hammer in his chest. "Is the gardener all right?"

"It seems that nothing was broken," the butler replied with a wince. "But Miss Docherty has not returned. What do you want us to do?"

Hurrying down the hallway towards the front door, Charles felt his anxiety rise with each step. "I will deal with this myself," he called back to the worried looking butler. "Take care of the gardener and, if you can, send Lord Walton out after me."

He did not wait to hear the butler's reply, but hurried outside into the freezing air. Thankfully, the frost had still not melted away, and Miss Docherty's footsteps could be clearly seen across the frosty grass. Breaking into a run, he followed her steps towards the wooded area, only to stop short at the sight of his aunt coming out of the woods, followed by one of the largest men he had ever seen.

Marching towards her, he glared at her. "What are you doing here, Aunt?"

"A fine way to greet your family," she replied with a roll of her eyes. "I just came for a visit, that is all. The woods seemed like they would provide a pleasant little walk, and after my long carriage ride here, I simply had to take a stroll."

"I did not know you intended to call on me," he stated, not believing her for a moment. "Is my uncle not with you?"

The flash of anger in her eyes told him that all was not well. "Your uncle and I have decided to spend the Yuletide festivities apart, and since I knew you were here, I thought I might beg to stay here with you instead of being entirely alone." She put on a somewhat morose expression, as though intending to tug at his heartstrings.

"I see," Charles murmured placatingly.

His mind worked furiously as his aunt continued to discuss her woes with him, wondering how best to get her into the house without alerting her to the fact that he intended to keep her under lock and key until he could send for his uncle. She was clearly mad, laughing one moment and looking close to tears the next. And, over and over, all he could think about was where Isabella might be and what his aunt had done to her.

"Well, let us not stand out here in the freezing cold," he said pleasantly, as Lord Walton came to join them. "Aunt, this is my dear friend Lord Walton. Walton, might you escort my aunt inside? I have had a report about an injured gardener that I must investigate. I will join you very soon." He saw Walton nod at once and murmur something to the lady who, to Charles' relief, began to walk towards the house. Her large manservant appeared to hesitate, as if aware what Charles' true intentions were, but eventually he followed his mistress.

"Walton," Charles called, stepping closer as his aunt continued to walk with her manservant beside her. "I forgot to tell you in which room to place my aunt."

Walton turned back at once. "Whatever is going on, Charles?" he asked in a low voice. "The butler said something about Miss Docherty?"

"Please take my aunt to the blue room, and ensure the butler locks the door from the outside. Dispatch a man to fetch my father and my uncle. The butler will know their addresses."

Walton goggled at him for a moment, but gave a swift nod of his head. "And what of that oaf?"

Charles lifted one shoulder. "I leave him to you. I must go in search of Miss Docherty. I thank you, Walton."

The light was fading fast. Charles had to find Isabella before the sun set, for then he could become lost within the woods. Running into the dense trees, he followed the path as best he could, glad that the coldness of the day allowed their footprints to remain visible.

"Where are you, Isabella?" he murmured, still moving forward. "Where are you?"

Something glinted, catching his eye. Frowning, he looked a little more closely, discovering to his horror that a small dagger was lying on the ground, as though thrown away. Streaks of red adorned the blade, making his breath catch. His aunt and manservant had shown no signs of injury, which could mean only one thing: Isabella was hurt.

"Isabella!" His cry rang out through the trees as he hurried forward, his heart in his throat.

His aunt had done something terrible, and he only hoped that Isabella was not gravely injured. He paused in his steps, wondering whether to go back to the house and demand that his aunt show him where Isabella had gone, but one glance at the darkening sky told him that he had no time to do anything of the sort. He simply had to find her.

Continuing to search, his eyes struggling to see through the ever-growing shadows, Charles tried not to allow regret to fill him, as though Isabella had already died. He had to believe that she was still alive and that, even if she was injured, she would recover.

How much of an influence she had already had on him, even though she had only been with him for a few days. She refused to back down, speaking to him in the way she always had, telling him truths that had hit him squarely between the eyes. He had been forced to consider what she said, only for his father's letter to prove her words. Only that very afternoon had he seen himself as he truly was, the black stain of his behavior spreading out in front of him. He needed her to be there beside him, needed her to guide him through this new path he was determined to make for himself.

"Isabella!" he cried, again and again, his voice growing hoarse as he called her name. He had to find her.

"Please," he whispered, as he looked to the heavens. "I have to find her. I need her."

A quiet sound made him pause, his heart hammering in his chest. "Isabella?" he asked softly, hoping to hear the noise again. "Isabella, is that you?"

"Charles," came a breathy whisper. "Charles, I am here."

Charles moved forward at once, his steps slow as he tried to find her in the gloom. To his horror, he saw her leaning heavily against a thick tree trunk, her cloak pulled around her as she gripped it. Her face was pale in the dim light, her eyes huge and filled with fear.

"Thank goodness, thank goodness," he whispered, hurrying to her and pulling her into his arms. "I have been so worried."

Her cry was muffled as he held her tightly, forcing him to step back with concern.

"I think I am injured," she whispered, her face contorted with pain. "Your aunt..."

"I found her," Charles replied grimly, bending down to look at where she pressed her hand. His stomach swirled as he saw the dark stain on her dress, suddenly terrified that she might yet die. "I have to get you back, Isabella." He put one arm under her knees and, even though she cried out, hoisted her into his arms. "You will permit me?"

She tried to smile despite her pain. "Of course. Thank you for coming to find me."

He brushed a kiss to her brow, alarmed at how her head rolled against his shoulder almost immediately, her eyes closing. "I am sure I swore that I would always be able to find you," he said, making his way back through the trees. "Do you not remember, Isabella? As children, we would play hide and go seek, and you were always so easy to find."

She did not respond, but a small smile crossed her face.

"Do not leave me now," he said softly. "Do not run away to a place where I cannot yet follow."

The smile drifted from her face, and Charles felt her go suddenly limp, overcome with the pain and exhaustion of being out in the woods alone. Fear clutched at his heart as he moved towards the entrance of the woods, relieved that he knew the forest so well. He hoped that Walton had managed to secure his aunt in her room, as well as taken care of the oaf that accompanied her. He did not want to risk Isabella's safety upon entering the house.

However, the house was eerily quiet as he entered, staggering now with the strain of hurrying with Isabella in his arms.

"Quickly," he said, as the butler stared at her prone form in alarm. "Send for the doctor and have the maids send up hot water and rags. She will be in my room."

"A...at once," the butler stammered, looking horrified at the sight of Isabella.

"Where is my aunt?" Charles called, as he began to make his way up the staircase.

"In the blue room," the butler replied. "However, she is making something of a racket. I believe Lord Walton is dealing with the situation."

Charles did not respond, but continued carrying Isabella up the staircase, a maid catching up with him with clean sheets in her hand.

"Put those on the bed at once, and place a towel on the left side," Charles instructed as he managed to discard Isabella's cloak. "Go and fetch Lord Walton. Bring him here."

The maid scurried away, and Charles was left alone with Isabella, placing her down gently on the bed. Her eyes remained closed with dark rings encircling them. The red stain on her dress was even more obvious now, although he did not think it had grown since he had first picked her up in the woods.

He did not know what to do. Should he try to remove her dress to see to the wound, or should he leave that to the maids and the doctor? Should he try to wake her? Should he leave her sleeping?

Brushing his hand down her cheek, he lifted one errant strand of golden hair and placed it behind her ear. Such a feeling of tenderness rose in his heart that it almost overwhelmed him, suddenly feeling quite desperate.

"Do not leave me," he whispered, leaning down to press a kiss to her cheek. "My dear friend, Isabella. I do not think I can be without you now."

14

Walton, the maids, and the housekeeper all arrived at once, and Charles found himself ushered from the room by his friend.

"Best to leave the maids to clean up," Walton said, firmly taking Charles by the arm. "The doctor has only just arrived and the butler is to show him up."

"She might wake," Charles protested, the urge to stay by her side pushing his steps back towards her. "I need to be with her."

Walton shook his head. "No, Sutherland. You must leave them to do their work. I am sure they will come to find you once she is recovered. The doctor will not want to be disturbed." He gazed at Charles with an inscrutable look on his face. "I must say, I have never seen you this way before."

"What way?" Charles asked, frowning.

"So caught up with a lady before," Walton explained. "Yes, I am aware that you have never before had a lady injured as she has been, but prior to that, you have been taken up with her. And to send all but me home is extraordinary."

Charles shrugged. The other guests and their feelings on the subject no longer seemed to matter. "She needed me."

Walton lifted one eyebrow.

"Very well, I care about her," Charles replied, sighing. "She is an old friend, and I treated her abominably. I want to make every effort to show her just how wrong I was."

"So, she has shown you the error of your ways, then?"

"Very much so," Charles repeated firmly. "I am afraid I shall end up being a very different man to the one you know, Walton."

To his surprise, Walton chuckled. "That is probably for the best, Sutherland. After all, we all must take steps towards a maturity that has been sorely lacking in our lives for some time, has it not? For what it is worth, as surprised as I was at your actions, I cannot disagree with them. There are those in our lives whom we must care for, no matter the circumstances."

Charles nodded. "I am just sorry it took me so long to see how important she is to me."

They walked along the hallway for some time, until the sound of shrieking suddenly met Charles' ears.

"Not to interrupt your thoughts, but that is your aunt, by the way," Walton said helpfully. "Two men were sent to fetch your father and your uncle, as you requested."

Charles cringed at the sounds that came from his aunt's room. "Clearly, she is not that impressed with her current circumstances."

"I ensured the windows were all locked, and there is no other door but this," Walton replied with a lopsided smile.

Charles nodded, wondering whether to speak to his aunt or not. "Thank you, Walton." Curiosity over what had happened to the stocky manservant overtook him, and he lifted one eye questioningly towards Walton. "What of the man?"

"Gregor, apparently," Walton replied amiably. "The cook's cast iron skillet took care of him. The staff does not take kindly to one of their own being so badly beaten, so I believe two of the footmen took pleasure in knocking him to the ground. He is locked in the pantry, bound hand and foot. The constable has been sent for."

Relived that he was not going to have to deal with the man himself, Charles slapped Walton on the shoulder. "You have really come through for me when I needed you, Walton. I cannot adequately express my gratitude."

"Not in the least," Walton replied with a seriousness that Charles had not often seen. "I know you will have a lot on your plate now, Charles, with the constable, your aunt, and the doctor, but I am more than happy to deal with anything you wish to give me. You do not have to struggle with this alone."

More grateful than he could express, Charles could only nod, his thoughts turning back to Isabella. "I shall speak to my aunt," he said quietly. "Although, be at the door, would you? I am not sure she will not try to make her escape. Although she does not have the dagger anymore, thank goodness."

A look of horror passed over Walton's face. "You mean it was your aunt and not her manservant who hurt Isabella?"

"Precisely that," Charles replied, his face grave. "I believe her mad, Walton, blaming Isabella and her mother for the fact that she was never able to provide my uncle with children." He shook his head. "It seems so strange to blame the woman who was forced to bear my uncle's child and sent from the house in disgrace."

"And that has affected her mind," Walton said slowly. "What are you intending to do with her?"

Charles shook his head. "She is not my responsibility. My uncle and father can deal with her. My only focus is Isabella. I will try to speak to my aunt to quieten her, but that is all I intend to do."

"Then I will guard the door," Walton said helpfully. "She might have more strength than you know."

Grimacing, Charles turned the heavy key in the lock and

walked into the room, shutting the door firmly behind him. His aunt stared at him with wild eyes, her hair in disarray and the room in a complete state behind her. It was evident she had been hurling whatever she could get her hands on in her fit of rage.

"Aunt," he said calmly. "What did you do to Isabella?"

She narrowed her eyes. "You mean that wench?"

"Please do not refer to Isabella so disrespectfully. She came to me for help after what you did to her home," Charles replied, making sure that he kept one hand on the door handle.

His aunt's face grew dark. "That woman stole my husband!" She launched into a stream of insults and attacks, her hatred for Isabella's mother more than evident.

Charles held up one hand, stopping her tirade. "Aunt, Isabella's mother was set upon by my uncle. She came here out of sheer desperation, and your attacks on her are untenable."

She glared at him, her eyes filled with a wildness that frightened Charles. "You are under the same spell that her mother cast over my husband. You believe you have affections for her." Stepping closer, her aunt grasped Charles' lapels, as though she could somehow convince him to turn his back on Isabella. "It is wrong, Charles. So very wrong. You need to stay away from her."

Charles knew it would do no good to explain to his aunt that since his uncle was only his uncle by marriage, that there was no wrong in his affection for Isabella. She was not able to listen and understand, so fixed on her vehemence over Isabella. Slowly, trying to extricate himself from his aunt's grip, he gave her a placating smile.

"Now, Aunt, you just rest here and—"

"You're on her side!" his aunt screeched, stepping back and raising her hand. "There is a sickness in this family, and it all stems from her." Her hand slammed across his face, her nails digging into his skin, and Charles felt a strong hand grab his arm and pull him, bodily, out of the door before Lord Walton slammed the door shut behind him.

Seeing Walton turn the key in the lock, Charles slumped against the wall, hearing his aunt ranting from within.

"Thank you, Walton," he muttered, pressing one hand to his cheek. "Her mind is lost. I can do nothing for her."

"You might want to go and clean that," Walton replied, frowning. "And one of the maids sent me to tell you the doctor is finished with Miss Docherty."

"Is she well?" Charles asked, a surge of energy racing through him. "Can I see her?"

Walton said nothing, but gestured along the hallway, another lopsided smile on his face as Charles practically ran the length of the hallway, desperate to see Isabella again.

Knocking once, Charles entered the room, seeing it lit with many candles. The doctor was busy tidying up his things, glancing up at Charles from under bushy brows.

"Ah, Lord Sutherland," he said, gruffly. "This lady is under your care?"

"She is," Charles replied, walking over to the bed at once and looking down at Isabella. Her eyes were closed with exhaustion written all over her face.

"She is very tired, of course," the doctor murmured quietly. "But with rest, she will recover. She has not woken yet, but she will, in time."

Charles picked up Isabella's hand and squeezed it gently, awash with relief. "Was she badly injured?"

"It was a bad wound, yes, but it is a flesh wound only. It is as if she dodged the attempt made to stab her, but caught the edge of the knife instead." The doctor looked up at Charles in question. "It was an attempt to rid her of her life, yes?"

"Yes," Charles muttered, shaking his head. "Have no fear, the culprit is safely under guard."

The doctor nodded. "Very good. Now, I have stitched and wrapped the wound, and your maid knows how and when to change the poultice and the dressing. Make sure she rests and remains abed for at least a week."

"A week?" Charles repeated, knowing that his plans for Christmas were now going completely awry. "Then it shall be a very quiet Christmas indeed."

Chuckling, the doctor put one hand on Charles' arm. "Have no fear, my lord. She will make a full recovery. You will see her smiling face very soon, I promise."

"Thank you, doctor," Charles said fervently. "Send me the bill, and I shall pay it at once."

The doctor nodded and, picking up his bag, left the room. Charles, wanting to spend some time alone with Isabella, sent the maid away to fetch him a tea tray. He had no intention of leaving Isabella's side again.

Once the door closed, Charles looked down at Isabella and felt his heart squeeze with pain. He had been so foolish. If only he had listened to her concerns sooner, then he might have discovered his aunt's intentions earlier and kept Isabella safe.

He pressed her hand to his lips, kissing it gently. She was the woman he needed in his life, the one who would show him how to live a life of kindness and generosity. He wanted to become the man she thought he could be, to become worthy of her—if she would have him.

Charles could not deny that his growing affection for Isabella had been swift and sweet, as if reawakened simply by her presence. He had tried to deny it, but his heart had refused to listen. Now, seeing how close he had come to losing her, Charles knew that he loved her.

She had endured so much, and he simply could not send her away again. The idea he had suggested to her, of settling her far away in a little home of her own, was now repulsive to him. He could not have her living apart from him. He had to have her by his side and in his life. There could not be any parting from her, not again.

"Isabella," he whispered, desperate for her to open her eyes. "Isabella, come back to me. I need you. I...I love you."

There was no reply.

15

Isabella frowned, her body aching. Pain filled her whenever she tried to move, and over and over, all she could hear was Charles' insistent voice. He kept asking her to open her eyes, but everything was hazy. It was as if she were surrounded by a thick fog, one that sapped her strength and demanded that she keep her eyes closed. Tired of fighting, Isabella gave in, drifting back into obscurity.

Eventually, Isabella stirred once more and found that things were not as cloudy as they had been. However, there was no insistent voice calling her name any longer. Had she dreamt it all?

Isabella managed to open her eyes, blinking to clear her cloudy vision. She saw that she was in a large, four-poster bed, and sitting in the chair next to her was Charles.

He was sound asleep, his face pale and dark rings under his eyes. Dressed in only his shirt and pantaloons, his hair in utter disarray, he looked the least distinguished Isabella had seen him since arriving at his estate. Something burst in her heart as she tried to sit up, a sharp gasp catching the back of her throat at the pain radiating from her side. Charles did not move, evidently exhausted.

"He's been like that for some time," came a quiet voice, and as Isabella managed to push herself back up on the pillows, she saw Lord Walton come towards her. "I told him I would keep watching you so that he might get some sleep, but he refused to move."

"How long have I been asleep?" Isabella asked, her voice hoarse and throat scratching. The pain in her side burned, but she did not give in to it, refusing the laudanum Walton indicated to her.

Lord Walton poured her a glass of water and handed it to her before settling down in another chair opposite Charles. "A day and a half," he said calmly. "The doctor was surprised that you were out for so long, but he put it down to your injury and the cold, as well as the shock of what occurred. However, you are healing well by all accounts."

The memory of Lady Johnston's actions hit Isabella in the stomach, tension rippling through her.

"All is well in that regard," Walton continued calmly. "Or as well as it can be. You need have no fear about your safety."

"I see," Isabella responded, her gaze returning to Charles. "And what of Charles? Is he well?"

"Exhausted, but otherwise in perfect health," Lord Walton said dryly. There was a twinkle in his eye as he leaned forward, as though about to impart a remarkable secret. "He has not told me much about you, Miss Docherty, but I must say that I have never seen someone have as big an effect on him as you have."

She stared at him, wondering what he meant.

He continued, obviously seeing her disbelief. "I mean that you have made him question almost everything about himself. Perhaps it is that you remind him of the man he used to be, the child he used to be." He shrugged. "Obviously, that did not particularly please the guests, but that cannot be helped."

"He sent them all away," she whispered, remembering how astonished she had been to discover such a thing. "I can hardly believe he did that."

Lord Walton chuckled. "I believe it goes to prove just how much he wishes to change his selfish habits. Not for me, of course. I quite enjoy my own self-indulgence and hope to spoil myself for as long as possible."

Isabella was not sure what to say to this, wondering whether the glint in Lord Walton's eye meant that he was entirely in earnest.

"Now," he said, standing up. "I shall go in search of tea tray for you, for I am sure you are in need of replenishment."

Heat hit Isabella's cheeks as she realized he meant to leave her alone with Charles.

"I will be back momentarily," Walton finished, walking to the door. "I am sure Charles will be very glad to see you awake again."

Isabella was about to respond, only for Walton to slam the door closed with such force that Charles jumped from him his chair at once, his eyes wide and staring.

"What...?" He looked around, only to catch sight of Isabella. "Oh, my," he breathed, sinking slowly back into his chair and reaching for her hand. "You are awake."

Such was the look of relief in his eyes that Isabella did not know how to respond. "As you see," she replied eventually. "Thank you for waiting on me with such patience."

"How do you feel?" he asked, his eyes searching her face for signs of pain. "Are you in discomfort?"

She lifted one shoulder, only to wince. "I will not pretend it is not painful, but Walton told me it is healing nicely."

He dropped his gaze, his expression growing sorrowful. "I

am only sorry I was not able to prevent your injury," he said quietly. "Had I taken your concerns with more severity, then I might have discovered the truth about my aunt's intentions earlier."

Whilst that was true, Isabella found herself wanting to relieve Charles of the burden of guilt he carried. "I think your aunt would have found a way regardless," she replied truthfully, trying to push herself up in bed a little more.

Pain had her sucking in air, and Charles immediately rose to assist her, his every gesture radiating concern. Once she was a little more settled, he sat down again and, to Isabella's surprise, reached for her hand. She found that the warmth of his skin against hers was both a comfort and a reminder of all they had shared as children and, now, as adults. It sparked the same feelings that she had been trying to hide from herself for the last few days, but this time, Isabella chose not to fight them.

"My aunt had a knife, it seems," Charles continued, his eyes searching her face. "She is mad, I believe. Had she managed to... to..." He twisted his head away, not able to complete his sentence.

Isabella squeezed his hand gently. "Do not think such things, Charles. I am alive now, am I not?"

He looked back at her, agony on his face. "What would I have done without you?" he whispered, his eyes piercing her. "You have come back into my life and shown me how utterly selfish a creature I am. I feel as though I am only just beginning to discover myself again, and to have lost you would have brought that to a shattering close."

"You need not distress yourself so," Isabella returned, her voice beginning to grow hoarse again, as the effort of speaking began to tire her out. "It did not happen, Charles, and I think I shall make a full recovery."

"Of course you will," he said firmly, pressing her hand. "You are to stay here with me until you are well enough to rise from your bed." A somewhat curious expression came over his face, as he looked at her. "I hope you do not mind spending Christmas here with me. Lord Walton intends to remain I think, for I cannot get rid of him, and my parents shall be arriving from London shortly."

"What of your aunt?" Isabella bit her lip, a swirl of anxiety in her chest.

Charles shook his head. "She will be taken care of by my uncle. You need not have any fear."

"I should not wish to see him, or her," Isabella said, hurriedly, not wishing to set eyes upon the man who had attacked her mother.

"Of course not," Charles replied at once. "Do not think that I have any strong connection with the man, Isabella. The only reason he has come is to fetch his wife, and my father will assist him in making arrangements for her. You must not worry."

Settling back against the pillows, Isabella felt her eyes drift closed. A feeling of relief and safety rested all through her, making her limbs heavy.

"Rest," came Charles' whisper as he released her hand. "I shall see you again very soon."

Isabella tried to answer but was too tired. His gentle kiss to her forehead brought a smile to her lips before she, once more, drifted off to sleep.

BY THE TIME Christmas day arrived, Isabella had already been up and about for two days. Her side, whilst still healing, did not pain her half as much, and she had made her way to the kitchens to help with all the preparation, much to Charles'

dismay. She had merely laughed and told him that he needed to remember that she was not of his station, and he had lapsed into silence.

Christmas came and was a very jovial affair, and Isabella could not remember the last time she had laughed so much. Lord Walton, for all his egotistical nature, was a remarkably humorous man.

They had shared a wonderful meal together, and Isabella had very much enjoyed spending time with Charles' mother and father, who, to her very great delight, treated her as though she was a long-lost relative. They had always been kind to her and her mother when Isabella had been a child, so it came as no surprise that that generosity and interest was still evident.

Charles, however, was a different matter. He said very little, although, whenever Isabella looked up, his gaze was firmly on hers. His eyes were warm, although his mouth did not smile, nor was there any kind of joviality in his expression. She could not understand why he looked so, although an uncomfortable feeling told her that she was the cause of it.

He had not taken her hand or even attempted to show her any kind of affection since the day she had woken. They had spent time conversing, and he had been more than attentive, having rarely left her side, but Isabella felt as though much was left unsaid.

Could it be possible that Charles was, truly, a changed man? Such a pronounced change would take time, but he was evidently in earnest. Isabella could not help but allow her heart to soften towards him, and with that softening came the first awakening feelings of love.

However, her future still remained unknown. Had Charles managed to secure her a small cottage somewhere, as he promised? He had not said a single word about it, and she had not wanted to raise the question, given just how happy and content she felt with him. However, Isabella knew that their current state could not last forever. Was that why he looked so troubled? Did he know that their friendship must, once again, be broken apart?

Come the end of the day, the family was tired. Lord Walton was busy playing cards with the duke, whereas the duchess retired to bed at an early hour. Isabella too, rose to excuse herself, exhausted from the day's events. There had been singing, games, gifts, and the most wonderful of dinners. Isabella could not have asked for more.

"Charles?" she asked softly, seeing him sitting by the fire. "I think I shall retire. I wish to thank you for such a wonderful Yuletide celebration, for I have very much enjoyed it."

He looked up at her, as though startled to see her standing before him. Clearing his throat, he rose, and to her surprise, took her arm and threaded it under his.

"Let me escort you to your room, my dear," he murmured. "You look pale, and I would not want you wearying yourself on the stairs."

Isabella was about to retort that she was more than capable of doing such a thing alone, but the sparks shooting towards her heart at his touch rendered her speechless. They left the drawing room together and walked in silence for a time until they came to the staircase. Isabella was just about to take the first step when he came to a sudden stop, dropping her arm and grasping her shoulders.

"I cannot do it."

Startled, Isabella stared at him, her breath catching in her chest at the need in his eyes.

"I cannot lose you again."

"Lose me?" she repeated as his hands dropped from her shoulders. "Charles, whatever are you talking about?"

"I am talking about you and me," he replied at once, the words tumbling from his mouth. "I know you slapped me good and hard the first time, but Isabella, you must know how I feel about you."

Her throat constricted as she tried her best to breathe, a burst of happiness in her chest.

"I am not worthy of you, I know," he continued, with a desperate tone to his voice. "But I am trying to become the man I ought to have been, pushing my selfish nature as far from me as I can."

Hardly able to get the words from her mouth, Isabella brushed his cheek, her touch stunning him into silence.

"Charles," she said hoarsely. "I have seen the way you have tried to change, and I admire you for it."

The hope in his eyes faded. "Admiration is not what I wanted," he muttered, his head dropping a little. "You have always reminded me that you are not of my station, but that is not in the least true." Raising his head, he looked at her again, his gaze focused. "You have shown me that title and fortune do not matter, for they can do more damage to one's character than one realizes. Kindness and compassion, such as my father and mother have shown and such as you have in abundance, are what matter. In that regard, you are of a greater station than I will ever be." Shaking his head, he caught her hand. "I have so much to learn from you, Isabella. Say you will not leave me."

"I...I..." Isabella's mouth was dry, her mind whirling with a thousand thoughts. "I have nowhere else to go, Charles."

That was not the answer he was searching for, it seemed, for his shoulders slumped as though she had killed his very last hope.

"I want you to know of the affection I have for you, Isabella," he murmured, making to turn from her. "The cottage in the country shall be yours as soon as I can make the arrangements."

Suddenly terrified that he was about to leave her forever, that they were never to share their innermost thoughts and feelings, Isabella did the only thing she could think to do. Grasping his hand, she pulled him back to her, and practically throwing her arms around his neck, she kissed him.

It was a startling revelation.

Having never kissed anyone before, Isabella was unprepared for the stars that seemed to break into brilliant light around her. Charles froze for a moment, only for his arms to slip around her waist as he returned her kiss.

It was one of the sweetest moments of her life.

It was only when Charles' arms tightened, and Isabella let out a squeak of pain, that she pulled her lips from his, his expression filled with apology.

"I am terribly sorry," he said, hastily dropping his hands from her waist. "I forgot your injury."

Isabella laughed, despite the ache in her side. "Charles," she murmured, keeping one hand on his shoulder. "I am quite well, I assure you." She saw the worry fade from his face and felt his hand catch her free one. "As you can see," she continued softly. "I do not wish for the house in the country."

He looked at her for a long time, as though he could not believe what she was saying. Isabella continued to smile at him, her heart almost bursting with happiness.

"You believe that I am no longer the man you first met, then?" he asked, brushing her hair back from her forehead. "You forgive me for the terrible way I treated you?"

"I believe you have changed, and that the recognition of your selfishness was a true one," she replied softly. "You have always had kindness and compassion in you, Charles. It just took a little time to come to the fore."

"You brought it to the fore," he replied at once. "You, my dear sweet Isabella. My oldest friend has shown me the man I should be." He smiled at her, his eyes filled with such a depth of emotion that Isabella felt her breath catch.

"Say you will live here with me," he said softly, as his fingers traced the curve of her cheek. "Say you will be my wife, Isabella. I find myself in love with you, truth be told." He swallowed hard and looked away for a moment. "We will not go to town, but live here, away from the social expectations that have grown so distasteful to me of late. I would have but your company, and yours alone. Say you will marry me, Isabella... My heart longs for no other. This is the only gift I wish for this Christmas and for all my Christmases to come. To have you by my side, for better or for worse."

Isabella's answering smile was beautiful, her heart so filled with joy and happiness that she thought it might burst from her. She wanted to laugh and cry all at once, finally feeling as though she had managed to find her way back home.

"But what of your parents?" she questioned. "Do you truly believe they will honor our union?"

"Yes," Charles answered without hesitation. "I will not marry anyone else, and being that I am an only child, I bear the full responsibility for the future of the dukedom. Besides, you have always been like family to us."

"Then, my answer is yes. Of course I will, my love," she replied, lifting her hands to his face. "You have sparked a love in my own heart, one that is deeper than just mere friendship. I will be your wife and live by your side for as many years as we are granted."

"And we shall be happy," he murmured, resting his forehead against hers.

"Yes," Isabella agreed, her voice filled with tenderness. "Yes, my love. We shall be very happy indeed and spend many more Christmas days together."

"But I cannot imagine that any will be as happy as this one,"
he whispered before lowering his head to kiss her tenderly.

THE END

UNEXPECTED EARL

By Joyce Alec

L ondon 1839

"Ah, there you are!"

Miss Catherine Hewson turned at once to see her mother bearing down on her with a particularly handsome gentleman by her side. Not in the least surprised at being interrupted in such a way, she sighed inwardly and pasted a bright smile on her face.

"My dear Catherine!" Lady Hewson exclaimed. "I have only just now been introduced to this particular gentleman, who, I believe, is new to town."

"I am," the gentleman replied, his fair hair falling over his brow as he inclined his head. "Your mother is being particularly kind to me."

"I can see that," Catherine murmured, catching the twinkle in the gentleman's eye.

As her mother continued to rattle on, Catherine allowed herself to carefully study the gentleman in question. He was tall, with broad shoulders and impeccably dressed. The cut of his clothing told her that he must be wealthy, if not titled, and she

found, much to her surprise, that she thought him quite handsome. His light blue eyes were warm, and a small smile creased
the corner of his mouth as he continued to pay rapt attention to
Catherine's mother, Lady Hewson. She considered that kindness
to say a great deal about him, for her mother could talk for all of
England!

"Mama," Catherine broke in, gently. "You have not yet introduced us."

Her mother's eyes flared as a hint of red brushed her cheeks.
"Oh, I quite forgot!" she cried, looking quite apologetic. "My
dear, this is Lord Kerr. Lord Kerr, this is my daughter, Miss
Catherine Hewson. Her father, my husband, is Viscount
Hewson."

"I have not had the pleasure of being introduced to him,"
Lord Kerr replied, sweeping into a deep bow as Catherine curtsied. "As I said, however, I am quite new to town."

"And are you enjoying London so far?" Catherine asked,
aware of her mother slowly stepping away from them both.

"Yes, indeed I am," he answered with a small laugh.
"Although it is very different from the country."

"Oh?" Catherine smiled, lifting one eyebrow. "Where do you
hail from?"

Their conversation flowed easily for some minutes.
Catherine discovered that the gentleman was, in fact, a baron,
and therefore held some property near the coast. Why he had
come to London, she had not quite managed to make out,
although he mentioned something about good company, which
made her smile. The music struck up behind them, making
conversation a little more difficult, but Catherine continued
their discussion regardless. She had to admit that she consider-
ably liked this man.

"Excuse me, excuse me!"

A short, slightly rotund gentleman appeared by Catherine's

side, catching her hand. Catherine jerked in surprise, only to realize that Lord Dunstable held her hand, ready to lead her onto the dance floor.

"It is our turn on the floor, I believe," he said, ignoring Lord Kerr altogether. "Come now, do not dawdle!"

Catherine wrenched her hand from his, her cheeks burning at his inappropriate behavior. "Yes, of course, Lord Dunstable," she managed to bite out, a spiral of disappointment running through her at the thought of having to leave Lord Kerr. Turning back to him, she dipped a quick curtsy. "I must apologize, Lord Kerr, but I have a partner for this dance."

He nodded, though there was a certain tightness around his jaw. "I am sorry to end our conversation. What a shame I was not introduced to you sooner, when your dance card was empty."

Lord Dunstable made some kind of encouraging noise, but Catherine was not to be moved.

"I believe if you look, my lord, you will see I have a few dances free at the moment," she said softly.

It was a bold move, to say the least, for young ladies certainly did not seek dances with particular gentlemen, but it seemed that Lord Kerr did not seem taken aback by her words. Instead, he smiled broadly and reached for her dance card, hurriedly signing his name in not one, but two of her four spaces. Catherine managed a quick smile and a 'thank you' before being whisked away by Lord Dunstable, who was not in the least pleased that she had dawdled.

Catherine did not care for Lord Dunstable in the slightest, but he was always quite insistent on dancing with her. He had attempted to call on her, but Catherine and her mother had made sure that he was quickly rebuffed. The man was a buffoon, and worse than that, he was a degenerate gambler.

Given that Catherine had something of a fortune that would come to her on her wedding day, she was careful not to be interested in anyone who only wanted her for her money. That would not be a good start to any marriage, she was quite sure. Besides, Lord Dunstable was not particularly attractive, and what good would it do to marry a man you could barely stand the sight of?

However, her obvious disregard had done nothing to push Lord Dunstable away. Although he did not call on her as often as he once used to, he would still seek her hand at every ball or soiree they attended, and Catherine had never found a way to avoid him. She groaned inwardly as they began to dance, hating the feel of his hand against hers. How grateful she was for gloves.

The dance continued slowly, and Catherine danced each step perfectly. Time seemed to drag on. Lord Dunstable's asked her many questions, but Catherine kept her answers brief. Without being rude, she made it apparent that she had no interest in him. He had to simply accept that she was not about to change her mind when it came to her opinion of him.

Thankfully, the music came to an end, and Catherine made her way from the dance floor back to where Lord Kerr had been. Much to her disappointment, however, she could not see him standing there any longer. Glancing down at the dance card that was tied to her wrist, she smiled to herself when she saw his name there. It would not be too long before they met again.

"You are an exceptional dancer, Miss Hewson."

Catherine smiled up at Lord Kerr, her cheeks warm. "I thank you, Lord Kerr. I would say the same about you, but my compliment would sound too trite, I think."

He laughed, making Catherine's smile broaden. "You are very quick-witted, Miss Hewson."

Catherine had to wait until it was her turn to partner with him once more before replying. "Indeed, my mother would say it is one of my greatest faults," she replied with a heavy sigh. "Although it appears you do not think so."

Lord Kerr regarded her for a moment, a thoughtful expression on his face. "No," he said softly, his gaze flickering over her. "No, I would not say it is a fault."

Something in his expression made heat curl its way up Catherine's spine, sending a wave of spiraling warmth into her very core. Lord Kerr smiled softly, and Catherine felt herself lost within it. There were no other dancers on the floor, no other hands that she had to touch. There was just Lord Kerr.

Their gazes remained strong and undeterred, as though fixed on one another as the dance came to an end. Catherine was drawn to his side once more as he accompanied her from the floor. She could not find anything to say, her tongue sticking to the roof of her mouth and her cheeks burning. Good gracious, she was quite overcome!

"I believe our next dance is a waltz," Lord Kerr murmured as they came to stand together on one side of the ballroom.

"It is," Catherine managed to say, aware that she sounded rather breathless.

"You are a little tired, I think," Lord Kerr replied, looking all about him. "I shall return in a moment with something to drink."

Catherine thanked him, glad that she would be able to stand alone for an instant. There were three dances before her waltz with Lord Kerr, and while she was meant to have partners for these dances, she hoped that, if she hid in the shadows, she might be able to rest for a few moments. It was late in the evening, and mayhap one or two of her intended partners had already found themselves lost in the card room. She did not mind in the least, however, for she only had thoughts of Lord Kerr.

"He is a wonderful man."

Catherine shrieked, clapping her hand over her mouth as a tall figure emerged from the gloom just behind her, his features half hidden by the candlelight.

"Now, now," he tutted, shaking his head. "Is that any way to greet an old friend?"

Catherine could hardly get her breath—such was her fright. Thankfully, the sound of her shriek had not caught anyone's attention, given the mixture of loud conversation and music, but still, she was quite overcome.

"Goodness, Kitty, it seems I frightened you." The gentleman grinned, coming a little closer and putting one hand on her arm. He leaned down a little, looking into her face. "Are you sure you are all right?"

Managing to draw in a shaky breath, Catherine nodded. Only one person called her Kitty, and that was Lord Linton.

"Yes, I am fine, thank you," she said. "Whatever are you doing here?"

"And I thought you would be happy to see me," Lord Linton responded, sounding hurt. "After all, I have not seen you in many years."

"I have been in town, as have you," Catherine replied firmly. "It is just that you have been quite caught up with your various..." She did not know how to say it, and so she lapsed into silence.

Lord Linton chuckled. "My various vices, shall we say?"

"Precisely," Catherine agreed, lifting one eyebrow. "We may have been childhood friends, Lord Linton, but that does not mean our friendship allows me to ignore your rather unpleasant behavior."

"Oh, tosh," he snorted, waving his hand nonchalantly. "You

listen to the gossipmongers too much, Kitty. I have not done half the things they accuse me of!"

Catherine's eyebrow was still raised. "So, it is not true that you were chased out of town only last Season?" she asked quietly.

Lord Linton tugged at his collar with one long finger, his dark brown eyes shifting from place to place. "I was not chased. I left of my own free will."

"Only because you were not welcome anywhere," Catherine finished with a shake of her head. "I am surprised that you were even invited here."

"Oh, but I have become a well-mannered gentleman now, Kitty," Lord Linton replied, a slight gleam in his eye. "Wealthy and titled; what more could a lady want?"

Catherine managed to prevent herself from snorting in disbelief, far too aware of Lord Linton's penchant for liquor, gambling, and women. "I am afraid I cannot believe that," she said quietly. "You may have managed to worm your way back into society, but I will not be fooled by your supposed change."

Lord Linton chuckled and lifted one shoulder. "You always see right through me. In short, money can calm all kinds of storms, my dear."

Catherine rolled her eyes, finding him quite distasteful. Lord Linton was an earl with a great deal of wealth, and whilst it was his to do with as he pleased, she could not help but feel disappointed at how he had turned out.

They had been friends growing up, and she had been quite enchanted by him for a year or so during her early teenage years, though that had all but evaporated. He was not a gentleman she particularly wished to be acquainted with any longer, such was his behavior. In fact, Catherine found herself wishing to distance herself from him as much as she could, worried that her reputation would be smeared by the mere association.

"I had best go in search of Mama. Do excuse me," she murmured, not even giving him a smile as she turned her back on him and began to walk away.

2

"Catherine!"

Catherine turned around at once, a delighted smile on her face as she saw her dear friend Alice approaching.

"Alice, darling!" she exclaimed, clasping her friend's hands. "How wonderful it is to see you!"

Alice smiled and embraced Catherine before straightening her bonnet. It was a windy day, but that had clearly not deterred Alice from visiting a few shops, just as it had not deterred Catherine, either.

"I am very pleased to see you, Catherine." Alice smiled, looping one arm through Catherine's. "It feels as though it had been an age since we last spent time together!"

"That is because you are a happily married lady now, Alice," Catherine chuckled, patting her friend's hand. "Tell me, how is married life?"

Alice's cheeks glowed, her eyes sparkling. "It is quite wonderful, I must confess—although the path that took us to the church was something of a difficult one."

Catherine nodded, the smile fading from her lips as she

remembered what Alice had endured before she could finally get married to the love of her life.

"And yet, it has been worth it," Alice finished with a bright smile. "I strongly encourage you to find a husband of your own, Catherine." She chuckled while Catherine laughed. "I can see you think me quite ridiculous, but I am serious. It must be someone that you love, though—to marry a man without love cannot be a happy state, I do not think."

Catherine nodded her head, her mind slowly turning back towards Lord Kerr. He had danced with her twice, but had not shown any further interest in her. That had disappointed her somewhat, for she had thought him both handsome and interesting. Her stomach had fluttered when she had been in his arms, and much to her surprise, Catherine had felt heat mount in her cheeks when he had smiled at her.

"You have someone in mind?"

Now blushing furiously, Catherine shook her head. "No, not at all."

"Are you sure?" Alice asked softly. "There is no shame in having a penchant for someone, Catherine."

"Oh, tis nothing!" Catherine exclaimed at once, shaking her head so violently that her auburn curls threatened to come tumbling down around her ears. Then she paused for a moment. "There is a Lord Kerr who Mama introduced me to last evening, but there was no particular interest from him there."

Alice arched an eyebrow. "But you for him?"

Catherine frowned, unable to find the words she needed to express herself clearly. "I suppose I thought him handsome and kind, a good conversationalist with a quick wit," she said. "But is that truly the beginnings of affection?"

"Did you find him good company, then?"

"Yes."

"And did your eyes try and find him in the crowd, even

though you were not aware you were doing it?" Alice wondered. "Did you enjoy every moment of being in his arms as you danced? Did your heart skip a beat?"

Catherine stilled for a second, blinking at her friend. "How did you know that?"

Alice laughed aloud, her eyes dancing with mischief. "Because that is exactly what happened to me, even though I repeatedly told myself that I did not care for him."

Despite wanting to believe her friend's words, Catherine's shoulders slumped. "But there is no hope, Alice. He did not show any sign of being keen to see me again. In truth, he danced with me twice and then bid me a good evening."

"That is no reason to lose hope!" Alice exclaimed as they began to walk once more. "When you see him again, try to engage him in conversation. Since he has done it before, I am quite sure he will ask you to dance again. Some men take time to ensure that their affections are truly engaged before they will show any kind of attention to a lady."

Catherine nodded, seeing the wisdom in Alice's words. "You are right, of course. It is just that I have not often felt this way towards a particular gentleman before, so it is taking me a little time to become used to what I feel."

To her surprise, Alice chuckled and shook her head. "I do recall how you declared yourself deeply in love with that friend of yours, only to realize that he was quite the rogue. I believe you then declared that you should never go near him again and that you had been quite mistaken in your affections."

Catherine cringed, a quiet groan escaping from her mouth.

"Do not remind me of my foolishness, Alice," she pleaded. "Particularly after I just met the very gentleman you are talking about."

She saw the surprise on Alice's face, sighing heavily as they stepped inside the bookshop. Of course, the shop itself was quiet and still, which meant that Alice had to wait until they drew near the back of the shop before continuing their conversation. In all honesty, Catherine would rather forget about her accidental meeting with Lord Linton.

"You mean to tell me Lord Linton is back in society?" she asked in a hushed whisper.

"So it seems," Catherine murmured, running her fingers over the spines of some dusty books. "He came to speak to me last evening, although I confess that I left his company as soon as I could."

"Little wonder," Alice said, a trifle more loudly than she had intended. "The man is a rake and a scoundrel. I am surprised the *ton* are so eager to have him back."

"Apparently, wealth goes a long way to smooth a once rocky path," Catherine muttered, rolling her eyes. "Linton has a great deal of wealth, and he likes to cling to it as best he can. I have heard rumors of his attempts to add to his funds through most undesirable means." She sighed heavily. "I cannot think much of him now, even though we were dear friends back in our childhood."

"And even though you once thought yourself in love with him," Alice commented with a smile.

"Alice, please, do not remind me of my mistake anymore!" Catherine begged, her hand on her heart as her green eyes filled with dismay. "I promise you now, I shall never be as ridiculous again. No, I fully intend to find myself a nice, honest, decent man who will hold my heart both gently and tenderly."

Alice's smile softened. "I am glad to hear it," she said quietly. "I think matrimony will suit you very well, Catherine. Just ensure you are not hasty when it comes to such things as courting and declarations of love. Some men hide their true nature and intentions behind a wall of accolades and compliments."

"You have no need to worry on that account," Catherine firmly declared. "I have been well aware of that kind of gentleman for some time, given my acquaintance with Lord Linton. I believe I can see through that kind of façade."

Alive, however, did not seem to agree, patting Catherine's hand. "Just be on your guard, that is all I ask."

"Of course I will," Catherine promised, surprised at her friend's concern. "And I promise that if Lord Kerr *does* decide to court me, then you shall be among the first of my friends that I shall introduce him to."

"Very well!" Alice laughed, beginning to peruse the books in earnest. "Come now, let us find a new title or two."

Catherine set about looking for a new book, only for a flicker of movement to catch her eye. Glancing out of the window, she was astonished to see none other than Lord Linton hastening across the street, looking like he was being chased by a terrifying band of mercenaries—although, from what Catherine could see, there was no one in particular chasing him.

"Good gracious," she breathed as he began to hurry towards the bookshop. "I do believe he intends to come in here."

"Who?" Alice asked, putting her book down and joining Catherine at the window. She gasped as she caught sight of Lord Linton. "Good heavens! Is that not the very man we were just discussing?"

"It is," Catherine answered grimly. "And here I am trying my very best not to be in his company."

Alice tutted and took Catherine's arm. "If we stay here at the back of the shop, there is a good chance he will not see us, and we will not even have to converse with him."

Catherine agreed and hurried away to the furthest recess of the room alongside Alice, but no sooner had they reached their hiding spot than Lord Linton appeared beside them, puffing and blowing for all he was worth. His eyes widened at the sight of them, his cheeks red with exertion as he placed his hands on his knees in an attempt to calm his breathing.

"Lord Linton," Alice murmured, still holding Catherine's arm. "How nice to see you. Do excuse us, we were just looking at a few new titles."

Catherine gave him a tight smile and made to move away beside Alice—who walked back to the door of the bookshop—only for Lord Linton to reach out and catch her hand.

"Can you see them?" he gasped, his voice harsh and rasping. "Are they there?"

Frustrated, Catherine pulled her hand from his. "Whatever are you talking about, Lord Linton? Who is coming?"

"Them!" he exclaimed, gesturing wildly to the window. "Do you see the gentlemen there? A lady with them, perhaps?"

Catherine rolled her eyes and gave the window a cursory glance. "There is nothing as far as I can see," she replied calmly. "Now, do excuse us, Lord Linton."

The bell at the door rang just as Catherine finished speaking, and Lord Linton quietened them both with a finger to his lips, once more clasping her hand with his. Catherine made to move away, but he still grasped her hand, crouching on his haunches as he peered around the bookshelves.

"They are coming!" he squeaked, his eyes widening. "Catherine, you must forgive me!"

Catherine blinked and opened her mouth to ask him what on earth he meant by such a thing, only for him to raise himself to his full height, catch her around the waist, and press his lips to hers.

Horror filled her. Her reputation would be in pieces should she be identified, and she began to struggle against him. Lord Linton did not stop his attentions, but rather caught her hands, stepped backward, and pressed her back against one of the deeper filled bookcases.

Thankfully, he released her mouth from his, though he kept his forehead against hers. "If you have ever thought of me as a friend, please stay here," he whispered, sounding more desperate than she had ever heard him. "Please, I beg of you. You will be quite safe. They will not be able to see your face."

Catherine wanted nothing more than to kick him in the shins, hard, and push him away, but knew from the oncoming voices that she might very easily be caught in a compromising position should she do so. Therefore, she had very little alternative other than to remain where she was, her body going rigid with anger.

The sound of footsteps caught her ears, followed by a few mutters and embarrassed exclamations on finding a couple so caught up with one another, and after a minute had passed, Catherine found herself released from Lord Linton's grip. She glared up at him, wanting to slap him hard for putting her in such a position. She knew, however, that the sound would carry throughout the quiet bookshop.

"How dare you!" she seethed, her voice barely louder than a whisper. "You are never to use me in such a way again!"

"Did you not find even the smallest amount of enjoyment in it?" Lord Linton replied, immediately at ease as he threw her a wink. "Come now, Catherine! Twas not all bad. You did me a very great favor, you know. I appreciate it more than I can say."

Fury burst through Catherine's veins, and she made to rage at him, only for Alice to reappear around the corner with a concerned look on her face.

"What stopped you?" she asked, ignoring Lord Linton completely. "I could not return to you since there were three gentlemen approaching, but then they departed rather quickly."

Catherine, who did not want to explain even to Alice what had occurred, simply shook her head, mute with ire.

"Come," Alice continued, looping her hand through Catherine's arm. "I think perhaps we should find another bookshop. This one has something of a stale odor, I think. Good day, Lord Linton."

Without bidding farewell to Lord Linton, Catherine strode from the shop, practically dragging Alice beside her. Her cheeks burned with fire, her face a mask of anger. She could not believe what he had done—using her in such an improper way! She was quite right to consider even his acquaintance a damaging connection. From now on, she would not even greet him unless absolutely necessary.

"I can hardly believe you used to be friends with that man," Alice whispered as they walked away from the bookshop. "He cannot always have been such a selfish, thoughtless creature, surely!"

"No," Catherine murmured, her face still red. "He was not. He used to be kind and gentle when we were children. Unfortunately, it seems he has strayed from the morals of his youth."

"It is an unfortunate connection," Alice sighed, shaking her head.

"You need have no concern in that regard!" Catherine firmly stated. "I intend to sever that connection here and now. I shall actively avoid him, for after such a display of behavior today, I cannot think of any good reason to maintain our friendship."

Alice nodded sagely. "Very wise, my dear Catherine. Very wise indeed."

atherine found her resolution to avoid Lord Linton more than a little difficult, given that he appeared to be at almost every social event that she attended. She had no other choice but to greet him on occasion, though she made sure to keep the conversation as short as she could manage. Alice, having been informed of what Lord Linton had done in the bookshop, was horrified at the situation and duly stuck by Catherine's side whenever she could.

However, Catherine was more than certain that Lord Linton was not about to do such a thing again, for he certainly did not have any true feelings for her—he had simply used her to get out of whatever situation he had managed to land himself in. Although, she did not have any inclination to know what that particular situation was either.

Shuddering slightly, Catherine tried her best to push Lord Linton from her mind and, instead, concentrate on the ball going on around her. It was a wonderful evening thus far, even though she had been forced to greet Lord Linton a few hours earlier. Thankfully, she had managed to extricate herself before he had requested a dance from her.

"Ah, my dear Miss Hewson!"

Catherine turned at once, her cheeks warming immediately as she saw the handsome face of Lord Kerr smiling at her. She managed a brief curtsy, wishing she could fan her hot face as she lifted her head.

"Lord Kerr," she greeted him, smiling back at him. "How good it is to see you again."

"I do hope you have some spaces on your dance card for me," he said at once, though his eyes were not on the card tied to her wrist. "I have not seen you in an age and would very much like to continue our acquaintance."

A tingling heat rippled up Catherine's spine as she handed her dance card to him, finding that her mouth appeared to be refusing to work. He signed his name in not one, but two of her three remaining spaces, his eyes fixating on her once more.

"I would sign my name to all three if I could, but I believe that would cause something of a scandal," Lord Kerr murmured, catching her hand in his and bending to press a light kiss to the back of her glove. "I very much look forward to our dances together."

Finding that she still could not speak—such was the astonishment that filled her—Catherine could only smile and watch him walk away, hardly able to believe what he had just said. Her heart slammed into her chest as she tried to catch her breath, her entire body buzzing with excitement.

I would sign my name to all three if I could.

The words ran around her mind over and over until she was forced to believe them. Lord Kerr had just made his partiality for her more than obvious, even though she had never expected such a thing. Since the last time they had danced together, she had not seen him at all. But now, it seemed he had thought of her whilst he had been absent from society, to the point that he was willing to state the depth of his affections to her.

Catherine danced the next few dances in something of a daze, her mind fixed only on Lord Kerr. When the time came for their dance, he found her immediately, as though he wished not to waste a single moment of their dance together.

"I do hope you do not mind the waltz," he murmured as Catherine took his arm and walked with him onto the dance floor. "I have heard that some ladies refuse to dance it."

"I am not one of those ladies," Catherine replied, a little breathlessly. "In fact, I must admit I find the waltz quite enjoyable."

Lord Kerr chuckled, placing one hand on her waist and taking her hand with the other. "I am glad to hear it," he murmured as the music began.

Catherine did as she had been taught and gave him the lead, finding him, once again, to be a prolific dancer. Lord Kerr twirled her around the floor, never once interrupting another couple's steps and always ensuring that he did not trod on her toes. They danced in silence, although Catherine braved a look into his eyes now and again, noticing he was always regarding her in an almost careful study. She could never look into his eyes for long, finding herself a little overcome by the intensity of his gaze.

When the music began to slow, a wave of disappointment rushed over Catherine, as if she had been doused with icy water. She kept her smile fixed as Lord Kerr bowed, ready to lead her back to her seat.

"Might you like to take some air?" he asked, abruptly taking her hand and placing it back on his arm. "It is a little stuffy in here, is it not?"

Catherine was about to answer that she should not, given that she was next due to dance with Lord Gregory, but she simply could not form the correct words. She did not want to dance with Lord Gregory, for he did not incite these feelings deep within her soul.

"Indeed, it is a little stuffy," she managed to say, looking up at him. "A few minutes of fresh air would be most welcome."

Lord Kerr grinned, and Catherine felt her heart practically spin in her chest. He was devilishly handsome, and she could not help but be drawn to him.

"Wonderful," she heard him say under his breath, and they walked towards the open French doors at the back of the ballroom. "Quite wonderful."

THE EVENING AIR was cool and damp, and Catherine's skin prickled almost immediately.

"You are cold," Lord Kerr stated, shaking his head. "Perhaps I should not have brought you outside after all."

"No, please," Catherine protested at once, growing even more chilled at the thought of him leaving her so abruptly. "I am quite at ease, I assure you."

He paused for a moment before smiling. "Very well, then. Just a few minutes, perhaps."

Catherine smiled back, relieved at his desire to stay with her. "It is very warm in there, is it not?"

"It is."

The silence grew between them for a few minutes, and Catherine began to feel a little uncomfortable. Other couples were present in the gardens, of course, and as they walked, Catherine was delighted to see the small lanterns lighting their path. It gave the grounds an almost magical appearance to them.

Lord Kerr cleared his throat.

"Miss Hewson," he began, "I confess that I have missed your company this last while."

"That is because you have been entirely absent from all the wonderful events," Catherine said, laughing. "Wherever did you go, Lord Kerr?"

In the lantern light, she could not quite make out his expression, but she saw that he looked away from her, a slight flicker of unease running through his features. He evidently did not want to answer her, and Catherine felt embarrassed for asking such a question, even though it was not meant to be impertinent.

"What I mean to say," she continued hastily, "is that I have also noticed your absence."

"Oh," he replied, his breath coming out in a rush, as though he had been holding it. "I see. Well, that is... that is good."

Seeing how disconcerted Lord Kerr was, unease swept through Catherine. She had thought he meant to speak to her privately, but mayhap she had been mistaken. It was possible he had asked her to get some fresh air just to be polite, not because he wanted to spend more time with her. Embarrassed beyond words at how quickly she had come to that conclusion, Catherine hung her head and inwardly railed at herself for being so ridiculous.

"And do you intend to be at any more balls?" Lord Kerr asked, hesitantly. Before Catherine could respond, he spoke again. "Forgive me, that came out quite incorrectly. What I meant to say was, your parents have no intention of leaving town soon, I hope?"

"Leaving town?" Catherine replied, surprised. "No, indeed. Why should you think so?"

"I had not thought that they would," he answered, coming to a standstill and looking as though he wanted to just take back what he had said. "What I mean is—oh, dear, I am making something of a hash of this."

Was... was this Catherine's doing? Did she make Lord Kerr nervous? A spark of excitement suddenly raced up Catherine's spine, her skin tingling all over as she paused in her steps, looking up at him. How was it possible that a man could make her lose her ability to speak so frequently?

"What I mean to say, in a very roundabout way, Miss Hewson," Lord Kerr eventually said, is that I would very much like to see you again. I would like to call on you, if I may?"

The hopeful expression on his face made Catherine want to laugh aloud, but instead, she simply clasped her hands together and smiled up at him. "Oh, Lord Kerr, I cannot tell you how agreeable I would be to such a thing," she answered, her heart almost skipping a beat as he stepped forward and caught her hand in his. "In fact, I would be delighted."

"Wonderful," he said, pressing her hand between his two. "I am sorry I got my words so terribly confused; it is not like me." His eyes warmed, his smile softening. "Perhaps it is your loveliness that has me struggling for air, my thoughts flung into such confusion that I know not what to say."

The air seemed to spark around her, and for a very brief moment, Catherine wondered if Lord Kerr might kiss her. He was so close, and his gaze was so soft yet so intense upon her. But then he dropped her hand, offered his arm, and walked back along the path in order to re-enter the ballroom.

"Our second dance shall be along very soon," he murmured as they entered the room once more. "I shall look forward to it now, with a much greater pleasure than before."

Catherine happily sighed to herself as Lord Kerr lifted her hand to his lips, pressing a gentle kiss to the back of it before finally taking his farewell. Catherine could not help but allow her eyes to follow him as he walked towards another group of gentlemen, finding Alice at her side almost immediately.

"Well?"

"Well," Catherine laughed, hearing the interest in Alice's voice. "I think Lord Kerr has come up to scratch after all!"

Alice drew in a sharp breath. "He intends to court you?"

"He intends to *call* upon me," Catherine answered, finally managing to drag her eyes away from him. "But yes, I have great hopes that we may show a particular partiality for one another, given time."

There was a short silence whilst Alice looked into Catherine's face, her eyes studying her carefully. Catherine grew a little uncomfortable at this, wondering why Alice had not yet replied to her words.

"If you believe he is a good man and the right kind of gentleman for you, then I will be vastly happy for you, my dear," Alice finally said, looping her arm through Catherine's. "I am glad that you are going to further your acquaintance with him first, however. That is always wise."

Catherine could not help but laugh. "Come now, Alice! It is not as though we are engaged already, nor are we likely to be any time soon. You need not look so severe. I shall continue to get to know him, and in time, I am quite sure my heart will make up its own mind about him."

"Good," Alice said, finally breaking into a smile. "He seems to be quite wonderful, and I am sure all will work out exactly as it is meant to."

Catherine nodded her head. She hoped her friend was right.

4

Catherine tried not to blush as Lord Kerr pressed a small bouquet of roses into her hands.

"You are too kind," she murmured, pressing her nose into the fragrant blooms for a moment. "Thank you for calling on me."

He smiled, bowed, and took a seat, clearing his throat whilst Lady Hewson began to chatter amicably with him. Catherine chose to sit quietly for a few minutes, simply watching the two of them talk.

This was now the third time Lord Kerr had called on her, and each time, he had stayed an appropriate length of time, engaged her in interesting conversation, and then taken his leave. They had never been allowed a moment together, given that Catherine's mother was something of a chatterbox. She had glowed on seeing her daughter so frequently visited by Lord Kerr, but had seemed completely unaware that, mayhap, they might like to talk together uninterrupted.

"Forgive me, Lady Hewson," Lord Kerr interjected. "But I do hope you might permit me to take your daughter out for a short stroll this afternoon?"

Catherine's eyes widened as Lord Kerr interrupted her mother mid flow—not that she could blame him, given that it was difficult to get a word in edgeways.

"A stroll?" her mother repeated, sounding quite breathless. "Well, now, I am not quite sure. The weather is a little chilly, and I—"

"I shall dress warmly, Mama," Catherine said quickly, rising to her feet as butterflies immediately began to flutter in her belly. She turned to Lord Kerr with a warm smile, watching him stand up from his seat.

"I shall meet you at the front door, shall I?" she asked, making her way towards the door. "I just need to make sure I am appropriately wrapped up."

Lord Kerr bowed, and even though Lady Hewson began to speak, Catherine excused herself and left the room at once.

Within a few minutes, Catherine and Lord Kerr were walking along the streets of London, not quite sure in which direction they were headed, but enjoying themselves nonetheless. Catherine's maid trailed discreetly behind them, and Lord Kerr seemed to be a great deal more at ease now that they were away from her mother's company.

"Shall we perhaps get an ice at Gunter's?" he asked, smiling at her. "I know it is a trifle cold, and your mama did seem concerned over the chill in the air, even though it is a summers day, but—"

"I think that is a wonderful idea," Catherine declared, laughing. "I would very much enjoy an ice, I think. And if it is too cold to stand outside, then mayhap we could sit down indoors?"

Lord Kerr smiled in delight, his eyes lighting. "Wonderful," he replied, offering her his arm. "I confess that it has been difficult for me to find time to converse with you as much as I would like."

Catherine took his arm immediately, delighted at his

manners. "You are quite right, Lord Kerr. You are too polite to say so, but my mother does delight in talking so. She is more enamored with you than I, if that were possible."

He looked down at her, pausing in his steps for a moment. Catherine, glancing up at him, realized what she had just said and felt her cheeks burn with heat.

"What I mean to say," she murmured, suddenly not sure where to look, "is... I am very pleased with your company. You have been very attentive."

"That is because I am quite enamored with you," came Lord Kerr's quiet reply. He stopped walking so that he could turn to her. "If I may be so bold, Miss Hewson, I have found your company more important to me than any other. I have thought of nothing other than spending time with you."

Catherine's heart squeezed with delight, her entire body humming with happiness. "I confess that I feel the same way, Lord Kerr. You are a most kind man, and I have very much enjoyed spending time with you. Although I will say that I wish Mama would allow us to talk at length without interrupting so very much."

He chuckled. "Mayhap if I make my intentions clear to your father and then also to your mother, they might be more inclined to allow us time together without their company. I know it is a little cold, but would you fancy a ride or two around town? Hyde Park, perhaps?"

"I am quite sure my father would be delighted to allow such a thing," Catherine said, slightly out of breath. "And yes, it is cold for the time of year, but that will not put me off spending time in your company, I assure you."

Lord Kerr clasped her hands, his expression growing serious. "I will be honest with you from the start, Miss Hewson; I am looking for a bride. I have no intention of playing games with you, nor do I have any intention of courting a great many other ladies, for my mind is made up. If you have no great desire for matrimony, then I should bring our acquaintance to an end."

Catherine, thrilled at his words, lightly squeezed his hands. She could almost not believe what she was hearing. "Lord Kerr, thank you for being so forthright. I find it most refreshing. As most young ladies, I am thinking of my future and considering my situation. Matrimony is what I seek. You need not have any fear on that matter." She smiled as his eyes warmed, his fingers tightening on hers.

"I am very glad to hear it," he murmured, letting go of her hands and turning to walk beside her once more. "You have made me very happy."

Not as happy as you have made me, Catherine thought to herself as they continued to walk towards Gunter's. She felt as if she were walking on air, the most blessed lady who had ever walked these streets. How wonderful that Lord Kerr was so willing to share the truth of his intentions towards her so early in their acquaintance.

She did not want to be toyed with, and, in speaking to her so, Lord Kerr had proven himself. Her estimation of his character and respect for the man himself grew immeasurably. Catherine was quite sure that her father and mother would be delighted with the prospect of having such a man for a son-in-law.

UNFORTUNATELY, Catherine's delight was to come to a swift end, for no sooner had they entered Gunter's than she saw Lord Linton sitting at one of the tables. He was accompanied by a young lady, who was laughing softly at something he said. His eyes glittered as though he were a cat sitting by a bowl of cream. Her stomach turned over as she recalled how he had behaved

towards her in the bookshop, her fingers tightening on Lord
Kerr's arm.

"Shall we sit?" he asked, evidently unaware of her concern.
"There is a slight bite to the wind this afternoon, I must admit."

She smiled tightly and gestured to a small table in the
corner. She would have to walk past Lord Linton, but that could
not be helped. Hopefully, he would ignore her entirely, given
that he was so taken with the lady at his table.

"Very well," Lord Kerr replied, patting her hand. "Why do
you not sit while I bring us a couple of ices?"

Catherine had no choice but to leave him and walk alone
towards the table. She kept her chin lifted and avoided eye
contact with everyone, trying her best not to react at all as she
walked past Lord Linton. Thankfully, he did not say a single
word, did not try to rise to greet her or even call her name.

Heaving a sigh of relief, Catherine quietly sat down at
her table.

Her eyes returned to Lord Kerr, who was about to order their
delicious ices. Catherine sighed joyfully to herself, refusing to
let the presence of Lord Linton disturb her happiness. The afternoon had gone wonderfully well thus far, and she was quite sure
that Lord Kerr was going to be the most wonderful husband.
Catherine had no doubt she would accept him, even though
Alice's warning about being too hasty nudged itself to the fore-
front of her mind.

"I am not being too hasty," she muttered to herself, carefully
smoothing her skirts. "He is a good man, kind and considerate.
Why should I not consider him?"

She lifted her eyes to him once more, her heart almost skipping a beat when he smiled at her, bringing their ices over.

"I thank you," she murmured, aware that she was blushing
furiously. "These look delicious."

"You are very welcome," Lord Kerr said warmly. "Your friend

asked to join us, but I am afraid I refused him. I do hope you do not mind."

"My friend?" Catherine repeated, frowning. "Who are you talking about?"

"A Lord Linton?" he said, turning slightly so that Catherine could see him. "He came over to introduce himself as I was fetching the ices. I do hope you do not think me rude for refusing his company."

"Lord Linton introduced himself to you?" Catherine asked, fury building up in her chest. "I am terribly sorry, Lord Kerr. That was most uncommonly rude."

Lord Kerr lifted one shoulder. "I did not think so, not since he is so dear a friend of yours, but I confess I wanted to have you entirely to myself for a few minutes." He smiled, and the anger instantly began to leave Catherine. "Was that so wrong of me?"

"No, of course it was not," Catherine murmured as a small smile began to overcome her lips. She frowned again, however, when she spoke her next words. "And Lord Linton is *not* a particular friend of mine. In fact, I would ask that you not go out of your way to become acquainted with him. I am doing everything in my power to avoid him at the moment."

Lord Kerr looked interested, his eyebrows lifting in surprise.

"It is not of any great importance, I assure you," Catherine insisted, wanting desperately to get off the subject of Lord Linton before she disclosed something she should not. "He and I used to be close friends, but I find that his recent behavior has pushed me quite far from him. I do not consider him a friend any longer."

"I see," Lord Kerr murmured, glancing over at him. "Well, I must say I trust your judgement, my dear. We shall say no more about it and continue talking about some other matter, shall we?"

Relieved, Catherine let out a slightly shaky laugh. "Yes, indeed. I would be glad to."

"And may I call on you again tomorrow?" Lord Kerr asked, briefly touching her hand with his. "Perhaps a walk in Hyde Park?"

Catherine practically glowed with happiness, her anger at Lord Linton forgotten in a moment. "That would be wonderful," she replied. "Thank you, Lord Kerr. I am already looking forward to it."

5

The following few weeks flew past in a blaze of sunshine, wonderful days, and private smiles shared between Catherine and Lord Kerr. He insisted that she call him Kerr, and given the intimacy growing between them, Catherine allowed him to simply call her Catherine, dropping the titles and propriety that came with new acquaintances.

Alice had met the man on two separate occasions and duly given Catherine her assessment. Lord Kerr was very good—amiable, handsome, and kind, which Catherine could not help agreeing with. It was only when Alice asked her what his background was that Catherine became stumped. She did not know very much about that, which, of course, she blamed herself entirely for. Shame had crept over her as she had realized just how little she had asked Lord Kerr about his family or background. He was always so good at asking her such things and was rapt with attention whenever she answered.

In regard to Lord Linton, Catherine was relieved to have seen very little of him lately. Lord Kerr had mentioned him on one more occasion, having met him at White's, an exclusive gentlemen's club, but he never came into their conversation again after that day. That was just as Catherine had wanted, and so she almost entirely forgot about him, entirely caught up in the whirlwind that came with Lord Kerr. Everything was going wonderfully well between them. Her parents approved, Alice thought well of him, and Catherine could not remember ever being so happy.

"YOU ARE LOOKING UTTERLY BREATHTAKING this evening, I must say!"

Catherine blushed as she greeted Lord Kerr, curtsying carefully. "Really, Kerr, you are too kind."

"Not at all," he replied at once, taking her dance card and jotting down his name. "It is quite right for me to express my feelings when it comes to you, my dear Catherine."

Butterflies burst into her stomach as he held out his arm for her, and together, they walked out onto the dance floor. Catherine held her head up proudly, knowing that there were already rumors about their ongoing attachment. She did not care for rumors at all, of course, even if there was some truth in them. Let the gossip mongers think what they liked. This was between herself and Lord Kerr, even if the rest of the *ton* were waiting with breathless anticipation for an engagement announcement to be made.

"I have something to tell you," Lord Kerr murmured as they danced.

"Oh?" Catherine looked up to see an expression of frustration on his face, and, surprised by it, she frowned immediately. "Something is amiss, then?"

Annoyed that they then had to wait for the next few dancers to take their steps before they could be reunited, Catherine continued to hold Lord Kerr's gaze, aware of the expression on his face. It was not one of happiness nor excitement, but rather of vexation and disappointment.

Once the dance was over, she hurried from the floor with Lord Kerr by her side, glancing up at him anxiously.

"Here," he muttered, leading her towards a small alcove a little away from the rest of the crowd. "At least we might speak a little more privately."

"You do look very put out," Catherine nervously murmured as they stood together. "Whatever is it?"

Lord Kerr let out a long, frustrated breath, shaking his head sadly. "I must return to the country."

Catherine's heart sank like a stone. Of all the various possibilities she had imagined as the cause of his disappointed gaze, she had never considered this one. "When?" she asked, her eyes widening.

"Tomorrow," he answered, sighing heavily. "I did not think I would be required, but urgent business has come up." He took her hand, careful not to let anyone see him do so. "I would take you with me if I could," he continued fervently, "but alas, I think your parents would have something to say if I did so."

"And how long will you be away?" Catherine asked, hoping it would not be too long a parting.

He shook his head. "I cannot say. It may be a few days; it may be a month."

"A month!" Catherine exclaimed, turning her head away in embarrassment as she saw others begin to look at her. "No, you cannot be serious."

Lord Kerr gently squeezed her hand. "I shall be as quick as I can, my dearest. I swear to you I do not wish to go, but I must." His grim expression faded as he tried to smile. "I have to be responsible, at times."

Catherine's heart ached at the thought of his leaving. "I

suppose you must," she replied dejectedly. "I shall miss you dreadfully."

"You will be the one thing that brings me back the moment my business is completed," he promised, smiling sweetly at her. "I would not be torn from you unless it was absolutely necessary. Can you forgive me, my dear?"

She managed a wobbly smile, her heart tearing asunder at the thought of his absence. "There is nothing to forgive. I shall endure, if I must, waiting for you to return to me."

To her very great surprise, Lord Kerr suddenly turned and, catching her hand, hurried her along the ballroom until they came to a door. He did not even look back as he pushed it open, pulling Catherine along with him. Finding themselves in a long hallway, Lord Kerr tried one door and then the next until he found one unlocked. Pushing it open and looking within, he stepped inside, slammed the door shut, and caught Catherine in his arms.

His mouth descended on hers with a hunger that took her breath away. Her heart exploded in her chest. Lord Kerr kissed her with such a great longing and passion that Catherine thought she might melt right there in his embrace. Her body burned with heat, her arms tangling around his neck as he angled his head to deepen his kiss. Everything came alive at once, the very air seeming to sparkle around them.

At length, he tore his mouth from hers and rested his forehead against her own, breathing heavily.

"I hope that will assure you of my deep and abiding affection for you whilst I am gone," Lord Kerr whispered, making her skin prickle with anticipation. "There is no one but you, Catherine. I swear it."

His lips pressed to hers once more, this time with a greater gentleness than before. Catherine sighed against him, pressing her hands against the firm planes of his chest. There was no doubt she would remember him after this!

"I had best return to the ballroom," he said after a few moments. "Shall you precede me or come after?"

Catherine let out a somewhat breathless laugh. "Come after you, I think. I need a little longer to compose myself."

He chuckled and pressed one tender kiss to her cheek. "Do not be too long, my dear. I do not wish to miss our second dance."

"Of course not," Catherine replied, smiling to herself as he walked from the room and left her alone.

After Catherine had managed to compose herself somewhat, she stepped from the room, firmly pulling the door closed behind her.

"Well, well!"

Catherine jumped in surprise, turning to see none other than Lord Linton standing idly against the wall, his arms folded and one eyebrow lifted. Her cheeks flamed, but she gazed back at him as calmly as she could.

"Linton," she said, "this is none of your business."

He did not smile. "I saw Lord Kerr leaving some moments ago and I simply had to see who he had left within. I did not imagine for one moment that it would be you."

Catherine lifted her chin a notch. "As I said, this is not your business." She made to leave to walk back to the ballroom, but he caught her hand, holding it tightly. "Lord Linton!" she exclaimed, trying to wrench her hand from his as anger burst into her veins. "What do you think you are doing? Unhand me!"

Lord Linton did not do as she asked, his brows settling low as he frowned at her. "I do hope you were behaving sensibly with Lord Kerr."

She glared at him. "Coming from you?"

"Yes, coming from me," he bit out, his own expression angry.

"Regardless of my own behavior, I do care for you still, Catherine."

Snorting in derision, Catherine shook her head. "After how you treated me in the bookshop, I would say the only person you care about is yourself. You have no right to quiz me on anything I do, especially when it comes to matters of the heart. Leave me alone, and I will be glad to do the same to you!"

A silence spread between them as Catherine continued to glower at him. Lord Linton's expression did not change. He appeared enraged and frustrated, but what he had against Lord Kerr, Catherine could not tell.

"He is not a good man."

Thinking that she had heard quite enough, Catherine pulled her hand from his grasp, spun on her heel, and marched along the hallway back towards the ballroom.

"I will force you to see the truth if I have to!" Lord Linton called, making Catherine's hands curl into fists. "He is not worthy of you, Catherine!"

Flinging the door open, Catherine walked into the ballroom and was immediately enveloped by the sound of music and conversation. Her anger faded, her anxiety evaporated. Soon it would be time for her second dance with Lord Kerr, and she did not want anything—or anyone—to spoil her time with him.

Catherine purposefully made her way towards where Lady Hewson stood, able to hear her voice even through the rest of the noise around them. She cringed inwardly as she heard her mother declare that Catherine was bound to be wed before the year was out, and she chose to stand a little away from where Lady Hewson was, not wishing to be caught up in her conversation.

She sighed to herself, thinking how different things would be after this evening. Lord Kerr would not be present for some time, but the way he had kissed her ensured she certainly would not be able to forget about him. She touched her lower lip absentmindedly, her cheeks blooming with color as her eyes landed on Lord Kerr himself, who was looking at her with a glint in his eye whilst he stood with an acquaintance of his.

Catherine dropped her hand at once, though she could not help but smile. It was only when her gaze drifted away from Lord Kerr and found Lord Linton that her smile faded, her stomach churned, and she found herself turning away from them both in search of Alice.

Yes, tonight had certainly been most unsettling!

6

"Catherine! Catherine!"

Catherine groaned and flung one hand over her eyes as the maid pulled back the drapes. The sunlight was most unwelcome, and Catherine groaned aloud as her mother rushed over to her, shaking her hard.

"Catherine! Will you please rise and explain yourself!!"

Her mind still fuzzy, Catherine opened her eyes and looked at her mother, desperate to sleep once more. Lady Hewson was still in her night things, her hair falling wildly about her shoulders and a horrified look in her eyes. She held a newspaper in her hands.

"Whatever are you talking about, Mama?" Catherine muttered, trying to push herself up on her elbows. "What is it that I need to explain?"

"I thought you and Lord Kerr had an understanding!" her mother exclaimed, her shrill voice echoing around the room.

Wondering if Lady Hewson had somehow discovered what she had been doing with Lord Kerr in the small, dark room yesterday evening, Catherine turned her head away and swung her legs out of bed in the hopes that her mother would not see the heat rippling into her cheeks.

"Lord Kerr and I do share an understanding, Mama," she murmured, pushing her feet into soft slippers and pulling a robe around her shoulders before walking over to sit by the fire. A tray of chocolate and warm croissants waited for her, and Catherine felt her stomach growl in anticipation.

Her mother, who had lapsed into silence for a few seconds, now hurried towards her.

"If you have such an understanding, then explain this to me!" She jabbed at something in the newspaper, and Catherine, who had taken a large bite of the croissant, narrowed her eyes to look at it. Unfortunately, Lady Hewson was shaking it as she continued to mutter under her breath that Catherine simply could not make it out.

"Mama, why do you not just tell me what it is that has you so upset?" she asked quietly. "I cannot read it if you keep shaking it about like that!" A small smile caught the corner of her mouth as she saw her mother splutter for a moment.

"You will lose that smile once I tell you!" Lady Hewson declared, her eyes flashing. "Here now, let me read it to you."

Catherine took another bite of her croissant and looked up at her mother expectantly.

"'This paper is proud to announce a surprising betrothal.'" Her mother lifted one eyebrow, but Catherine simply waited, not sure who she was about to announce. It could not be Lord Kerr, could it? A sense of uneasiness coursed through her as she waited for her mother to continue.

"'It is between Robert, the Earl of Linton and Miss Catherine Hewson, daughter of Viscount Hewson. This paper understands that they have long been close friends, and we wish them nothing but happiness in their future lives together.'"

The croissant suddenly tasted like ashes in her mouth.

Catherine stared at her mother, her hands beginning to tremble as she put the remainder of the croissant down on the plate. Her mind was screaming, but she simply could not take in what she had heard.

"How *dare* you engage yourself to a man without seeking your father's permission!" Lady Hewson cried, slamming the paper down on the table. "He is quite furious—your father, I mean—and demands that you speak to him at your earliest convenience!"

Hot tears burned in Catherine's eyes. "I did not— He did not —" She tried to speak, feeling moisture trickle down her cheeks. "Mama, I am not engaged to him."

Her mother opened her mouth only to close it again, a puzzled frown on her face. "Whatever do you mean?"

"He did not ask me. I have barely spoken to the man!" Catherine continued, suddenly reaching for her mother's hand. She needed some reassurance, such was the shock racing through her body. "I do not understand!"

Thankfully, her mother's shrewd gaze took in Catherine's astonishment and realized that what her daughter said was true. Keeping a hold of Catherine's hand, she sat down next to her and regarded her carefully.

"Are you trying to tell me that Lord Linton has done this of his own accord?" she asked, more gently than her previous question. "That you are as surprised as I am?"

"Indeed," Catherine replied, sniffing heavily. "I do not know why he has done this. I... I cannot marry him!" Her eyes widened, panic racing through her heart. "Oh, my goodness! If Lord Kerr reads this, then..." She dropped her mother's hands, raced to the corner of her room, and began to prepare a piece of parchment.

"Catherine!" Lady Hewson exclaimed, rising at once. "What are you thinking?"

"I have to let him know this is entirely false!" Catherine cried, writing as quickly as she could. "He is due to leave this very day and I must catch him!" Finishing her letter, she rose to ring the bell, leaving it to dry. "Oh, Mama! Whatever am I to do?"

For the first time in her life, Catherine felt as though she might give in to hysterics, as though she were about to weep and wail all over her astonished mother.

"Well," Lady Hewson murmured as the maid came in. "This is quite extraordinary."

Catherine, wiping her eyes, managed to give directions to the maid about her note, repeating multiple times the urgency of its delivery to Lord Kerr before hurrying her from the room. Then she shut the door, leaned back against it, and began to cry in earnest.

"Oh, my dear!" Lady Hewson came over to give her distraught daughter a warm embrace. "Do not cry so. We shall sort this whole matter out, I am sure of it."

"How can we?" Catherine wept, her body racked with pain. "An announcement such as this shall bring gossips and rumors, and were I to break it—even though I never acquiesced in the first place—there would be a scandal! My name will be sullied!"

Her mother patted her back reassuringly. "Now, that will only be until something of a greater scandal comes along," she said, as if that was comforting. "We might go to the country and try again next Season."

"No!" Catherine exclaimed, horrified at the idea. "Lord Kerr and I..." She trailed off miserably, not knowing what to say. "I am not sure what the situation will be with him now, I confess," she whispered, her head dropping. "Goodness, this is all such a muddle."

Her mother gently led her back to the seats by the fire, encouraging her to drink her chocolate. "I just cannot fathom what Lord Linton meant by such a thing," she said, handing Catherine her cup. "He is a long-term acquaintance, certainly, but he has not often been in your company."

"I have actively avoided his company!" Catherine yelled, a streak of ire suddenly racing through her. "Mama, might you go explain this situation to Father, so as to assuage some of his anger? I... I must go for a walk."

Catherine managed to keep a somewhat morose expression on her face, despite the anger burning in her veins.

"Oh, of course, my dear," her mother said immediately, looking entirely sympathetic. "I shall speak to him at once. Take your time outside, but ensure you are back home before the fashionable hour." She frowned, her mouth a thin line. "You will be the talk of the town, and it is best not to be seen."

"Of course, Mama," Catherine mumbled, waiting impatiently for Lady Hewson to leave the room before bounding to her feet as an unexpected bout of energy began to course through her veins. "I must go speak with him." Her hands clenched into fists as she stormed to the window, her brows furrowed. "He will see that I am not to be trifled with!"

The memory of his words from last evening came back to haunt her, reminding her that he had vowed he would force her to see Lord Kerr's true nature. Was this how he intended to do it? Her jaw set, her anger was burning through her like a furnace growing hotter and hotter with each passing moment. Ringing the bell, Catherine waited impatiently for her maid, ignoring her mother's protests. She would speak to Lord Linton herself, demand that he rectify the situation somehow and, hopefully, return to discover that Lord Kerr had received her note and quite understood the entire situation. She would not allow her reputation to be sullied in this way.

Lord Linton had a great deal of explaining to do.

〜

CATHERINE MADE her way down the street with her confused maid in tow. Thankfully, it was early enough for the streets not to be particularly busy, which meant that Catherine did not have to avoid unwanted whispers or knowing looks.

However, as her steps began to slow, Lady Hewson's warnings began to dig into her mind, reminding her that she could not exactly walk into Lord Linton's home and demand an audience with him.

"Then again," she murmured to herself, "I am his 'betrothed.'" Glancing back at the maid, Catherine smiled to herself and pushed her unease to one side. She would do as she had intended and ignore the potential consequences. She would simply have to make sure to leave his home before town began to grow too busy.

Hailing a hackney, Catherine and her maid climbed in, and Catherine gave directions as to where to go. Knowing where Lord Linton lived, she gave an address one street away, thinking it would be best not to appear on his doorstep. The hackney rolled through the streets of London, giving her time to think about what was to come.

What was she going to do if Lord Kerr had not received her note? She did not know where his country estate was, exactly, so she could not write to him there. She would then have to wait until he was able to return in order to explain things to him, and it mayhap be too late. Biting her lip, Catherine's anger began to boil once more as they drew closer to Lord Linton's home.

Alighting from the hackney, Catherine paid the driver and began to hurry along the street towards Lord Linton's townhouse. However, on rounding the corner, she discovered that there was a carriage outside it, and as she drew closer, she recognized that carriage to be none other than Lord Kerr's.

"Oh, goodness!" she whispered, her eyes widening as she hurried closer and saw the carriage was empty.

"It seems that he has gone inside, Miss Hewson," the maid said to her unspoken question.

Catherine could only stare at her maid for a moment, her heart sinking into her boots. This could not be good. Giving herself a slight shake, she made her way to the front door. Her knock was answered almost immediately by a frazzled-looking butler, and much to her dismay, Catherine could hear two very loud and very male voices floating down the hallway towards her.

"Good morning. I am Miss Hewson and I come in search of Lord Linton," she told the butler, attempting to keep an innocent look on her face. "I must see him at once."

The butler bowed and opened the door for her. "Of course, Miss Hewson." He took her things from her. "However, I must ask you to tarry here for a moment. His lordship is currently speaking to another gentleman."

"Yes, Lord Kerr," Catherine said. "I am well aware of that, and I believe I must see him regardless. Now, if you could just tell me where they are?" She looked enquiringly up at the butler, lifting her chin and keeping her stance firm so that he would not attempt to delay her any further.

Thankfully, the butler did not seem inclined to do so, and he led her down the hallway.

"Just in the study, Miss Hewson," he murmured, indicating the door in front of them. "Might I get you some refreshments?"

"No, thank you," Catherine replied crisply. "I can show myself in, I thank you." She did not give the butler any time to argue, stepping ahead of him and opening the door at once.

Two pairs of eyes met hers the moment she stepped inside. Lord Linton was standing behind his desk, his hands planted firmly on top of the mahogany wood. His cheeks were red, his eyes were filled with anger, and his dark hair was in a state of complete disarray. Lord Kerr, on the other hand, looked immaculate in every way, aside from how his hands were clenched into fists. He was standing opposite Lord Linton, and had been in the middle of bellowing something when Catherine had walked into the room.

"Catherine!" Lord Kerr exclaimed, coming towards her immediately. "Whatever are you doing here?"

Catherine caught his hands, relieved beyond measure that he had not left. "Oh, Lord Kerr, did you receive my note this morning?" she asked desperately, looking into his eyes. "Please tell me you did not believe a word of what was written in the paper!"

Lord Kerr looked back at her with uncertainty in his eyes. "I am not quite sure what to believe, Catherine," he murmured. "This is all very peculiar." He squeezed her hands gently. "What are you doing here?"

"I came to ask Lord Linton what on *earth* he was thinking in sending in such a notice to the newspaper!" Catherine answered, turning to frown at Lord Linton, who was, much to her surprise, still glaring at Lord Kerr. "Linton, what is the meaning of this?" Her fury had her dropping Kerr's hands and marching to Lord Linton's table, her fingers itching to slap him. "We are not engaged! We have *never* been engaged, and yet you go and do this! Do you need me to get you out of yet another situation, is that it? I told you before that I would not be your plaything, to use as you wish!"

Lord Linton lifted one eyebrow, his gaze drifting from Catherine to Lord Kerr. "My dear Catherine," he murmured, his gaze still fixated on Lord Kerr. "I consider it my duty to marry any lady I kiss in public."

Catherine's mouth fell open, her heart practically stopping in her chest.

Lord Kerr slowly turned to look at her, his expression growing severe. "Is this true, Catherine?"

"No!" Catherine exclaimed crossly. "I mean, yes, but not in that particular way."

Lord Kerr sighed heavily and passed one hand over his eyes.

"Is it not as Lord Linton is suggesting, I swear to you!" Catherine protested weakly, grasping onto Lord Kerr's arm in desperation. "He is correct in saying he kissed me, but I did not accept his attentions, nor did I want them." She turned her head to look at Lord Linton, who stood with a small smirk on his face. Her anger grew, mingled with nervousness and anxiety as she looked back at Lord Kerr. "Please," she continued quietly. "Please, do not think of this as love or affection between myself and Lord Linton. He kissed me so that I might save him from three gentlemen who were chasing him."

Lord Kerr closed his eyes for a moment, looking thoroughly confused. "I am not quite sure what to make of all this."

Catherine held her breath, moisture beginning to cling to her lashes. "Do not believe him," she pleaded, terrified that she might lose the man she cared so much for. "I promise you he means nothing to me. His reputation alone should tell you that I would not allow myself to even consider him as a potential husband. I have even pushed myself away from his acquaintance. Please, trust me. Believe what I am saying, I beg you."

Lord Kerr's expression softened, his eyes meeting hers. Catherine heaved a sigh of relief as he briefly ran his fingers along the curve of her cheek.

"I *do* believe you, Catherine," he murmured gently. "I am still mightily confused, but you are quite right to remind me of Lord Linton's reputation. I do not know much of him, but what I do know is not particularly good."

Catherine let out a long breath, pressing away her tears with shaking fingers. "I am so glad."

"I am afraid this does cause some difficulties, however," Lord Kerr continued, returning his steely gaze to Lord Linton. "And whilst I am afraid I must continue with my plans to return to my estate, I fully expect there to be a retraction in tomorrow's paper."

Lord Linton snorted. "And what makes you think I would do such a thing? Simply because you ask it? You are not worthy of Kitty."

Lord Kerr paused, his eyes glinting. Catherine continued to hold onto his arm, feeling his muscles tense beneath his coat sleeves. "You are an arrogant man, to say the least. You will do as I ask, Linton, or I shall call you out. I shall have you know that I am a particularly good swordsman."

"No!" Catherine exclaimed, clasping Lord Kerr's arm with both hands. "You cannot!"

"I will, and I shall," Lord Kerr replied firmly. "Linton, you shall ensure that the retraction is made and that there is no damage to Miss Hewson's reputation. Do you understand me?"

Lord Linton's jaw clenched, his eyes narrowing.

"I can stand to be in your presence no longer," Lord Kerr spat, putting one arm around Catherine's shoulders. "Do it, Linton, or it will be all the worse for you."

And with that, he swept from the room, taking a shaking Catherine with him.

7

"Are you all right, my dear?"

Catherine leaned into Lord Kerr for a moment, drawing from his strength. "Yes," she said. "I believe I am." She looked up at him, grateful beyond words that he had not let himself be deceived. "I cannot thank you enough for believing my words."

His expression became grim. "The little I know of Linton told me that I could not trust him. Just as well you appeared when you did, my Catherine! I loathed the mere idea of returning to the country without speaking to you first."

"My relief is overwhelming," Catherine admitted as he stepped back and took her hands in his. "Must you still go?"

He nodded, crestfallen. "I am afraid so. As much as I would love to tarry with you, my business cannot be put off any longer. You will write to me, will you not?"

Catherine's face lit up. "Yes, of course! I was distressed when I realized I did not know where to send my letters."

Lord Kerr's eyes widened. "Oh, how foolish of me!" he responded, sounding both horrified and frustrated. "My dearest Catherine, I shall write to you the very moment I reach my estate, so then you will know where to send your replies. I very much look forward to our correspondence."

Catherine blushed as he pressed his lips to the back of her hands, her heart soaring in her chest when, only minutes before, it had sunk lower than she had ever thought possible.

"I must go," Lord Kerr murmured. "Might I give you a ride home?"

"No, I thank you," Catherine replied, glancing about her. "I realize my maid must still be indoors, and I am quite able to hail a hackney. Do not let me keep you."

His warm smile delighted her. "You are very good, Catherine. I shall see you again anon."

Catherine waited until his carriage had turned down the street, waving one last time at him before stepping indoors once more, hating that she had to return to Lord Linton's home in search of her maid. The butler appeared by her side the moment she came through the front door, looking most apologetic.

"I have just now sent for your maid, Miss Hewson," he said with a short bow. "Do forgive me for the oversight."

"There is no oversight," Catherine reassured him. "I did not expect to be leaving in such a hurry."

She waited patiently, but just as her maid rushed towards her from the back stairs, Lord Linton appeared in the doorway of his study.

"Kitty," he said hurriedly. "Do not go. Please. I need to talk to you."

Catherine felt her anger begin to burn once more, and she turned her back and waited for her maid, refusing to answer him.

"Please!" he begged, sounding more contrite than she had ever heard him. "I have done this for your own good, Kitty."

She rounded on him, burning with anger. "My good?" she

shouted, her voice echoing down the hallway as her maid and the butler melted away almost at once. "There is nothing good about this, my lord! You tried to ruin things between Lord Kerr and myself, and I simply cannot understand why you would do such a thing! You are a wicked, cruel man, and I cannot believe that we were ever truly friends!"

Much to her shame, Catherine felt tears spring to her eyes as she choked back a sob. His excuses would not do. Not this time.

"Kitty," Linton said softly, stepping a little closer to her. "I know I have not treated you well, and I cannot fault you for your anger, but I know that Lord Kerr is not who he claims to be."

"Nonsense!" Catherine spat, her eyes ablaze even as tears fell onto her cheeks. "He is honest and true and—"

"He is almost bankrupt."

His words took her breath away. She stared at him, a twist of fear in her gut.

"I had a word with some of my acquaintances after I saw you with him," Linton continued. "They have told me that the man owes a great deal of money. His estate is in dire straits."

Catherine shook her head, a bubble of laughter rising up within her. "You spoke to some of your acquaintances?" she asked, mockery in her tone. "Come now, you shall have to do better than that."

"Please, Kitty!" he exclaimed, stepping closer and catching one of her hands in his. "I know I have not been a good friend to you, that I have not been a particularly good man, even, but I promise you this is true. I did what I had to so as to sever the connection between you and Lord Kerr because I care about you, truly."

Catherine was robbed of speech for some moments, going from anger to laughter to confusion in such rapidity that she was hardly able to think.

"I am telling you the truth about Lord Kerr," Linton insisted, his eyes looking into hers as his fingers gently rubbed the back of her hand. "Can you not trust me on this, even for old times' sake?"

Slowly, Catherine pulled her hand away from his, stepping back and shaking her head. "No. I cannot."

The desperation in his expression deepened.

"I cannot believe a word you say, my lord," she went on. "You are not a trustworthy man. You have not been a friend to me in a long time, and since your return to town, I have tried to distance myself from you—with good reason, I might add." Tears began to pour down her face, unchecked. "Fix what you have done, as Lord Kerr directed."

Lord Linton made to move forward, but she stepped back from him, numbness spreading through her limbs. "No!" she cried through her sobs. "It is done. Fix this now. As much as you deserve it, I would not like to see you badly injured by Lord Kerr's swordsmanship."

Turning her back on him, Catherine made her way to the front door and hurried down the steps, pulling a handkerchief from her sleeve. She wiped her eyes quickly, drawing in one sharp breath after another in an attempt to calm herself. Her maid seemed to materialize out of nowhere, falling into step behind her as Catherine quickened her steps away from Lord Linton's home. She hailed the first hackney she saw, and once inside, she sank back onto the seat. Her maid sat opposite her, her gaze fixed on the window and not looking at Catherine at all. Catherine was grateful for the silence, her mind whirling with all the events that had taken place.

~

RETURNING home was something of a relief, even though Catherine had to pour out the whole story to her mother and then her father, leaving her quite exhausted. Her father muttered darkly about calling Lord Linton out himself, which made Catherine smile in spite of her distress. He had never been a man of many words, but there were times when he proved that he cared about her in his own way—and this was one of those times.

"But how shall he fix such a thing?" Lady Hewson queried, still looking dreadfully worried. "I mean, there shall be a scandal if it is not done properly."

Catherine lifted her shoulders. "I cannot say, Mama, but Lord Kerr put the fear of God in him, so I am quite sure Lord Linton will do what he must."

"I should hope he does," her mother replied, her face a little paler than usual. "You shall have callers this afternoon, no doubt, but I do not know what we shall tell them."

"We shall go out then, Mama," Catherine declared, not wanting to have any kind of visitors today. "A carriage ride, mayhap, or a visit to one of your trusted friends. Tomorrow, when the truth of the matter is known, then we might allow callers."

Her mother nodded slowly. "You must appear to be the distressed victim, who has been the plaything of Lord Linton and is most upset by it. That is the only way we can alleviate some of the rumors that will inevitably follow."

Catherine tried to smile, but found the growing ache in her throat made it almost impossible. "Yes, of course, Mama. I do not think that will be particularly hard to do."

Lady Hewson smiled sadly. "I am sorry for all this, Catherine. I am quite sure Lord Kerr will return to you as soon as he is able. I have the greatest of hopes for you both."

"As do I," Catherine replied firmly, doing her best to push away the nagging question that dogged her mind.

What if Lord Linton was right?

She shook her head and excused herself, desperate for the quiet of her own room. Her mother watched her go with concern in her eyes, her shoulders slumping as Catherine left the room. This was not what either of them had expected.

8

The following morning, Catherine was awake early, having had something of a restless night. Her mind had been tormented with thoughts about what Lord Linton had meant when he had said Lord Kerr was up to his neck in debts.

Lord Kerr had always seemed so true, so devoted to her. A man could not fake such a thing, could he? The depths in his eyes had to be real, surely?

And so, troubled by her thoughts, Catherine had risen early and made her way down to the dining room to break her fast, but found she could barely eat. Nibbling on a piece of toast, which slowly grew cold and hard in her hands, she drank cups and cups of warm tea.

The butler, who had been instructed to bring the papers to her the moment they arrived, soon appeared, and Catherine rose from her chair to take them from him immediately, her eyes filling with sudden tears as her anxiety rose. Leafing through the papers, she tried desperately to find her name amongst the many notices, but, as her vision blurred, she had to pause in her search to calm herself down.

"Come now, Catherine," she told herself, dabbing at her eyes with a napkin. "This will never do. Get a hold of yourself!"

A vision of Lord Kerr and Lord Linton dueling sprang to her mind, making her breath catch. Closing her eyes tightly, Catherine pushed down her nerves and drew in one long breath after the other, hoping her stomach would soon stop rolling.

"Catherine?"

Looking up, Catherine saw her mother framed in the doorway, still in her night things. Her face was filled with worry and anxious expectation, and Catherine felt her heart burst with warmth over her mother's ongoing concern for her.

"I am just looking now, Mama," she managed to say, her throat constricting with apprehension at what she might find. "I am sure Lord Linton has done what Lord Kerr instructed."

This time, Catherine slowed down her pace. She still struggled to find her name anywhere in the pages of the paper, though, growing almost frantic as she neared the end.

"It is not here!" she exclaimed, her heart thumping within her. "I cannot find it anywhere!" She turned to the very last page, scanning it quickly, only for her attention to catch on a small notice at the very bottom of the page.

"Did you find it?" Lady Hewson breathed, coming to sit next to her. "Is it the retraction we hoped for?"

"'This newspaper is sorry to say that there has been some confusion over the previously printed engagement between Lord Linton and Miss Catherine Hewson,'" Catherine read aloud, her entire body growing cold. "'At this present time, it is not known for certain what the current situation is, but readers will be informed in due course.'" She stared at the notice for a good few minutes, re-reading it over and over, as though she might find something different there.

She could not believe that Lord Linton had done this. Instead of rescuing her from the scandal he had caused by his previous advertisement, all he had done was make things worse. Now she would have visitors demanding to know what had occurred, rumours flying around about her and her supposed betrothed. Closing her eyes, Catherine let her tears trickle down her cheeks unhindered, moisture landing on the paper in front of her. This was not what had been meant to happen.

"Oh, my dear!" Lady Hewson exclaimed, pulling the paper away from Catherine. "This is not good at all. Whatever is Lord Linton thinking?"

"He thinks he is doing this for my best," Catherine answered through her tears. "I know it seems quite untoward, but he believes that he is somehow saving me from a most imprudent match."

"He has no right!" her mother cried indignantly. "He was your friend, of course, but you have not been close with him for some time. What makes him think he has any right to involve himself now?"

Catherine could not answer, aware that if she said anything, her mother would find out that she had kissed Lord Kerr and been seen leaving by Lord Linton.

"He wants you for himself," her mother suddenly declared, as though that were the obvious reason for this scandal. "That is what all this is about! Lord Linton means to have you for his own, and this is the only way he can push you away from Lord Kerr."

"No, Mama," Catherine replied, shaking her head. "That is nothing to do with it, I am quite sure. For whatever reason, he believes Lord Kerr is unworthy of me, and thinks it is his responsibility to prevent our connection. What he means by this," she continued, gesturing at the paper, "I cannot say. Lord Kerr threatened to call him out if he did not remove the engagement entirely from my shoulders, and since he has not done it, I cannot help but think that it will be so."

Despair filled her as she thought of the inevitable duel, terrified that one or both men would be gravely hurt or even killed over her. It was not as though Lord Linton did not deserve such a consequence over what he had done, but she did not want to see blood spilled, much less because of her.

"Your father may well do the same," her mother added. "I should go and speak to him at once." She rose and put a gentle hand on Catherine's shoulder. "Take some time and compose yourself, my dear. Eat something. Drink some tea. I will return shortly. We must come up with a plan for what to do next."

Catherine barely heard her mother go, an inner trembling beginning to get a hold of her very soul. Her life had been so easy before, so simple. She had hopes and dreams for the future, believing that she would, one day, be the wife of Lord Kerr.

Now, thanks to Lord Linton, she was going to be the talk of the town, her future with Lord Kerr marred and possibly gone forever. People would be wondering what the truth was, and she would undoubtedly have a great many visitors, desperate to find out what was going on between herself and Lord Linton.

What could she say to them that would make the situation any easier? Could she really just tell them the truth—that Lord Linton had done this all of his own accord? No, for then the rumors would begin in earnest, and Catherine knew exactly what would be said. There would be talk of a liaison between them, mayhap when they were first friends. It would not matter whether or not she refuted him, whether or not there was any truth in the matter, her reputation would be tarnished. So what was she to say?

Groaning softly, Catherine put her head in her hands and battled more tears. This was not what she had expected, and she certainly had no idea how to deal with such things. Lord Kerr had not yet written, thus leaving her unable to sit at her desk and scribe a letter to him, begging him for his help. Even worse, she was unsure whether he intended to call Lord Linton out, as he had threatened to do. Whatever Lord Linton was doing, it could not be for her good, despite what he had promised. He had always been able to wangle his way out of any misdemeanor, using his silver tongue to the best of his ability.

"Miss Hewson?"

The door opened, and the butler walked in, a slightly puzzled look on his face. Catherine sniffed once and looked up at him, knowing she could trust him not to tell the rest of the staff that she had clearly been crying.

"Forgive me for disturbing your breakfast, Miss Hewson," he said, "but you have a visitor."

Catherine frowned. "A caller? At this hour?"

"Indeed," the butler replied, frowning. "He is most insistent; otherwise, I would not have interrupted you."

A cold hand gripped her heart. "It is Lord Linton, is it not?"

The butler inclined his head. "It is, miss. What shall I do?"

Catherine wanted to have him sent away at once, wanted to refuse to speak to him or even see him, but sense told her that it would be best they had a discussion. He was the only one who could bring a little clarity to this situation, the only one who could sort it out as best he could.

"I suppose I should see him," she sighed heavily, anger beginning to burn in the pit of her stomach. "You may send him in."

The butler nodded. "Very good, miss." He opened the door, murmured something, and closed it behind him, leaving Lord Linton standing just inside the door.

Catherine found she could not even look at him, her ire rolling like heavy waves over her.

"Kitty," he began. "I came to tell you—"

"To tell me what?" she burst out, rising to her feet and glaring at him. "To tell me that you have made this even more serious than before? To tell me that I should expect a great number of busybodies enquiring about my health, under the pretense of discovering what there is between us?"

"I came to tell you that I am sorry for what I have had to do," Lord Linton replied, his voice quiet. There was a gravity in both his eyes and his expression that gave her pause, her mind clouding with worry.

"Your apologies will make no difference now," she told him, shaking her head at him. "Do you truly intend to make things more difficult for me, simply because you dislike Lord Kerr?"

Lord Linton pressed his lips together for a moment, as if battling his temper. "Oh, Kitty," he said eventually. "I am trying my utmost to save you."

"He is not what you think!" Catherine protested, slamming her hand down on the table. "How you can say so is beyond me! I know him!"

"I am aware of that," he said drily. "But you only see what he wants you to see. Trust me, Catherine, I have discovered things you would never have been able to find out for yourself. He is up to his neck in debt. He intends to marry you only for your inheritance."

Heat rushed up Catherine's neck, her hands balling into fists. "How dare you!" she cried, her eyes blazing with fire. "Lord Kerr means more to me than anything, and he cares for me with a deep, intense affection that you could never understand!"

Her voice echoed around the room, bouncing off the walls. Lord Linton did not move, did not speak, but he kept his gaze fixed on hers. Catherine, suddenly weary, chose to sit back down in her chair, hopelessness filling her.

"I do not know why you have done this, Linton," she muttered, almost to herself. "You seem intent on ruining my happiness."

"I am intent on shattering the illusions Lord Kerr has built up around you," Linton said.

"And you propose to do that by breaking the two of us apart with your lies, is that it?" Catherine replied, her words dripping with mockery and disdain. "I can tell you now, my lord, that you have failed in your task already. You have only driven us closer."

"Is that the case?" he asked, walking to the table. Uninvited, he took a seat and helped himself to a cup of tea. "Have you already written to him with the news of what has taken place?"

"I expect to hear from him very soon," Catherine retorted angrily.

Lord Linton regarded her for a moment. "Kitty, we were friends for a long time. Is it truly so hard to believe that I might be doing what is best for you?"

"You cannot be serious!" Catherine exclaimed, seeing the flash of hurt in his eyes but not caring about it in the least. "I believe you think of no one but yourself. Somehow, this situation must improve your own status. Am I to save you yet again from another father, brother, or even husband searching for you after your appalling behavior with another woman? Am I to be used in an attempt to show you are decent or even moral?"

"No!" Lord Linton's hand came slamming down onto the table, the anger and frustration in his expression startling Catherine into silence. "No," he said more quietly, sinking back into his chair. "No, Catherine, you are not to be used in any of the ways you have suggested, I swear it."

Much to her surprise, he put his head in his hands and groaned aloud, as though aware of just how terribly he was handling the entire situation.

"I know I am not a good man," he continued, not raising his head to look at her. "I know you have every right to be as angry with me as you are, but I *know* that Lord Kerr is not the gentleman he claims to be. I only wish to prove it to you."

"Prove it to me?" Catherine repeated, completely taken aback by the change in Lord Linton's tone and demeanor. "You expect to be able to prove your accusations to me somehow? What is it that you plan to do, exactly?" Her tone became somewhat mocking, her eyes narrowing. "Do you intend to find a copy of his accounts and bring them to me?"

"No," Lord Linton said calmly, his head rising from his hands. "I have other ways of doing such a thing. I intend to use you as a bargaining chip."

9

Catherine's stomach rolled. "You intend to barter me?" she whispered, breaking out into a cold sweat of fear and revulsion. "I will go to the highest bidder, is that what you intend? I tell you now, Lord Linton, I will *not* be used in such a way!"

Linton shook his head, holding up one hand to quieten her. "Now, now, there is no need for such vehemence. I have a much simpler plan in mind. I will write to him and offer him a great deal of wealth, so long as he will break off his acquaintance with you."

Catherine recoiled at once, utterly horrified at the idea. "How dare you," she whispered, tears pricking at her eyes. Her voice rose when she spoke again. "I am not something you can simply buy and sell!"

He gave her a wry smile. "And well I know it. This would only be to prove to you what I have said about Lord Kerr." He tilted his head just a little, regarding her carefully. "Do you not wish to know the truth?"

"I already know the truth," Catherine replied, hating that her words faltered, just a little. "I know that Lord Kerr cares for me, that he intends to marry me, and that we shall have a future together filled with love and affection."

Lord Linton smiled softly. "Then you need not worry about what I will write him," he said, arching one eyebrow. "If you are so certain of his reply, then nothing I say will induce him to do what I ask, will it?"

Catherine lifted her chin. "No, it will not."

"Good," he replied, lifting his tea cup as though toasting her. "Then, if he replies in indignation and anger, I shall step out of your life for good and wish you nothing but the best."

"And, if he does not?" Catherine asked, cringing inwardly as the words escaped her mouth without her realizing it.

Lord Linton chuckled, aware she had not meant to ask such a thing. "If he accepts my wealth, then our agreement stands."

Catherine frowned, confused as to what he meant. "Our agreement?" she repeated. "We have made no agreement."

"Our engagement, Kitty," he reminded her, lifting one shoulder. "It shall stand."

Spluttering, Catherine set down her tea cup, unable to quite believe what she was hearing. "You expect me to wed you if Lord Kerr accepts the offer you make him?" she asked, shaking her head at him. "Goodness, it seems you have gone quite mad!"

"Those are my terms," Lord Linton said, as calmly as if he were making a business proposition. "If you wish to discover the truth, which I know deep in your heart you do, then you shall wed me if Lord Kerr proves to be as unfaithful and as untrue as I know him to be."

Catherine shook her head. "Why would you want to wed me? You have no affection for me—that, I know for certain."

"Mayhap you do not know me as well as you think," he said, something burning in his gaze. "I wish to wed you, Catherine, for I need to settle down and produce my heir. Who better than with a lady I have known for a great many years, a lady I know will suit me very well?"

She snorted in derision. Of course he would only desire to wed her for his own purposes. "If I was your wife," she warned him, "you would not live as you do now. There would be no pleasures, and certainly no mistresses. Your life would not be one of enjoyment."

Lord Linton chuckled, his chest rumbling. "I think I would quite enjoy that. It may come as a surprise to you, but I believe I can be a faithful and true husband, regardless of how much my wife intends to make my life a misery." His eyes glittered. "The only question is whether you will accept my proposal."

There was a short silence, the air humming with expectation. Catherine did not know what to think, whether she should agree or not to his proposal. She knew that the possibility of Lord Kerr being so untrue was virtually impossible, yet in order to prove it, she would have to accept Lord Linton's terms.

"Very well," she said softly, looking up at him with a clear, firm view. "I accept your terms, my lord."

The slow smile across Lord Linton's face gave Catherine a rather uncomfortable feeling, as though he knew for certain this would not bode well for her. Her mind worked over what she had just agreed to, a niggle of doubt ringing through her mind regarding Lord Kerr's true intentions.

"Very good," Linton murmured, getting up from the table and coming over to her. "I look forward to proving myself correct in this matter."

Catherine looked up at him, her fingers tightening on her napkin as she twisted it in her lap. "Is that all that truly matters to you?"

He paused for a moment, thinking, only to shrug his shoulders, bend down, and plant a gentle kiss on her cheek. "This means I can save you from a marriage to a man who does not care for you, but only for your fortune," he answered, and his voice was gentler and more tender than she had ever heard before. "I will inform you when I receive a reply, Kitty. Good day."

Catherine sat quietly for some moments after Lord Linton had left the house, her stomach rolling still with what had transpired. Her skin burned where Linton had kissed her, heat spreading across her features and into her cheeks. The way he had spoken to her before he left had taken her aback, for his words had been filled with a tenderness she had not expected. She was forced now to consider the fact that Lord Linton might not be using her for his own gains, as she had convinced herself. There could not be any truth in what he said about Lord Kerr, however—he was quite mistaken on that count.

Catherine sighed heavily and poured herself another cup of tea, finding it a little too cold for her liking. She rang the bell and resumed her seat, not quite ready to go in search of her mother and father to discuss what had taken place.

The truth was, up until Lord Linton had spoken to her, she had no qualms about Lord Kerr. She trusted him wholeheartedly. He had never spoken to her of his past, nor of any difficulties, but then again, she was not expecting such discussions until they were engaged. She did not doubt that Lord Kerr's intention was towards matrimony, given that he himself had told her such a thing, and he had never once discussed her dowry.

Of course, she had something of an inheritance because of her father's status, but that had never once come to her mind when she had thought of Lord Kerr. As far as she was aware, he was running a profitable estate, and had never shown any specific interest in any vices whatsoever. He had been fixed on her, showering her with his particular attentions so that she would have no doubt of his intent.

Catherine had no reason to believe he was lying to her. So

why did the niggle of worry continue to push its way into her mind now? She had not been close with Lord Linton for a number of years, even though they had known each other since childhood, so she owed him nothing. Recalling how she had been embarrassed to be in his company only a week or so ago, Catherine drew in a deep breath and chose to push him out of her memory.

Lord Linton was using her for his own ends, although what those ends were, she could not say. Mayhap having her as his betrothed, even for a short time, would convince those he had wronged that he was, in fact, a respectable and honorable man. Possibly they would stop chasing him for whatever it was he had done to them.

It was not as though she could expect him to have any true consideration for her reputation, or what the notice in the paper would do to her—even if he admitted it to be false much later. The damage had been done. Thank goodness Lord Kerr had believed her entirely. It meant that no matter what happened with Lord Linton, both she and Lord Kerr knew the truth and would cling to one another through the inevitable storm of rumors, whispers, and gossip that would come upon them very soon.

Satisfied in her own mind that she was right to believe and trust Lord Kerr, Catherine settled back into her seat and smiled at the maid as the fresh tea tray was brought in. She would push all doubt from her mind and would wait, already triumphant, for Lord Linton to return with news of his defeat. Lord Kerr would respond as she expected, telling Lord Linton to cease his nonsense.

"Catherine?"

Lady Hewson appeared in the doorway, looking quite horrified. "I heard Lord Linton came to see you. You should have sent him away at once, or at least sent for me while you discussed matters!" She settled herself at the table and looked expectantly at Catherine, waiting for her to respond.

"Everything is quite all right, Mama," Catherine replied. "You need not worry about Lord Linton. He intends to fix what he has done."

"But the newspaper—"

Catherine held up one hand, silencing her mother. "Mama, let us not worry," she repeated. "He is to write to Lord Kerr this very day, and I am quite sure that there will be both a retraction and a public apology to me. All will be well very soon. I assure you."

Catherine poured tea for both herself and her mother before turning the conversation to other things, quite ready to put Lord Linton away from her mind entirely.

10

"You have a visitor, my lady."

Catherine tried to smile as her mother rose to greet their next caller: a Lady Melrose, who was one of the best-known gossips in town. To Catherine's knowledge, Lady Melrose had never called on them before, which meant that Catherine's engagement was the only reason for her visit.

Sighing inwardly, Catherine rose to greet their guest, knowing that it was expected, but also finding it more and more difficult to keep appearing jovial. She had endured more than enough over the last three days, and yet the visitors kept coming.

"Ah, Lady Melrose!" her mother cooed, as though greeting an old friend. "How good to see you!"

"And it is good to see you, Lady Hewson. I simply *had* to call on you both, in lieu of the exciting news that has all of London talking," Lady Melrose said, sitting down at once. "Goodness me, Miss Hewson, you have got London in an uproar!"

"Do I?" Catherine asked a bit nervously. "That is a surprise. I was never so interesting before."

"Oh, but you are now!" Lady Melrose exclaimed, her dark brown eyes fixed on Catherine. "Everyone is wondering whether or not you are engaged to Lord Linton, and there is such confusion that we talk of nothing else! You were great friends, were you not?"

Catherine cleared her throat delicately. "Lord Linton and I were friends many years ago, yes."

"But now you are *more* than friends, are you not?" Lady Melrose asked with a twinkle in her eye. "How wonderful!"

Catherine did not know what to say, her frustration rattling through her.

"And when is the wedding? When are the banns to be called? And what is with all the secrecy?" Lady Melrose questioned. There was a calculating look in her eyes, and Catherine felt as though Lady Melrose was writing everything down in her head, storing it away so that she might repeat it to all and sundry once their visit was over.

"Lady Melrose," she began, sitting a little further forward in her chair and fixing the lady with her gaze. "Lord Linton has deceived you all, myself included. This is some prank, that is all."

Lady Melrose stared at Catherine for a moment before blinking rapidly, her face alive with excitement. "A sham? A prank? You cannot be serious."

"And yet I am," Catherine replied firmly, ignoring her mother's flapping hands. "Lord Linton has caused a great deal of confusion for me, as I seem to be a part of his game. I cannot tell you how difficult this has been."

Seeing the flash of sympathy in Lady Melrose's eyes, Catherine shot a glance at her mother, who, much to her surprise, was looking somewhat relieved.

"Goodness me," Lady Melrose murmured, her eyes still fixed on Catherine's face. "You have been treated quite ill, have you not? Whatever were his reasons for doing so?"

"I cannot say," Catherine answered, sighing heavily. "He is, as you know, something of a scoundrel. I believe he has been chased down the streets by those he has wronged on a previous occasion, which shocked a great many people." She had no qualms in sharing such details with the lady, thinking that Lord Linton deserved every bit of gossip and rumor that came his way after what he had done to her.

Lady Hewson reached across and patted Catherine's hand, her eyes bright with sympathy. "My dear Catherine has been so poorly treated, and even when she demanded it, Lord Linton did not write an explanation in the paper. My daughter has been left to pick up the pieces, for what can a young girl do when a gentleman uses her name and connection in such a way?"

"Indeed," Lady Melrose agreed, shaking her head. "And has this turned Lord Kerr away from you, Miss Hewson?"

Her words made Catherine pause, her eyes widening slightly.

"You will excuse my boldness," Lady Melrose hurriedly added, "for it has been quite apparent that Lord Kerr has had something of an attachment to you."

Catherine did not want to talk about Lord Kerr in great detail, so she satisfied Lady Melrose with a slight shrug. "Lord Kerr has had some business to deal with at his estate," she murmured. "Although I know for certain that he understands Lord Linton just as well as I do."

Thankfully for her, Lady Melrose seemed quite taken with this news, and she rose from her chair in a flurry of skirts, thanked them both for their kindness, and took her leave of them.

"No doubt to pass on what she discovered to her great many friends," Catherine muttered, slumping back in her chair.

Lady Hewson, looking quite exhausted, said, "That should be all around town by the morning, Catherine! I do hope you know what you are doing, my dear."

Catherine smiled softly. "I do, Mama. I think it best to be as honest as possible, whilst still hiding the truth in its entirety. Remember I am to garner sympathy from the *ton* instead of having my name dragged through the mud by Lord Linton. I think speaking to Lady Melrose in such a manner was necessary."

Her mother nodded slowly. "Let us hope that it will be enough to satisfy the gossips until Lord Linton does... whatever it is he intends to do to clear this whole mess up." She looked inquiringly at Catherine, who had to sigh and shake her head.

"He has not put in any kind of retraction yet, Mama," Catherine said woefully. "For the moment, we must wait."

She did not want to go into details with her mother about the letters that were to be exchanged between Lord Linton and Lord Kerr, for the less she knew of that, the better. In the end, Catherine was sure it would all be quite settled soon enough.

"There should be no more callers now," Lady Hewson said. No sooner had she finished speaking, though, than another scratch came to the door. "It is almost six o'clock!"

"I am sure we can refuse them, Mama," Catherine told her after calling the butler to enter. "We will simply say we are no longer at home."

The butler entered the room, and much to Catherine's surprise, he did not hand her mother a calling card but rather held out a small tray with a note for Catherine. She took it at once with a murmur of thanks, wondering who it might be that had written to her.

"Is it from Lord Kerr?" her mother asked.

Catherine looked up at her mother's question, holding the letter in her hand still. "I hope so, Mama," she responded. "Might you excuse me so I can read this alone?"

Her mother's expression softened. "But of course, my dear. I believe our morning calls to be at an end, regardless, so I shall take my leave of you and rest for a time before dinner." She rose, dropped a light kiss on Catherine's cheek, and left the room.

Catherine stared down at the letter in her hands, her heart turning over as she broke the wax seal. For whatever reason, there was no mark pressed into the wax, leaving no indication as to who could have written the letter. She had to hope it was Lord Kerr, for Catherine still had not heard from him, which had left her with a growing anxiety over his lack of correspondence.

"It has to be from him," she murmured to herself as a flurry of excitement flooded her veins. She smoothed out the letter and, getting to her feet, walked to the window in order to see it a little better.

""My dear Kitty,'" she read aloud, her heart sinking into her toes as she realized the letter was from Lord Linton, and not from Lord Kerr. ""I am writing to inform you that I have received a reply from Lord Kerr. Might I call upon you at your earliest convenience to discuss the matter? Yours, Linton.'"

Catherine's heart thumped wildly in her chest as she read and re-read the letter, not sure what it meant. Had Linton received a reply that he disliked? Had Lord Kerr proved his worth, as she had expected him to? She could not tell.

Glancing at the clock, Catherine realized that it was much too late to go calling on him now, even though she was almost desperate to hear what had passed between both them. She would write back at once and tell him to come tomorrow at his earliest convenience. Frustration rattled through her as she set off in search of parchment.

11

The following morning, Catherine was awake before dawn, pacing up and down her room in a state of nervous anticipation. Lord Linton had not replied to her letter, but she fully expected him to appear soon after breakfast. It was not as though he would wait for the proper time in which to call, given that he was not exactly a stickler for propriety. Besides, she had expressly instructed him to call as soon as he could, assuring him she would be quite ready to greet him.

However, given that the sun had only just begun to rise, Catherine did not think that he would appear any time soon.

Sitting down by the fire, she rubbed her arms to ward off the morning chill, stifling a yawn as she did so. The truth was, she had spent the night tossing and turning, worrying about Lord Kerr's response. Although she tried to convince herself he was honorable, she could not be completely sure about his intentions.

He had not written to her as he had promised. She had been unable to correspond with him because she had no idea where to send the letter, and she had been anxiously waiting with each passing day for his letter to arrive. But to know now that he had written to Lord Linton and not to her struck fear into her heart. Even if he was unwilling to continue their association after all that had gone on, she did not want to believe he had accepted Lord Linton's offer.

Her stomach churned with unease and anxiety as she got to her feet to ring the bell, ready for her breakfast tray. She was not particularly hungry, but it was probably best to eat something, no matter how small. It might stop her from feeling so ill.

Chewing on her bottom lip, Catherine tried to settle her mind and her heart. She had to believe in Lord Kerr. Mayhap he *had* written to her, but his letter was delayed somehow. Perhaps, after receiving Lord Linton's note, he had wanted to respond to him first, furious that Linton could even suggest such a thing! Or, maybe, he had been so caught up in the business of his estate that he had simply forgotten he was to write to her.

"Yes, I am sure that is it," Catherine said to herself, quelling her growing anxiety. "All will be well, I am quite sure."

SOME HOURS LATER, Catherine was still feeling as nervous as ever, even though she had given herself a stern talking to. There was still no sign of Lord Linton, and she began to wonder if he was likely to appear at all. Maybe he was going to leave her waiting, prolonging the torture for no other reason than to frustrate her.

Perhaps she should go and do something else in order to prevent her from thinking only about what Linton had to say. It might help her anxiety if she played the pianoforte or attempted to read a book. Getting to her feet, Catherine brushed down her skirts, only for the door to open as the butler walked in.

"Lord Linton, Miss Hewson," he said, directing a questioning look at her.

"Yes, yes," Catherine said hurriedly. "Send him in at once."

"Of course." The butler bowed, and after asking if she wanted a tea tray, swiftly left the room, leaving Lord Linton to enter.

Catherine could hardly speak, such were her trembling nerves. She looked up at him as he stepped inside the room, trying her best to keep her gaze direct.

"Kitty." Linton smiled, sitting down opposite her. "You look well."

"I do not have time for trivialities," Catherine bit out, already frustrated with him. "You know quite well that I have been anxiously waiting to hear from you."

His expression grew sympathetic. "I am aware of that, yes."

"And yet you sit here and expect me to be able to have a calm conversation with you?" she asked, growing angrier with each passing second. "Just get it over with, if you please. I cannot bear the anticipation any longer!"

He gave her a rueful smile. "I was aware that you would have a great many callers, and I am sorry for that, but at least now we can put this whole thing to an end."

Clearing his throat, Linton pulled out a few letters from his pocket and set the first one aside. "Here is the first letter that I wrote to Lord Kerr. It is a copy, of course, but an exact one." He lifted one eyebrow. "Would you like me to read it to you?"

Catherine nodded, her fingers twisting in her lap as she waited. She could hardly breathe, her anxiety rising with each breath she took.

Lord Kerr cleared his throat. "It reads as follows: 'Kerr, I am writing to explain my reasons for the article in the newspaper recently, announcing my engagement to Miss Catherine Hewson. I will not apologize for doing so, and you should not expect such a thing from me. If I am to be truthful, I would do the same thing again if I had to, for Kitty is my dear friend, and I would be lying if I did not admit that I cared for her a great deal.'"

He glanced up at Catherine, who found she could say nothing, her throat constricting and her heart hammering. She did not believe that Lord Linton truly cared for her, even though his expression was most sincere. She had seen him use that expression in order to get what he wanted in the past.

Lord Linton looked at her for another moment before continuing, his voice a little softer than before.

"'I believe that I would make Kitty very happy, although she is not likely to forgive me any time soon for my actions of late. In addition, I know of your current financial circumstances and the difficulties you have endured, although I will not lecture you on the misappropriation of funds through gambling and the like. However, I would ask that you relinquish your association with Miss Hewson and allow me to take your place. In recompense, I will pay the largest of your debts without question, helping you to regain some of your financial assets and no longer move close to bankruptcy.'"

There was a short pause, and Catherine struggled not to cry, feeling hot tears press against her lids. She did not want to let him know just how upset she was on hearing herself traded in such a way.

"'Do let me know of your decision as soon as you are able,'" Lord Linton finished, his eyes lifting to meet hers. "And that is all I wrote."

"And you received a reply," Catherine stated, hating that her voice was so thin and weak. "When did it appear?"

"I received it only yesterday, and I wrote to you at once," he answered, looking at her with something akin to sympathy, as though he was expecting her to be grievously upset. "Are you sure you want to hear his response? I know Lord Kerr himself will be writing to you very soon, regardless of this." He held up the other note.

"Yes," Catherine replied firmly. "Yes, I want to hear the reply."

"You still have faith in him?"

She lifted her chin. "Of course I do," she said, far too aware that her voice was wobbling. "You are doing this to tease me, my lord, to try and make it appear as though I have something to worry about when I know that I do not." Catherine could not help but admit to herself that the fear she felt in her heart was growing steadily.

Lord Linton cleared his throat gruffly, shaking out the second letter. "This is in his hand, and you may check it afterwards if you wish." He glanced at her, his expression grave. "In fact, you may do whatever you wish after you hear this, to prove to yourself the correspondence is genuine."

"Just read it, please," Catherine begged, her voice now an anguished whisper. "Do not torment me so."

Lord Linton eyed her for a moment longer before turning his attention back to the paper. "'Lord Linton,'" he began, "'I do not know where you have heard such news about my financial affairs, nor am I in any way pleased about what you put in the newspaper about my dear Catherine.'"

Catherine's breath came out in a whoosh of relief, her body practically bursting to life again. "I knew it," she said, her delight overflowing. "I knew he would not betray me so!"

Lord Linton held up one hand, a silent gesture to ask her to wait. Catherine sank back into her chair, her happiness slowly evaporating as he continued.

"'However,'" Linton went on, "'I will not pretend that paying off my largest debt would not be precisely what I need to pull me from the mire I find myself sinking into. I have enclosed the details. Once you have paid the sum, I will write to Miss Hewson myself, informing her of my change of heart. You need not change the notice in the paper, it seems, and I can no longer threaten to call you out. However, if this information becomes known throughout society, I will have no hesitation in throwing the blame for it on you. I do not want to be a laughing stock. Yours...'" Lord Linton looked up at her. "Well, you know the rest."

Catherine sat frozen in her chair, her blood slowly turning to ice in her veins. Could it really be true? Had Lord Kerr truly chosen wealth and payment of debts over her? Had he never really cared for her in the first instance, had never once held the deep affection he had tried his best to make so apparent?

"Kitty," Linton said softly, coming over to sit by her. He took her cold hand and wrapped another arm around her shoulder, trying his best to look into her eyes. "Are you all right?"

"No," Catherine whispered, sobs beginning to shake her form as she spoke through the tears falling down her cheeks. "No, I am not all right. I do not think anything will be right ever again."

12

The very same afternoon, Catherine received a letter from Lord Kerr. The maid brought it to her, but Catherine could find no happiness in its appearance. She knew what it held. Instead, she sent for yet another tea tray and sat quietly in the drawing room, simply looking down at the letter in her hand.

Lord Linton had left her soon after his revelation, aware that he had caused her a great deal of anguish. Catherine had wanted to be left alone, and had refused his request to stay longer and comfort her. She found that she was growing cold and weary from his presence.

However, being alone had not exactly brought her any relief. Instead, it had only intensified, making her heart ache with such a terrible pain that she thought her very soul might break in two. She had wept countless tears, her shoulders shaking as she gave into the grief she felt, growing angry at times over how abysmally Lord Kerr had treated her.

Then she would become upset with herself for her foolishness, her belief in Lord Kerr and the words of affection he had spoken to her. Catherine railed at herself for thinking that he had meant every word he had said, for not even being cautious when it came to giving him her heart. Slowly, her tears had abated, and she had sat quietly, wrapped in a shroud of heartache and sorrow.

Now, as she finally opened the note, his words seemed dull and devoid of emotion. He told her, in no uncertain terms, that there was no longer any connection between them. His reasons made no sense whatsoever, for he stated that since returning to his estate, he had realized that the number of responsibilities he had entirely overwhelmed his desire for affection and love and a life in matrimony. Therefore, he had chosen not to seek out a wife at this present time. In a way, Catherine was relieved that Lord Linton had come to her first, to soften the blow that was Lord Kerr's letter.

"It is as if I never knew him," she murmured to herself, getting up only to throw the letter onto the fire.

The door opened, and her maid set the tea tray in front of her before the maid went away. There Catherine sat, the hours drifting away as she became lost in her sadness and pain. The maid came to light the lamps and to set a dinner tray by her, and still she sat, refusing all company—including her mother's. Her hope of matrimony to a loving and kind man was gone entirely, and in its place now was a simple acceptance that she was to marry Lord Linton.

If only she had never made such an agreement. She might now be free of him, be free of all gentlemen. There would be no requirement for her to marry. She could live her life as an old maid, relying on friends and family for company and friendship until she died, entirely alone. That seemed a good option at the present, but the sensible part of Catherine's mind told her that she would not live happily that way for long.

She wanted a home of her own. She wanted children. But she could not risk seeking out the affections of another gentleman without being sure of his intentions. The pain was too great.

Mayhap marrying Lord Linton was a good thing. She could marry without love, knowing exactly who he was, and he knew her just as well. After all, they had been friends for a long time, even though she had pulled herself away from him of late. She would be in the position to bargain with him, to demand that he change some of his habits so as not to bring shame and embarrassment to the family.

Catherine could not help but think just how much Lord Linton had proven his kindness to her, despite the odd way he had gone about it. He had wanted to show her that Lord Kerr was not the man she had thought, and he had indeed managed to do so, but in such a way as to secure her hand for himself.

That had been clever of him, though Catherine knew that when he told her he cared about her, that sentiment had been genuine. It had been written all over his face, although she had chosen to ignore it. His eyes were sympathetic and kind.

What lengths he had gone to in order to save her from an imprudent marriage. And now, since he had been proven correct, he was to give a great deal of money to Lord Kerr to pay off one of his debts. As far as she was concerned, Lord Linton did not have to honor his word, given how much of a rogue Lord Kerr had turned out to be, but she had no doubt that Lord Linton would do just as he had said.

At least she knew he could be honest when he tried.

"Catherine?"

Jerking from her seat, Catherine turned to see her mother framed in the doorway, looking resplendent in all her evening finery. "Mama," she said, managing a smile. "You look utterly beautiful."

"I thank you," Lady Hewson replied, coming into the room and looking at Catherine with some concern. "You were meant to be joining us this evening, dear."

Catherine frowned, unable to recall what it was she was meant to be attending.

"The ball?" her mother continued after a short pause. "Lord and Lady Haye's ball?"

"Oh, yes," Catherine murmured, looking away from her mother. "Forgive me, Mama, I have something of a headache. I shall probably retire early."

Her mother worriedly looked down at her. "My maid tells me you have been sitting here almost all day," she said softly. "Are you sure it is only a headache?"

"Quite sure," Catherine answered in a rush. "Have a good evening, Mama, and do give my apologies to Lady Haye."

Her mother touched her hand briefly, an unspoken concern written across her features. Inwardly, Catherine willed her to go, hoping that she would be left in peace once more. She did not want to speak to her mother about what had happened, finding the wound too fresh, too painful to discuss.

"Very well," Lady Hewson murmured after a few quiet minutes had passed. "I want you to know you can always come to me, Catherine. Do not carry burdens alone—it is not good for you."

A lump lodged itself in Catherine's throat as she looked up at her mother, trying her best to give her a bright smile. Her mother patted her hand gently before leaving the room. Catherine let out a sigh of relief.

She welcomed the quiet and the darkness. Her pain and hurt wrapped around her heart, burying her in it. Catherine went willingly, letting it shroud her very soul. Her entire future had been shattered in a moment, her hopes gone entirely. How was she to emerge from this?

Catherine remained where she was, not moving or having any desire to do anything else but sit quietly, staring into the fire that burned and crackled in the grate. The door opened, and—thinking it was the maid—Catherine neither moved nor spoke.

"Kitty?"

Jerking in her seat, Catherine turned to see Lord Linton approaching, his expression grave.

"I wanted to see how you were feeling," he murmured.

Catherine glared at him. "You do not need to pretend to care about my feelings now," she retorted, even as a sudden rush of tears came to her eyes. "I am not in need of any company. Please, go away."

"No."

Much to her surprise, Linton sat down opposite her, his eyes searching her face as he took his seat.

"You do not mind if I take the liberty of ringing the bell, do you?" he asked, reaching across and tugging at it. "I have not had too much to eat today, although I see that your food is barely touched."

Catherine, wanting to give the impression that she was quite well and did not need his company, tugged the tray over to her lap and began to eat with ferocity. They sat in silence as she ate, interrupted only by the maid, who took Linton's request and then returned downstairs.

Her stomach soon full, Catherine set the tray to one side and handed it to the maid, who returned with one for Linton, as well as setting down a fresh pot of tea for Catherine. Catherine glared at Lord Linton as he began to eat, growing angry with his incessant need to be in her company.

"We shall eat a great many meals together when we are wed," Lord Linton said pleasantly. "I think you shall be very good for me, Kitty." He studied her for a moment before sighing heavily, setting his tray to one side. "I can tell you are unhappy."

"Of course I am!" she exclaimed, hot with rage. "Lord Kerr has proven himself to be the worst of men, and as if that were not terrible enough, I find myself engaged to the man I tried to avoid!"

"I will not continue as I have been," Linton promised. "You mean more than that to me."

She let out a snort of derision. "Forgive me if I do not believe you."

There was a short pause. "Would you like me to release you from our agreement?" he asked, suddenly and quietly.

Catherine stared at him, her mouth forming a fine line.

Had she heard him correctly?

"I know that you are unhappy," Lord Linton continued after a moment. "I want you to be happy. That is all I have ever wanted, truly. I will release you if you wish it."

"I... I do not know what to say," Catherine whispered, her anger and frustration dying away as she looked at him in a sudden new light. He had been so insistent on having this arrangement, on having these as the conditions of their agreement, and now he was offering her a way out? "Are you truly willing to allow this to come to an end?"

He chuckled, his expression gentle. "My dear Catherine, I suppose I must be honest with you. As much as I am willing to allow our engagement to come to an end, I do not wish it." Leaning a little closer, he reached across and took her hand.

Catherine was startled by the tenderness in his expression.

"The moment I saw you with Lord Kerr emerging from that room, my heart froze within me," he murmured. "I have been a fool, running around in the way that I have been. I had never considered anything like matrimony or the like before now, but I know that there can only be one woman who would make me happy." His fingers gently caressed the back of her hand. "And that woman is you, Catherine."

"I do not know what you mean," Catherine replied, butterflies beginning to flurry about in the pit of her stomach in the midst of her confusion. "We have only ever been friends."

"That is quite true," Linton said, a half-smile on his face. "But seeing you with Lord Kerr made me realize that I did not want that any longer. I admit that posting the engagement in the newspaper like that was selfish, although it did bring about my desired goal, but I do not want to be without you any longer. The years we shared together as friends are dearer to me than ever before. I *want* a future with you, as my wife and not just my friend."

He remained as such for a few minutes, not saying anything more but still keeping a hold of her hand. A great swell of opposing emotions ran through Catherine, making it hard for her to think clearly. She was not quite sure what Lord Linton was saying, but it had more depth and more feeling than anything he had ever said to her before.

"You will need some time to think, of course," he finished, getting up from his chair and moving closer to her. "I will come and call on you again next week. Or do you need more time than that?"

"Next week will do," Catherine answered in a somewhat breathless voice.

"Good." He grinned, putting one hand on her shoulder. "One final thing I should say, Catherine, is that I fully intend to court you. If you agree to wed me, then we will behave as any other betrothed couple might. Balls, soirees, carriage rides, walks in the park—whatever you wish. I intend to show you that I am a changed man."

Catherine blinked up at him, her thoughts tumbling like raindrops.

"It is all very sudden, I know," Lord Linton continued, more quietly. "But you have brought about such a desire—nay, a *need* to change, that I will do anything I have to in order to prove it to you." Bending down, he pressed a kiss to her cheek, lingering close to her for just a fraction too long. "Good evening, Catherine. I look forward to speaking to you next week."

13

However, Catherine's mind went from one thing to another over the following week. She simply could not come to a decision. One moment, she was terribly upset over Lord Kerr and grateful towards Lord Linton, and the next, she thought she could simply never allow herself to wed a man such as her old friend, no matter how much he promised to change.

What did not help was that her mother insisted on dragging her to all kinds of social occasions, refusing to allow her to sit at home and mope as she wished. The recitals and soirees did very little to help Catherine's state of mind, although at least she could throw herself into dancing for a time and forget about the whole thing entirely—although she still had to dodge those who wanted to get some kind of gossip from her. More eyes looked at her with curiosity than ever before, as though she was the latest morsel offered up to the hungry crowd.

"Are you enjoying your evening thus far, Miss Hewson?"

Catherine neatly avoided her foot being stepped on and tried to smile, wishing that she had managed to avoid Lord Dunstable's request for a dance.

"Yes, very much," she murmured.

"And is it true that you are engaged?" he asked bluntly, making her breath catch with surprise. "I must advise you against such a course of action."

"Is that so?" she returned, disinterestedly.

"Lord Linton is not an honorable man, and you require an honorable man as a husband."

Catherine bit back the harsh retort that formed on her lips and instead gave him a tight smile.

"After all, there are a great many honorable men within society, most of whom would be a much better choice than Lord Linton!" Dunstable laughed, shaking his head. "It will not be difficult for you to find such a man."

Catherine's lips thinned in distaste, already aware of what Lord Dunstable was getting at.

"I am such a gentleman," he said, glancing down at her. "A gentleman already willing to step in to remove you from this union, should you wish it."

Choosing to remain silent, Catherine stared firmly over Lord Dunstable's left shoulder, gritting her teeth so that she would not say another thing. Lord Dunstable mumbled something, apparently a little put out by her silence, but Catherine paid very little attention.

"Excuse me!"

Catherine blinked as the orchestra began to slow the music. Someone was shouting over the top of the music, over the buzz of voices, and bringing the dance to a sudden, unexpected end.

"Might I have everyone's attention?" the voice boomed, and as the music died away entirely and the clamor of voices began to diminish, Catherine turned to see Lord Linton standing where the orchestra was, looking out at the crowd.

Her heart turned over as his eyes searched the crowd. She knew who he was looking for, and she was torn between the desire to run away entirely or to wait and let him find her. She knew that, with her red curls, she would be quite conspicuous, and it would not take him too long to spot her.

"Whatever is he doing?" Lord Dunstable spluttered, releasing her from the dance hold. "He is about to make a fool of himself yet again!" He snorted and folded his arms. "Not that it should come as much of a surprise."

Catherine's blood roared in her ears as Linton's eyes met hers, lingering on her for a long time. He gave her a small smile, and Catherine felt her cheeks burn. *What are you doing?* she wanted to call, but she was forced to simply remain standing silently instead.

"My lords and ladies," Lord Linton boomed, dragging his eyes away from Catherine. "I come to you this evening with a request."

A murmur ran through the crowd, leaving Catherine fraught with anxiety. Was he about to make a fool of her? Was he about to declare that they all join in a toast to congratulate their engagement when he had not yet heard a response from her?

"It is a request I do not make lightly," Linton continued, his voice echoing around the room. "It is one I make in the hope that you will realize just how much I wish to change." He gave a slight smile, although his eyes grew serious. "I have recently become aware that my behavior over the last few years is not what should be expected of a gentleman such as I claim to be. I intend to make up for that in some small way, though I am aware that it will not cover all the hurt I have caused."

"So what is it that you are offering, exactly?" a gentleman shouted. "The chance to take a shot at you without retaliation?"

A small ripple of laughter ran around the room, despite the fact that Catherine's heart thundered with worry. As much as she was frustrated with Linton, she did not want to see him dead! She never had.

"As much as I am aware that there are those who would delight in slicing me to ribbons, I am not, in fact, able to offer such a thing," Linton answered with a wry smile. "However, to those I have cheated, to those I have hurt, to those I have caused harm to, I offer a financial settlement."

There was a stunned silence followed by a buzz of voices.

"But that will cause you to be almost bankrupt!" one voice cried, surely in jest, only for Linton to smile quietly.

"It will not push me to bankruptcy, but it will force me to live more quietly," he said as the room slowly quietened again. "And that, I think, must be a good thing." He looked directly towards Catherine, who stared back at him in disbelief. "No matter what should happen in my future, I am determined to live in a better way," he finished. "Now, if you wish to speak to me, Lord Seagate has allowed me the use of his study, where I might be able to discuss any matter you wish, one at a time."

Catherine watched with utter astonishment as Linton made his way through the crowd, which parted for him like a sea. Something in Catherine wanted to follow, wanted to see if he would truly follow through with what he had said. She had no choice but to remain where she was, though, watching him depart with a trail of gentlemen following after.

"My goodness," she breathed, hardly able to believe what she was seeing. "Whatever has he done that for?"

THE FOLLOWING MORNING, Catherine, with her maid in tow, made her way to Linton's home. It was just about time for morning calls, and given that she had barely slept a wink last night over what he had done, she had been terribly anxious to go and speak to him.

The prior evening at the ball, she had waited as gentlemen

began to reappear one after the other, each with a small smile on their faces. Catherine, not wanting to appear to be gossiping, had no choice but to eavesdrop on certain conversations, eager to find out what exactly Linton had done.

"Recompensed me for what he had taken from me the last time we played cards!" one gentleman had declared, his smile broad. "I always knew that there was something funny going on at that game—although he has never admitted it."

"Promised to send back my greys in the morning," said another, delight in his eyes as he spoke about the horses he had lost to Linton. "I am quite thrilled, I can tell you!"

More and more gentlemen had spoken of Linton's generosity, to the point that Catherine had no other choice but to believe that he was doing exactly as he had promised.

Which meant he was now a poorer man, although his fortune was large enough that she knew it would not push him towards insolvency or the like.

"Linton?" she asked the moment the butler allowed her entry. "Linton? Where are you?"

"The study, my lady," the butler murmured as her maid took Catherine's bonnet. "Just this way."

Catherine, in her urgency, did not wait for either her butler nor her maid and hurried into the room, seeing Linton busy at his desk.

"Kitty!" he exclaimed, shutting the door firmly behind her. "Whatever are you doing here? I thought I was to call on you?"

"Whatever did you do that for?" she asked breathlessly, refusing to answer his questions.

He frowned and rose to his feet. "Do what?" he replied. "Are you referring to last evening?"

Catherine let out a small frustrated noise, her eyes narrowing.

"I did that because I know that I need to be a better man," he said calmly. "You have shown me that."

"But you did not need to do such a thing!" she exclaimed, throwing her reticule down onto the nearby chair. "You could have just started afresh, determining not to behave in such a way any longer."

Lord Linton gave her a soft smile, his expression gentle. "I could have, but I had to prove to myself that the change in me was real. When I made amends to those I had hurt—and, to my shame, there were a great many of them—some of the guilt in my soul was assuaged."

Catherine nodded slowly, a spiraling disappointment in her chest. "So you did not do it for me, then," she murmured, unable to explain why she felt so let down by such a revelation. "You did it for yourself."

The sentiment should have brought her happiness, but Catherine found that she had wanted him to do such a thing in the hope of proving himself to her.

"You sound a little frustrated," Linton commented. "As I said last evening, I am determined to make amends so that I can live my life in a little less comfort but with a little more sense." His smile broadened. "I will not pretend that it has been simply my own thoughts and desires that have brought me to this place. I think you know that this has come from you."

"From me?" Catherine repeated, swallowing the sudden ache in her throat.

He chuckled. "Of course from you! Had I not seen you with Lord Kerr, then I do not think any of this would have happened."

Linton came around from behind his desk and took her hand, standing close to her. Catherine felt her breath catch in her chest, butterflies sweeping through her stomach as he stared at her with such an intensity that Catherine found she simply could not look away.

"My dearest Kitty," he said softly, his breath brushing lightly against her cheek. "I have you to thank for beginning the transformation in me from rogue to gentleman. Whether you agree to wed me or not, I will always be grateful to you. My wealth may be a little less, but my heart is no longer as cold."

Catherine looked into his eyes and realized that it was not only his heart that had changed; it had also been her own. By trying his best to make amends to those he had cheated or hurt, he had proved to her that he truly wanted to change. For years, Linton had enjoyed his wealth and had never given it away willingly. To do so now, at great loss to himself, was the proof she needed to know for certain that he was never going to revert to the behavior she had found so indefensible.

"I will," she found herself saying, almost without thinking. "I will marry you, Linton."

Something sparked in Lord Linton's eyes, his hand tightening around hers. "Are you sure, Kitty?" he asked, as though wanting to give her more time to consider his proposal. "Do not be hasty in this decision."

Catherine shook her head, feeling the certainty of her answer deep in her soul. "I am not being hasty, although I appreciate your concern in that regard."

"Then," he said, his eyes glittering, "you will be my wife?"

Looking up, Catherine gave him a small smile, her confusion, at last, finally abated. "Yes, Linton. I will be your wife."

14

"What do you mean, you are going to marry him after all?"

Catherine winced as Lady Hewson's shrieked exclamations bounced around the room. "Linton is here this morning, Mama. We had a brief discussion, and now he has gone to Papa to seek his permission."

Catherine had no doubt that her father, whilst certain to be surprised, would agree to the engagement. After all, there were still questions over her supposed engagement announcement in the paper, and this would be the best way to avoid a scandal. That had left Catherine with the task of breaking the news to her mother, who, all in all, was not taking it particularly well.

"Catherine!" her mother continued, still shrieking. "Why would you do such a thing?"

"Because it is not a particularly bad arrangement," Catherine answered. "Lord Linton is a childhood friend, Mama, and he has proved himself quite changed as of late, which I know you cannot deny." She raised one eyebrow and looked directly at her mother, well aware that she had been present at the time of Lord

Linton's announcement at the ball. "Besides," she finished, "you know it would be a good match."

That took some of the angst from her mother's face. "I suppose," she said a little more calmly, staring at Catherine as though she had lost her mind. "And I will not deny that I was as surprised as you to hear Lord Linton's announcement at the ball. But still, you cannot be happy with him, Catherine. I would not want you to go into a marriage that will make you miserable."

Smiling gently, Catherine tried to reassure her mother, knowing she was unable to express all the deep emotions in her heart. "Mama, Linton will not make me miserable. I am quite sure of it. He has changed, or is trying to, at the very least, and I find that I trust him." Even saying such a thing out loud brought a smile of both surprise and happiness to Catherine's face. It was as though Linton was slowly becoming the person she had once known, before he had turned into a scoundrel, and that could not help but make her glad.

Lady Hewson shook her head at her. "Catherine, we have been trying to get through all that has happened with Lord Linton for some time. You have been upset, you have cried, *I* have cried... and now I discover that you intend to marry him after all?" The frustration on her face grew. "My dear, did we go through all that for naught? I thought... I thought Lord Kerr was..." She trailed off, looking at Catherine with a mixture of irritation and puzzlement.

"Lord Kerr is not the man I thought," Catherine replied crisply, determined not to talk about the man more than necessary. "Lord Linton was kind enough to show me that."

Her mother frowned in confusion, and Catherine sighed inwardly, knowing she was going to have to explain a little more. "Mama, I thought that marriage to Lord Kerr would be one of love and shared companionship, but it now seems that he was only interested in the wealth I would bring with me."

Lady Hewson's eyes widened as she drew in a sharp breath. "Surely not, Catherine!"

Catherine's lips tugged with a sad smile. "It is so, Mama. I did not believe it at first, either, but it is quite true. Lord Kerr told me as much himself."

"And so you will marry Lord Linton instead? Even though you do not care for him?"

"But I do care for him. I know him entirely," Catherine said. "There is no disguise with Lord Linton, no pretense. I know him through and through. It is quite right that I do not love him in the way I once thought I loved Lord Kerr, but that does not seem of such great importance now. He will be a good and kind husband, and we can rekindle the friendship we once shared. I think it will be enough for me."

"So?"

Linton grinned down at Catherine as they sat in the carriage, riding around Hyde Park at the fashionable hour. It was only their first public excursion since news of their engagement had gone around society only the prior day, and Catherine could not help but feel a little nervous.

"You know what I am asking you," she chuckled when Linton did nothing but smile at her. "Did my father draw up a reasonable contract?"

Catherine had been both embarrassed and pleased to discover that her father had drawn up a contract for Linton to sign, one which would only allow him access to Catherine's fortune in small increments. It would also be handed over to Catherine entirely should he prove himself unworthy of her. Catherine's heart had swelled with love over such a thing, aware that this was how her father showed his care for her.

"It went very well, and all is in hand," Lord Linton replied with a broad smile. "And yes, of course I signed it. In fact, I signed it without hesitation. Your fortune is of no importance to me. And, as you know, I intend to prove myself to you in whatever way I can."

"Yes, I am aware of that," Catherine murmured, glancing out of the carriage window. "In fact, you have already done so, although it clearly is not enough for my father."

Linton chuckled. "And rightly so! It honors him to show such a great level of concern for his daughter.

Their eyes met for a moment, and Catherine was filled with warmth, feeling quite content with her engagement and upcoming marriage. It was as though Lord Linton, in proving himself to her, had become the answer to all of her problems, solving them in one single act.

"It is a good thing you know me so well, Kitty," Linton said, leaning across the carriage to take her hand. "You know my foibles and my shortcomings and have never once held your tongue in order to correct me." He grinned at her, his eyes alight. "Do you recall when you caught me taking apples from Lord March's apple tree?"

Catherine could not help but laugh, remembering the incident all too clearly. "Yes, and I recall the way I told you off in such a loud tone that you fell from the tree with a thump!"

Linton grinned at the shared memory, his eyes never leaving hers. "I think I lost my way when we drifted apart," he said quietly. "Mayhap if I had always had you by my side, then I would not have become such a rogue."

Catherine did not know what to say, growing very aware of how his fingers were tracing the back of her hand. Something curled in the pit of her belly, spreading heat through her limbs.

"I suppose I had to go to Eton, of course, but I should have ensured my behavior remained tempered," he finished. "Your voice was always my conscience, Kitty. I just became used to ignoring it."

"I have never heard you speak in such a way before," Catherine murmured. "This is quite new to my ears."

His smile was warm. "I suppose I never wanted to admit it to you. But now that we are to be wed, I shall always have you as my conscience, and I do not think I will be easily able to ignore you."

Catherine tilted her head and looked at her friend, seeing him in an entirely new light. He appeared more than earnest, and there was no hint of guile in his expression.

This was the Linton she knew, the one from her growing years. The one who was kind and compassionate, even if he did steal apples from Lord March. He was quite right to say that she had been his conscience, for she had never held back from telling him what he ought not to do. Her heart broke open with a warmth and a kinship long forgotten, her entire being desperate to believe that he really had changed back into her friend from childhood.

Linton patted her hand, smiling at her before dropping a firm kiss onto the back of her hand, making heat rush up her arm and into her core. He sat back and looked out of the window, apparently quite at ease with what he had done whilst Catherine sat there, entirely stunned at such a feeling.

This was now the second time she had experienced such a strong reaction to Linton's gentle display of affection. It meant nothing, of course, for she was quite sure Linton did not love her, and she certainly could have no feelings towards him. The idea was quite ridiculous. They were friends and nothing more, and Linton had already promised her—while her cheeks had burned furiously—that he would not press any kind of physical attentions on her in their marriage until she was quite ready.

"Ah, look!" Linton exclaimed, rapping on the carriage roof. "There is your dear friend waving at us."

"Alice!" Catherine exclaimed, seeing her friend walk towards her, leaving her husband talking with some other gentlemen. She quickly descended from the carriage whilst Linton instructed the driver to keep driving through the circuit so as not to hold up any of the other carriages.

"My dear Catherine!" Alice exclaimed, catching Catherine's hands and squeezing them gently. "How wonderful to see you! It has been so long since you last called upon me!"

A stab of guilt pricked Catherine's heart. "I am sorry for that, Alice. I meant to call, but there has been a great deal going on."

"So I see," Alice replied with a slight smile as Lord Linton approached them. "And are you happy, Catherine? You think this is the right path for you?"

"I do," Catherine stated quietly, aware of Lord Linton's presence drawing near to her. "I have not changed my mind yet."

Alice lifted one eyebrow as Linton gave her a deep bow. "And are you proving yourself, my lord?" she asked, not even waiting to greet him. "I will not have you hurt Catherine."

Linton did not seem in the least bit offended. "I have every intention of proving myself to both Catherine and to her friends," he answered with another short bow. "I do hope you will attend our wedding."

"Of course I shall," Alice replied, never taking her eyes from Linton. "Unless I can convince Catherine of her folly, first."

Catherine's eyes widened in shock at Alice's candor, but to her very great relief, Lord Linton only laughed, putting one hand around Catherine's waist. "I see I shall have to work hard to show you how much I have changed," he said, still laughing. "I have not made a good impression on you, have I?"

"No, you have not," Alice declared. "Do you not recall your terrible behavior towards Catherine at the bookshop? I cannot have a good opinion of you since I saw you use her for your own ends."

"Not even when he has done so much in recompense?" Catherine asked her friend, finding herself a little protective of Lord Linton. "Surely you have heard what he has been doing recently?"

Alice's expression grew surprised as she saw the sudden flash of defensiveness in Catherine's green eyes. "Yes," she murmured, glancing at Lord Linton. "I suppose that does make a difference."

"Good," Catherine stated as Linton tightened his arm around her waist just a fraction. "Now, shall we walk for a while? The air is warm, and the day is pleasant, so there is no need to sully it with angry words."

Alice kept her eyes on Lord Linton for another moment or so before turning back to her, the fight gone from her expression. "I must return to my husband," she said, pressing Catherine's hand. "Do call on me soon, will you not?"

"I will," Catherine promised, smiling at her friend as the tense atmosphere around them lessened. "Very soon, I assure you."

"I look forward to it," Alice muttered, inclining her head towards Lord Linton before taking her leave.

Lord Linton watched her go, a small smile on his lips. "You defended me valiantly, Kitty. You did not need to do so."

Catherine looked up at him and tucked her arm into his as they began to walk around the park. "Of course I did," she said. "You are to be my husband, are you not? Alice need not worry about me any longer. I have made up my mind."

Linton's eyes grew warm, his expression tender. "You are a marvel," he murmured, walking away from the trail of carriages. "A wonder, in fact. I am truly blessed."

Catherine could not help but blush at his compliments. As

she walked alongside him, she began to feel quite settled within herself. The friendship she had once shared with Linton was beginning to grow yet again, and with it, warmth had begun to blossom in her heart. She felt more than happy with him, which came as a rather alarming surprise.

Could she possibly feel something more for him? As much as she did not want to even consider it, Catherine had to admit that there was the chance she might grow fond of him. Had she not already been feeling a few strange sensations when he had taken her hand or kissed her cheek?

Her thoughts in disarray, Catherine stumbled suddenly as they entered a small, secluded copse of trees, only for Linton to catch her. Carefully setting her on her feet, he eyed her carefully, his hands now on her waist.

"Are you all right?" he asked, sounding worried. "You are not growing weary, I hope? I know this has all been rather sudden, and I would not blame you if—"

"I am quite all right," Catherine interrupted hastily. "I simply was not looking where I was going."

Linton's hands remained settled on her waist, his dark brown eyes piercing her own. Catherine drew in a shuddering breath, aware that they were quite secluded. She could not account for the way her body was bursting to life, her heart thundering in her chest as he raised one hand and ran his fingers lightly down her cheek.

"You are such a beautiful woman," he murmured, his hand gently brushing her auburn curls. "Your eyes are like emeralds surrounded by a blaze of fire."

Her heart beat all the faster, and Catherine found she could not look anywhere but his face. His mouth was so close to her own, and for a moment, Catherine realized she had a strong urge to kiss him.

It was too much.

"I am feeling a little wobbly after all," she said quickly, stepping out of his embrace. "Might you take me home? I think a cup of refreshing tea would do me the world of good."

A strange little smile crossed his face as he held out his arm to her, as though he knew she was trying to run from her own feelings. They walked back towards the carriages, still doing their slow circle of the park in search of their carriage whilst Catherine found that, all of a sudden, she was quite desperate to get home.

15

"And so the final banns are to be read come the morrow!" Lady Hewson exclaimed as she sat down heavily in a chair opposite Catherine, who was trying her best to continue with her embroidery.

"Yes, Mama," Catherine said. What was it her mother wished to say about it? Catherine knew she would not make such a comment without having something to say about it.

Her mother sighed heavily. "And are you quite sure, Catherine?"

"Yes, Mama," Catherine repeated, shaking her head to herself. "You need not keep asking me."

"I simply want to ensure you are prepared for this, my dear," her mother replied, sounding quite frustrated. "I must admit that Lord Linton has shown himself to be somewhat worthy of late, but that does not mean he will remain so."

Catherine smiled at her mother, aware that her exasperation came out of concern for Catherine's wellbeing. "He *has* changed, has he not?" she mumbled to herself, thinking over the last two months. The banns had only been called a sennight ago, once all had been settled, and Catherine had only one last opportunity to break off her engagement, should she wish it. She was due to be married in five days' time, the Thursday after the final banns were called. It was to be a very quiet affair, but that was just as Catherine wanted it.

What had surprised Catherine lately was to realize that Linton was becoming quite the gentleman. He had called on her almost every day since their engagement had been announced, and Catherine had grown more and more eager to spend time in his company. She had not mentioned her growing feelings to either her mother or Alice, finding them most confusing and quite unexpected.

When Linton smiled at her, her heart seemed to stop for the briefest of moments. When he called her 'Kitty' in that affectionate way of his, it spread warmth all through her, even though he had called her that name for almost as long as she had known him.

She did not even consider Lord Kerr, nor did she feel any kind of hurt over what he had done. Linton's actions did not cut deeply any longer, and she found herself strangely grateful towards him, as though she was glad that she was to marry him. He no longer had any rumors chasing after him, given that he had sorted out a variety of substantial monetary amends to each one—and that was on top of the debt he had paid on behalf of Lord Kerr! He was not clinging to his wealth but rather doing good with it, as though he wished to keep his future with Catherine a bright one.

She no longer worried in the least that he would go back to his former ways, and instead, she saw him as a strong, astute gentleman who would do anything he could to make her happy. How much she appreciated that! How much he had done for her. Catherine could not help but feel gratitude and, she had to admit, a slow burning affection for the man she had once been determined to avoid entirely.

"Catherine?"

Glancing up at her mother, Catherine realized she had become lost in thought. "Yes, Mama?"

Lady Hewson closed her eyes and shook her head. "Do not tell me you have fallen for the man, Catherine! Too often I have caught you with your head in the clouds these last few weeks!"

The laugh died in Catherine's throat. "Love?" she croaked as a burst of heat climbed its way up her spine. "I am not that foolish, Mama."

"I should hope not!" her mother exclaimed, tossing her head. "Lord Linton has shown he can change, yes, but that does not mean that the change will be long standing."

"Well, I have Father's contract in place, if the worst should happen," Catherine reminded Lady Hewson. "Please, Mama, you are driving me mad with your constant worrying. I trust Linton. We shall be happy together, I promise you."

Her mother sighed heavily. "I shall miss you, my dear," she said, a little more gently. "Once you are wed, there will be no need for us to remain in town."

Catherine swallowed the lump in her throat. She was close to her mother and had never truly considered what being apart from her would be like.

"I suppose you shall live here, given that Linton enjoys the town life so much, whilst we return to the country," her mother continued woefully.

"I presume so," Catherine murmured, trying not to think of it. "Life will be very different after I am married. That is to be expected, I suppose."

Lady Hewson huffed and muttered under her breath for a few minutes more, but then she was interrupted by a knock at the door.

"Are you expecting someone, Catherine?"

"No, I do not think so," Catherine answered, setting her embroidery aside. Once they were both sitting properly, her mother called the butler to enter, only for Lord Linton to stride in ahead of the butler, his gaze fixed on Catherine.

Her breath caught as he bowed, his eyes never leaving her face. Catherine smiled as she got to her feet, her heart swelling with happiness as he kissed her hand gently.

"My dear, Kitty." He smiled after he had greeted her mother. "The wedding is only a few short days away, and I have come to see that all is in order."

"Of course all is in order!" Lady Hewson exclaimed, her eyes flashing. "Do you not think us capable of organizing a wedding?"

Catherine hid a smile as Linton bowed heavily, his expression a mixture of surprise and embarrassment.

"I never doubted you for a moment, my lady," he said, attempting to appease her. "What I meant to say—and you will have to forgive me for being so ineloquent—is that I wanted to see if there was anything I might help you with." He flashed a smile, which Catherine knew was an attempt to mollify her mother. "After all, this is to be my wedding, too, and I cannot help but feel excited at the prospect of marrying your daughter."

Lady Hewson glared at him for a moment longer before giving him a tight smile and resuming her seat. Catherine laughed quietly to herself as she got up to tug the bell pull for tea.

"If you do not mind," Linton interjected hastily, "I wondered if you might like to take a turn around the gardens, Kitty?"

Catherine paused, her hand freezing as it neared the bell pull. "You want to walk with me?"

"I do," he replied, a slight twinkle in his eye. "Is that all right? I thought it might be nice if we had a few minutes to talk."

"You can talk here!" her mother interrupted, looking as though she were about to disagree with every single thing Linton would say. "There is no reason you cannot speak freely in my presence."

Catherine moved away from the bell pull, bent down to kiss her mother's cheek, and stepped towards the door. "A walk in the gardens sounds quite wonderful," she said, ignoring her mother's hiss of discouragement. She had dealt with more than enough of Lady Hewson's frank speech that afternoon, and a walk with Linton might be just the thing to give her a little relief.

"Wonderful!" Linton boomed, walking across the room to meet her. "I shall not be too long. Mayhap we can have tea with your mother once we return?"

"A very good idea," Catherine declared, laughing at the look of relief on Linton's face as they quit the room. "We will not be long, Mama!" she called as they began to walk along the corridor. Once they stepped outside, she turned to Linton. "I am sorry for my mother's behavior towards you. She does not trust you still, I am afraid."

Linton shook his head, a rueful smile on his lips. "I have no doubt that she cares for you a very great deal. I do not hold her attitude towards me against her."

"Then you are very good," Catherine declared with a quick laugh. "She has been most trying the last few days. She intends to put me off our nuptials, I am quite sure of it!" She squeezed his arm gently. "As I said, she is having a somewhat difficult time trusting you."

He looked at her for a moment as they walked, his gaze concentrated on her face. "And do you trust me?"

Catherine paused in her steps, caught by the intensity of his gaze and the seriousness of his question. "Of course I do," she answered. "I would have thought it would have been more than apparent as of late."

"It is," he said fervently, turning to face her a little more. "I suppose I just wanted to hear it from your lips. I cannot explain it even to myself, but something about you drives me to become the man you deserve."

Catherine caught her breath as the warmth in his eyes grew, and then she turned herself back towards the path and began to stride away. She was too confused to speak, her stomach filled with fluttering butterflies as she moved away from him.

"Kitty!" Lord Linton called, catching her arm. "Is something the matter?"

Catherine found herself breathless as she turned back to face him, unsure of what to say.

"You are worrying me now," he said, his expression concerned. "You are not having second thoughts, I hope?"

"No, no, nothing of the sort!" Catherine exclaimed, shaking her head. "You need not worry yourself on that account."

"Need I not?" he asked, his voice a little softer as he drew closer to her. "Then, are you going to tell me what is on your mind?"

Pursing her lips, Catherine struggled in vain to think of what to say, her thoughts more jumbled than ever. "I am quite all right."

"No, you are not," he protested. "You forget just how well I know you. Come now, be honest with me. Whatever it is, I want to know." He smiled gently at her. "Mayhap I can help you."

Groaning, Catherine shook her head and stepped away from him again. "Please, Linton, do not press me so."

A light seemed to burn in his eyes, but he remained silent, taking her hand in his own and beginning to walk slowly amongst the garden shrubs.

"This is a beautiful garden, I must say," he commented, turning the subject away from her entirely. "When we are wed, I thought to move back to my country estate."

"Really?" Catherine breathed, surprised.

"Of course!" he replied, his eyes still twinkling at her. "I know just how much you love the countryside."

It was true, of course. While Catherine did enjoy the hubbub of the town, nothing quite compared to the quiet loveliness of the country.

"I thought you might also like to be close to your parents," he continued, surprising her still further. "Given that my estate borders your father's, it means that we will be close to them and able to see them whenever you wish it."

"Oh, Linton!" Catherine whispered, her eyes blurring with sudden tears. "I can hardly believe it!"

He chuckled, pressing her hand a little. "No doubt you thought I would wish to remain in the town, close to the things I love."

"I did," Catherine admitted, brushing away her tears with her fingers. "I even said so to Mama. I thought you would wish to remain where all the excitement can be found."

Linton shook his head, his eyes serious. "No, Kitty. I chose you, which means I chose to live in a way that would please you. And, for what it is worth, I do not believe living in the country to be any kind of penalty. I think that life will be quite exciting enough with you by my side." Seeing a small path leading between various rosebushes, Linton led her in that direction, and the air was soon filled with beautiful scents.

"Does it please you?" Linton asked, stopping her in their walk and turning her so that she had no choice but to look into his eyes. His eyes searched hers, a small line of worry creasing his forehead.

"Does it please me that you are doing whatever you can to make me happy?" Catherine asked, astonished that he would worry about such matters. "Of course it does! It does surprise me, yes, but I am more than delighted to know that we will be living so close to my parents. I had not considered until earlier today just how much I would miss them."

Linton smiled, the worry gone from his expression in a moment. "I am glad to hear it," he said. "I do not want you to ever doubt the affection I have for you."

Catherine followed his hand with her eyes, her fingers suddenly itching to be where his were, delving into the thick locks of his brown hair. Heat rushed into her cheeks at the thought, her heart beating almost painfully as he moved closer to her, his hands now resting gently around her waist.

"I must be honest with you," he continued, his voice quiet. "I want you to know how I feel before we go into the church to become man and wife."

"Speak freely, please," Catherine replied, trying to sound as nonchalant as she could despite the hurrying of her heart. She looked up into his face inquiringly, wondering to herself when he had become so handsome.

"I love you, Kitty."

Her world stopped turning at his words. Stars began to sparkle in her vision as she saw the earnestness in his expression, becoming painfully aware that her feelings went in much the same direction.

"I believe I have loved you all my life," he went on, his hands now a little tighter around her waist. "I threw myself into all these vices, trying to drown out your quiet voice in my head, trying to kill the love I held for you in my heart, but it has proved entirely impossible." Dropping his head, Catherine saw Linton's gaze move to her lips before returning to her eyes once more. "I can only apologize for all the hurt and pain I have caused you, and I promise you that, from this day forward, I will love you with all that I have, never preventing myself from feeling such a way as I have done in the past."

Letting out a long breath, Catherine closed her eyes for a moment, trying to steady herself.

"Kitty?" he asked, the quietness in his voice replaced with concern. "Have I upset you?"

"Upset me!" she exclaimed, her eyes opening at once. "No, you have not. It is just that I have been tormented in much the same way."

As she watched his face, she saw his expression turn from worry to a slow dawning understanding, his features coming alive with happiness.

"I cannot say when this came about, and it certainly has not been as of long standing as your own feelings," Catherine admitted, a sense of peace washing over her, "but I have to confess that I think I love you in return." It was as though saying it aloud, even to herself, brought about a deep relief.

"I see," Linton replied hoarsely. "I cannot believe this. I…" He trailed off, shaking his head. "I never thought this would happen to me. I feel as though I am not worthy of you."

"You are proving yourself worthy with every day that passes," Catherine whispered, boldly stepping forward and putting her arms around his neck, her fingers threading into his hair. "You are not to torment yourself with such a thought any longer. You wish to make me happy, and I find that I wish to do the same for you. I know now that our marriage will be one filled with all the love and affection I once longed for."

Catherine saw him swallow once, twice, before his eyes closed and he held her tightly. She rested her head on his shoulder, peace running through her. This was where she was meant to be. This was where she belonged.

"I love you, Kitty," Linton murmured, his lips searching for hers.

Catherine smiled gently, ready to close the distance between them. "And I love you, Linton," she murmured, just as she pressed her lips to his.

≈

THE END

CLEAN HISTORICAL ROMANCES

If you loved reading this book, discover other clean, historical romances that will warm your heart. All books are stand-alone stories and can be read in any order.

Heart of a Marquess
A plan born of deception... Can Charlotte overcome her stepsister's cruel actions and find the love she deserves?

A Marquess and a Secret
Lord Rivenhall and Miss Richards both have secrets they do not want society to know about. Will their secrets bring them together or keep them apart?

Finding Hope
A mail order bride is left at the train station by her betrothed. Alone and afraid, Grace is offered a second chance at happiness.

The Bride's Heart

Hazel is a free spirit. Stephen likes order in his life. Can they learn how to compromise, or did they just make the biggest mistake of their lives?

LOVE LIGHT FAITH

Receive a FREE inspirational romance eBook by visiting our website and signing up for our mailing list. Click the link or enter www.LoveLightFaith.com into your browser.

The newsletter will also provide information on upcoming books and special offers.

THANK YOU

Thank you for reading this book! Avid readers like you make an author's world shine.

If you've enjoyed this book, or any other books by Joyce Alec, please don't hesitate to review them on Amazon or Goodreads. Every single review makes an incredible difference. The reason for this is simple: other readers trust reviews more than professional endorsements. For this reason, we rely on our readers to spread the good word.

Sending you endless appreciation, plus a little love, light and faith!

ABOUT THE AUTHOR

Joyce Alec grew up in Colorado and graduated from college with a degree in business. After developing a passion for books, she spent countless hours reading a variety of genres, but fell in love with sweet, historical romances. Joyce's passion for reading eventually cultivated into a love for writing, so creating Regency-era tales of love is a dream come true for her.

After planting her roots in Florida, Joyce found another passion: the ocean! In her free time, you can find Joyce at the beach with a big floppy hat, flip-flops, and a vanilla iced coffee in hand. She lives in the Sunshine State with her prince charming and wildly vivacious son.

Printed in Poland
by Amazon Fulfillment
Poland Sp. z o.o., Wrocław